TEMPTING THE LAIRD

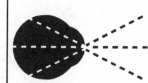

TEMPTING THE LAIRD

JULIA LONDON

THORNDIKE PRESS

A part of Gale, a Cengage Company

Farmington Hills, Mich • San Francisco • New York • Waterville, Maine
Meriden, Conn • Mason, Ohio • Chicago

GALE
A Cengage Company

LIBRARY OF CONGRESS CIP DATA ON FILE.
CATALOGUING IN PUBLICATION FOR THIS BOOK
IS AVAILABLE FROM THE LIBRARY OF CONGRESS

ISBN-13: 978-1-4328-5782-0 (hardcover)

Published in 2018 by arrangement with Harlequin Books S.A.

Printed in Mexico
1 2 3 4 5 6 7 22 21 20 19 18

CONTENTS

Mackenzies of Balhaire

John Armstrong,
Lord Norwood

Anne Armstrong

Knox Armstrong *(bastard son)*

Bryce Armstrong

Margot Armstrong, b. 1688

m. 1706

Arran Mackenzie, b. 1680

Conall Mackenzie

Cailean Mackenzie, b. 1711

m. 1742

Daisy Bristol, b. 1713
Lady Chatwick
(previous marriage)

Georgina Mackenzie, b. 1747

Ellis, *Lord Chatwick*

m. 1751

Avaline Kent, b. 1732

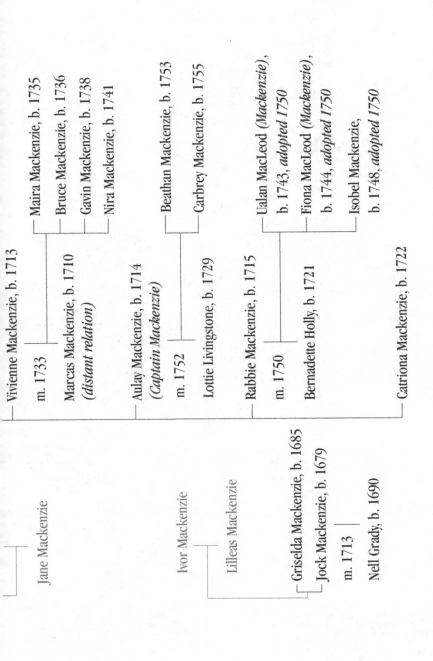

CHAPTER ONE

Kishorn Lodge, Scottish Highlands, 1755

There'd been a spirited debate among the Mackenzies of Balhaire over where to bury the remains of the venerable Griselda Mackenzie. Arran Mackenzie, her much beloved cousin, wanted her buried at the clan's seat at Balhaire alongside two hundred years of Mackenzies. But Catriona, his youngest daughter — who had been as close to her "Auntie" Zelda as her own mother — wanted to bury her at Kishorn Lodge, where Griselda had lived most of her remarkable life.

In the end, a compromise was struck. Auntie Zelda was buried in the family crypt at Balhaire, but a *fèille* in her honor was held at Kishorn a month later. This arrangement satisfied Catriona, as it was the celebration she wanted for a woman who had lived life very much on her own terms.

Unfortunately, the weather turned foul on

the eve of her *fèille.* Kishorn was remote, far into the Highlands, reachable practically only by boat. Therefore, only the most immediate Mackenzie family was able to attend, rowing up from Balhaire, past the Mackenzie properties of Arrandale and Auchenard, and across Loch Kishorn to the point where the loch met the river for which it was named.

There was scarcely anything or anyone this far into the Highlands. A village and prime hunting grounds had once graced the banks of the river, but they were long gone. A Mackenzie ancestor had built the lodge on the ruins of the village. Zelda, who had always preferred her freedom to a confining marriage, and had been indulged by her father, had taken possession of the abandoned lodge as a young woman and had made it her home, lovingly repairing and adding to it over the years.

The only thing left of that ancient village was a crumbling abbey, built on a hilltop overlooking the river glen. It was small as abbeys went, and no one could say whose abbey it had been. Zelda had decided it was hers and had made half of the original structure habitable again. The other half — what had once been the sanctuary — was missing its walls, and only a few beams and

10

arches remained of the roof. It served no useful purpose, other than to provide a wee bit of respite from the weather for the cows that wandered in from time to time.

If only they'd had a respite from the cold rain that continued to beat a steady rhythm against the paned windows on the day of the *fèille*.

Catriona was quite undone by it — she'd planned this event to rival all such celebrations for years to come. "I'm bloody well cross with God this day, that I am," she said to the women gathered around the fire blazing in the hearth. They included her mother, the Lady of Balhaire, and Catriona's sister, Vivienne. Also present were her sisters-in-law, Daisy, Bernadette and Lottie. "It rained the day we buried her, and here it rains again. She deserved better, she did," Catriona said as she carelessly held up her wineglass to be refilled.

"Zelda would not care a whit about rain, Cat," her mother assured her. "She would care only that you carried on with the *fèille* in spite of it. Can't you hear her laughing? She'd say, 'Did you expect cherubs and bluebirds to herald my arrival? No, lass, heaven weeps when I knock at the door.'"

"*Mamma,*" Catriona said gravely, but she couldn't help a small smile. Zelda would

11

have indeed said something like that.

"I miss that old crone," her mother said fondly, and lifted her glass in solemn salute. "She was incomparable."

That was high praise coming from Margot Mackenzie. She and Zelda had maintained a fraught relationship through the years, had never quite seen eye to eye for reasons Catriona still didn't fully understand. She knew that Zelda couldn't bring herself to forgive her mother for being English, which, to be fair, was a sin in the eyes of many Highlanders. But Zelda had also seemed determined to believe the absurd notion that Catriona's mother was a spy, of all things. Once, Catriona had asked her father why Auntie Zelda said her mother was a spy, and he'd given her a strange look. "Some things are better left in the past, aye?" he'd said. "You canna believe everything Zelda says, lass."

He had not, Catriona had noted, denied it.

In spite of the ancient discord between the two women, in the last months of Zelda's life, when she'd been ill more often than she'd felt well, Catriona's mother had come once a week from Balhaire to sit with her. The two of them would argue about events that had occurred during their long lives, but they'd laughed, too, giggling with one another about secret things.

One of the serving women refilled Catriona's wineglass. She drank it like water.

With all the Mackenzies crowded into the lodge, there was little room for the games Catriona had planned, and little else to occupy them. Frankly, Catriona had fallen into her cups. No, that wasn't correct — she was *swimming* in her cups, an idea that made her giggle.

"There ought to be dancing," Lottie complained, and shifted uncomfortably under the weight of the bairn she was holding. Another boy. *"Something."*

"What do you mean?" Vivienne said. "You canna dance, Lottie." She nodded to the bairn. Lottie had only recently delivered Carbrey. The birth of a second son had Catriona's brother Aulay strutting about Balhaire like a bloody peacock.

"Aye, but *you* can dance," Lottie said, nudging Vivienne. "And I should like to watch."

"Me? I'm too old and too fat for it, that I am," Vivienne complained, and slumped back in her chair, one hand across her belly. Bearing four children had left her with a full figure. "Bernadette will dance."

"By myself?" Bernadette, wife of

13

Catriona's brother Rabbie, bent down to stir the logs in the hearth. "Shall I hum the music, as well?"

"And what of me?" Daisy asked. She was wed to Cailean, Catriona's oldest brother. "*I'm* not too old for a reel."

"Or too fat," Lottie agreed.

"No, but your husband is too old," Vivienne said, and nodded toward Cailean. He was seated near a brazier with their father, his legs stretched long. A tankard of ale dangled from two fingers.

" 'Tis a pity that Ivor MacDonald is no' here to dance with our Cat," Catriona's mother said, and smiled devilishly at her daughter.

Catriona's inhibitions had been drowned by the good amount of wine she'd drunk, and she groaned with frustration. "You'll no' rest from seeing me properly wed until you meet your demise!"

"And what is wrong with that, I ask you?" her mother asked sweetly.

"Yes, what is wrong with that?" Daisy asked. "Why will you not accept Mr. MacDonald's attentions, Cat?" she asked curiously. "He seems rather nice. And God knows, he is smitten with you."

Ivor was a thick man, the same height as Catriona, with hair that drooped around his

14

face. In the weeks since Zelda had died, he'd offered his condolences so many times she'd lost count. "He may smite all he likes, but I'm far too restless to tie my lot to a *shipbuilder,*" Catriona said imperiously, and drained the rest of the wine from her glass. Actually, his occupation had little to do with it — it was most decidedly his lack of a neck.

"I think that's incorrect," Lottie said, looking puzzled as Catriona held her glass up again. "He hasn't smited you, but rather, you're the one who's done the smiting, are you no'?"

Catriona clucked at her. "You know verra well what I mean, aye?"

"Aye, I know verra well," Lottie agreed. "But you're three and thirty, Cat. Sooner or later you must accept that the last sheep at market must take the price offered or be turned to mutton."

"Lottie!" Bernadette gasped. "What a wretched thing to say!"

Catriona gave the remark a dismissive flick of her wrist. "Aye, but it's the truth, is it no'? I am firmly planted on the bloody shelf of spinsterhood. I've quite accepted I'm to remain without husband or child all my life, aye? That's what Zelda did, and quite by choice. I know what I'm meant to do — I'm meant to carry on Auntie Zelda's work."

"I should like to think you are destined for something other than living at Kishorn, removed from all society," her mother said. "You are not Zelda, after all."

Well, that was just the thing — there *was* no society for her. There was nothing for her here but endless days stretching into more endless days, with nothing to occupy her but this blasted abbey in the middle of nowhere. "What society, Mamma? Do you mean the Mackenzies and all their married men? Or perhaps you mean the MacDonalds and their representative, Ivor?"

"If you don't care for Mr. MacDonald, there is more society for you to explore," her mother argued. "But spending all your time at Kishorn has isolated you from the world."

"Mmm," Catriona said skeptically. "I think I may safely say I have explored all available society in the Highlands, and like my dearly departed auntie, I've found it wanting, I have. And besides, the women and children of the abbey need me, Mamma. Why should I no' have a grand purpose?" she asked, and gestured so grandly that she spilled wine onto the stone floor. "I've learned all that I could from Zelda. The women of the abbey have no other place to go, and I'm determined to carry on, that I am, for there is still so much to be done, and Zelda would have wanted it so. Donna try and dissuade me, Mamma." She sat up and turned around. "Where is that serving girl?"

"Catriona, darling," her mother pleaded.

But Catriona was in no mood to discuss her future plans. "*Diah* save me," she said, and stood up, swaying when she did, and catching herself on the back of the chair before she tumbled. She was exhausted from discussing her situation. She felt as if she'd been discussing it for years and years. *Poor Catriona Mackenzie, whatever will they do with her? She's no prospects for marriage, no society, nothing to occupy her but a run-down abbey full of misfits.* "I think I should like to dance, then. Is Malcolm Mackenzie about? He's brought his pipes, I'm certain of it."

"For the love of God, *sit,* Cat." Bernadette caught Catriona's hand and tried to tug her back into her seat. "You're pissed —"

"I've scarcely had a drop!" Catriona insisted. "That's the English in you, Bernie," she said, and wagged a finger at her sister-in-law. "We Scots are far better dancers with a wee bit of wine in us, aye?"

"You could hurt someone," Bernadette

said, and tugged on her hand again.

"You really shouldna drink so," Vivienne said disapprovingly.

"I shouldna drink, I shouldna dance," Catriona said irritably. Her few drops of wine were enough to make her feel a wee bit stubborn, and she yanked her hand free of Bernadette's. But in doing so, she misjudged her balance and stumbled backward into someone. She managed to right herself and turn about and laughed with delight when she saw who had caught her. Rhona MacFarlane was the abbess at Kishorn. Rhona wasn't *really* an abbess — she had a heart of gold, but she was no nun. Nevertheless, everyone called her the abbess, as she had been working alongside Zelda for twelve years.

"Aye, look who has come to jig with me, then! Thank you, Rhona, dearest. You've saved me from a scolding, and I should verra much like to dance." Catriona made a flourish with her hand and bowed low, very nearly tipping over.

"There's no music," Rhona said.

"A fair point," Catriona conceded, and grabbed Rhona's arms and teased her by trying to make her dance. "We donna need music!"

"Miss Catriona!" Rhona said, and pulled

18

her arms free.

"Aye, all right, I'll find Malcolm," Catriona said petulantly.

"Miss Catriona, we have *visitors*," Rhona said.

Catriona gasped with delight. "Visitors! Who has come?" She whirled around to the door, expecting to see the MacDonalds from Skye, all of whom had known Zelda well. But the men at the door were not Mac-Donalds — Catriona could tell by their demeanor they were no friends of the Mac-kenzies or Kishorn. She was suddenly reminded of the two letters Zelda had received in the last months of her life. Let-ters written on heavy vellum, with an of-ficial seal. Letters that Zelda had waved away as nonsense.

Fury swelled in Catriona, her heart calling her to arms and swimming against the tide of wine she'd drunk. How *dare* they blacken the *fèille* for Griselda Mackenzie with their presence! If they thought the abbey was easy picking now that Zelda was gone, Catriona would show them that was not the case — she'd die before she'd let these men take the abbey from her and Zelda's memory.

"What visitors?" her mother asked, rising to her feet.

"Bloody bastards, that's who," Catriona

19

said, and began striding for the door before her mother could stop her. As she neared the men, the one in front bowed his head.

"Who are you?" Catriona demanded.

"Ah. You must be Miss Catriona Mackenzie," the man responded in a crisp English accent. He removed his cocked hat, slinging water onto the floor and one of the Kishorn dogs, who shook it off his coat.

"How do you know my name? How did you get here?"

"It is my occupation to know your name, and a man at Balhaire was kind enough to bring us." He removed his dripping cloak and handed it to the gentleman beside him. His coat and waistcoat were so damp and heavy that they smelled of wet wool and hung nearly to his knees. "I am Mr. Stephen Whitson, agent of the Crown. Would you do me the courtesy of informing the laird that I have come to present a matter of some urgency to him?"

"My *laird*?"

That man calmly returned her gaze. "As I said, it is a matter of urgency."

"Is it the same matter of urgency that compelled you to badger my ailing aunt on her deathbed with your letters, then?"

"I beg your pardon, Miss Mackenzie, but this is a matter for men —"

20

"It's a *matter* of bloody *decency* —" She was startled out of saying more by the firm clamp of a very big hand on her shoulder. Cailean had appeared at her side and squeezed her shoulder as he gave her a look that warned her to hold her tongue.

"I beg your pardon, what's this about, then?" he asked calmly.

"Milord, Mr. Stephen Whitson at your service," the man said, bending over his outstretched leg.

"He wants to take the abbey, that's what," Catriona said angrily.

"Cat." Aulay had come around on the other side of her. He took her hand and placed it firmly on his forearm, then covered it with his hand, squeezing so tightly that she winced. "Allow the man to speak, aye?"

"It is true that the abbey is a concern for the Crown," Whitson said, and casually flipped the tail of his bobbed hair over his shoulder. "I have been sent by the Lord Advocate's office."

"The Crown?" Cailean repeated skeptically, and stepped forward, putting himself before Catriona. "I beg your pardon, sir, but we are in the midst of a wake for Miss Griselda Mackenzie."

"My condolences," Whitson said. "I regret my arrival is inopportune, but our previous correspondence went unanswered. As I attempted to explain to Miss Mackenzie, I've come with an urgent matter for the laird."

"Aye, bring them forth, Cailean," Catriona's father called from the other end of the room.

Whitson did not wait for further invitation. He neatly stepped around Cailean and began to stride across the room, heedless of the others gathered.

The room had grown silent, all ears and narrowed gazes on this man.

Cailean followed Whitson, but when Catriona tried to move, Aulay tugged her back. "Stay here."

"I'll no' stay back, Aulay! That's *my* abbey now."

But Aulay stubbornly tugged her back once more. "Then I would suggest, if you want to keep it, you mind your mouth, Cat. You know how you are, aye? Particularly after a wee bit too much to drink."

She was not going to debate how much she'd had to drink with him. "What of it?" she snapped. "Zelda is gone and I have drunk my sorrow." She shook his hand off and hurried after the others.

Her father had come to his feet. He leaned heavily on a cane, but he still cut an imposing figure and was a head taller than Mr.

Whitson. Her father was a good judge of character, and he had judged this man's character quickly, for he did not offer him food or drink. He said curtly, "What is your business, then?"

Mr. Whitson lifted his chin slightly. "As you are to the point, my lord, so shall I be. Kishorn Abbey was used unlawfully in the aiding and abetting of Jacobite traitors who sought to displace our king in the rebellion of '45, and in return for that treason, the property as such is forfeited."

Catriona and her family gasped, but her father, Arran Mackenzie, laughed. "I beg your pardon? Kishorn Abbey sits on land that has been owned by the Mackenzies for more than two hundred years. There was no *aiding* and *abetting.* We've been loyal subjects, sir, that we have."

"Kishorn Abbey was used to house fleeing rebels after the loss at Culloden and was operated by a known Jacobite sympathizer in the form of Miss Griselda Mackenzie. It is pointless to deny it, my lord — we have the witness of two of the sympathizers. As the property was used to house traitors, it is forfeited to the Crown by order of the king."

"By order of the king?" Cailean echoed incredulously. "Are you mad, then? Ten years have passed since the rebellion."

Mr. Whitson shrugged. "It was a crime then and is yet, sir."

"What does the Crown care for that old abbey?" Rabbie scoffed. "It's falling down and too remote to be of any use."

"There is interest in it," Mr. Whitson sniffed, and paused to straighten his lace cuffs. "There are those who believe any use would be better than housing women of ill repute."

Catriona gasped with outrage. "How *dare* you! Have you no compassion?"

Whitson swiveled about so quickly that she was caught off guard. "There are many in these very hills who do not appreciate the likes you seek to house, Miss Mackenzie. Some are very much against it."

"It is no one's affair what we do with our property," Catriona argued. She was acutely aware of Rhona's nervous fluttering behind her, and even more acutely aware of the anger that was seeping into her bones and warming her face.

"I will ignore your discourtesy, Whitson, that I will, for you are no' from these parts, aye?" her father said. "But if you ever deign to speak to my *nighean* in that manner again, you'll find yourself at the receiving end of Highland justice, that you will."

Whitson arched a thick brow. "Do you

threaten an agent of the king, my lord?"

"I threaten any man who dares speak to my family in that manner," her father snapped. "Have you an official decree, then, or are we to take the word of a *Sassenach*?"

Whitson's eyes narrowed. "I rather thought you were a man of reason, Mackenzie. You've a fine reputation as it stands, but it's best for all concerned if you do not push too hard, if you take my meaning. An official decree was delivered to Miss Griselda Mackenzie. I've not a copy of the decree on my person, but I can have one drawn up, if that is what you prefer."

"Griselda Mackenzie has departed this life," her father said to Whitson. "Until *I've* seen official notice of it, I've no reason to believe you."

Mr. Whitson clasped his hands behind his back. "I shall have it delivered posthaste. In the interest of expediency, allow me to inform you the decree grants you and your people six months to vacate the premises of the abbey, and if, by that time, you've not vacated, it will be taken by force. The property is forfeited, my lord. The king's orders are quite clear."

Catriona's head began to swim; she thought she might be sick. There were twenty-three souls at the abbey, all but one of them women and children who had been cast out of society. Where would they all go?

"Aye, and you've a quarter of an hour to vacate these premises, sir, or be removed by force, as well," her father said, and with that, he turned his back on the strangers.

"Expect your decree to be delivered by week's end," Mr. Whitson said icily. He turned about and started for the door.

"Have you no conscience?" Catriona blurted as he walked past her.

He paused. He slowly turned his head and set his gaze on hers, and Catriona felt a shiver run through her. "My advice to you, madam, is that you keep to the charitable works of proper women."

"Get out," Rabbie said in a voice dangerously low.

Whitson walked out of the room, his assistant hurrying after him with his soggy cloak.

All of them remained silent for several moments after the intruders had gone. Catriona's head was spinning. She thought of the women of the abbey: there was Molly Malone, who had been beaten so badly by her husband that she'd lost the child she was carrying. She'd slipped away in the dead of night with her two young children and a single crown in her pocket. And Anne

Kincaid, who, as a lass, had been cast out by a father who had no regard for her. She'd been forced into prostitution to survive. And Rhona, dear Rhona, such a godsend to Kishorn! When her husband had died, there had been no one to take her in. She had done piecework for a year but couldn't pay her rents. Her landlord had offered her a bargain — her body for a roof over her head. Rhona had endured it for three months before refusing him. He'd forced her onto the streets without a second thought.

There were more of them, many of them with children, and Catriona could not bear to think of what would become of them. She sank onto a chair, her gut churning with disbelief, her heart racing with fear and her head beginning to pound.

"Well, then," Catriona's mother said.

"*Airson gràdh Dhè,* what are we to do with this news?" Aulay asked.

"What can we do that has no' been tried before?" her father returned as he carefully resumed his seat. "The MacDonalds fought to have property seized by the Crown returned to their heirs and were no' successful."

"Aye, but the land they wanted returned was arable land," Cailean reminded him. "It

27

was more valuable than this," he added, gesturing vaguely toward the window.

"Aye, 'tis no' worth a farthing for planting," the laird agreed. "But this is a valuable glen for a *Sassenach* who means to run sheep."

"Can they no' put their sheep in the glen and leave the abbey?" Catriona asked.

Vivienne snorted. "They donna want the abbey or the women who live here." She paused and glanced sheepishly at Rhona. "My apologies, Rhona."

" 'Tis no' necessary," Rhona said. "We know verra well who we are."

"I've a suggestion," Catriona's mother said. "I think Catriona ought to deliver Zelda's letter to my brother sooner rather than later."

Her father looked at his wife curiously. "A letter? What letter?"

"Zelda wrote a letter to my brother that has not yet been delivered. You know Knox nearly as well as I, Arran. If there is anyone who might help us, it's him. He knows everyone in places high and low, and it so happens he is summering in Scotland."

All of Catriona's brothers groaned.

The Earl of Norwood's *summering* had been a sore spot for them all. He was one of the wealthy Englishmen who had benefited from the forfeitures and seizures of Scots' land after the rebellion. He'd bought a small estate near Crieff from the Crown and had once crowed he'd purchased the property for as much as a horse.

"Zelda's letter has naugh' to do with this," Catriona said as she looked around for her wineglass.

"Nevertheless, you promised Zelda to see it personally delivered, didn't you, darling? That's why you must go to him, and while you are there, you can appeal to him for his help with the abbey."

"Go to him!" Catriona said, and having located her wineglass, she swiped it up. It was empty again? "I canna leave the abbey now, Mamma. *Diah,* we've only just lost Zelda!"

"They have Rhona," her mother said, and took the empty wineglass from Catriona's hand. "Rhona is quite capable of seeing after them."

Catriona shook her head. " 'Tis no' the same —"

"Aye, Mamma is right," Vivienne chimed in. "Auntie Zelda would have gone to Uncle Knox straightaway, if that's what it took, Cat. You're the abbey's only hope, you are, and Uncle Knox is *your* only hope. And besides . . ." She paused and exchanged a

29

look with her mother. "You could do with a bit of distance, could you no'?"

"Distance?" Catriona repeated, confused, as she tried to retrieve her wineglass from her mother. "From what, pray?"

"From Balhaire. From Kishorn," her father said.

"Pardon?" The churning in her gut was taking on a new urgency. Something wasn't right, but she was having a wee bit of trouble thinking clearly.

"You were a blessing to my cousin, God knows you were," he said. "But you've tended her deathbed for months, and now it is time you saw to your own life."

Catriona blinked. Her thoughts were suddenly very clear — they'd been discussing her. Her own family, talking in secret about her! She could see it in the faces of her parents, of her siblings, of her sisters-in-law. They surrounded her now, looking at her with varying expressions of determination and sympathy. "What's this, then, you've discussed my life and determined a course, have you? How *dare* you speak ill of me behind my back."

"*Criosd,* Cat, no one has spoken ill of you!" Rabbie said. "But for the last few months, you mope about and drink your fill of wine and brandy every night, aye?" Rabbie said. "You donna attempt to have any society about you."

"What society?" she exclaimed loudly. "Where is it, Rabbie, do point me in that direction, aye? And in the course of it, perhaps you might point to something that I might *do*."

He frowned. "Do you no' see what we all see? You're letting your life slip between your fingers, you are."

She felt strangely exposed. Uncomfortable. Not angry, really, but . . . but she didn't like this, not at all. What did they expect of her? None of them had ever been a spinster, with nothing to look forward to, without any hope of ever being a mother, or a wife. "What would you have me do? I've no occupation, no' a bloody thing to do with my time but mope about and drink wine and brandy!" She felt on the verge of tears. She felt annoyed, she felt betrayed, she felt as if they'd all left her behind. Every one of them had families and loves and occupations, and *purpose,* for God's sake, but she, by virtue of being born female and at a time when suitable men were scarce, could do nothing but float from one gathering to the next, looking for something to do with her time.

The only meaningful thing in her life at

present was the abbey. Zelda had given a purpose to Catriona's life, and they would take it away?

Blast it, but the tears began to slip from her eyes again.

"*Diah,* I didna say it to make you cry," Rabbie said gruffly.

Her mother walked to Catriona's seat and wrapped her arms around her daughter. "Go to your uncle Knox, allow him to help you, and please, darling, take a bit of time to care for yourself."

"I canna leave them," she said tearfully, and took the handkerchief Daisy offered her and blew her nose.

"Aye, Miss Catriona, you can."

Catriona stilled. The mutiny was complete, then. "You, too, Rhona?" she asked in a whimper.

Rhona colored slightly. "We'll be quite all right for the summer, aye?" she said nervously. "Your lady mother, she . . . well, she's right, she is. You deserve happiness, Miss Catriona. You've no' had it at Kishorn."

Catriona wanted to argue that she was happy, but it was a lie. She was desperately unhappy with her situation, and apparently, in spite of her best efforts to hide it, they all knew it.

"Rhona and I had opportunity to speak," her mother said. "We agree everyone might look after themselves. But I very much miss my bright daughter."

Her "bright daughter" had withered away a very long time ago, and in her place, a lonely Catriona stood.

"I'll help at the abbey while you're away," Lottie said.

"So will I," Bernadette offered.

"Me, too!" Daisy joined in. "All of us."

"Aye, well, you'll no' know what to do, any of you," Catriona said petulantly. "You'll make a mess of things."

"We verra well might," Aulay agreed, and leaned down to kiss the top of Catriona's head. "But you'll put it all to rights when you return, aye?"

Catriona rolled her eyes. "I've no' said I'll go," she warned them.

But by the end of the week, Catriona was on a Balhaire coach bound for Crieff and Uncle Knox.

CHAPTER TWO

The journey from Balhaire to Crieff was tiresome, particularly given that the roads were single track and many of them used so infrequently that the coachmen were forced to stop more than once to clear debris from their path. Every day for a week they bounced along to a mean inn, then woke up and started the day over again.

Contrary to her family's wishes, Catriona's bleak mood was not improved by the travel.

It seemed weeks had passed instead of days when at last the coach rolled onto the High Street at Crieff and came to a halt at the Red Sword and Shield Inn. It was midday, but Catriona was so weary she all but fell out of the coach and into the hands of the young Mackenzie coachman who caught her and set her upright.

"Here you are, then, Miss Mackenzie," he said. "We'll be back for you in a fortnight, perhaps three weeks, aye?"

In that moment, she didn't care if they ever returned for her, because she could not fathom putting herself in that coach once more.

"There she is!" called a voice very familiar to her.

She turned about and smiled at her uncle Knox, who strode across the cobblestones to her, his coat flapping in time to his gusto. "My dear, dear girl, you've come at last!"

Her beloved uncle met her with such verve and enthusiasm that she was propelled a step or two backward, and her cap was knocked from her head. He wrapped her in a hearty embrace, smashing her face against his chest, then laid several kisses on her cheek before standing back, holding her at arm's length, admiring her as the coachmen tried to hand her the hat. "Still a beauty, my little one," he said proudly.

Still? She supposed that now she was three and thirty, he was expecting her looks to have begun to fade away into spinsterhood. "It's so good to see you, Uncle Knox," she said. "You've no idea."

Her uncle had grown a wee bit more corpulent since the last time she'd held him. What was it, a year or so ago? He'd come from England to visit his sister, Catriona's mother — and to pay a call to Auntie Zelda at Kishorn. Aye, he was a wee bit rounder, but quite handsome with his glittering pale green eyes and graying hair, which he'd bobbed with a black velvet ribbon. His coat was fine wool, and his waistcoat had been embroidered with gold thread that matched the embroidery along the center front of his coat. His neckcloth was snowy white and tied into an elaborate knot. Catriona felt quite plain in comparison.

"Come, come, you must be thirsty. And hungry, too, are you? Here you are, my good men, a night's lodging and all the wine and women you might want," he said, tossing a bag of coins to the driver. "Don't hasten back now. I should like time with my most favored niece." He wrapped an arm around Catriona's shoulders and wheeled her about. "It's such a dreadfully long way from Balhaire, is it not? I've always said to Margot that there ought to be an easier way to reach her, but alas, she has long loved your father and refuses to leave him."

"*Leave* him?" Catriona exclaimed.

"You've come alone, have you? No girl to tend you? Nothing but those brutes to drive you and handle your trunk?" he asked as he hurried her along the cobblestones toward the entrance of the inn's public room. Bright red poppies graced the window boxes, and tables and chairs had been arranged outside, yet there was no one enjoying the sun.

"I've a girl for you if you haven't one, although I can't vouch for her skills. She seems to do well enough to my eyes, but my guest, Miss Chasity Wilke-Smythe, claims she is wretched, and yet Chasity looks rather pretty to these old eyes."

Guests! Catriona should have known — Uncle Knox constantly surrounded himself with a retinue of friends and acquaintances, gathered from far-flung corners and questionable establishments. Catriona felt suddenly self-conscious as he bustled her along. She could smell herself, felt wretched in her traveling clothes and wanted nothing more than a hot bath and a wee bit of brandy.

"Between you and me, love, the Wilke-Smythes are a bit demanding," Uncle Knox said in a low voice. "And a bit too far on the side of the Whigs, if you take my meaning." He waggled his brows at her.

She did not take his meaning.

"But you will find great company in them, I am certain of it, and if not, there is Countess Orlov and her cousin, Vasily Orlov. Now, there is a colorful pair if ever there was." He leaned his head to hers and whispered, very dramatically, *"Russians."*

"I beg your pardon, Uncle. You didna mention you were already entertaining guests in your reply to my request to join you."

"Why, I've hardly any!" he declared. "And besides, I should have an entire assembly under my roof and turn them all away if it meant I might spend a summer with my much beloved niece."

"No' a summer, Uncle. A fortnight —"

"Here we are!" he declared, ignoring her, and with one arm around her, he used the other as a sort of battering ram and shoved open the door of the inn, then loudly proclaimed, "She's here!"

The small group of people gathered at a table in the center of the room looked at her. Those were her uncle's guests, she gathered, as the only other people in the inn were two men standing at the counter in the back with tankards before them.

Uncle Knox dragged Catriona forward to the table and introduced her to his company: Mr. and Mrs. Wilke-Smythe and their daughter, Miss Chasity Wilke-Smythe. Miss Chasity Wilke-Smythe resembled her mother so much that the pair looked a wee bit like twins in their powdered hair and matching coats. The former, at first glance, seemed scarcely old enough to be out.

38

She then met Countess Orlov, an elegant woman with a discerning gaze, and her cousin, the handsome, yet foppish, Mr. Vasily Orlov. "You must call me Vasily," he said, his name rolling off his tongue as he bowed over her hand.

Next was Mrs. Marianne Templeton, whom Catriona knew as the widowed sister of Uncle Knox's neighbor in England. Her mother had mentioned her once, had said she was quite eager to make Uncle Knox her next husband. She looked a wee bit older than Uncle Knox and examined Catriona from the top of her head to the tips of her boots. And last, an elderly gentleman with thick, wiry brows. Lord Furness, an old friend, her uncle said, scarcely glanced at her.

Uncle Knox sat her between Lord Furness and Miss Chasity Wilke-Smythe and ordered tots of whisky for them all. "In honor of my niece. The Scots are fond of whisky, is that not so, Cat?"

"Ah . . . . many are, aye," she agreed.

"When in Scotland, lads, we drink as the Scotch do," Uncle Knox said, and held his tot aloft. "To Scotland!"

"To Scotland!" his guests echoed.

Catriona tolerated whisky well enough, but she was so parched today that she downed the tot and set the small glass firmly on the table. That was when she noticed everyone was staring at her. "It was just a wee tot," she said a bit defensively. She was still bruised from the apparent censure she'd received from her family on that rain-soaked afternoon at Kishorn.

"Another!" shouted Uncle Knox. "Another round for us all!"

The whisky had the effect of making the group a bit merrier. They began to laugh and talk over one another, correcting each other's accounting of what had happened the night before, which, from the sound of it, had been a game of Whist gone horribly wrong. Catriona listened, and she smiled and nodded where she thought she ought, but she felt nothing but fatigue weighing her down. She leaned far back in her chair so that Lord Furness could speak over her to Miss Wilke-Smythe. The inn was beginning to fill, and she prayed that meant Uncle Knox would soon see them to Dungotty, the estate he'd allegedly purchased for a song. Unfortunately, he showed no sign of leaving, ordering kidney pies for all, and moving them from whisky to ale when Mrs. Templeton began to laugh a little too loudly.

Another hour passed. Catriona felt herself

sliding down her wooden seat and glanced at the watch pinned to her gown to gauge the time. When she wearily lifted her gaze, her eyes landed on the back of a man. He was quite tall. He was wearing a cloak that, from even a bit of distance, she could see was made of the finest wool. His snowy-white collar covered the back of his neck, and his hair, as black as his cloak, was bobbed into a queue with a single green ribbon. She had not seen him come in. He had taken a seat near the window, quite alone, and sat with one leg crossed over the other, one arm slung across the back of an empty chair, and gazed through the windowpanes at the goings-on in the street.

Catriona was suddenly nudged with an elbow. "I can't believe he's come in," whispered Miss Wilke-Smythe.

"Pardon?"

The young woman nodded in the direction of the tall man with the green ribbon. "That is the *Duke* of *Montrose*," she whispered excitedly. "Look, there's the coach from Blackthorn," she said, nodding toward the window.

Catriona looked at the man's back again.

"You've no doubt heard of him, haven't you?" asked Miss Wilke-Smythe.

Catriona shook her head. "Should I have?"

"Yes!" Miss Wilke-Smythe said in a near squeal. She clamped her hand down on Catriona's arm and squeezed with alarming strength. "He's quite notorious," she said, her brown eyes glittering.

He didn't seem so notorious to Catriona. "Why is that, then?"

Miss Wilke-Smythe leaned even closer, so that Catriona could feel her breath on her neck, and whispered, *"They say he murdered his wife."*

"What?" Catriona blinked. She turned her head to look at the young woman. "You jest," she accused her.

"Not in the *least*! Everyone says so — they say she simply disappeared. One night, she hosted a table set with so much china and silver that armed guards stood before the mansion. And the next day, she vanished, just like that," she said with a snap of her gloved fingers. "One moment she was here, and the next, *vanished.* No one has seen her since."

Catriona looked at the broad back of the man at the window. "That's impossible."

"You must hear it from Lord Norwood!" Miss Wilke-Smythe said, referring to Uncle Knox, who happened to be the Earl of Norwood. "He relayed it all to me."

"All right, then, that's enough of this," her

42

uncle suddenly said, and stood up, swaying a bit on his feet. "Time I see my darling niece home, I should think. Where are her trunks? Has someone got her trunks?"

"Well, I haven't got them," Lord Furness said, and staggered to his feet, too. In fact, there was a lot of rattling about as they all stood, casting around for discarded cloaks and reticules, hats and bonnets. In the flurry, Catriona tried to get a look at the duke's face, but his back was very much to the door, and Vasily Orlov chose that moment to sidle up to her with a leering sort of smile. "Norwood was *remiss* in mentioning the *beauty* of his niece," he purred.

Catriona stepped away from him and followed her uncle as he and his party stumbled into bright sunlight.

The Balhaire coach was gone, and in its place, a large barouche coach waited. It sported red plumes at every corner, and the gold seal of Montrose was emblazoned on its doors, much like the sort of coach Catriona had seen at Norwood Park when she was a child.

"By devil, has Montrose shown his face in town?" Uncle Knox said as he linked Catriona's arm through his.

"He has indeed," Lord Furness said as they stood together, admiring the coach.

43

"Did you not see the gentleman in the inn? It can be no one but him, not with the garish signet ring he wore."

"What? In the inn? I did *not*," Uncle Knox said. "Jolly well brave of him to come round, I'd say. Come along, Cat darling, you are with me. I've a new buggy, a cabriolet. From *France*," he said, as if that pleased him.

"What of my trunks?" she asked, looking back over her shoulder for them.

"Someone will bring them."

"Uncle, I —"

"There now, darling, don't fret about a thing. All is taken care of. I should not be the least surprised to see your trunks already delivered safely to your suite at Dungotty. The Scotch are surprisingly efficient."

She wondered if she ought to be offended by his surprise or his generalized view of her fellow countrymen, but her attention was drawn to her uncle's new carriage. It had two seats, a hood and two horses to pull it.

Uncle Knox helped her up first, but as he was unsteady on his feet from the ale and whisky, it took two attempts for him to haul himself into the seat beside her.

"Do you mean to drive?" she asked, alarmed.

"I had a mind to, yes. Don't look so

44

frightened of it, darling! Do you not trust your dear old Uncle Knox?"

"No!"

He laughed. "Well, then, if you prefer, *you* may drive," he said gallantly.

"I prefer."

He clucked his tongue at her. "So like Zelda you are. It's uncanny." He gladly handed her the reins. "Look here, look here!" he called to his companions. "My niece means to drive! That's the way of it in Scotland, the women are as hard as brass!"

"Uncle!"

"I mean that in the most complimentary way," he said as he settled back against the leather squabs. "My own sister is more Scot than English now, can you believe it? To think how she fought against being sent to Scotland to marry your father," he said, and laughed heartily before pointing. "Take the north road."

Catriona set the team to such a fierce trot that Uncle Knox had to grab on to the side of the carriage to keep from being tossed to the ground.

He was eager to call out points of interest as they drove, but Catriona scarcely noticed them, she was so tired. But when the road rounded a thicket, she did indeed notice, sitting at the base of a hill, an estate so

45

grand, a house so vast, that she thought it must belong to the king.

The stone was dark gray, the dozens of windows, even from this distance, glistening in the afternoon sun. There were so many chimneys that she couldn't possibly count them as they rolled by. "What is it?" she asked, awestruck.

"*That,* my dear girl, is Blackthorn Hall, the seat of the Duke of Montrose."

The house disappeared behind more thicket. They climbed a hill in the cabriolet, and the road twisted around, at which point they were afforded another view of Blackthorn Hall and the large park behind it. A small lake was in the center, the lawn perfectly manicured. There was a garden so expansive that the colors of the roses looked like ribbons in the distance. The stables were as big as Auchenard, the hunting lodge near Balhaire that belonged to Catriona's nephew, Lord Chatwick.

"Quite grand, isn't it?" Uncle Knox remarked.

The road curved away from Blackthorn Hall, and Catriona returned her attention back to the road. "Did he really kill his wife, then?"

"You've heard it already! That is indeed what the locals say, but I don't know that he did. Perhaps he sent her off to a convent. Whatever happened, it seems to be fact that she disappeared one night and no one has seen hide nor hair of her since."

"And no one has looked for her?" Catriona asked.

"Oh, I suppose they have," he said. "She was, by all accounts, a ginger-haired beauty, beloved by the tenants. I have heard it said she was a bright spot of light in a dismal man's shadow. How he must have resented her," Uncle Knox mused.

"Why?"

Uncle Knox laughed. "Don't you know, Cat? Gentlemen of a certain disposition do not care to be overshadowed by the weaker sex."

"But murder?" Catriona asked skeptically.

"Yes, well, some men are driven to mad passion by the right woman, darling." He tapped her hand. "Mind you remember that."

Catriona rolled her eyes. "Have you met him, then?" she asked. "The duke?"

"What? Why, *no,*" he said, sounding as if he'd just realized it and was surprised by it.

"If I lived here, I should make a point of meeting him," Catriona said. "I'll no' believe such rumors without meeting the man."

47

"So much like your aunt Zelda, aren't you?" he said, shaking his head. "She would have walked up to Blackthorn and banged the knocker and asked his grace, 'Did you murder your wife?'."

Catriona smiled.

Her uncle suddenly sat up. "There it is, there is Dungotty!" he said, swiping his hat off his head to use as a pointer.

Dungotty was a glorious house. It was half the size of Blackthorn Hall, but quite bigger than Catriona had expected, and rather elegant. It was at least as big as Norwood Park, her uncle's seat and her mother's childhood home. Dungotty was nestled in a forest clearing, and a large fountain spouted water from the mouth of three mermaids in the middle of a circular drive. They were arranged with their arms around each other, their faces turned up to the sun as if they were singing.

As Catriona steered the team into the drive, two men in livery and wigs emerged and took control of the team and helped Catriona and her uncle down.

"I've the perfect suite for you, my love," Uncle Knox said, wrapping his arm around her shoulders. "It was once inhabited by the dowager of Dungotty."

"Who was the family, then?" Catriona

asked, casting her gaze up at the frieze above the grand entry.

"What family?"

Catriona gave him a sidelong glance. "The family that was forced to forfeit."

"Ah, of course! You still harbor tender feelings, I see. I believe they were Hays. Or perhaps Haynes. Well, no matter. It was a very long time ago, and we should allow bygones to be bygones."

"Spoken like an Englishman," she muttered.

Uncle Knox laughed. "You might change your thinking when you see the rooms I've set aside for you."

Well, as it happened, Uncle Knox had a point. The rooms he showed her to were beautiful — a bedroom, a sitting room and a very large dressing room. The suite had been done in pink and cream silks, and a thickly looped carpet warmed the wood-planked floors. The bed had an elaborate canopy, and the view out the three floor-to-ceiling windows featured a trimmed lawn and a picturesque glen with hills rising up on either side beyond. In the sitting room, a fire blazed in the hearth. It boasted upholstered chairs, a small dining table and a chaise. But perhaps the most welcome site was the brass tub in the dressing room.

"What do you think?" Uncle Knox asked.

"Aye, it's bonny, uncle," Catriona said, and looked up at the ceiling painted with an angelic scene. "Thank you."

He smiled with pleasure. "Rest now, love. I'll send a girl and a bath to you before supper. We've a fresh ham in honor of your arrival!"

Catriona wasn't certain if he was more excited by her arrival or the prospect of fresh ham. She was excited by the prospect of a nap and a bath. "Before you go, uncle," she said, catching her uncle before he disappeared through the door. "I've a letter," she said, reaching into her pocket.

"My sister is determined to rule my life," he said with a chuckle. "This will be the third letter I've received from her in as many weeks. What now?"

"No' Mamma," Catriona said. "It's from Zelda."

Uncle Knox's expression softened. He looked at the letter Catriona held out to him. "She *wrote* me," he said, his voice full of wonder.

"Aye, that she did. She left three for me to deliver, she did. One for my father. One for the reverend. And one for you."

Uncle Knox took the letter and ran the tip of his finger over the ink where she'd written his name. "Thank you, my darling Cat," he said, and hugged her tightly to him.

Catriona was suddenly overcome with a wave of emotion. "You'll help me, will you no', Uncle Knox?" she asked into his collar. "You'll help me preserve what Zelda worked so hard to build, aye?"

"There now, lass, of course I will. But we will save talk of it until later, shall we? You need to rest from your journey and your loss."

"But I —"

"We've plenty of time," he said, and kissed her temple. "Rest now, darling." He went out, his gaze on the letter.

Catriona closed the door behind him, then lay down on the counterpane of her bed and closed her eyes with a weary sigh. But as she drifted off to sleep, she kept seeing a broad back, a neat queue of black hair, held with a green ribbon, an arm stretched possessively over the back of an empty chair.

It was impossible to imagine that a man who looked as virile as he would find it necessary to kill his wife. Could he not have seduced her instead? Of course he could have — he was a duke. She'd never known a woman who could not be seduced with the idea of being a duchess.

What, then, had become of her?

51

CHAPTER THREE

Hamlin Graham, the Duke of Montrose, Earl of Kincardine, Laird of Graham, was brushing a ten-year-old girl's hair. It was not his forte, nor his desire.

These were the true troubles of a notorious duke.

"It's too *hard*," the girl, his ward, complained.

"What am I to do, then?" he asked brusquely, annoyed with the task and his clumsiness at something that seemed so simple. "You've a bird's nest on your head."

The girl, Eula — Miss Eula Guinne, to be precise — giggled.

"Why do you no' have your maid brush your hair, then? She's surely better than me."

"I donna like her," Eula said.

"Aye, and why no'?"

"Because she's quite old. And she smells of garlic."

52

Hamlin couldn't argue — he'd caught a whiff of garlic a time or two from Mrs. Weaver.

"I should like a new maid."

Hamlin rolled his eyes. "I'll no' let Mrs. Weaver go, Eula. She came all the way from England to serve me and has been in my employ for many years, aye?" There was also the slight problem of finding a suitable replacement were he to lose Mrs. Weaver, given his black reputation.

"But she's no' a maid, no' really. She's a housekeeper. I want a *maid.*"

Eula was very much like her cousin, Glenna Guinne, the woman Hamlin had once called wife. Glenna had wanted for things, too — all things, and always more things. It had been a loathsome burden to try to please her.

He took one of the jewel-tipped hairpins from an enamel box and set a thick curly russet tress of Eula's hair back from her face. He did the same on the other side of her head.

"They're no' *even,*" Eula said petulantly, examining herself closely in the mirror.

It took Hamlin two more attempts before she was satisfied. When she was, she turned around and eyed him up and down. "You're no' properly dressed, Montrose."

"I've told you, 'tis no' proper for a young miss to address a duke by his title," he said. He glanced down at his buckskins, his lawn shirt and a pair of boots that needed a good polish. "And I'm perfectly dressed for repairing a roof."

"Which roof?"

"One of the outbuildings."

"What happened to it?"

"It's gained a hole."

"Why must you do it, then? A footman or a groundskeeper ought to be the one, no' you."

Hamlin folded his arms and cocked his head to one side. "I beg your pardon, then, lass, but are you the lady of Blackthorn Hall now?"

She shrugged. "Cousin Glenna said dukes are no' to work with their hands. Dukes are meant to think about important matters."

"Well, this duke happens to like working with his hands, he does." Hamlin put his hand on her shoulder and pointed her toward the door. "It's time for your studies."

"It's *always* time for my studies," Eula said with the weariness of an elderly scholar.

"Off with you, then, lass."

Before Eula could skip out the door, Hamlin stopped her. "Are you no' forgetting

54

something, lass?"

She stopped mid-skip, twirled around, ran back to her vanity, picked up her slate and quit the room.

Hamlin walked in the opposite direction, striding down the carpeted hallway lined with portraits of Montrose dukes and their ladies. He swept down the curving staircase to the marble foyer and strode through the double entry doors a footman opened as he neared, and onto the portico.

He jogged down the brick steps and onto the drive, where he paused to look up at a bright blue sky. The summer had been unusually dry thus far, which created crystal clear days such as this.

He struck out, walking purposefully to a group of outbuildings that housed tools and a tack room. Men were waiting for him, their workbenches and tools arrayed around the edge of a storage building that had been damaged by a late spring storm.

"Your grace," said his carpenter, inclining his head.

"Mr. Watson," Hamlin said in return. "Fine day, aye?"

" 'Tis indeed, milord." He handed him a hammer.

Hamlin took it and ascended the ladder that had been placed against the wall. There was a time the servants of Blackthorn had spoken to him as if he were a person and not someone to be feared. *Good day to ye, your grace. Been down to the river? Trout are jumping into the nets, they are.*

When he had positioned himself on the roof, he leaned to his side. "A plank, Watson."

"Aye, milord." With the help of a younger man, Watson climbed the ladder with a plank of wood and helped Hamlin slide it into place. Hamlin held out his hand for nails. Nails were placed in his palm. He set them in his mouth save one, which he began to hammer.

He had not been entirely clear with Eula. It wasn't the work he enjoyed, it was the hammering. He liked striking the head of a nail with as much force as a man could harness. He liked the reverberation of that strike through his body, how powerful it made him feel. Wholly in control. Capable of moving mountains and forging rivers. He'd not always felt that way. He'd not always been able to pound out his frustrations to feel himself again.

"Your grace," Watson said.

"Hmm," he grunted through a mouthful of nails.

"Your grace, someone comes, aye?"

56

Hamlin stopped hammering. He glanced up, saw a sleek little cabriolet behind a team of two trotting down the drive toward his house. He was surprised to see any conveyance coming down the road at all — no one called at Blackthorn now. There was no such thing as a social call. He spit the nails into the palm of his hand. "Who is it, then?" he asked of no one in particular.

"I donna recognize it," Watson said.

Hamlin sighed irritably. He wanted to hammer nails. He wanted to repair this hole and feel as if he'd done something meaningful today. He wanted to feel his strength, and then his exhaustion. But he handed everything to Watson and climbed down the ladder, reaching the ground just as the carriage was reined to a halt . . . and not a moment too soon, as it happened. If the driver hadn't reined when he did, the team would have run him over. As Hamlin waved the dust from his face, he squinted at the pair in the cabriolet. It was a woman who held the reins.

A gentleman, older than Hamlin by two dozen years or more, soft around the middle, climbed down, then held out his hand to help the driver. But that one had leapt like a stag from her seat on the opposite side of the cabriolet. The force of her landing knocked her bonnet slightly to one side, and he noticed she had hair the color of wheat. She righted her hat, then strode forward to join the older man.

There was something about the woman that struck Hamlin as odd. Perhaps it was the way she walked as they approached him and his men — confidently and with purpose, her arms moving in time with her legs. He was accustomed to women walking slowly and with swinging hips, in ways that were designed to attract a male's eye. This woman moved as if she had someplace quite important to be and not a moment could be spared.

The other notable thing about her was that she looked him directly in the eye, and not the least bit demurely. She was not complicated, but rather easy to read. Women used to smile at him in ways that made him question if he knew anything at all. But this woman gave him pause — generally, when anyone looked at him with such undiluted purpose, it was to request something or to accuse him.

"How do you do, sir?" the older man asked.

Hamlin shifted his gaze to the gentleman.

"Be a good man, will you, and send someone to inform the duke we've called.

Knox Armstrong, Earl of Norwood," he said, and bowed his head.

Hamlin stared at him. *Norwood.* He was English, quite obviously. Should he know him? He didn't recall the name and wondered what in bloody hell he was to be accused of now.

The woman cleared her throat.

"Ah. And my niece Miss Catriona Mackenzie of Balhaire," he added.

Hamlin looked again at the woman. She smiled prettily.

A moment passed as Hamlin considered the two of them. Miss Catriona Mackenzie of Balhaire arched a brow as if to silently remind him he was to fetch the duke. And then, in the event he did not recall what he was to do, she said, "If you would be so kind as to tell the duke we've called, then."

Her voice lilted with a Scottish accent. It was a lovely, lyrical voice, and he imagined her reading stories to children, soothing them to sleep. It was a voice quite at odds with her direct manner.

"You might tell him yourself," Hamlin said.

Norwood's eyes widened with surprise, and he exchanged a look with his niece. The two of them suddenly burst into laughter, startling Hamlin and his men.

59

"Good God, man, we cannot simply waltz into a grand house and announce our presence, can we? That is not the way things are done. One must inform the duke we've called, and he must decide if he shall receive us."

"Is that how it is done, then?" Hamlin drawled, aware that the niece was looking at him with amusement shining in her eyes.

"Well," the earl said, smiling jovially, "perhaps I should say that is how *we* do it."

Aye, the English thought themselves superior in every wee thing. Hamlin folded his arms across his chest. "*I* am the duke."

The niece looked startled, but Norwood seemed quite diverted by it, as if they were playing a game. "*You* are Montrose?"

"I am."

He looked at the men behind Hamlin, and whatever he saw there convinced him that Hamlin was telling the truth. "The devil you say. Well, then!" he said, smiling broadly now. "A pleasure to make your esteemed acquaintance, your grace." He bowed low. "You will forgive me for not recognizing you straightaway, but you can imagine my confusion, seeing you whale away at a nail as you were."

"Why should that confuse you, then?"

Norwood blinked.

"Because we've never known a duke to lift more than a cup, have we, uncle?" the niece said, and laughed.

Hamlin shifted his gaze back to her. This woman had not an ounce of conceit in her. Nor an ounce of manners, as one might expect, given that she was the niece of an English earl.

"Aye, well, this duke is no' afraid of a hammer. Or a cup."

"Apparently no'," she said with a pert smile, and her gray-blue eyes glittered like the surface of the lake in bright sunlight. Hamlin was momentarily blinded by it . . . until he realized that all gathered were waiting for him to speak.

He turned toward Watson. "Go, then, and inform Stuart we've visitors, aye?" he said low. He turned to his guests and said, "If you will be so kind as to carry on to the entrance. My butler will show you in. I'll join you shortly."

"Thank you, your grace," Norwood said, and gestured for his niece to come along.

Hamlin watched her ascend to the driver's seat once more, then stepped out of the way of the cabriolet, which proved to be a wise decision, for the niece started up the team with such enthusiasm that they practically launched into space with the small carriage flying behind them.

Hamlin looked around at his men. They were all staring at him as if they'd seen a comet. "Aye," he said, in taciturn agreement. No other words were needed — to a man, they all understood that what they had just witnessed was not the natural way of things.

CHAPTER FOUR

Stuart, a prim and proper butler, as thin as a reed, his neckcloth tied as tightly as a garrote, showed Catriona and her uncle into a small drawing room with brocade drapes, furnishings upholstered in silk and a wall of books. A clock on the mantel ticked away the minutes for them.

"He means to make us wait," Catriona said as she made her third restless trip around the room.

Uncle Knox had made himself quite comfortable on the settee and was currently examining a porcelain figurine of a small Highland fiddler. "Well, darling, we did make a rather unfortunate mistake in thinking him someone other than the duke."

"Who could blame us?" Catriona asked. "He looked like a carpenter, he did." A strong, strapping, handsome carpenter. His eyes were as black as his hair, his lashes as black as his eyes. His shoulders were as broad as a horse and his hips as firm as a —

"We should not judge a man by his appearance," her uncle absently opined.

It was too late. She'd judged him by his appearance and had found him ruggedly appealing. "No," she agreed. "But might we judge him a *wee* bit? He doesna look a murderer, does he?"

"I hardly know, darling. I am not acquainted with any murderers. I'm uncertain what to look for, precisely."

Well, she'd never known a murderer, either, but she was convinced the duke did *not* look like a murderer. He looked like someone who ought to be wearing a crown, or leading an army of Highland soldiers, or breaking wild horses. He had a commanding presence — even more so once she'd realized with a wee thrill that he wasn't a tradesman after all, but a *duke* and all that entailed — but not for a moment did he look the sort to murder. Catriona would be bitterly disappointed if she discovered he was.

She made her fourth trip around the room. She'd never been very good at waiting. In fact, she had coaxed her uncle into calling at Blackthorn Hall today because she couldn't bear to wait another moment to discuss the abbey, which Uncle Knox was reluctant to do. He wanted her to put it out of her mind for a time, and enjoy her visit. But Catriona could not put it out of her mind for any length of time, really, and certainly not without something to divert her instead. So she'd cajoled him into calling on the mysterious Duke of Montrose.

She paused at the shelving to examine his books. The duke had a collection of tomes concerning history, astronomy and philosophy. No plays, no sonnets. A serious man, then. Daisy brought Catriona novels from England, tales of chivalry and love and adventure on the seas. Did the duke read nothing for pleasure? Was the man who inhabited that physique opposed to the simplest diversion?

"Sit, Cat, my love. You're wreaking havoc on my nerves."

"I canna sit and wait like a parishioner for the end of the sermon," she complained.

Just then, the door swung partially open. A russet-haired head popped around the edge of the door about knob high. The head slid in just so that two brown eyes were visible. And then the door slowly swung open.

Uncle Knox gained his feet, clasped his hands at his back, then leaned forward, squinting at the creature who peeked around the door. "Good day," he said.

65

The child moved, presenting enough of her body to know that it was a lass who eyed them. The other half remained hidden behind the door. "I'm Eula," she said. "Who are you, then?"

"Good afternoon, Miss Eula," Uncle Knox said. "Lord Norwood." He bowed. "And this is my niece Miss Mackenzie."

Catriona curtsied.

The lass looked at Catriona, her gaze sweeping over her, lingering on the hem of Catriona's gown, which had been embroidered with vines and bluebirds. "Did you come to call on Montrose?"

Uncle Knox exchanged a look with Catriona.

"That's the duke," the lass said. "He lives here, too."

"Aye, we have," Catriona confirmed.

"Are you his friends?"

"Not as yet," said Uncle Knox. "But we do mean to change that."

The girl slid all the way into the room, her back to the wall. "He doesna have any friends," she said, staring at them suspiciously.

Uncle Knox covered a laugh behind a cough.

"Aye, we've heard it said," Catriona agreed.

The lass pushed away from the door and came closer to Catriona, peering at her curiously, her gaze taking in every bit of Catriona's gown, her face, her hair. "You're verra bonny."

"Thank you kindly," Catriona said. "So are you, Miss Eula. Do you live here, then, with his grace?"

She nodded. "I've my own suite of rooms."

"How wonderful. I should imagine them quite grand, aye?"

"They are," the lass agreed matter-of-factly, and traced her finger over the figurine that Uncle Knox had been examining. "I have *two* rooms, I do, but one is for sitting, and one for sleeping. That's the way of proper ladies."

"I see," Catriona said.

"Eula."

The deeply masculine voice was quiet but firm, and Eula was so startled that she knocked the figurine to the carpeted floor. Catriona bent down and picked it up. She smiled and winked at Eula before she rose, and returned the figurine to the table. She looked over the lass's head at the duke. He'd donned a proper coat, but he was still lacking a collar or neckcloth. And he had not, she noted, combed his thick, black hair.

"You're to be at your studies," he said coolly.

"But we have callers," Eula said.

"Rather, *I* have callers. *You* have studies. Go on, then."

"Aye, all right," Eula said with dejection, and began to slink to the door, but at the pace of a slug, pausing to examine the tassel on a pillow, an unlit candle. When she at last reached the door, she glanced back.

"Feasgar math," Catriona said with a smile.

The lass's pretty brown eyes widened with surprise.

"Good afternoon," Catriona translated.

Eula smiled with delight. She waved her fingers and sort of slid around the duke. As she went out, the duke ran his hand affectionately down her arm. So he cared for the wee minx. Which meant he wasn't entirely reprehensible.

The duke closed the door behind Eula and looked at Catriona and Knox expectantly.

"Very kind of you to receive us, your grace," Uncle Knox said. "I should have sent a messenger —"

"Aye," he said curtly.

Catriona arched a brow. Was he miffed with them still, or merely unpleasant?

"Well, then, we are agreed. In our considerable defense, we've only just arrived at Dungotty."

The duke said nothing.

"It's ours now, you see," Uncle Knox said.

Still nothing.

"It was an exceptionally good investment," Uncle Knox added quite unnecessarily. Catriona politely cleared her throat, which caught her uncle's attention.

"Yes, well, I have come for the summer, which is what brings us here today, your grace. I should like to extend an invitation to you to dine at Dungotty. I have invited my neighbors to the north, the MacLarens. Are you acquainted?"

The duke regarded Uncle Knox a long moment before responding. "I am."

"Splendid! We will have a fine evening of it. I've brought a cook from France, and I do not overstate his culinary skill, I assure you. You will not be disappointed, your grace."

The duke folded his arms across his chest as if he anticipated Uncle Knox would say more. His eyes, black as coal, moved to Catriona and flicked over her.

"You need not answer straightaway, of course," Uncle Knox continued. "You will need time to consult your diary, quite obviously, busy man that you must be. We should like to dine on Thursday evening if it pleases you, so if you would be so kind to grant us the favor of your reply by Wednesday, it would be most appreciated."

The duke stared at Uncle Knox with a clenched jaw. It was curious that he should be so tense in the face of an invitation to dine. Curious and rude. Uncle Knox, quite unaccustomed to taciturnity in anyone, looked helplessly at Catriona.

She stepped forward and took her uncle's arm. "At any other time we would be delighted to stay for tea, your grace, but as it happens, we've many calls to make today."

His gaze narrowed. "I didna invite you to tea."

"No?" she said cheerfully. "Then I do beg your pardon. I must have assumed you would as it would be the courteous thing to do, aye?"

"Oh," Uncle Knox muttered, and squeezed her hand. "Oh, no. *No,* Cat," he muttered.

But the duke was not bothered by her pointed remark because he said, "I donna disagree," and moved to one side and opened the door, thereby giving them a clear path to an exit.

"Thank you," Catriona said, and curtsied deeply. "We do look forward to your favorable reply, despite your obvious displeasure

70

with the invitation."

"Oh, dear me," Uncle Knox said. "Your grace," he said with a nod of his head, and with his hand firmly on her elbow, he escorted Catriona past the duke. She wouldn't know if the duke watched them go or not, for she refused to look at him.

In the hallway, Stuart appeared seemingly from nowhere, and with a sweep of his hand, he indicated the path to the main doors, then walked briskly ahead of them. When they reached the foyer, a footman was on hand to open *that* door so they would not be hindered for even a moment in their departure with a bothersome wait for someone to turn a knob. And no sooner had they stepped onto the landing than the door closed behind them so suddenly that Catriona turned her head to assure herself that her gown had not been caught.

"Well," Uncle Knox said, yanking on his sleeves, "I've scarcely met a ruder man."

"He's absolutely *diabolical,* is he no'?" Catriona asked with gleeful terror as the two of them began their walk down the steps. "I'm more determined than ever to know if he is a murderer, that I am."

"I would caution you in pressing your cause, darling, for if he is indeed a murderer, he may very well determine *you* ought to be murdered."

"True," she said thoughtfully. "Then again, he might no', aye?" She winked at her uncle.

"I've indulged you in this chase, but I've done all that I can for you, darling. You should have heard the hue and cry Mrs. Templeton unleashed when I said we meant to invite him to dine. One would think she was being murdered that very moment. If you want my opinion, you should not concern yourself with him at all. He has a black reputation. They say he is a candidate for the House of Lords, but I can't see how that could possibly be, given his sour demeanor and penchant for disposing of unruly wives." He paused. "Or perhaps that is the very thing that recommends him."

"You believe it!" Catriona said triumphantly. "You believe he's done something awful to his wife. You *do,* Uncle Knox!"

He patted her hand. "I've not yet made up my mind, but after today's interview, I am leaning toward the affirmative. Hopefully, he will agree to dine with us so that we might glean something."

Catriona laughed.

They climbed into the cabriolet. She took the reins from a groomsman and guided the team around. She had the strongest desire to look back at the massive ducal seat as they rode away, but she wouldn't allow herself to do it. Still, she had the strangest feeling they were being watched. Perhaps he was studying her back, determining where, precisely, to insert the dagger. Perhaps the ghost of the duchess was watching her.

Their next order of business was to call on the MacLarens. Uncle Knox had only recently met the influential laird MacLaren, and he was rather taken with him. Catriona could instantly see why when she was introduced — MacLaren had the same build as her uncle, was roughly the same age and possessed a booming laugh that he employed frequently. "You will be amazed at my collection of American tobacco products," he crowed as he and his wife led Catriona and her uncle into a receiving salon.

"Ah, American tobacco. A finer cheroot I've not enjoyed," Uncle Knox said as he took up a position at the hearth.

Catriona looked at him curiously. "How have you come upon American cheroots?"

"My dear, my acquaintances stretch round the globe," he said, and drew a large circle in the air.

Mr. MacLaren burst into loud laughter.

"Then you must have a look at my American tobacco, sir, aye? You've no' had as fine as this, on that you may depend." And with that, he whisked Uncle Knox away to some lair to admire tobacco.

Mrs. MacLaren summoned tea for the two of them. Like her husband, she was jovial, and the small salon felt as gay as its mistress.

"How long will you grace us at Dungotty, then?" she asked Catriona as she poured tea.

"No' long at all," Catriona said. "Perhaps a fortnight, but no more. I've pressing business at home."

Mrs. MacLaren did not inquire as to the pressing business as Catriona had hoped — she welcomed any chance to talk about Kishorn. "No' for the summer? Dungotty is so lovely this time of year, what with all the peonies. The Hayses, the former occupants, took great pride in their gardens."

She had no doubt they did before they were summarily ousted. "They are indeed bonny," she said. She picked up her teacup. "By the bye, we invited the Duke of Montrose to dine with us Thursday evening."

Mrs. MacLaren's surprise was evident in the manner her dark brows rose almost to her powdered hair. *"Really,"* she said, and put down her teacup, as if she couldn't hold the delicate china and absorb the news at the same time. "That's . . . surprising. He so rarely leaves Blackthorn."

"Oh?" Catriona asked innocently. "Perhaps, but he's our neighbor all the same. It would be rude not to have extended the invitation, aye?" She sipped her tea, then said coyly, "I've heard what is said of him."

Mrs. MacLaren looked a wee bit nonplussed. "Aye, he's been the subject of wretched gossip." She stirred sugar into her cup and added, "I canna imagine there's a soul in these hills who's no' heard what is said of him."

"Do you believe it?" Catriona asked.

Mrs. MacLaren frowned. "I donna know what I believe, in truth. Lady Montrose was *much* beloved in and around Blackthorn."

"It seems impossible that anyone can simply vanish, much less a duchess, aye?"

Mrs. MacLaren nodded. "Particularly such a bonny young woman. A true beauty, that she was. *Och,* but she was full of light and love, and younger than the duke. Quite young, really. And him so *brooding,*" she said with a shiver.

"Is he?" Catriona asked. She had thought him rude. But brooding?

"Rather distant, he is. But I suppose that's to be expected from a duke."

Catriona didn't suppose any such thing, but she kept that opinion to herself. "What did the duchess look like?" Catriona asked.

"Oh, she had *beautiful* ginger hair and piercing green eyes," Mrs. MacLaren said, happier to speak of the duchess. "A true beauty, that she was. He must have believed so, too, for he had her portrait made and hung it in the main salon at Blackthorn."

"Why would anyone assume he'd murdered her, do you suppose?" Catriona asked. It seemed so curious to her that murder should be everyone's assumption, rather than believing the duke had cast his wife out. A woman who'd been cast out by her husband had turned up at Kishorn Abbey a year or so ago. Did someone somewhere believe that woman had been murdered?

"I can hardly guess the workings of a deviant mind," Mrs. MacLaren said with a slight sniff. "What I *do* know is that passion can often be a dangerous thing between two people. But I shall no' speak ill of the duke," she said, in spite of having just spoken ill of the duke. "He's no' been charged with a crime, has he? To speculate would be to malign his reputation, and no matter what else, he's done a lot of good for his tenants. But he's made no friends for himself, that is true. And besides . . ." Mrs. MacLaren's voice trailed away.

"And besides?" Catriona gently prodded.

"Well . . . it was no secret that there was great unhappiness at Blackthorn."

That was a foregone conclusion. Happy homes did not lose a member here and there. "What sort of unhappiness?"

"I know only it's been said," Mrs. Mac-Laren demurred, and sipped her tea. "Ah, but she was a bonny woman, indeed she was. Devoted to the staff and their families. And he, well . . . he was rarely seen about. Quite cold, that one. It will be a curious thing to see him in society."

"I saw him in the common room at the Red Sword and Shield on the day I arrived," Catriona said.

"Did you? Perhaps he's changed his ways. God knows he needed to. All right," Mrs. MacLaren said, putting her teacup down again. "Enough of the duke. Is it true that your uncle has brought *Russians* to Dungotty?" she asked.

Catriona said it was true, and as Mrs. MacLaren began to speak of a chance meeting with a Russian count several years ago, Catriona thought of the dark-eyed man with the stern countenance and the portrait of his wife — *Dead wife? Missing wife?* —

hanging in his salon.

Catriona hoped he would come to dine. She hadn't been as diverted by a terrifyingly slanderous tale in ages.

Fortunately for her, they received the duke's favorable reply on Wednesday.

CHAPTER FIVE

"You're certain of this, are you?" Hamlin asked.

"Aye," Eula said. She was standing on a chair before him, working on the knot of his neckcloth, her brow furrowed in concentration.

"I was speaking to Mr. Bain," he said, and touched the tip of his finger to her nose.

"Aye, your grace, that I am," a voice behind Hamlin said.

Hamlin eyed the reflection of his secretary, Nichol Bain, in the mirror. He was leaning against the door frame, his arms folded across his chest, watching Eula's ministrations. The auburn-haired, green-eyed young man was ambitious in the way of young men. He didn't care about the rumors swirling around Hamlin, he cared about performing well, about parlaying his service to a duke to a better position. What would that be, then? Service to the king? Hamlin could only guess.

Bain had come to Hamlin through the Duke of Perth, the closest friend of his late father. As Hamlin had been a young man himself when he'd become a duke, Perth had taken him under his wing, and twelve years later, like his father before him, Hamlin considered Perth his closest adviser. Perth had brought Bain to him, had vouched for what Hamlin had thought were rather vague credentials.

Bain's expression remained impassive as he calmly returned Hamlin's gaze in the mirror. The man was impossible to discern. Whatever he thought about any given situation, he kept quite to himself unless asked. But he'd made up his mind about tonight's dinner at once when Hamlin had asked. Frankly, he'd hardly thought on it at all. He'd said simply, "Aye, you must attend."

Hamlin looked at himself in the mirror, eyeing his dress. He'd not seen about acquiring another valet since the last one had "retired" from his post after the fiasco with Glenna. He'd never been anything but perfectly civil to the man, and yet he'd believed the talk swirling around his master. Fortunately, Hamlin was quite capable of dressing himself and had donned formal attire. His waistcoat was made of silver silk, his coat and breeches black. Alas, Eula's attempt to tie his white silk neckcloth had not met with success.

"I think it a waste of time," he said to his reflection, returning to his conversation with Bain. "Nothing of consequence can come of it."

"It is well-known that the Earl of Caithness is unduly influenced by MacLaren's opinion. A vote from Caithness will be instrumental, if no' decisive," Bain said. "It could verra well be the vote to put you in the Lords, aye? The more familiar you are with the Caithness surrogate, the better your odds."

Hamlin responded with a grunt. If he secured a seat in the House of Lords, it would be nothing short of a small miracle. Scotland was allowed sixteen seats, and those seats were determined by a vote of the Scottish peers. Four had opened, and his name had been put forth by virtue of his title. But his appointment, which had once been seen as a *fait accompli,* was now tenuous at best. People did not care to be represented by a man rumored to be a murderer.

"You see this as an opportunity to be familiar with MacLaren. I see it as an opportunity for a lot of scandalmongers to

81

invent a lot of scandal."

"What does it mean, scandalmonger?" Eula asked.

"It means busybodies have been invited to dine, that's what."

She shrugged and hopped down from the chair, her task complete. "Will the lady attend?"

"What lady?" Hamlin asked absently as he tried to straighten the mess she'd made of his neckcloth.

"The bonny one with the golden hair."

And the gray-blue eyes. He could not forget those eyes sparkling with such mischievous delight. She was a minx, that one. It seemed of late that when most women viewed him at all, it was with a mix of horrified curiosity and downright fear. But Miss Mackenzie had looked at him as if she wanted to either challenge him to a duel or invite him to dance. He didn't know what to make of her forthright manner, really. He wondered if anyone had ever tried to bring her to heel. She was not a young debutante, that much was obvious, but a comely, assured woman, scarcely younger than he. Which raised the question of how a beautiful woman of means was not married? "I believe she will be, aye," he said to Eula.

"I rather like her," Eula said.

Of course she did — Eula was a wee minx herself, and with no woman to properly guide her, she was turning into a coquettish imp. "Where is your maid, then, lass? 'Tis time for your bed, I should think."

"Already?" Eula complained.

"Already." He leaned down and kissed the top of her head.

"You look very fine, Montrose," she said, eyeing him closely.

"Your grace," he reminded her.

"Your grace Montrose," she returned with a pert smile. In the mirror's reflection, Hamlin caught Bain's slight smile of amusement.

"Off you go, then. I'll come round to see you on the morrow, aye?"

"Good night," she chirped, and skipped out, intentionally poking Bain in the belly as she passed him.

When she had gone out, Hamlin undid his neckcloth and began to tie it again. "You're convinced, are you, that given all that has happened, I still stand a chance at gaining a seat?" Hamlin asked bluntly.

"No' convinced, no, your grace," Bain said. "But if anyone will consider a change of heart, 'tis MacLaren. He would keep the seat close to home and his interests rather than stand on principle."

Apparently, Hamlin was the unprincipled choice for the seat. He mulled that over as he retied his neckcloth. He was not shocked that MacLaren might advocate for him for less than principled reasons — a seat in the Lords wielded considerable power in Scotland, and Hamlin would be expected to return favor to whomever had supported him. But he wasn't convinced that MacLaren's lack of principle would extend all the way to him. He could very well have another candidate in the wings.

Never mind all this dithering about the evening on his part. He'd sent his favorable reply to Norwood on Bain's recommendation and would attend this bloody dinner. He was, if nothing else, a man of his word.

His butler appeared in the doorway and stood next to Bain. "Shall I have your mount saddled, your grace?"

It was a splendid night for riding, the moon full, the path through the forest that separated Blackthorn Hall and Dungotty pleasant and cool. But before Hamlin could answer, Bain lifted a finger. "If I may, your grace."

Hamlin nodded.

"To arrive on horseback to an important supper such as this might give the appearance of having suffered a diminishment in your standing. I'd suggest the coach, then."

A *diminishment of standing.* Is that what was said of him now? Hamlin sighed with irritation at the lengths he had to go to present himself to a society he'd once ruled and that had been quick to turn its back on him. Before he'd been married, invitations to Blackthorn Hall had been sought after throughout Scotland and even in England — the prospect of marrying a future duke, particularly one with the revered name of Montrose, had brought the lassies from far and wide. Hamlin had had no firm attachment to any of them, and he'd agreed to marry the woman his father had deemed suitable to carry the Montrose name and bear its heirs.

After his marriage, Hamlin and Glenna hosted dinners and balls for the country's elite in his ailing father's stead, as was expected of him, the heir. And when his father died, and the title had passed to him, Hamlin had stepped into his father's shoes. He and Glenna had dined with peers, appeared in society when it was expected. He opened a school and presented funds to a theater troupe. He sat on councils and hunted game and joined men at the gentleman's club in Edinburgh to complain about the government.

85

He had performed the duties of a duke in the same distant manner as his father had before him. Not because he was the same distant person his father had been — Hamlin liked to think himself as warmer than his father had ever been — but because he was already having trouble with Glenna and he didn't want anyone to know.

The trouble with Glenna was not apparent to anyone else before the disaster fell that ruined his life and his spirit, and left him desolate and questioning everything he thought he'd ever known about himself or this world. What had happened at Blackthorn Hall was a disgrace to any man.

That astounding fall from grace was the reason he'd taken Nichol Bain into his employ. The first thing Bain had said to Hamlin the day they met was *I am the man who might repair your reputation, I am.*

Normally, Hamlin would have taken offense to that. But he was intrigued by Bain's lack of hesitation to say it, and he was acutely aware that his reputation was in critical need of repair. This was, in fact, the first invitation he'd received in several months.

"Aye, Stuart, do as he says, then," Hamlin conceded. "The coachmen and the team will no' care to stand about waiting for a lot of fat Englishmen to dine, but that's their lot in life, it is."

The emblazoned Montrose coach drew to a halt in the circular drive at the Dungotty estate, and two footmen sprinted to attend it. The door was opened for Hamlin, a step put down for his convenience to exit the coach. The front door likewise opened for him before Hamlin could reach it, and a man wearing a powdered wig and a highly embroidered, fanciful coat stepped forward, bowed low and said, "Welcome to Dungotty, your grace."

"Thank you." He handed the man his hat as he stepped into the foyer. The grand house had had a bit of work done to it since Hamlin had last seen it, which he recalled was at least a decade ago, before his marriage. Marble flooring had replaced wooden planks, and an expansive iron-and-crystal chandelier blazed with the light of a dozen candles overhead. The stairs leading to the first floor were dressed in expensive Aubusson carpets, the railing polished cherry.

Hamlin removed his cloak, handed it to yet another footman and wondered just how many footmen an English earl actually needed for summering in Scotland. He'd seen more tonight than he had on staff at

Blackthorn Hall, which was twice the size of this house.

The sound of laughter suddenly rose from a room down a long hall. Hamlin immediately tensed — it sounded as if there were more souls laughing than the four he expected, which were the MacLarens, Norwood and his niece.

"This way, if you please, your grace," the butler said, and walked briskly in the direction of the laughter, down a corridor and to a set of double doors. He placed both hands on the brass handles, paused and gave his head a bit of a shake, then practically flung the doors open. He stepped inside and loudly cleared his throat. Standing behind him, Hamlin could see a number of heads swivel around. Damn it to hell, he'd been waylaid by that old English goat. There was a crowd gathered in this room.

The butler bowed and said quite grandly, "My Lord Norwood, may I present his grace, the Duke of Montrose."

Hamlin moved to step forward, but the butler was not quite done.

"And the Earl of Kincardine," he added, just as grandly.

Hamlin waited a moment to ensure that was the end of it, but as he moved his foot, the butler added with a flourish, "*And* the

Laird of Graham."

Well, that was definitely the end of it, as he held no other titles. But Hamlin arched a brow at the butler all the same, silently inquiring if he was done. The butler bowed deeply and stepped back.

Hamlin walked into the room and looked around at the dozen souls or more gathered. He made a curt bow with his head, and almost as one, the ladies curtsied and the men bowed their heads back at him.

"Welcome, welcome, your grace!" Norwood appeared through what felt a wee bit like a throng, one arm outstretched, the other hand clutching a glass of port. He was dressed in the finest of fabric, his waistcoat nearly to his knees and as heavily embroidered as the butler's. They shared a tailor, it would seem.

"We are most pleased you have come. May I introduce you to my guests?" Norwood said, and gestured to the MacLarens. "Mr. and Mrs. MacLaren, with whom, I am certain, you are acquainted."

"Your grace," Mrs. MacLaren said, and curtsied, her powdered tower of hair tipping dangerously close to Hamlin.

"Montrose, 'tis good to see you about," MacLaren said, eyeing Hamlin shrewdly as he gripped his hand and shook it heartily.

"Thank you," Hamlin said.

When MacLaren had taken a good long look at him, he shifted his gaze to Norwood, and something flowed between those two men that Hamlin didn't care for. That was precisely the reason he hadn't wanted to come here this evening — the unwelcome scrutiny, the assumptions about what had happened at Blackthorn.

"My dear friend Countess Orlov and her cousin, Mr. Vasily Orlov," Norwood continued, introducing him to a middle-aged woman with dark hair and rouged cheeks, and her fastidiously dressed cousin, who wore a sash across his chest with several medals pinned to it.

He was then introduced to an English family, the Wilke-Smythes, whose relation to Norwood was quite unclear. Lord Furness, a corpulent man who, from what Hamlin could glean, was an old friend. He seemed already well on his way to being thoroughly pissed. Next was Mrs. Templeton, a woman with a full bust and a painted fan, which she employed with great verve in the direction of her décolletage.

"Lastly, my dear niece Miss Mackenzie, who has already had the great pleasure of making your acquaintance," Norwood said, and waved airily at his niece.

She had made it quite clear it was not a pleasure, as he recalled. Miss Mackenzie rose elegantly from her inelegant perch on the arm of a settee. "It was indeed a *great* pleasure, your grace," she said with a wee lopsided smile that made it seem as if she was teasing him. She was wearing a shimmering gown of silver silk cut so daringly low across her bosom that standing over her, Hamlin had a most enticing view of creamy, full breasts. Her eyes, the remarkably brilliant gray-blue orbs, were shining at him a mix of mirth and curiosity. Her golden hair had been fashionably arranged on top of her head, pinned with a pair of tiny ornamental bluebirds, and a pair of long curls dangled across her collarbone.

He inclined his head. "Miss Mackenzie."

She sank into a curtsy at the same moment she offered her hand to him. He reluctantly took it, bowing over it, touching his lips to her knuckles. It struck him as somehow incongruent that a woman with such an audacious manner should have such an elegant hand that smelled of flowers.

He lifted her up and let go of her hand.

"There, then, the introductions are done," Norwood said. "You are in want of a whisky, your grace, are you not? I know a Scotsman such as yourself enjoys a tot of it now and again. My stock has come from my sister, Lady Mackenzie of Balhaire, and she assures me it has been distilled with the greatest care."

"No, thank you," Hamlin said. He would prefer to keep all his wits about him this evening.

Miss Mackenzie arched a brow. "Do you doubt the quality of our whisky, then, your grace? I've brought it all the way from our secret stores at Balhaire."

"I've no opinion of your whisky. I donna care for it," he said, but really, it was the whisky that didn't agree with him. The worst argument he'd ever had with Glenna came after an evening of drinking whisky. Hamlin had sworn it off after that night. He'd never believed himself to be one who suffered the ravages of demon drink, but a bad marriage could certainly illuminate the tendency in a man.

The lass smiled and said, "There you have it, uncle — that is two of us, both Scots, who donna care for whisky."

"What? I've seen you enjoy more than a sip of whisky, my darling," the earl said, and laughed roundly.

She shrugged, still smiling.

"Will you have wine?" Norwood asked Hamlin.

"Thank you."

"Rumpel! Where are you, Rumpel?" Norwood called, turning about and wandering off to find someone to pour a glass of wine.

His niece, however, showed herself to be more expedient. She walked to a sideboard, poured a glass of wine and returned, handing it to Hamlin.

He took it from her, eyeing her with skepticism. "Thank you."

" 'Tis my pleasure, your grace. I find that a wee bit of wine eases me in unfamiliar places. It helps loosen my tongue." She smiled prettily.

Did she think him uneasy? She stood before him, her hands clasped at her back. She made no effort to move away or to speak. No one else approached, which didn't surprise Hamlin in the least. He'd been a pariah for nearly a year and knew the role well.

"Will it surprise you, then, if I tell you I didna believe you'd accept our offer to dine?" she asked.

He considered that a moment. "No."

"Well, I didna believe it. But I'm so verra glad you've come."

He arched a brow with skepticism. "Why?" he said flatly.

She blinked with surprise. She gave a

cheerful little laugh and leaned slightly forward to whisper, "Because, by all accounts, your grace, you're a verra interesting man."

That surprised him. Was she openly and, without any apparent misgivings, referencing the untoward rumors about him? "You shouldna listen to the tales told about town, Miss Mackenzie."

"What tales?" she asked, and that mischievous smile appeared again. "What town?"

"Here we are!" Norwood said, reappearing in their midst. He'd brought the butler, who carried a silver tray on which stood a small crystal goblet of wine. Norwood spotted the wine Hamlin already held. "Oh," he said, looking confused. "Well, never mind it, Rumpel," he said, and waved off the glass of wine the butler was trying to present to Hamlin. "You may take that away. I beg your pardon, Montrose, if my niece has nattered on. Have you, darling?" he asked, smiling fondly at her. He probably doted on her, which would explain her impudence. She'd probably been allowed to behave however she pleased all her life.

"Whatever do you mean, uncle?" Miss Mackenzie asked laughingly.

"Only that you are passionate about many things, my love, and given opportunity, will

94

expound with great enthusiasm."

Miss Mackenzie was not offended — she laughed roundly. "You dare say that of me, uncle? Was it no' you who caused your guests to retire *en masse* just last evening with your lengthy thoughts about the poor reverend's most recent sermon?"

"That was an entirely different matter," Norwood said with a sniff of indignation. "*That* was an important matter of theology run amok!"

"Milord." The butler had returned, sans tray and wine. "Dinner is served."

"Aha, very good." Norwood stepped to the middle of the room and called for attention. "If you would, friends, make your way to the dining room. We do not promenade at Dungotty, we go in together as equals. And we dine at our leisure! I'll not insist we race through our courses like the Empress Maria Theresa of Austria, whom I know firsthand to be *quite* rigid in her rules for dining. Countess Orlov has been so good as to help me determine the places for everyone. You will find a name card at each setting. Catriona, darling, will you see the duke in, please?" With that he turned about and offered his arm to the young Miss Wilke-Smythe.

Miss Mackenzie held her hand aloft in

midair. "You heard my uncle — I'm to do the escorting of our esteemed visitor, who, it would seem, is no' our equal after all, but above us mortals and worthy of a special escort."

The woman was as impudent as Eula.

She smiled slyly at his hesitation. "Please donna give him reason to scold me."

With an inward sigh, Hamlin put his hand under her arm and promenaded her into the dining room ahead of everyone but Norwood.

The dining room was painted in gold leaf and decorated with an array of portraits of men and women alike. The table had been set with fine china, sparkling crystal, and silver utensils and candelabras polished to such sheen that a man could examine his face in them. A floral arrangement of peonies graced the middle of the table, and as Hamlin took his seat, he discovered that one had to bend either to the left or right to see around the showy flowers.

On his right was the Wilke-Smythe miss, and on his left, Mrs. MacLaren. He was not entirely sure who sat across from him, given the flowers. Norwood was seated at the head of the table, naturally, and anchoring the other end was Miss Mackenzie. She had the undivided attention of Mr. Orlov to her right, and Lord Furness to her left.

The dinner began with carrot soup, progressed to beef, potatoes and boiled apples, and was, Hamlin would be the first to admit, quite well-done. The earl had not exaggerated his cook's abilities.

In the course of the meal, Mrs. MacLaren asked after Hamlin's crops. Yes, he said, his oats were faring well in spite of the drought this summer. Yes, his sheep were grazing very well indeed.

When he turned his attention to his right, Miss Wilke-Smythe was eager to speak of the fine weather, and how she longed for a ball to be held this summer at Dungotty. "I miss England so," she said with a sigh. "I'm invited to all the summer balls in England. On some nights, I keep a coach waiting so that I might go from one to the next."

She made it sound as if there were scores of summer balls, dozens to be attended each week. Perhaps there were. He'd not been to England in years.

"Alas, there are none planned for Dungotty," she said, pouting prettily, and Hamlin supposed that he was supposed to lament this sad fact, and on her behalf, either make a plea to her host to host one or offer to arrange one himself. But Hamlin couldn't possibly care less if there were a hundred balls planned for Dungotty this summer, or none at all.

His lack of a response seemed to displease Miss Wilke-Smythe, for she suddenly leaned forward to see around him. "My Lord Norwood, why are there no balls to be held at Dungotty this summer?"

"Pardon?" the earl asked, startled out of his conversation with Countess Orlov. "A ball? My dear, there are not enough people in all the Trossachs to make a proper ball."

This answer displeased Miss Wilke-Smythe even more, and she sat back with a slight *huff*. But then she turned her attention to Norwood's niece. "Do you not agree, Miss Mackenzie, that we are in need of proper diversion this summer?"

Miss Mackenzie was engaged in a lively conversation with Mr. Orlov and looked up, her eyes dancing around the table as if she was uncertain what she might have missed. Her cheeks were stained a delightful shade of pink from laughing, and her eyes, even at this distance, sparked. "I beg your pardon?"

"I was just saying that Dungotty is so very lovely," Miss Wilke-Smythe explained, "but there are very few diversions. How shall we ever survive the summer without a *ball*?"

"Oh, I should think verra well," Miss Mackenzie said. "We survive them without balls all the time, do we no', Mrs. Mac-Laren? *I* intend to survive the summer by returning home," she said. "You must all take my word that the journey to Balhaire is diverting enough for a dozen summers."

Her announcement caused Miss Wilke-Smythe more distress. *"What?"* she cried, sitting up, her fingers grasping the edge of the table. "You mean to leave us? But . . . but *when*? How long will we have your company at Dungotty?"

This outburst had gained the attention of everyone at the table, and they all turned to Miss Mackenzie, awaiting her answer.

"A fortnight," she said. She smiled and turned her attention back to the Russian, apparently intent on continuing her conversation, but Miss Wilke-Smythe pressed on.

"But why must you *go*?"

"Yes, why indeed?" Mr. Orlov seconded as his hand strayed near Miss Mackenzie's, his fingers touching her thumb. "You do not mean to deprive us of your lovely company, surely. You must stay the summer, Miss Mackenzie, for I shall be highly offended if you do not."

Miss Mackenzie laughed. "You might be offended for all of an afternoon, sir, but I've no doubt you'd find suitable company, aye?"

"Oh, she means to stay," Norwood said

dismissively. "She's been too long in the Highlands."

"Too long in the Highlands, as if that were possible!" Miss Mackenzie playfully protested. "You know verra well that I've an abbey to attend to, you do, Uncle Knox. I intend to leave in a fortnight."

"An abbey!" Mrs. Templeton said, and snorted. "I would not have guessed you a *nun.*"

Miss Mackenzie did not take offense to that purposeful slight. She laughed again, delighted by the remark. "On my word, I've no' been accused of being a *nun,* Mrs. Templeton. But I've wards that need looking after, aye?"

"You're far too young for wards, Miss Mackenzie," Mrs. Wilke-Smythe said graciously.

"She is indeed, but she speaks true," Norwood says. "My niece and her dearly departed lady aunt have provided shelter for women and children for a few years now."

Shelter for women and children? Wards? Hamlin looked curiously at Miss Mackenzie. He himself had a ward. That she had a ward — several of them, by the sound of it — aroused his curiosity.

She looked around the table at everyone's sudden attention to her. Her laugh was suddenly self-conscious. "Why do you all look at me this way, then? Have you never done a charitable thing, any of you?"

" 'Tis more than charity, my darling," Norwood said.

"What women?" Mrs. Templeton demanded. "What children?"

"Women who've no other place to go, aye?" Miss Mackenzie explained. "They've taken up rooms at an abandoned abbey on property my family owns, that they have."

"Why have they no place to go?" Miss Wilke-Smythe asked with all the naivete of her age.

"That's . . . that's no' an easy answer, no," Miss Mackenzie said, and shifted uncomfortably. For the first time since Hamlin had made her acquaintance, she seemed at a loss for words and looked to her uncle for help. "It's that they are no' welcome in society or with families for . . . for various reasons."

"Good Lord," Furness said. "Do you mean —"

"Aye, I mean precisely that, milord," she said quickly before he could say aloud who these women were. "Women who have been cast out, along with their children."

That was met with utter silence for a long moment. Mrs. Wilke-Smythe looked at her husband, but he was staring at Miss Mackenzie.

Privately, Hamlin marveled at her revelation. The sort of charitable work she was suggesting she did was the kind generally reserved for Samaritans and leaders of the kirk. Ladies of Miss Mackenzie's social standing might embroider a pillow or collect alms, but they did not generally participate in a manner that would put them into direct contact with such outcasts. Or at least, they would not *house* them. It appeared that Miss Mackenzie was more than a pampered woman of privilege.

"What do you make of it, Montrose?" MacLaren abruptly asked him. "Seems the sort of thing you'd run across now and again in the Lords, does it no'? Social injuries, poor morals and the like?"

"They donna have poor morals," Miss Mackenzie said, her voice noticeably cooler. "Or if they have poor morals, it is because the poor morals were forced onto them."

MacLaren ignored her, his gaze on Hamlin. "Well? What would you say to someone with Miss Mackenzie's passion for the depraved?"

"They are no' depraved!" she said, her voice rising.

"Yes, your grace, what do you say to it?"

the countess asked him.

One reason Hamlin was intent on gaining a seat in the House of Lords was to address social injustice, to move Scotland forward, away from the rebellions of the past. Change was needed. Many people had been displaced by the rebellion, he knew, but even he was taken aback by this. Women and children living in a run-down abbey? He glanced at Miss Mackenzie, who was watching him without any discernible expectation. He realized she didn't care what he thought of it. That also intrigued him. "One canna dictate or impose on the charitable intentions of another, aye?"

"One can if it's wrong," MacLaren said.

Miss Mackenzie's gaze narrowed slightly, and she looked away.

"For God's sake, Rumpel, take that arrangement away, will you?" Norwood complained. "I can't see Cat from here."

The butler moved at once to remove the offending peonies.

"Catriona is a philanthropist," Norwood continued, looking around at them all.

"*Philanthropy!*" Countess Orlov suddenly laughed. "Of course, that explains it! I understood something much different, but now I understand it plainly. The Orlov family is among the greatest philanthropists of

Russia."

Miss Mackenzie's face had turned a subtle shade of pink. " 'Tis no' philanthropy," she said low. "My family is verra generous with their resources, aye, but 'tis a wee bit different for me. I verra much want to help them. By the saints, I donna understand anyone who'd no' want to help them. Their lives have unfurled in ways through no fault of theirs, and life can be verra cruel to women, it can."

"Oh, *dear*," Mrs. MacLaren muttered despairingly. "Do you mean that life has been cruel to you, then?"

"To me?" Miss Mackenzie clucked her tongue. "No' to *me*. I've had every privilege. But to women born to less fortunate circumstances, aye? Women without a family fortune to gird them, aye? I've wanted for nothing in my life, no' a thing. But these women? They've wanted for compassion and love, a place to call their own. They've wanted food for their children and shoes for their feet. Some of them have come with hay stuffed into their shoes to keep the damp from seeping in. Can you imagine it, any of you?"

It was the height of indelicacy to speak of these things at a supper table, but Hamlin found her response to be intriguing and, frankly, righteous. Everyone needed to understand the inequalities that existed in their world.

"I wouldn't know about that, but life has certainly been cruel to *me,*" Mrs. Templeton said bitterly, prompting Norwood to pat her kindly on the hand before she swiped up her wineglass and drank. Mrs. Templeton seemed to have forgotten she was dressed in silk and dripping in jewels. She clearly didn't understand what cruel meant.

"What madness is this?" Furness demanded of Norwood. "How is it your family has allowed one of your own to . . . to *consort* with such women and in such a public manner?"

"I beg your pardon, sir, but my uncle doesna speak for me," Miss Mackenzie said calmly, although the color was high in her fair cheeks, and her grip of the table so tight that Hamlin could see the whites of her knuckles from where he sat. "Griselda Mackenzie, God rest her soul, turned an old abbey into a safe haven for the forlorn and the lost, aye? I donna know all the circumstances that brought these women to Kishorn, but it never mattered to her, it did no' — what mattered was that they'd lost their husbands and fathers and brothers, with no one to provide for them, or had escaped situations in which their bodies were used for the pleasure of men."

Mrs. Wilke-Smythe gasped with alarm. Her daughter's eyes rounded.

"None of them had a place to go, no' until Zelda revived the old abbey for them."

"But that's . . . that's hardly *proper,*" Mrs. Wilke-Smythe said uncertainly.

"Neither is it proper to leave them in the cold with no hope," Miss Mackenzie retorted.

"But what do you *do*?" Miss Wilke-Smythe asked, clearly enthralled by this unexpected side of Miss Mackenzie, while her mother withered in her seat, clearly undone by the world beyond ivy-covered walls. "Do you mean you are with them?"

Miss Mackenzie let go her grip of the table and touched a curl at her neck. "Aye, I am. I see after them, that's what," she said with a shrug. "I see that they have all they need."

"My niece is to be commended," Norwood said firmly, but it was clear to Hamlin that few others in this room, with perhaps the exception of Vasily Orlov, shared his view. "Frankly, it is unconscionable that there are those who would cast out these women and children from the safety of an old abbey when they can't properly fend for themselves," he continued.

"Who would cast them out?" asked Mac-Laren.

"Highland lairds," Miss Mackenzie said. "They donna like them so close, aye? They can find no pity in their hearts, can see no value in them. They view them as hardly better than cattle."

"How do you presume to know what is in the hearts of the lairds?" Lord Furness demanded.

"Englishmen, too," she continued, ignoring him. "They want the land for their sheep. They mean to seize the property. The Crown has determined it forfeit."

"On what grounds?" MacLaren asked gruffly.

"I'll tell you the grounds," Norwood said grandly. "My niece will not tell you the whole story, I'm certain of it. Her aunt, who I may personally attest was as daring a woman as I've ever known, and if I might say so, quite beautiful," he added wistfully, "in her own way assisted the Jacobite rebels who fought to overthrow our king by hiding them when they fled to escape the English forces."

There were gasps all around, which Norwood clearly relished.

"Treason!" MacLaren uttered.

"Uncle, perhaps you ought no' —"

"Perhaps they ought to know the truth, darling."

Hamlin's curiosity about this abbey was entirely kindled. He had not been on the side of the Jacobites — he was loyal to the king. But like most Scots, he was not particularly fond of the English and their ways.

"This woman's aunt was a traitor to the king and the Crown," Furness said angrily, pointing at Miss Mackenzie.

"Furness, for God's sake, man, she was a *benevolent*," Norwood said impatiently. "When the rebellion was put down, and these men faced certain death, she took it upon herself to help them escape with their lives instead of seeing them slaughtered. Find fault with it if you will, but I think it a very noble thing to do for one's country-men."

No one argued with Norwood's impassioned defense, but Hamlin privately wondered if it was truly noble to aid traitors, no matter if they were countrymen.

"Shall I tell you what else?" Norwood asked, leaning forward now, one elbow on the table.

"No, Uncle Knox," Miss Mackenzie said, sounding slightly frantic.

But Norwood had the room's rapt attention, and Hamlin knew he would not relinquish that attention. It seemed even the servants were leaning a little closer to hear his answer.

"Our own Catriona Mackenzie *helped* her."

"Airson gràdh Dhè," Miss Mackenzie muttered, the meaning of which was not known to anyone in this group. "I beg you, Uncle Knox, donna say more!"

"She's a daring girl in her own right," he said. "Her own father expressly forbid her to associate with known Jacobites, and yet my beautiful, compassionate niece could not let those young men die! She brought many of them to Kishorn herself." He sat back, nodding at the looks of shock around him. Miss Mackenzie looked as if she wanted to crawl under the table. "What's the matter, darling? You're not ashamed, are you?"

"No!" she said emphatically. "But you are needlessly distressing your guests, uncle."

"They've no grounds for distress!" he proclaimed. "I will have you all know that I mean to help her. What sort of men are we to punish a woman's true compassion? Is that not what we all seek from the fairer sex? The Lord Advocate contends the property is forfeit for housing those traitors a decade ago, but by God, I shall have something to say for it."

Miss Mackenzie groaned softly and bowed her head.

"And what have you to say for *that*, Montrose?" MacLaren challenged him. "Is the property forfeit?"

"I'll no' pass judgment on events for which I donna have all the facts, sir, and I'll no' do so here for your entertainment."

A ghost of a smile appeared on MacLaren's lips. If he wanted to find reason to deny him the vote, then so be it. But Hamlin would not be goaded into making a pronouncement on Miss Mackenzie's good intentions.

"I beg your pardon, Lord Norwood, but what have these women to do with the rebels?" Miss Wilke-Smythe asked.

"You see, don't you, my dear, that once the rebels slipped away, it was only natural that women and children who had lost their protectors and providers to the same battlefield and desertion would follow? And once they were gone, others who had no place to go, no way to feed their children came behind them. It was a noble calling that Zelda and Catriona undertook."

"I would argue that," Furness sniffed. "Seems rather foolhardy and ill-advised to me. Precisely the sort of thing one can expect to happen when one leaves aunts and daughters to their own devices without proper arrangements for marital supervision."

It was quite obvious to Hamlin — and everyone else, for that matter — that Furness's misogynistic view of a woman's place in the world irked Miss Mackenzie, because her head came up and her sparkling eyes fixed like a pair of burning lances on the old man. Hamlin was not surprised by Furness's stodgy views — he doubted the doughy English nobleman had ever risked as much as a hair on his wig for a cause in which he believed. But if Furness couldn't agree with her mission, he might at least commend her for her conviction.

Miss Mackenzie suddenly swept up her wine and drank long from it, then put the goblet down and leaned back in her chair, her gaze averted from the table, as if she was longing to be anywhere but here.

The sour Mrs. Templeton seized the opportunity to pounce, as well. "I daresay Miss Wilke-Smythe would *never* be caught riding about with rebels," she said haughtily. "*Here* is a young lady who is *very* well accomplished in the ways a debutante *ought* to be."

"More's the pity. She looks the type to be

quite diverted by it," Norwood said with a chuckle.

The lass's parents both gasped, but Norwood continued without a thought. "But she is indeed an accomplished little songbird. Will you not amuse us with a tune on the pianoforte, Chasity?"

"Aye, you must," Miss Mackenzie said, and stood so abruptly that all the gentlemen had to hasten to their feet. "Shall we retire, then, ladies, and leave the gentlemen to their ports and their cheroots and judgments of us? Donna leave us alone too long, lads — we'll be without proper supervision, after all."

The gentlemen stared at her in quiet astonishment, but Norwood smiled broadly. "Just so, just so," he said, and to Furness, "What did I tell you just yesterday, Furness? My niece is a quick-tempered woman."

If Furness made a reply, no one heard it, for the women were walking out, Miss Mackenzie leading the way, her gait determined. As they moved into the corridor, Hamlin heard her laugh rise up.

The lass was not quick-tempered. She was quick-witted. And she did not appear to allow fools to dismay her for more than a moment.

Hamlin couldn't help but admire that in a person.

CHAPTER SIX

Catriona had suspected Furness was an old swine, and tonight, he'd confirmed it. Now that she'd taken his measure, she'd not waste another moment fuming about him. That was another thing she'd learned from Zelda — never spend a moment of precious sunlight on the likes of him.

She and the other ladies entered the drawing room, where Catriona very unceremoniously collapsed on a settee. The Wilke-Smythe women retreated to the far end of the room and pretended to examine the sheets of music there, no doubt thoroughly scandalized and concerned they'd tarnished Chasity by virtue of being in the same room with Catriona. She knew very well how the English viewed things — Catriona's mother was English.

Mrs. Templeton examined a few books on the shelf. She'd made it clear from nearly the moment Catriona had stepped off that

114

coach that she didn't care for Catriona's appearance at Dungotty, no doubt because it divided the attention Uncle Knox had apparently been giving her. Mrs. MacLaren sat on a chair near the hearth and picked up a poker to stoke the embers.

Countess Orlov was the only one who dared to speak to Catriona, sidling up to her to sit daintily beside her. "What *guile* you have, Miss Mackenzie. I would not have thought you the sort to take such dangerous risks."

Catriona eyed her with reservation.

"I am impressed," the countess said. "Were you frightened?"

"Frightened?"

"Of the rebels. Were they perfectly awful?" she asked, her eyes glistening with anticipation of Catriona's answer.

"Oh, no, I wasna frightened. I was *intoxicated* with excitement."

Of course she'd been frightened. She'd defied her family and risked her own fool neck. But she'd been caught up in the wake of her aunt Zelda's fierce loyalty to the Highlands.

Her answer seemed to please Countess Orlov. She leaned closer and whispered, "Then you *enjoyed* it, no?"

Catriona blushed. She sat up. "It was a

115

verra long time ago."

"Were they very handsome, these rebels?"

Diah, those men had been as frightened as her, running for their lives. "I beg your pardon, but the circumstance did no' make it possible to study their faces, aye?"

"Oh," the countess said, and sagged back against the settee with disappointment. "I suppose not. Nevertheless, I can't help but admire what you've done. I pity those poor women. I had to send a maid away once when my husband had impregnated her." She shrugged a bit. "I don't know where she might have gone."

Catriona stared at the countess. It was a callous remark, said without the least bit of emotion. How many had come to Kishorn after being tossed out on their arse by a lord or lady who no longer had any use for them? "I can only hope she made her way to Kishorn Abbey, aye?"

Countess Orlov smiled a little. "I rather suppose she didn't survive the Russian winter." She stood up and glided away.

If Catriona could have fled that room without disappointing her uncle, she would have. She didn't want to be near these people. She stood and moved restlessly about, her fingers trailing over the furnishings, and was only brought to a halt when

116

Miss Wilke-Smythe said breathlessly, "I can't bear it another moment if I don't inquire — what do any of you make of the duke?"

Five coiffed heads turned toward the lass.

"Chasity! You've only just made his acquaintance," her mother said. "None of us know him well enough to pass judgment."

Catriona would have bet all she had that every one of them had already passed judgment.

"Well, I rather like him," Miss Wilke-Smythe said. "And I think him quite handsome."

"He is much older than you," Countess Orlov said, and fidgeted with an earring. "I, too, find him quite appealing, but he must be near to forty years. Has he an heir? If he has no heir, he must be desperately in want of a new wife."

"Countess Orlov!" Mrs. Wilke-Smythe said sternly.

Countess Orlov shrugged.

"You donna believe he killed his wife then, aye?" Catriona asked idly.

"*I* do," said Mrs. Templeton without a moment's hesitation. "You can see it around the eyes. They're too dark."

As if the duke could control how black his eyes were. Catriona turned her head so no

117

one would see her roll her eyes.

"And he's very cold in his demeanor," Mrs. Templeton continued. Apparently, she believed *she* knew him well enough to pass judgment. And a lot of it. "He's scarcely said a word."

"Well, it was rather impossible," said Mrs. Wilke-Smythe. "Miss Mackenzie took up a fair bit of the table conversation."

Catriona laughed at the slight. " 'Twas no' I, madam. 'Twas your curiosity that filled the time."

Mrs. Wilke-Smythe lifted her chin and pressed her lips tightly together. But she did not deny it.

"I mean to discover the truth about the duke," Catriona announced to Mrs. Templeton's back. "It is passing strange to me that a man's wife can go missing and no' a thing is done about it. What of her family? Have they nothing to say?"

"Oh, her parents were killed in a tragic fire, and her only other relative, a cousin, died in childbirth. Lady Montrose had no one but the duke," Mrs. MacLaren said. "Even if she had, what could be done about it, I ask you? Who would dare question a duke? He may say what he likes of his wife's absence and there is no' a man in Scotland who would dare defy him. How do you

118

mean to discover the truth, then, Miss Mackenzie, without putting yourself in harm's
way?" asked Mrs. MacLaren. "And well
within a fortnight at that, as you yourself
said this very evening you'd no' be long at
Dungotty."

All fair questions. "I donna know how,"
Catriona admitted. "But I've quite a lot of
idle time between now and my departure,
and if I donna at least try, I'll perish from
curiosity, that I will. It's a wretched rumor,
and I, for one, donna think he seems even a
wee bit murderous. And yet, a duchess
doesna go missing all on her own, aye? If he
is a murderer, he ought to be made to ac-
count for it, aye?"

"Are you some sort of authority on traitors and murderers?" Mrs. Templeton
scoffed. "Is that another of your gifts?"

"Only traitors," Catriona said. "But I
mean to become an authority on murderers, too."

"You're a hoyden, that's what you are,"
Mrs. Templeton said icily. "You've been
indulged by your uncle in your fantastical
thinking and left to roam the countryside
like a pilgrim."

Catriona burst out laughing, picturing
herself with a staff and a rough robe,
wandering the Highlands.

Her laughter only angered Mrs. Templeton more. "What is your age, Miss Mackenzie?" she demanded. "I find it curious a woman of your considerable years has not yet married. Were you my daughter, I would have made you a proper match long ago."

Her remark was met by stunned silence from everyone except Catriona. "*Diah,* Mrs. Templeton, how I incense you without any effort on my part at all," she said cheerfully.

But in truth, Catriona was a wee bit surprised that Mrs. Templeton had seen fit to state the obvious so openly. It was the question that followed Catriona wherever she went. Why wasn't the daughter of a powerful laird, the sister of noblemen, the daughter of an English heiress, married? Never mind what she'd accomplished without benefit of being married in her thirty-three years, it seemed that none of it mattered to the world if she was not wed. She was expected to have a husband, provide an heir, set his table and mend his shirts. She was to be dutiful and supportive of the head of her household and submit to his desires. She was *not* to have adventures of her own, or desires of her own, or dreams and ideas and likes and dislikes all on her own.

Anything less than what was expected made her less of a person in the eyes of proper society.

Aunt Zelda had scoffed at such thinking, but even she had lamented more than once that the world thought less of her than any man, and would never think any more of her until she had a husband.

"You do incense me," Mrs. Templeton agreed. "You seem to think it perfectly all right to shirk your duty."

"If you'd care to see me wed, Mrs. Templeton, I'll no' stand in the way of your attempts," Catriona said. The irony in Mrs. Templeton's observation was that she seemed to think Catriona had refused to be married when, in fact, she longed to *be* married. She did want a husband to love, a family to raise. She wanted the happiness her siblings found in sharing their lives with their spouses and children. For whatever reason, fate had not seen fit to lead her to drink from the trough of marital bliss, and now, frankly, it was too late.

Fortunately, Zelda had taught Catriona to think beyond everyone's expectations for her. To think beyond marriage and the sort of life she'd been taught to expect. "Life didna turn out as you thought it might, aye?" she'd said to Catriona once. "Never mind it, lass — yours is still a life that can bring you as much joy as you allow. This

121

world belongs to you as much as anyone. You're fortunate, you are, *mo chridhe,* for you have been blessed with a family that allows you to live as you choose. No' many women are given such an opportunity, are they? But choose your path wisely, aye? Donna make the same mistakes I did."

When Catriona had pressed her on what mistakes she'd made, Zelda had shaken her head and waved her away. "*Och,* too many I've made, then," she'd said. "Too many long forgotten."

Well, Catriona had chosen her path, all right — she'd followed her aunt on some of the greatest experiences man or woman could imagine. She was thankful for the life Zelda had shown her, and while she worried about the responsibility Zelda had left for her, she was grateful it was her responsibility, and not one of her brothers.

It seemed a far more important calling than marriage.

"You'll not stand in my way?" Mrs. Templeton repeated snidely, then laughed with a twinge of outrage. "Perhaps *you'll* find the duke a suitable match, Miss Mackenzie, seeing as how you are convinced he'd no' harm a hair on anyone's head. As the Countess Orlov has pointed out to us all, he does not have a wife."

"Mrs. Templeton!" Mrs. MacLaren chided her.

But Catriona couldn't help laughing. By God, the woman was as bold as she was. And she obviously loved Uncle Knox very much, for nothing else could explain her contempt for Catriona. "Perhaps," she said jovially.

The conversation was thankfully ended as Uncle Knox fairly exploded into the room, swaying a wee bit and in jolly spirits thanks to all he'd imbibed this evening. The other gentlemen filed in behind him, the duke entering last and remaining at the back of the room, his hands clasped behind him, his weight shifted onto one hip. He said not a word but kept his head down, studying the room with his black eyes. When that black gaze met Catriona's, she felt a strange shiver course through her unlike anything she'd ever felt in her life. She wasn't entirely certain what it was — a natural response to Mrs. Templeton's suggestion that she should marry those black eyes? A shiver of revulsion? Or was it something else? Whatever it was, it was intense and hot and prickled at the back of her neck.

She wondered, as she turned away from him and let her gaze settle on mother and daughter at the pianoforte, if the duke had ever looked at his wife like that. She wondered if he'd looked at his wife like that as he squeezed the breath from her throat.

Another, more potent shiver ran down her spine.

"Chasity, darling, we'll have a song from you, shall we?" Uncle Knox asked.

"It would be my pleasure," Miss Wilke-Smythe answered.

As she and her mother arranged themselves at the pianoforte, Catriona moved around the perimeter of the room so that she could steal another glimpse of the dark duke.

His gaze was locked on the performers.

Miss Wilke-Smythe cleared her throat and began to sing along to her mother's accompaniment. Catriona wandered to the back of the room and paused, pretending to listen, standing with her back to the wall. Miss Wilke-Smythe sang passably, her voice light and pure, like her. Catriona surreptitiously watched the duke take in the performance. His expression was inscrutable, but his attention apparently rapt, as he never turned his eyes from the magpie.

After polite applause praised Miss Wilke-Smythe at the conclusion of her song, she decided to perform a second. Catriona sighed beneath her breath and rested her hands on her middle on her belly, pretending to enjoy the warbling and stealing glimpses of the duke.

He never glanced in her direction.

When the second song concluded, Lady Orlov suggested something a bit livelier. She relieved the Englishwomen of the pianoforte, then settled in, speaking in Russian to her cousin, who seemed to disagree with the countess's suggestion. In the midst of the familial argument, Montrose wandered to where Catriona stood, set his gaze on the Russians and said under his breath, "I take it you are no' the sort of woman to present your accomplishments in song."

His remark surprised Catriona. "No, alas," she said. "My accomplishments run to the masculine."

He glanced at her for a single, searing moment. "To the masculine? Pray tell, what are your accomplishments, other than rescuing widows and lightskirts?"

Catriona couldn't help a pert smile. "The sort of accomplishments of a duke."

He slowly turned his head toward her. His eyes flicked the length of her. "As lofty as that?" he murmured as Countess Orlov arranged the music on the stand and settled in.

"I didna say a duke's accomplishments

125

were *lofty.*" She smiled coyly, pushed away from the wall and walked away. She took a seat. Countess Orlov began to play with such a heavy hand that the flames of the candles shook.

Halfway through the countess's playing, Catriona glanced back. But the duke was not in the room. Neither was Mr. Mac-Laren. They had slipped out, unnoticed.

She turned around and fixed her gaze on the mantel clock. What a strange and curious man the dark duke was. What had he done with the beauty of Blackthorn Hall?

Catriona didn't know how she'd discover the truth. She might have to simply resort to inquiring of his grace. *What have you done with your wife, milord?*

A curl of heat settled in her chest when she imagined how dark his eyes would look if she ever found the courage to ask him.

CHAPTER SEVEN

For MacLaren to whisper in Caithness's ear, Hamlin would have to pledge his support for keeping the Scotland bank under the control of Scotland.

MacLaren had explained this rather succinctly a couple nights past as Hamlin had prepared to take his leave of Dungotty. "The earl will no' abide the choke hold the Crown keeps on the English banks, no' here, no' in Scotland," he said with such vitriol that Hamlin wondered what sort of encounter MacLaren or Caithness had experienced with an English bank. "Our regulations serve us well enough without the meddling of the exchequer or Parliament, aye?"

"Aye," Hamlin agreed.

"I am favorably inclined to voice my support of a candidate who vows to keep as much of our independence as possible, that I am," MacLaren said. He'd kept his gaze, shrewd and suspicious, on Hamlin, as if he thought he might see something in Hamlin's expression to warn him off.

But Hamlin had learned through years of a tumultuous marriage how to keep his thoughts and emotions to himself. He steadily held the man's gaze and said, "My aim is to keep Scotland for the Scots and move forward from the disputes of the past, aye? I donna mean to bring more rule into Scotland, if that is your fear."

MacLaren's smile had been slow. "Well, then," he'd said. "You may verra well have my Caithness's vote after all. I'll have a word with him."

Hamlin related the conversation to Bain this morning, who stood across the continental desk with its inlaid wooden design of blackthorns. It had been a gift from Glenna's family to Hamlin on the occasion of their wedding. He had liked Glenna's parents. He had been appalled when he'd received word that the viscount and his wife, as well as a chambermaid, had died in an early morning fire at their estate. An unattended candle was the culprit, setting fire to half the house.

The desk was a constant reminder of their tragic end, but it felt too dismissive of their lives to remove it. He'd once asked Glenna for her opinion. She'd glanced at the desk rather absently, then at him, and had shrugged. "I donna care what you do with it," she'd said.

Was it grief that had made her so callous? He knew grief came to people in different ways. Some made light of it to protect themselves from more hurt, he thought. Others let it grip them by the throat until it felt almost as if there was no point in breathing any longer. He could count himself in the second group.

He'd kept the desk.

His study was his favorite room in the sprawling ducal estate — it was filled with books and maps, and rugs he'd purchased from Flemish weavers. He had floor-to-ceiling windows from which he had an excellent view of his extensive garden.

Bain was staring out the windows as Hamlin told him about the supper at Dungotty and what MacLaren had said. "Did he give you his commitment, then?" Bain asked when Hamlin had finished.

"He said he'd discuss it with the earl."

Bain tapped absently on the windowpane. "I should think it worth a wee inquiry, aye?"

"What?"

"The sort of bank business MacLaren may wish to keep under wraps, that's what. If you donna have his firm vote, perhaps it would behoove you to have something that might help persuade him." He'd turned and looked at Hamlin then, his green eyes dark and intense.

Hamlin understood. Bain's point was unsavory, but he understood why he made it. "The Bank of Scotland was once believed to be supportive of the Jacobites, is that no' so?" Hamlin asked.

A ghost of a smile appeared on Bain's lips. "Aye, your grace, that is so."

Hamlin nodded. He drummed his fingers on the desk, thinking. "How difficult would it be to learn MacLaren's business, then?"

"I've an acquaintance, a banker. A Scottish banker."

Hamlin chuckled. "How fortuitous for me, aye?" He stood up and walked to the window and stood beside Bain. His eye caught the ruby-red color of a rose bush in full bloom. He was suddenly reminded of another, similarly bonny day, when the roses also had been in full bloom. He'd been in the garden with Glenna. He recalled her crying. Forever tearful she was, her complaints and displeasure with him piling higher with each passing week. He could not, for the life of him, remember what had vexed her so that day.

"There is to be a meeting held of the

Gentlemen of Science, Thursday next," Bain said. "Among them are the agents of some of our more illustrious countrymen, and in particular, the dukes Argyll and Lennox. And Caithness."

In addition to Caithness, Argyll and Lennox would also vote on the empty seat in the Lords. "What is the meeting about, then?"

"Bridges, your grace."

"Bridges," he repeated.

"There is need of a bridge on the south end of Loch Ard to ease travel."

"I see," Hamlin said. "And now I must be a proponent of bridges, is that it?"

"It would be helpful."

Hamlin nodded. "What else?"

"Mr. Palmer has informed us he intends to leave his post by month's end."

Hamlin turned his attention from the window to Bain. "My gamekeeper?"

Bain nodded.

"Why?"

His secretary shrugged. "He's been quite taken with religious sensibilities."

Hamlin frowned. "Religious sensibilities? Or does he find it reprehensible to be in my employ, perchance? 'Tis been a year, has it no', and still they quake in their boots at the sight of their employer?"

131

"As I understand it, a reverend from Kippen attended the parish fair and there expounded on the battle of good and evil in our world. He advised his flock to avoid evil at all costs. Mayfield House has been searching for a suitable gamekeeper and Mr. Palmer was moved to inquire after it, aye?"

"The news catches me by surprise, aye? For a day or so, I have forgotten I am the evil, black-hearted Duke of Montrose. Mayfield House will no' pay a wage as well as I've paid his bloody hide," Hamlin groused.

"No," Bain agreed.

"For God's sake. Verra well, find another. And a lady's maid for Eula."

Bain started. "Beg your pardon, your grace?"

"She needs proper supervision, aye?"

Bain stared at him.

"What?" Hamlin asked impatiently.

"*You're* proper, your grace."

"No' *me*. Someone who knows about hair and . . . and gowns, I suppose. And the way of women."

Bain looked utterly confused. Hamlin clucked his tongue at the young man. It wasn't as if Bain was naïve about the fairer sex. He was often out catting around at nights — Hamlin had seen him slinking back to Blackthorn Hall in the misty hours of the early morning. "Their courses, lad," Hamlin said low.

Bain slowly lifted his chin, his gaze suddenly defiant. "I beg your pardon, your grace, but I am no' versed in the requirements of a *lady's maid.*"

"I just told you the requirements. She must brush hair and . . ." He made a whirling gesture with his hand.

Bain and Hamlin stared silently at each other for a moment until Hamlin relented and said, "Aye, verra well, then. Inquire of Mrs. MacLaren."

"Aye," Bain said, his voice full of relief. "I'll call today, I will. Speak of the wee devil," he said, and nodded toward the window.

On the road that ran alongside the garden walls, Eula appeared, leading her pony with one hand, and dragging a stick in the dirt behind her with the other. Aubin, Hamlin's cook and resident equestrian — the Frenchman possessed many talents and had no qualms about taking his wage from purported murderers — was riding his mount behind her.

"Is there more?" Hamlin asked as he watched Eula walk along.

"No, your grace."

Hamlin walked out the French doors of

his study and onto the terrace, then headed down the flagstone steps and around the side of the house, where he intercepted Eula and her instructor.

"Good afternoon," he said.

"Good afternoon," she responded, and bobbed a lopsided curtsy as she waved her stick at him.

"Why do you no' ride?"

"I donna want to ride him anymore," she said, looking at the pony. "He's too small." She dropped her stick and the reins and looked at Hamlin with an edge of defiance he'd only recently begun to notice. It rivaled only Mr. Bain's.

"He looks the perfect size for you, he does," he said, and stroked the pony's mane.

"He's no'. I saw the lady today, and she rides a horse as big as Mr. Aubin's."

"What lady?" Hamlin asked, although he suspected he knew the answer.

"Miss Mackenzie."

He suspected correctly. No one else would dare come so close to Blackthorn Hall. "You saw her where?"

Eula suddenly gasped. "She was wearing *breeches*!" she said with delight, as if she'd discovered a new litter of puppies.

"Was she indeed," Hamlin drawled,

"I believe they are called trews, your

grace," Aubin reported in his thick accent. "She wore them beneath her mantua gown in place of a petticoat."

Hamlin stared at Aubin as he tried to picture it. Was that . . . acceptable?

"She wears them for riding," Eula patiently explained. "She said a lady canna ride properly if she sits on only half her bum —"

"Pardon?" Hamlin asked.

"She says that if you mean to ride, you must ride properly, and ride astride."

"She said all that, did she?" he said, folding his arms across his chest.

"She rides verra well, Montrose. You should see her."

"Sir," he corrected her.

"Sir," she obediently repeated. "I want to ride like her. May I?"

"No." He looked at Aubin. "Where did this happen, then?"

"At the river, your grace. Miss Guinne and I had stopped to water our mounts, and she came galloping across the meadow, riding so recklessly I thought certainly she was being chased by highwaymen. She is indeed a fine rider. She might, perhaps, have a point."

"Perhaps, but that is no' the way of things at Blackthorn Hall, aye?" Hamlin said, and picked up the reins of the pony and handed them to Aubin. "Come, then, Eula." He put his hand on her back and ushered her forward, toward the back terrace.

"She wore her hair down, and it fell all the way down her back, just like the tail on Mr. Aubin's horse when he brushes it," Eula said, her small hands fluttering to demonstrate just how long this tail of hair was. "She said lassies ought to learn how to ride and shoot and fish for themselves, because sometimes there are no men to do it for them and sometimes a lassie doesna want a man to do it for her."

Good Lord, had they taken tea? Whiled away the morning? "It would seem the lady is full of opinions," he muttered.

"May I *please* ride astride?" Eula asked, turning her face up to his. "Please? She's verra good, and I'm no'."

"You may no'. It is no' considered lady-like to ride in that fashion, Eula."

"But she rides that way."

Yes, but she was a different sort of lady. One whose accomplishments ran to the masculine — oh, yes, he recalled that bold, inexplicable claim. "What the lady does is her affair — no' yours."

"It's no' fair," Eula complained. "I quite like her. She's bonny. Do you think she's bonny? I like the way she laughs. She laughs a *lot.*"

"I've noticed, aye." He had a sudden image of Eula, several years in the future, wearing trews and leading rebels to some hideout in the Highlands and laughing as she went. Good God. "For now, you will put aside your desire to ride like a highwayman and have your bath, aye?"

"Aye," she said, clearly disappointed when he sent her on to her room and Mrs. Weaver. He remained at the open French doors, staring out into the gardens of Blackthorn Hall. He did not want to think about Miss Mackenzie in her trews. He had trained himself to suppress any thoughts of women. Of their innate beauty. Of sex. After the tragedy of his marriage, Hamlin was persuaded he would never know happiness. No matter that he was a duke, he was damaged, a social leper, and would never know the sort of intimacy he craved. Better not to think of it at all.

And yet, he was thinking of the hoyden with the golden hair and the gray-blue eyes, sparkling as if she believed the entire world existed for her amusement. She was a traveler, passing through life and enjoying the sights, the tastes, the scent of it all. And putting ideas in young girls' heads about riding astride as she went.

Putting ideas in a grown man's head about riding astride, as well.

He could picture her riding a horse like a man. Vividly. Too vividly.

He suddenly felt the need to hammer something. He needed to hammer for a good hour, something hard and unbendable so that he might expend the unwanted vigor that had suddenly invaded his body.

The stable. Surely something needed hammering there.

Two days later, Hamlin rode into the small village of Aberfoyle to meet with his solicitor. It was a short meeting; his solicitor, like so many others, obviously did not care for Hamlin, what with all the rumors. But he did not despise Hamlin so much that he was willing to part with the compensation he received for handling ducal affairs. If Hamlin had had another choice in this part of Scotland, he gladly would have taken it. It was his misfortune that the surly Mr. Peterboro was the only decent solicitor for miles.

When he quit that office and walked outside, he struck out across the village green toward the stables to fetch his mount. He didn't look right or left — what was the point? He would not be acknowledged — had not been acknowledged in months, even by those who might still call him friend. Better to pretend not to see the ignominious duke than shock anyone by greeting him. The people of this region had loved Glenna. She had a way of ingratiating herself into one's good graces by showering them with the affection only a duchess could afford. She bestowed gifts in the way of large purchases from the shopkeepers, favors of employment or benevolence to the less fortunate, trinkets of value to her friends. And he was the man whom they believed had removed that angel from their midst in a most nefarious manner. None of them would say that to his face, fearing the power he wielded, which, as Bain had once pointed out to him, was considerable. Because he was a duke, an accusation of murder would have to be brought to Parliament. The lords would not entertain it. "It strikes too close to home, as it were," he'd said casually.

It hardly mattered to Hamlin if they accused him — what mattered was that they believed it of him.

Aye, Hamlin was very well aware how his presence was received in the village, and, no, he did not look about for a friendly face that afternoon.

So it was to his great surprise that he heard his name called out as he reached the far side of the green. He paused and curiously turned about to see Miss Mackenzie hurrying across the green to him, her reticule bouncing merrily against her hip. *"Madainn mhath!"* she called cheerfully from a distance twenty or so feet away, as if she couldn't bear to wait the few steps to greet him.

Hamlin glanced around, expecting the full Dungotty entourage to appear, a host of Englishmen who cared nothing about what was said about the Duke of Montrose, but that they might boast about their titled "friend" when they returned home.

Yet no one else appeared but the Mackenzie lass, reaching him with cheeks pinkened from her near sprint, wisps of her hair curling around her face beneath the wide brim of her hat. And her eyes, shining with mirth, always full of vitality and happiness. How in blazes was she so happy? How was anyone so bloody happy?

"Madainn mhath!" she said again. "I greet you in Gaelic."

"I gathered."

She clasped her hands before her and smiled expectantly, presumably thinking he might offer his own greeting. When he did not, as he did not trust her intentions, she was not the least deterred. "What brings you to the village this bonny morning, then?" She glanced skyward as if he might not have noticed the bright sun overhead, the azure-blue skies.

He wondered if she didn't know or perhaps didn't care that it was ill-mannered to inquire after a gentleman's business. He found himself glancing at the petticoat of her gown, also wondering if she wore trews beneath it and having a sudden and ferocious urge to see her legs in trews. So ferocious, in fact, that his heart began to pound with curiosity.

"Where is your ward?" she asked when he didn't speak. "Has she come with you?"

Now she would ask after Eula? Hamlin didn't know what to do with this bonny woman. He didn't trust her interest in him, and yet he couldn't help but feel drawn to her. "Perhaps I've been misinformed, but I thought it was no' done for a passing acquaintance to make such a personal inquiry."

"A passing acquaintance!" She laughed. "Have you forgotten that we've dined together? That makes us practically friends! I should go so far as to say we *are* friends. You should agree to this, as I have heard it from your ward's own lips that you donna have many."

"She said that, did she?"

"Without any misgivings." She smiled. "My sincere apology if I've managed to offend you, your grace, but I happened upon Miss Guinne earlier in the week and thought to ask after her. She's a bonny lass, and I like her verra much."

"Aye, she is," he agreed, but he was looking at her when he said it, and for a sliver of a moment, he was confused as to who was the bonny one. "By the bye, she mentioned your bit of advice to her."

"What advice was that?" Miss Mackenzie asked. "That she should aspire to a meaningful life? That is no' a bit of advice, but rather important. I think you must mean my advice on how to properly sit a horse," she said cheekily. "I wasna wrong in that. How can anyone believe a woman might handle something as big as a horse perched so precariously on its back? I dare say you couldna ride in that manner, either. Have you tried it?"

"Of course no'," he said.

"Of course no'," she mimicked him, making her voice deep and her brows furrow.

"I amuse you," he said.

"You *do* amuse me," she admitted. "And

you intrigue me. I find it curious that a duke has no friends at all. One would think your title and your verra big house would bring you scores and scores of dear, close friends." Her smile broadened.

Hamlin was aware of his heartbeat again. It wasn't racing per se, but reminding him that it was very much present and willing to work in any manner necessary in the presence of this woman.

"You're no' in a talkative mood, are you? Verra well, then, I'll leave you to your stomping about the green and all the mysterious reasons you've come to Aberfoyle," she said, and touched two fingers to the brim of her hat. "I'll no' wonder long, for I'm certain the reasons will be known far and wide across the Trossachs before the day is through. I have discovered that I'm no' the only one who is intrigued with you, aye?" A devilish little smile of amusement twinkled in her eye.

He didn't smile outwardly, but he could feel a smile inside of him. "I warned you against paying any heed to the latest gossip, did I no'?"

"Gossip! I donna listen to gossip, your grace. I meant only that you're a *verra* important duke."

His gaze narrowed on her smiling face.

"You didna mean that at all, Miss Mackenzie. What is *your* business here, then?"

"Why, I am *delighted* to tell you." She leaned forward as if she meant to share a secret. He leaned closer to hear it. She whispered, "If you look very closely over my shoulder, I'm sure you'll spot Miss Chasity Wilke-Smythe. I left her cowering near the millinery, for she was quite reluctant to approach you without invitation or chaperone."

He forced himself to look away from Miss Mackenzie's very kissable lips and over her shoulder. He could see the young woman clutching her reticule and watching them on the green. "She's been properly brought up, then."

"Oh, aye, she has indeed. So have I, in truth, but as the years have flitted by, I have found less and less use for rules. Now, here is my true confession," she said, and leaned even closer to him to whisper, *"I have come to Aberfoyle to seek diversion from the tedium at Dungotty."* As soon as she said it, she covered her mouth with her gloved hand, and her eyes crinkled with laughter above it. She swayed back and dropped her hand. "I hail from Balhaire. Do you know it, then? It's a great fortress in the Highlands, and my family has ruled from there for centuries.

There is quite a lot to do there on any given day."

"Such as hiding rebels?"

She laughed. "*Mi Diah,* you surely donna believe we hide our rebels every day, your grace! Generally, we hide them only on Fridays. Sometimes on Saturdays, but on Saturdays, we prefer to drink our wretched whisky and dance our rowdy reels and plot against the throne." She winked.

Her grin was infectious, and damn it if Hamlin didn't feel a tiny bit of it spreading to his own lips. He clasped his hands behind his back and inclined his head. "As today is Wednesday I may rest assured I will no' encounter any rebels on my return to Blackthorn Hall, then."

"I should think no' today," she agreed. "Good day, your grace! Please give my regards to Miss Eula, will you?"

"I will think on it," he said, and bowed. He walked away, the sound of her giggling trailing behind him like the vapor of a dream slipping away with the morning sun.

When he reached the stables, he glanced back. She had crossed the green to the Wilke-Smythe lass, and their heads were bowed together, their tongues most certainly wagging. What did she say of him? What had she proved with such a display?

He would rather not know, he decided. His curiosity about such things had been beaten down by the untoward things said about him. And he would prefer to hold the cheerful Miss Mackenzie in a box all to herself.

He thought about her cheekiness all the way to Blackthorn Hall. *Rebels on Friday, indeed.*

By the time he reached Blackthorn, her infectious smile had invaded all of his lips. He could feel his smile cracking the planes of his cheeks.

CHAPTER EIGHT

Catriona rather liked Chasity Wilke-Smythe, but the young woman's habit of announcing far and wide every wee thing Catriona had said was beginning to wear thin.

When they returned to Dungotty, Chasity threw open the doors of the green salon and said dramatically to the women gathered there, "Miss Mackenzie intercepted the Duke of Montrose on the *street* of Aberfoyle! The *street*! And then she inquired as to his reason for being there!"

"Did he give you a satisfactory answer or did you receive only his dark look?" the countess asked idly from her chair near the window.

Catriona tossed her hat onto the settee. "He spoke. But he'd no' reveal why he'd come to the village, and reminded me it was impolite to ask."

Mrs. Wilke-Smythe dropped her sewing with a gasp. Chasity giggled with delight.

She giggled now, but she'd been so over-wrought when she and Catriona had spotted the duke in the village, and Catriona had announced her intention to speak to him, that the skin of her chest had turned to rash. The moment Catriona had left the duke and returned to Chasity's side, Chasity had practically beat the news from Catriona with the kid gloves she'd held in her hand. She'd hung on every last word.

"Surely you didn't ask him *why* he'd come to the village!" Mrs. Wilke-Smythe's shock and disapproval was loudly evident.

"Aye, I did," Catriona said pertly. "Everyone avoids his gaze, they do, and I wanted verra much to wish him a good day. Unfortunately, one can only remark on the weather so many times before one is judged to be a dullard."

Chasity colored a bit, as if she feared she'd remarked on the weather too many times. "You are *incorrigible,* Catriona," she said with a twinge of admiration. "I've never known such an audacious woman as you, on my word!"

"Thank heavens for that," her mother muttered.

Catriona went to the sideboard and poured a glass of water. That moment in the village when she'd returned to Chasity, she'd happened to glance back at the duke. He was so quick to his horse that he was already riding out of the village. But he'd turned his head, and Catriona would swear that he was looking back at her, too. She was certain of it — she swore she could feel his gaze boring through her from even that great distance.

"Perhaps he'd gone to the village to find a lady's maid," Mrs. Templeton drawled from her seat at the writing table.

"Why do you say so?" Chasity asked.

"Norwood and I called on the MacLarens earlier today, and she informed me that his man had come to inquire if she might know someone up to the task. I would guess that he has a lady at Blackthorn who is in need of the services of a maid."

"A *lady*," Chasity said, as if she were unfamiliar with the word. She slowly sank onto a seat next to her mother. "What *sort* of lady?"

"Well now, there you have me. One can only imagine, can't one? Would you not agree, Miss Mackenzie?"

Catriona ignored her.

Mrs. Wilke-Smythe picked up her needlework with a snort. "No one will send their daughter or sister to him, not with what has been said of him."

"I agree," the countess chimed in. "There is something quite unsettling about that house."

" 'Tis for his ward," Catriona said.

She suddenly had the attention of the room. "His what?" Mrs. Templeton asked.

"His ward. The lass who resides with him."

"How do you know this?" Mrs. Templeton demanded, tossing down her quill pen to better study Catriona.

"My uncle and I have made her acquaintance."

"Were I you, Miss Mackenzie, I should cut a wide berth around Blackthorn Hall. No good can come of calling there."

"So I should no' plan to wed him, after all?" Catriona asked, and smiled irreverently at the woman.

Mrs. Templeton grumbled something under her breath.

It was entirely possible that Mrs. Templeton had a point. But Catriona was far too intrigued by the black duke to even consider it. "His crime is inquiring after a maid," she said. "That doesna seem sinister to me."

Mrs. Templeton eyed her over the rims of her spectacles. "Then by all means, help the poor gentleman find a lady's maid for his mysterious ward."

"Who has said his ward is mysterious?

She's bonny, she is. Has anyone seen my uncle, then?"

"He's in his study," Mrs. Wilke-Smythe said. "But he doesna wish to be disturbed."

Catriona didn't care. She walked out of the room and pretended she didn't hear Mrs. Templeton's muttering as she passed.

She found Uncle Knox in his cluttered study, in his favorite armchair, which he'd brought with him from England. He did not forbid her entry and in fact waved her forward. He wore his spectacles perched on the edge of his nose, his legs stretched onto the ottoman before him. He was reading Zelda's letter — Catriona recognized the familiar handwriting. He carefully folded it and slipped it into his coat pocket as Catriona neared him.

He rubbed his face, then managed a smile for her.

Catriona knelt beside his chair and put her hand on his knee. "What happened between you and Auntie Zelda?" she asked.

He smiled. "That was a long time ago, darling."

Zelda had never spoken to her about Uncle Knox, but Catriona knew something had happened between the two of them. She had asked about him through the years, and now Catriona had seen her uncle read

Zelda's letter more than once.

"Did you find something to amuse you in the village?" he asked.

"Nothing, really." She rose up, walked to a settee and collapsed onto it. "I saw Montrose."

"Did you?"

"Aye. I spoke to him, too. I asked what brought him to Aberfoyle today."

Her uncle's brows rose with his amusement. "And did he share the details with you?"

Catriona laughed. "No. He chastised me for asking."

Uncle Knox grinned. "I think there is no one in all of Scotland who has gotten under the man's skin as you have, my darling."

She tried not to smile, but his comment pleased her. "Do you know where one might find a lady's maid in need of work?"

"You've had a change of heart, have you?" he asked eagerly. "You swore you'd not need one for the short time you were here."

"No' for me, uncle. For Montrose's ward."

"Ah. Mrs. Templeton was eager to pass that along, was she?"

"Verra eager," Catriona agreed. "I should like to introduce him to one."

Uncle Knox cocked his head to one side. "Why?"

She shrugged. She didn't know why, really, other than she wanted an excuse to see him again. "I am determined to discover what became of his wife. Perhaps I might gain entry to Blackthorn Hall were I to present him a lady's maid for Miss Eula."

"I see," her uncle said. Catriona avoided his gaze in case he saw right through her. "Do you mean to help him? Or stir up a bit of trouble?"

"Well, that, I canna say, uncle. I donna know what I think of him, no' yet. Or the Trossachs. Or Dungotty. Or any of your guests." She sighed to the ceiling. "I donna know what I think of anything anymore, other than I must pass the time before I return to Balhaire and Kishorn or go mad."

"There, there, girl, don't be cross," her uncle soothed her.

"I'm no' cross, uncle. I'm . . ." What was she, really? Weary. *So* weary. Bored? Lethargic? But lethargy did not explain why she'd been so brazen with this duke, and, frankly, shameless. "They all think I'm bloody barmy, aye?" she said softly.

Her uncle smiled fondly at her. "You *are* a bit barmy, love. But that's what makes you such a lively, interesting woman. You must be a bit mad to do the good work you're doing at Kishorn, is that not so? Be proud, Cat. Take comfort in the knowledge that you aid those who are less fortunate than you, and don't allow a lot of pampered English prey on your spirit. With a bit of salt, they'd devour it."

Catriona smiled ruefully.

"I think you should stay the summer at Dungotty," he said.

"Stay! With Mrs. Templeton determined to see me gone?" She shook her head. "The driver will return for me soon. I canna stay on, uncle. I'm needed at Kishorn." She was suddenly reminded what Zelda had said to her, in those final hours as life slowly leaked out of her. "*You must be strong for the others, aye,* m'eudail," she'd said, using an old term of endearment. "*The women and children at the abbey, they'll need you more than ever.*" Her voice had been rough with pain, but she'd gripped Catriona's hand with surprising strength. "*Rhona is a fine abbess, that she is, but she doesna have entry into the world as you do. She'll need you.*"

"*How will I ever carry on without you?*" Catriona had asked tearfully.

"*Och, well enough, you will. Life doesna end when I'm gone. It will begin again every morning, and they'll need you, Cat. Donna weep for me, aye? Carry on for me.*"

Uncle Knox must have guessed what Catriona was thinking, because he said, "Your mother's letter informed me that the denizens of Kishorn Abbey are quite well at present, and that one Mrs. MacFarlane can manage without you for a month or two."

Catriona rolled her eyes. "Mamma is determined to remove me from Kishorn."

"She is determined that you not lose sight of your own destiny, darling. You've given the poor souls a place to reside. You need not give your life to them."

"Auntie Zelda did."

"And you are not Zelda, love. It's been a long struggle for you and Zelda, what with her illness and the responsibility of seeing after your wards."

That was true. As much as Catriona missed Zelda, there was some relief in her passing. The suffering had ended for them both.

"You should have a summer away," Uncle Knox continued. "You ought to find your own desires again. Which is why I've instructed the driver not to return for a month."

Catriona gasped and sat up. *"What?"*

"You're young, Catriona, with your life ahead of you, and unless you've taken the vows of an abbess, you need not spend every moment at the abbey. They will survive well enough on their own. Your mother agrees with me. So does your father. And your brothers and sister."

They had conspired against her *again.* Catriona thought about the women who arrived on foot or in mean wagons, in threadbare clothing and shoes so worn they could scarcely keep them on their feet. She thought about the way those poor women had looked with eyes wide as moons at that decaying abbey, an opulent comparison to their own lives. She thought about how they'd brought with them those few things that held some value to them — a tiny portrait of a loved one. A chipped teapot. A bit of lace. The last coins they had to their name.

They'll need you, Cat.

But in the same breath she thought about the duke with the black eyes and piercing gaze, and the mysterious missing wife, and how he was the one thing that had captured her attention in a very long time. "I want to stay at Dungotty, I do," she admitted weakly. "But I fear what might happen in my absence, aye? The English mean to take Kishorn."

"Yes, I know. And you will be more use to me here than there, will you not? I can't

156

very well argue for Kishorn without your help, can I? Robert Dundas is a friend of mine. He's the Lord Advocate, you know, and he'll arrive in Edinburgh at month's end. He comes every year during the summer months to tend to the Crown's business. We make it a point to meet."

Catriona's mother was right — Uncle Knox knew everyone. The Lord Advocate was the top legal adviser to the Crown for both English and Scottish matters.

"We'll plan a visit, shall we? We'll see about this forfeiture."

What her uncle said made sense. The women and their children would still be at Kishorn at the end of summer, and Rhona would look after them. In the meantime, she could help Uncle Knox press her case here. It was only a month or two — it wasn't as if she was abandoning them, was it?

She thought again of the enigma, Montrose.

"Cat?"

Catriona shifted her gaze to her uncle. He had the same eyes as her mother. "I'll no' stand for a ball, uncle. Promise me that no matter how badly Chasity begs, you'll no' attempt a ball."

Uncle Knox laughed. "You have my word — no ball. At least not one that I will host."

"And promise you will help me find a lady's maid."

He sighed and gave her a look of fond exasperation. "Why is it that all the women I love must play with fire?"

"I'm quite used to the flames. Will you help me, then?"

"If it will amuse you, darling, of course I will. God knows I've never been able to deny you the simplest thing."

CHAPTER NINE

After a long meeting in Glasgow with the Gentlemen of Science, at which Hamlin was forced to learn the complications of building a bridge across a body of water — one tended to take such things for granted — Hamlin arrived at Blackthorn Hall with the dust of the road covering his greatcoat, a dry throat, and a desire for nothing more than a meal, a bath and his bed. But as he strode into his ornate foyer, something black against the white marble caught his eye. A small valise had been carefully placed on the floor, wool gloves laid neatly across, and above it hung a worn lady's coat.

A swell of panic filled Hamlin's throat when he saw those trappings of a woman. He imagined the worst, particularly when he heard the feminine voices in the distance.

She's come back. By some phenomenon, she's come back.

He heard a sound and turned to his right;

Stuart was closing the door to the green salon very quietly behind him, hurrying down the long corridor to the foyer. But as Stuart approached, the tension in Hamlin eased somewhat. His butler did not look unduly alarmed, which certainly he would have had the nightmare Hamlin feared actually occurred in his absence. "What is this, then?" Hamlin asked gruffly, gesturing with his gloves to the things tucked in a corner before handing them to his butler.

"A lady's maid has come, your grace," Stuart said. He took Hamlin's hat.

"Pardon?" Hamlin repeated uncertainly as he removed his greatcoat. "From where?"

"Dungotty, your grace."

Hamlin stilled in the straightening of his waistcoat and frock coat. He stared at his butler. And then he struck out for the room at the end of the hall, his pulse beginning to race with umbrage and something else that felt, strangely, like a wee bit of anticipation.

When he entered the room, he first saw Eula, speaking with a woman only an inch or two taller than her, and as homely a woman as Hamlin had ever seen in his life. She had a broad, flat nose, and eyes that were too far apart. She wore a gown of brown muslin, carefully patched in at least two places that he could see.

Then he saw Miss Mackenzie. She was across the room, looking quite pleased with herself, smiling at Eula and the woman with an air of approval, like one of the celestial angels that smiled down at them from the ceiling in the ballroom. The moment Miss Mackenzie saw Hamlin, she sank into a graceful courtesy.

So did the homely woman.

Eula was bouncing with excitement. "She's a *lady's* maid!"

Hamlin looked at the homely woman. "Good day, madam." Then he slowly turned his full and unbridled attention to Miss Mackenzie. "A word, madam?"

"Aye, of course," she said brightly, and came gliding forward like a vision from a dream. He marveled at it — how was it that this woman had no trepidation before him? He couldn't step foot into Aberfoyle or Crieff without people hurrying to the other side of the street, and yet this woman, come down from the Highlands, had no such feelings. On the contrary — she seemed to challenge him at every turn.

It was maddening. And oddly refreshing.

When she reached him, her smile was shining in her eyes. "Your grace?"

"What is this about, then?" he asked.

"This?" She glanced over her shoulder at

161

Eula and the woman. "Well, it seems I was right, your grace. Your business has spread far and wide across the Trossachs, and when I heard of it, I thought I might help you."

"Far and wide, has it? How noble of you to want to help, madam, but alas, you were no' *invited* to help," he said, as if he needed to explain once again that one did not step into the business of a duke without invitation.

"Oh, aye, I know," she readily agreed. "Only sometimes, I canna quite help myself." Her smile broadened.

His breath shortened. "Is this, perchance, one of your wards?" he asked coolly.

She gasped with delight. "Would it no' have been wonderful if she *was*? But alas, your grace, she is no'," she said, and stepped back from him, turning toward Eula and the woman. "May I introduce Miss Jean Burns, from Glasgow. She comes with two letters of recommendation. Is that no' so, Miss Burns?"

Hamlin looked at the homely woman.

"Aye," she said, her voice soft.

"She was last in service to Mrs. Culpepper of Glasgow."

Hamlin was speechless. What was wrong with Miss Mackenzie? What did she think, bringing this woman to him? "You are too presumptuous," he said low.

"Hmm," she said thoughtfully. "Perhaps we might think of it as helpful."

What cheek! "I said *presumptuous.*"

"Neighborly," she countered. "It's impossible that I should be any other way, for that's the way of it in the Highlands. We help those who canna help themselves."

"Are you suggesting that I canna help myself?" he asked incredulously.

"Of *course* no'," she said, quite unconvincingly.

The audacity of this woman was shocking. He looked again at the mouse who had been presented to him as a lady's maid. "You've served a lady," he said dubiously, looking at her worn clothing.

"Aye, milord. Nigh on fourtin years, that I did."

Her voice was heavily accented with the Glaswegian dialect. "Why have you left her employ?" he asked.

The mouse blinked. "Why, she's deid, milord," she said. "Choked herself to deeth on a chicken boon, milord."

"He prefers your grace," Eula said. "And he doesna like to be called Montrose. Only the gentlemen may call him that, aye? I'll teach you all the things he doesna like," Eula said confidently.

163

It was bad enough to have one presumptuous woman in the room, but Hamlin had
two, and it was almost his undoing. "Thank
you, Eula. Perhaps we might discuss proper
forms of address at another time, aye?"

"May I show her my rooms?" she asked
excitedly.

Hamlin opened his mouth to speak, but
Eula was already inching toward the door.
"Please?"

Hamlin knew he was defeated. "Aye, go
on," he said. "But I've no' made a decision."
It was useless to say more — Eula wasn't
paying him the slightest heed. She'd
grabbed the mouse's hand and was pulling
her along, chattering about her rooms.

Miss Mackenzie, the cunning little bird,
attempted to walk behind the pair, as if she,
too, would see Eula's rooms. But Hamlin
put his hand on her arm and said, "No'
you."

Miss Mackenzie looked at the two women
as they went out of the room, and said,
"Shall I wait in the foyer, then?"

"No." He walked past her, shut the door,
then turned and folded his arms tightly
across his chest, braced his legs apart and
demanded, "What in blazes do you think
you are doing here?"

The slightest bit of color began to seep

into her cheeks. "I told you, aye? I mean to help you."

He moved forward until he towered above her and forced her to lift her chin to maintain eye contact. "I didna want your help, Miss Mackenzie. Had I wanted it, I would have asked for it, aye?"

"So you've said," she agreed. "But I'd no' mind if you did ask it of me."

She was incorrigible. He shifted even closer. She tilted her head back even farther. She smiled pertly. She was not intimidated by him. Not the least bit cowed, which, admittedly, and perhaps to a wee bit of his shame, was his intent. She said, "Perhaps you ought to ask for help more often, aye? You could make do with a friend like me, particularly in light of your wretched reputation."

He glared down at her. "Has anyone ever told you that you are too impudent by half?"

A tiny laugh escaped her throat. "Aye, of *course,*" she said.

His presence, his words, his title, his disapproval — none of it could fluster this woman. And Hamlin was utterly intrigued by it. She was smiling at him as he glared at her. She found him amusing in that way she found everything amusing. She was truly remarkable in a way he'd never known another person to be.

"Miss Burns comes highly recommended," she said, her gaze falling to his mouth. "She needs a post, quite obviously, as her former employer choked on a chicken bone." She winced. "Can you imagine a worse way to meet our Maker?"

"I can," he said low.

Her lashes fluttered, and the bit of pink spread down her neck to her throat. But she did not step away from him, did not look away from his eyes, his mouth, his chest. "She has no one in this world. She'll be loyal to Eula."

Hamlin clenched his jaw against the knowledge that he'd been defeated in this. Miss Mackenzie had solved a problem for him and for that mouse of a woman. He resented the way she'd done it, but there was something in the back of his mind that was whispering he would not have accepted it had she presented it any other way. "She's competent?"

"Verra competent."

Hamlin sighed. He turned away from the heat he was beginning to feel radiating between them. He walked to the sideboard, poured two whiskies and held one out to her.

She looked at the glass, then at him, and

slowly came forward to take it. "I thought you didna care for whisky."

"I lied," he said. "Did you?"

She gave him that strange little lopsided smile that made him feel as if she could read his thoughts. "No." She touched her glass to his and sipped.

Hamlin tossed his whisky down his throat. "On my word, Miss Mackenzie, I donna understand you. You're far too brazen for your own good, aye?"

"Aye."

"What do you want from me, then?" he asked as he refilled his glass.

"Want? Nothing at all," she said as she set her tot aside. "I'm passing time in the best way I know, that's all." She began to move around the room and paused for a moment under Glenna's portrait. Hamlin looked at it. It had hung there so long that he didn't see it anymore. He should store it, put it away, out of sight. Eula would ask where the painting had gone, and again ask where Glenna had gone, and he preferred to avoid that conversation. She was young yet, too young to understand the wickedness that dwelt in the hearts of some.

"Will you take her into your employ?" Miss Mackenzie asked.

Hamlin realized she'd moved again, was

looking at him as he looked at the portrait of Glenna. He'd spent too many evenings in this very room with too much whisky and suddenly lost the taste for it. "Have I any choice?" he asked, setting his tot aside, too.

"One always has a choice."

"I beg to differ," he said. "But I'll keep her." He leaned back against the sideboard, his gaze on the bonny Miss Mackenzie again. There was still a hint of a blush on her smooth skin.

"You'll no' regret it." She smiled.

He wasn't so certain of that.

"Verra well, your grace, I'll take no more of your time, then." She curtsied.

"You've helped me all you can, have you?"

She laughed. "For today."

For today. He couldn't begin to guess what other help she had in store for him. He pushed away from the sideboard and walked to the wall and tugged on the bell pull. The door opened a moment later, and a footman entered, bowing at the waist. "See Miss Mackenzie out," he said.

"*Feasgar math,*" she said, and with a flurry of her fingers, she quit the room.

Hamlin stood for a long moment after she'd gone. He was imagining things, obviously, for it was almost as if he could feel warmth sliding out of the room in her wake.

168

■ ■ ■ ■

Just as he suspected — all right, then, maybe hoped — it was not the last Hamlin saw of Miss Mackenzie that week. Not two days later, a messenger arrived with a letter. In a sprawling script, with blots of ink in places they ought not to have been, as if the note had been dashed off at a great hurry, Miss Mackenzie wrote and inquired if she might call on Eula at week's end. As the lass had said she enjoyed painting best of all, Miss Mackenzie would very much like to introduce her to a friend, an artist, who might show her a thing or two.

As Hamlin was at breakfast with Eula, he lowered the letter and looked at her over the edge of it. "Did you say to Miss Mackenzie that you enjoyed painting more than any other diversion, then?"

Eula nodded eagerly. "I like to make colors. Did you know that yellow and blue make green when mixed altogether?"

He lowered the letter to his lap. "I thought your favorite diversion was your music lessons, aye? When did painting rise to supremacy?"

"I donna remember."

"No memory whatsoever?"

169

"No."

"No, what?" he asked, trying to remind her that, if nothing else, she ought to at least remember her manners.

"No memory whatsoever," she said, mimicking him.

He couldn't help smiling and abandoned this morning's attempt at manners, which were clearly beyond his ability to teach, or beyond his student's willingness to learn. He lifted the letter once more and studied the sprawling, blotted script.

Later that morning when he met with Bain, he asked him what he thought about Miss Mackenzie's desire to bring an artist to Blackthorn Hall.

Bain didn't have to think about it as much as a moment. "I see no harm."

No harm? Aye, well, Bain had not yet had the pleasure of making the notorious Miss Mackenzie's acquaintance. He'd understand once he met her.

"She's brought us a lady's maid. Are we to take an instructor from her, as well?" Hamlin asked irritably.

Bain looked confused. "Aye. I would recommend, your grace, that as your attention is necessarily turned elsewhere —"

"Aye, aye," Hamlin said, waving his hand before Bain could remind him that he was quite well occupied in being every man to everyone. "Send a favorable reply, then." He tossed the letter across the desk at his secretary. It skidded over the highly polished surface and fluttered to the floor. With a sly look, Bain picked it up off the floor between finger and thumb. "Of *course,* your grace."

Miss Mackenzie appeared two days later with a man she boasted had come all the way from Stirling. He wore a tattered coat and waistcoat, a cap that looked as if it had once been jaunty but was jaunty no more and a leather satchel that he wore across his body, stuffed with paintbrushes. His hands, Hamlin noticed, looked permanently stained with paint.

Miss Mackenzie was all smiles, of course, lighting the bloody room. "May I introduce *Monsieur Kenworth,*" she said with flourish.

"French?" Hamlin asked the gentleman.

"No, your grace. A proud Scotsman, like you, aye?" the man said, lifting his chin.

"I was jesting," Miss Mackenzie said, as if she and Hamlin were so familiar as to trade jests. "Mr. Kenworth tells me that all the best artists are French, but I assure you, he's as good as any of them." She punctuated this statement with a wink, as if she and Hamlin shared a secret. She bloody well *winked* at him. It happened so quickly that

171

Hamlin wasn't certain he'd seen it. Except that he was quite certain he had.

Eula was enthralled, of course, and by the end of the session, Hamlin was pressed to purchase paints and canvases from *Monsieur Kenworth,* as well as agree to twice-weekly lessons for the course of the summer. "The lass might attend her skill at landscape while the weather is warm," Kenworth had suggested, and had gestured to the open doors to the gardens.

Hamlin muttered his opinion of landscape paintings in general under his breath but gave the man a curt nod, for there was no man who could look at the upturned face of Miss Eula Guinne and believe he had a fighting chance at denying her.

In the course of Miss Mackenzie and her artist taking their leave, Miss Mackenzie happened to notice an archery field just below the gardens. There ensued quite a lot of discussion about archery, and her general chastisement of Hamlin's failure to instruct Eula in the art. And naturally, Eula was suddenly very keen to learn.

"I donna have the time just now to teach you, lass," he said. "And Aubin has injured his elbow, aye, Eula?" Hamlin reminded her. The mysteriously talented man had taken a tumble off his horse last Sunday, the day all the servants had to themselves. Hamlin suspected he'd been returning to Blackthorn Hall well into his cups when the mishap occurred.

"A Frenchman! For archery!" Miss Mackenzie exclaimed, and clucked her tongue.

"I canna bear the suspense, Miss Mackenzie. No doubt you've a lad who is in want of an instructor position," he drawled in her general direction as he studied the back of his hand.

"A lad!" She laughed as if that were preposterous. "I grant you, I've brought Mr. Kenworth round to teach Miss Guinne art, that I have, for I've no talent for it. But my father and my brothers have trained Highland soldiers, your grace. I can teach her archery as well as any man, on my word."

He looked at her. "You."

"Me!"

"With a bow and arrow?" he added skeptically, in the event she meant something else entirely.

"Is there any other way to teach archery, then? Why do you look so disbelieving?" she asked laughingly, without offense. "I happen to be an excellent shot."

He snorted.

Miss Mackenzie began to fit her hands into gloves as she prepared to take her leave

173

with Mr. Kenworth. "If you donna believe me, then perhaps you ought to attend the lesson, as well."

The woman never failed to disappoint him with her cheek.

"Aye, please, your grace!" Eula begged him.

He looked at Miss Mackenzie. She smiled. "I mean only to help," she said, but that smile of hers suggested otherwise.

It was the memory of the smile that haunted him for the remainder of the day and well into the night. It made him privately rage with fury and desire all at once. He could not recall ever being so curious about a woman. His thoughts before his marriage had been almost entirely prurient, and after his marriage, his thoughts had become increasingly resentful about the woman he had married. The prurience was still there and thrumming to the point of discomfort. But it was his interest in the way her pretty head worked, in her fearless approach to life, that flummoxed him. He had not felt such a burning interest in a woman as this that he could recall. Miss Mackenzie had laid siege to his thoughts and was setting up camp in his brain and other regions of his body, and Hamlin didn't know what to do about it.

CHAPTER TEN

Catriona appeared for breakfast Saturday morning dressed for riding and a bit of archery. She wore her hair in a loose tail down her back so that she might fit a proper hat on her head, and leather boots for trekking down to the archery field at Blackthorn.

She swept into the breakfast room for a quick bite. Her uncle was at his usual spot at the table and had been joined by everyone but Mr. and Mrs. Wilke-Smythe, and Mr. Vasily Orlov, who had come sneaking into Dungotty at half past three in the morning. The only reason Catriona knew this was because he'd been so drunk he'd crashed into the wall just outside her room and had let forth a colorful string of what she surmised was Russian cursing.

Uncle Knox looked up from his paper and over the tops of his spectacles. "Where are you off to this morning, darling?"

"To Blackthorn Hall," she said as she bit into a piece of ham. "I'm giving an archery lesson to the duke's ward." She leaned over Chasity's shoulder and snatched a biscuit from the table.

"A better instructor she could not have," he said. "I recall when you were scarcely as tall as a reed, piercing the smallest targets from thirty paces."

This news caught the old goat Furness's attention, and he looked up. "What sort of target?"

"An apple," Catriona said. "A rotten one, but an apple all the same."

"I don't believe it," Furness said, his gaze on Uncle Knox.

"Then perhaps we might place a rotting apple on top your head and allow her to prove it," Uncle Knox said.

"I thought we might ride into Crieff," Chasity said with a bit of a pout. "There is a modiste there, and I am desperately in need of a new gown for London's Little Season."

The Little Season, as Catriona understood it, was a social calendar that filled around a short parliamentary session in the fall. It was months away yet. "Another time, aye? I promised Miss Guinne."

"So there is indeed a ward," Countess Orlov said. She was still in her robe and bedclothes, her dark hair loose around her shoulders. "What else have you learned about our secretive duke?"

"Surprisingly little," Catriona answered truthfully.

The countess gave Catriona a pert smile. "But we are depending on you to solve the mystery for us."

"I've seen the portrait of his missing wife. Will that appease you?"

"Really?" Chasity asked. "How did she appear? As pretty as they say?"

Quite pretty. So pretty that Catriona had felt a wee bit faded in comparison. "Quite bonny. Ginger hair, green eyes. She was portrayed with a mischievous gleam in her eye."

"Where is the portrait?" Chasity asked.

The portrait was in the main salon. She wondered why. Was it possible that he missed her? She had seen a glimpse of a softer side. Her brother Rabbie was like that — very gruff on the outside, and as soft as butter on the inside. Was it possible the duke was the same sort of man? He obviously cared a great deal for the lass. Wouldn't that indicate a warm heart? Perhaps what had happened to his wife was the very opposite of what everyone believed.

Perhaps his wife had been the one to end it.

But that made no sense to Catriona. How could a woman sharing the intimacy of marriage with a man who was handsome, rich and perhaps even kind want rid of him? No, she couldn't imagine it. There was something more there. "The portrait?" she said when she noticed Chasity waiting for her answer. "In the main salon. It's as tall as a window, it is. Well, then, I'm off," she said, and gave them all a wave as she made her way to the door.

"Mind you have a care, Cat!" Uncle Knox called after her. "The last time you rode, you gave poor Mr. Bartles a fright when you went thundering by. He thought the Grim Reaper had come calling for one of them."

Catriona laughed roundly at that as she strode from the room.

Catriona arrived at Blackthorn to find Eula sitting on the steps of the portico. She was dressed in a smart little coat and cap, her boots polished to a sheen. Miss Jean Burns was waiting with her, bundled in a brown wrap and a faded cap.

Eula stood up as Catriona slid off her horse, waving as if perhaps Catriona had not seen her.

"Madainn mhath!" Catriona said, and

178

tapped her crop against Eula's cap. "You're ready, then, are you?"

"Aye," said Eula.

Catriona glanced at the door. She expected Montrose to come out and greet her. Maybe she had indeed worn out her welcome here. It wouldn't surprise her if she had — she knew how impetuous she was, both in action and in speech, and no matter what else she suspected about the duke, he did not care for her impetuosity — he'd made that abundantly clear.

"Aye, good day, Miss Burns," she said, nodding at the small woman. "How do you find Blackthorn Hall, then?"

" 'Tis as bonny a hoose as I've ever seen, aye," Miss Burns said. "You're to wait, you are, for Mr. Aubin."

Catriona looked at Eula.

"Montrose said he's to carry our arrows," the lass said.

"What's this?" Catriona exclaimed. "We're strong lassies, are we no'? We'll carry our own arrows, aye?"

Eula shrugged. Miss Burns shook her head. "She's no' to go doon to the field withoot him, no."

Catriona groaned. "Where is he, then?"

"There," Eula said, and pointed at a man walking toward them with two quivers on

179

his back. He was taller and thinner than she recalled, and possessed an air of confidence about him that seemed a wee bit too much for the task of carrying quivers and a small bow. He paused directly before her, clicked his heels, bowed deeply at the waist and said, "A pleasure to see you again, Miss Mackenzie."

"Aye, and you as well, Mr. Aubin. How is your elbow?"

"On the path to recovery." He cast his arm in the direction of the path that led round the side of the house. "Shall we proceed?" With another bow, he walked on, his stride long and sure.

Catriona glanced at Eula and wrinkled her nose. "Will he interfere, do you suppose?"

Eula nodded.

"That's our lot in life, lass — there will always be gentlemen to interfere. They think they know better by the mere virtue of being male. Is that no' so, Miss Burns?"

"Aye," Miss Burns agreed, and with a cheery wave, she disappeared back inside Blackthorn Hall.

Catriona and Eula followed Aubin, who was yards ahead of them now.

"What do you mean, then, that gentlemen know better?" Eula asked.

"Well, they are the stronger sex, that

180

canna be denied, aye? But men often make the mistake of assuming that their physical strength means that their minds are stronger, too. Do you see, then?"

Eula giggled. "No."

"That couldna possibly be true, could it?" Catriona said airily. "Our minds are all the same in the beginning, and it hardly matters if it is male or female. My late aunt once told me that because we are physically the weaker sex, we must be more clever than men to get what we want, aye? 'Tis the only way we might outdo them, to use our minds instead of our physical strength to match them."

Eula wrinkled her nose in confusion. "Pardon?"

"Say, for example, that you want something verra badly."

"A cat!" she declared. "I should verra much like a kitten, for I've no one to play with, aye? But no' a barn cat. One that might come into my room."

"You should have a cat, lass, if that's what you want."

"Montrose willna allow it. He says animals belong outdoors and no' indoors."

For heaven's sake, Blackthorn Hall was as large as a small village. What difference would a cat make to the duke? "A beastly thing to say, if you ask me," Catriona whispered. "Why, you've never seen so many dogs as those that wander about my home at Balhaire."

"In your house?"

"In our house. In our *beds,*" Catriona whispered.

Eula gasped with surprise.

"So how might we get your cat, *leannan?* You canna fight him for it, can you?"

Eula shook her head.

"You must be clever, then. You must devise a plan that somehow leads Montrose to believe it's all his idea. You must be smarter than the duke."

"I donna think *anyone* can be smarter than Montrose," Eula said.

Perhaps not, but Catriona chafed at the benefit of thought men were given simply for breathing. "I shall cover my ears and sing loudly if you say so again. Never believe you are less than a gentleman because you are female, lass. Promise me this."

Eula thought about it a moment, then nodded. "I promise."

They had reached the archery field, where Aubin had set up three straw targets covered in burlap, on to which concentric circles had been drawn. But in the center of each target, different figures had been added.

One looked like a chicken. Another, a deer. And the third, the figure of a man. Catriona squinted at the figure. "Who is that, then?" she asked Aubin.

"A thief, madam," Aubin said.

She glanced curiously at the Frenchman. He shrugged nonchalantly, handed her the two quivers and the bow, then removed himself to a bench, where he sat and slipped his hat over his eyes, as if he meant to nap.

"What are you doing?" Catriona asked.

"I am not to help," he said. "By order of the duke."

Oh, was that the way of it, then? Catriona turned about with a small *harrumph*. The duke didn't believe she could teach Eula to draw a bow. Wouldn't he be surprised, then?

"How do you know how to shoot a bow and arrow?" Eula asked curiously as she watched Catriona tighten the tautness of the bowstring.

"When I was a child, my father would organize archery contests between me and my brothers and sister. I was the youngest of them all, but I often took the trophy. My father said I was naturally inclined."

"A trophy! May I see it?" Eula asked.

Catriona laughed. "It wasna really a trophy, lass. It was an old earthen jug my father had christened a trophy, for it had no other use, really. And it is no more — one day, my brother Rabbie accidentally shot the jug and shattered it." She laughed. "My father vowed he'd make a better trophy, but he never came round to it."

"I've never had a trophy," Eula said. "No' before I came to Blackthorn Hall or since I came here."

"Oh?" Catriona said. "Have you been at Blackthorn Hall verra long, then?"

"A long time," Eula said with a roll of her eyes. "My cousin said that days seem like weeks here. Can I shoot the arrow now?"

Catriona was momentarily taken aback by the comment. She debated asking Eula more, but the lass was studying her bow, was eager to begin. "Here now, see how I hold the bow high like this? That way, when I pull my arm back, even with my mouth, I may sight my target without bending my head."

Catriona showed Eula how to set the notched end of her arrow against the bow-string, how to hold the limb of the bow, how to draw the arrow back and take aim.

Eula was a good student, studying intently each thing Catriona showed her. Her first few arrows were quite short of the target, scarcely leaving the bow. But then Catriona stepped behind her, helped pull the lass's arm back so that she knew just how far to draw it, and demonstrated the featherlight release her father had taught her that sent the arrow sailing.

At last, with Catriona's help, Eula hit her target and squealed with delight. "Again!" she said breathlessly.

Catriona gave her an arrow and helped her set it against the bowstring, then removed her hand and allowed Eula to fire. That one just missed the target. "Aye, then, now that you know how to draw the arrow, you need work on your aim."

They made their way down the three targets, Catriona helping her, and allowing her a little more freedom each time. When they came to the last target, they gathered the spent arrows, put them in the quiver and walked back to their marks before the target. "Would you like to attempt it all on your own, then?" Catriona asked.

"Aye, please," Eula said. She removed an arrow from the quiver. It took her a few minutes to properly set the arrow against the bowstring, as it kept slipping.

"Steady," Catriona said to her.

The lass was tiring, was losing patience with the game. "You're standing too close," she complained.

Catriona moved several feet away.

Eula tried again. This time, she managed to set it against the bowstring and hoist the bow up. She pulled her arm back, but it was difficult for her — the bowstring was taut and the strength required to hold it steady was more than she could manage on her own. Eula turned toward Catriona and opened her mouth as if to say something, but her gaze moved past Catriona, and she shouted triumphantly, "Look what I've learned! Watch me!"

Catriona never turned to see who had come, for Eula's arm wobbled, and she inadvertently launched the arrow in Catriona's direction. She had scarcely registered what had happened when she was knocked to the ground as the arrow whizzed by her ear.

A moment of stunned silence passed. Catriona's heart was pounding so hard at the prospect of what could very well have been a shot between the eyes that it took her a moment or two to realize that something very heavy was draped across her.

It was another moment before she realized that an arm was clamped around her waist, and a hard chest was pressed against her back.

"I'm sorry!" Eula cried. "I didna mean it!"

186

"Aye, all right, you may let go, Aubin," Catriona said, her voice shaking, and struggled to free herself. She was unsteady, and her shoulder hurt, and Aubin did not let go but pulled her up so that she was sitting on her rump in the grass, feeling a wee bit dizzy and bewildered.

That was when Catriona realized that the person who had saved her from certain death-by-arrow was not Mr. Aubin at all — it was Montrose.

He was not shaking. He was crouched beside her, staring intently into her eyes for a very long moment. Something was humming, Catriona realized. What was it, a bee? No. *No,* it was inside her, that humming. In her breast. Near her heart.

Montrose abruptly leapt to his feet and dusted off his knees, then offered Catriona his hand, pulling her up with such vigor that she bounced on her toes and landed so close to him that she could plainly see the folds of his neckcloth, and the lighter flecks of brown in his black eyes.

"Are you all right?" he asked quietly as his gaze raked over her, presumably looking for an arrow protruding from her body somewhere.

Was she? She glanced down at herself, at her trews, her blue-and-white gown tied with ribbons across her stomacher. All still there, all limbs accounted for. "I think so," she said a little breathlessly. She noticed leaves on her sleeve and moved to brush them off, but he was still holding her hand, his fingers wrapped securely around hers. He seemed to realize it at the same moment and let go.

She brushed the leaves from her sleeve and noticed a rivulet of blood down her forearm.

"You've been hurt," he said.

" 'Tis nothing," she said. "A scrape, that's all." She gave him a sheepish look. "Thank you. You verra well may have saved my life."

He shook his head. "I owe you an apology for knocking you to the ground, for her aim was far, *far* off the mark."

Her aim had seemed deadly true to Catriona, but everything had happened so fast.

"I suppose we should both be thankful for your expert instruction," he said, and a single, dark brow arched. She realized that he was attempting humor, and she couldn't help but smile at his effort.

"I didna mean it!" Eula sobbed, suddenly appearing, her bow discarded. She fell into the duke, burying her face in his coat. "It was an accident!" she wailed, although her voice was muffled by the wool of the duke's coat.

"Aye, lass, of course you didna mean it," Catriona soothed her, but Eula only wailed louder.

"There now," the duke said, caressing her back. " 'Twas an accident, that it was. No harm has come to anything but Miss Mackenzie's Highland pride, so dry your tears." He glanced at Catriona and the tiniest hint of a smile shadowed his face. "Perhaps we should see after Miss Mackenzie's scrape and take tea, aye?" he suggested.

Catriona had in mind something a bit more potent to soothe her badly shaken nerves but said, "Aye, thank you."

They started back to the house while Aubin, who had been God only knew where in the moment Catriona saw her life flash before her, was left to pick up the quivers, the bows and the arrows. They walked along, Eula still sniffling, but Montrose had his arm around her thin shoulders, was holding her tightly to his side.

Some would have been angry with the lass for nearly shooting a guest, but the duke understood Eula's distress. This man had saved Catriona's life and was comforting a lass who had made a grave mistake. That was not the heart of a murderer. It was impossible — she was certain of it.

The intrigue she'd viewed him with in this last fortnight was beginning to feel like billowing esteem.

CHAPTER ELEVEN

Hamlin was mortified by what had happened, even more by the cut on Miss Mackenzie's arm. The trail of blood was a stark, ugly red next to her fair skin. He instructed Stuart to fetch a basin with soap and water and bandages to tend to Miss Mackenzie's arm the moment they entered the salon.

"I donna need a bandage," she protested, but Hamlin would not hear it. He was grateful that at least he'd been close enough to save her. He'd lied to both Eula and Miss Mackenzie — the arrow had narrowly missed her, and inwardly, he was still shaking. He should never have let them go on their own. He'd been stubbornly determined to keep his distance from the feelings that were prospering in his blood and tissue, but in the end, having watched them from behind a window, he'd not been able to keep away. Thank the saints for that.

As they waited for the soap and bandage,

Miss Mackenzie would not sit still and wandered about the room, holding Hamlin's handkerchief to her arm. She paused beneath Glenna's portrait and looked up at it.

"That's my cousin," Eula volunteered. "My father said I look verra much like her."

Hamlin had not known Eula's mother, but the lass looked nothing like Glenna, other than perhaps the color of her hair. Eula's was russet; Glenna's was more of a ginger color.

"What's her name?" Miss Mackenzie asked.

"Cousin Glenna," she said, then glanced at Hamlin. "I mean, Lady Montrose," she amended quickly. "She's no' here at Blackthorn Hall, you know. She's gone away."

Miss Mackenzie stood very still, her gaze fixed on the portrait of Glenna. Hamlin wondered frantically if he ought to say something, to clarify. He didn't. He hadn't spoken of it in so long to anyone but Bain that his thoughts were jumbled between indecision about how much to say and shame that anything had to be said at all.

"I miss her so." Eula sighed.

Miss Mackenzie cleared her throat then and turned away from the portrait, her gaze on anything in the room but Hamlin. He could feel the tension between them rising at the mention of his wife — he'd felt it with others many times before. What did Miss Mackenzie think of the rumors? Did she believe them? Did she ignore them? Why did she continue to call at Blackthorn Hall?

"I miss my aunt verra much, too," she said. "I know how you feel, Miss Guinne. But I've weathered the loss by keeping my companions close. Perhaps you lack a proper companion, aye?"

Was that some sort of indictment against him? Hamlin did the best he could for Eula — God knew he'd agonized about her lack of proper playmates and had tried to rectify it. But no one wanted to bring their children to Blackthorn Hall, not where a man who might have murdered his wife would be present. He'd also searched Scotland far and wide for anyone she might call family but had not been able to find anyone who would lay claim to the girl.

"There are no other children at Blackthorn Hall," Eula said. "I'm the only one, I am."

The door opened; Stuart held it for a footman, who carried in a basin of warm water. Another came behind him with a bandage and a cloth.

"Please sit, Miss Mackenzie," Hamlin

said, gesturing to the settee. He directed the footmen to put the things on the table.

"Shall I call Mrs. Weaver?" Stuart asked.

"No, thank you. Miss Eula and I can attend our guest."

Miss Mackenzie looked uncertain of that, however. He pointed to the settee again and added a perfunctory "Please."

She swept past him, her gown brushing against his legs, and sat on the very edge of the settee, her back ramrod straight, as if she was prepared to launch herself across the room if necessary.

Hamlin went down on one knee beside her and noticed the slight part of her lips, the breath of incredulity. He peeled her fingers back from where she held his handkerchief and examined the cut just below her elbow. She must have landed on a rock or root. The wound was not deep, but enough to need bandaging. "If you would hold the fabric of your sleeve."

She pushed the bell sleeve up and held it in place as he dipped the cloth in the soapy water, took hold of an elbow that felt entirely too delicate for this woman and dabbed the cloth against her skin.

She let out a hiss of breath between her teeth, then turned her attention to Eula, who was seated beside her, watching with great fascination as Hamlin carefully cleaned the cut. "Perhaps no' a person, then," she said, a wee bit breathlessly as he carefully dislodged grass from the cut.

"Pardon?" Eula asked absently.

"Perhaps your companion need no' be a person," Miss Mackenzie said.

Eula slowly turned her attention from Hamlin's cleaning of her cut to Miss Mackenzie. "No' a person?"

Miss Mackenzie shook her head. Her brows arched, and she smiled at Eula. "*No'* a person."

Hamlin glanced up from his attention to her arm.

"Do you mean a horse?" Eula asked.

"Perhaps a wee bit smaller than a horse," Miss Mackenzie said with a laugh.

Eula pulled a sad face and said, "I *do* wish I had a friend."

What she wished she had was a kitten, and Hamlin knew subtle coercion when it was played out before him, particularly when one of the actors was not particularly good at it.

"Perhaps you ought to take up reading," Hamlin suggested, and slowly drew the wet cloth down Miss Mackenzie's arm, wiping away the blood. It was odd, because he felt her shiver, but her skin felt warm to his touch. She had the arm of a dancer, slender and long. "Your tutor believes you would benefit from more reading, he does," Hamlin added, and stroked the cloth up Miss Mackenzie's arm again, just as slowly.

She glanced at him, her gaze strangely dark.

"He makes me read psalms," Eula complained. "I donna like to read psalms."

"Aye, well, he doesna wish to see you become a heathen, lass."

"Perhaps Miss Guinne might like a novel," Miss Mackenzie murmured, her gaze still locked on his. "I've the perfect one in mind. If my uncle can find it with his bookseller, I could come round and read it with you."

"Montrose says novels are frivolous," Eula said.

"His grace," Hamlin muttered. He stretched Miss Mackenzie's arm long, resting the back of her hand against his thigh as he wrapped the bandage just below her elbow. Her skin was as soft as down. The tips of his fingers were tingling. He began to imagine what else about her was as soft and warm as down.

"I beg your pardon, but I must disagree," Miss Mackenzie said, and looked away from him. "They illuminate the world around us in ways that we've no' always seen."

"But I wish I had a *friend,*" Eula said. "Then I wouldna have to read at all."

"You would still have to read," Hamlin said. He had finished bandaging Miss Mackenzie's arm, and carefully picked up her hand from his thigh, and moved it to rest on the settee beside her.

She glanced down at his work, then at him, her eyes moving over his face. "Thank you."

Hamlin came to his feet. He felt slightly unsteady.

"I'll ask my uncle's help in finding the book," she said airily, and stood, straightening her sleeve, as if her hand had never rested on his thigh, and his fingers had never attended her wound. "You'll see, *leannan,* reading can be quite diverting . . . if his grace allows it." She glanced over her shoulder at him, the sparkle having returned, and practically dared him to deny it.

Hamlin gave her a look to convey he would not be challenged in this manner in his own home. "Now that we've wrapped Miss Mackenzie up, it is time, Eula, to wish her a good day and return to your lady's maid, aye? You will have your music lesson in less than an hour."

Eula sighed. Hamlin arched a brow at her,

and she obediently turned and curtsied at Miss Mackenzie. "Thank you for coming," she said politely.

"Thank you for allowing me to call," Miss Mackenzie said graciously.

"I'm sorry I almost shot you," Eula said softly.

Miss Mackenzie smiled so warmly that Hamlin could feel it all the way to his toes. It seemed sorcery that she could dispel any sort of mood with that smile. "You must no' give it another thought."

"Come along, Eula," he said, and took Eula by the hand to deliver her to Stuart. At the door, she turned back and waved at Miss Mackenzie.

Hamlin sent her off with explicit instructions she was to be delivered to Miss Burns. A footman entered to take the basin away, and then, suddenly, Miss Mackenzie was the only one remaining in the room. She was standing next to a gaming table where Hamlin had a game of chess in progress.

He joined her there and looked down at the board. He and Bain had played a time or two, but the truth was that, like Eula, Hamlin also lacked proper companions. At present, he was engaged in a chess battle with himself. He came at night, when Eula had gone to bed, and played himself.

How things had changed for him since Glenna. There was a time when this salon had been filled four nights of the week with guests. There was a time he'd been weary of it, had wished that a week might pass quietly. But Glenna despised quiet. She had a voracious need to surround herself with people. One would think he would be quite content with the quiet now, but that was not true. He missed society. He wished he could still issue an invitation and receive guests. But once his invitations began to be turned down, he stopped inviting.

He studied the board as he'd last left it. "Do you know the game, then?"

"Aye, of course. The winter nights are long at Balhaire."

How long were the nights at Balhaire? What things did she do in the evenings? Who did she see, who came to call? "Have you any skill at it?"

Miss Mackenzie turned toward him, her brow arched, her eyes were shining with the heat of a challenge. "A wee bit, aye."

Hamlin smiled as if he'd just spotted a buck through the sight of his hunting rifle. He couldn't help himself — he touched the bandage of her arm, then traced a line up to her neck. "Then we must have a match someday, aye?"

199

"Aye," she agreed. She shifted closer to him as he traced the path of her collarbone. Her mouth was tantalizingly close to him, her eyes glittering.

He moved his hand to her ear, tracing the outline of it as he studied her lips, full and plush and darkly pink. He could think of scarcely anything other than touching his lips to hers. He wondered which he would appreciate more — bedding this hoyden, or spending time in her company, watching the light change her eyes, feeling the force of her smile rifle through him? At present, the impulse to kiss her was winning over rational thought. He needed to know how her lips would feel beneath his.

How her body would feel beneath his.

"You are verra confident, your grace. You think highly of your gaming skills."

He could feel a corner of his mouth tipping up in a wry smile. "I am *entirely* confident in *all* my skills, madam," he muttered. Lust was flaring and burning in him, the desire to touch more of her skin, to feel the beat of her heart underneath his lips. He imagined the warmth of her body as he slid into her, and raised his hand, touched the curl at her collarbone, then moved his hand around to her nape.

The shine in Miss Mackenzie's eyes had

gone molten. Her lips parted with the tiniest gasp of breath. Hamlin was mesmerized, and he was going to kiss her, consequences be damned. She moved closer, so that her bosom brushed against his chest, and whispered, "If you intend to do it, your grace, then, *Diah, do* it."

Heat surged through Hamlin. He pulled her head close and touched his lips to hers. It seemed almost a dream, as if he was watching himself take this liberty with this woman. By all rights, she should have denied him, should have pulled away, should have promised to relay this egregious lack of decorum to her uncle. He deserved all of that.

But Miss Mackenzie hadn't done any of those things — she had unabashedly invited him to do it, and he could not possibly have been more aroused. She made a sound like a soft sigh, then sort of sank into him, her hand going to his waist, another sliding up his chest.

A fire began to build in Hamlin that he knew he'd not be able to douse. He slipped his tongue between her lips to meet hers. She kissed him back with the passion of a woman who'd been waiting for a long-lost lover. The power of desire was building in him rapidly, turning his thoughts to ashes, turning his body to rock. He could think of nothing, see nothing, but this woman before him. It was startling, but inherently familiar.

He suddenly lifted his head. He gazed down at her, brushed the pad of his thumb across her wet bottom lip, then turned away from her. He walked across the room and away from the temptation that was suddenly roaring in him. "I beg your pardon."

"Why?"

Why? A million reasons, and none of them good. He turned his head to look at her. Her cheeks were pink, and she was breathing quickly, her hand on her chest, as if trying to push the air down.

"I should go," she said.

Yes, she should go, go at once, before he took things even further, past the point of redemption. He opened the door for her. She swept past him, hesitating only briefly to look up at him as she passed, her eyes still shining with desire. How extraordinary that this woman would not even feign offense. She was as aroused as he.

That served only to stoke the flames in him higher.

Miss Mackenzie took her leave, insisting to Stuart that her bandaged arm was no impediment to her riding, and proving thus by galloping away with such reckless abandon that Hamlin assumed he'd have to send an army of men to pick up the pieces and stitch her back together.

When she'd gone, he went directly to his rooms and took himself in hand, trying desperately to relieve himself of the raging desire. And though he was successful in the immediate, that desire for Miss Mackenzie did not leave him. It was different. It wasn't just physical. It was much more than that.

That night, he and Eula sat down to dinner as if nothing at all had happened this day.

Eula seemed exhausted by the day's events. She picked at her food, moving carrots around on the plate. Hamlin had told her more than once not to play with her food, to eat what was before her, but this evening he was distracted. "Did you enjoy your archery lesson, then?" he asked.

Eula looked up from her plate. "Aye. I quite like archery."

"Aubin can instruct you if you like."

She frowned at him. In that respect, she was very much like Glenna. Hamlin put down his fork. He sipped his wine, dabbed at his mouth with his napkin, then leveled a look on Eula. "Well, then, let's have it, aye? What has made you cross?"

She cast her eyes to her plate. "Nothing."

"Here now, sit up like a proper young lass, and tell me what has you wrought."

She sat up. "I have no friends," she said. "I should verra much like a friend, a *real* friend."

"I thought you esteemed Miss Mackenzie."

"I *do*!" she exclaimed, as if he was being intentionally obtuse. "But she's as old as my cousin, Glenna."

"I grant you, she is older than you, but friends come in various ages and —"

"She'll *leave*," Eula interrupted him. "And then I'll have no friends again."

Hamlin's heart clutched a little at that. Eula was right — Miss Mackenzie would indeed leave. Eula would miss her just as she missed Glenna. Perhaps more — Miss Mackenzie had paid her more heed than Glenna had in the last months she'd been at Blackthorn Hall. It was little wonder Eula was cross, and frankly, Hamlin was surprised she wasn't cross more often. She wanted companionship, and she should not be forced to live without it.

It galled Hamlin that he was a bloody duke, and yet he could not give Eula the one thing she wanted and needed.

So he did the next best thing. The next morning, he dispatched Bain to find a pair of kittens. The day after that, he set off for Dungotty to issue an invitation on behalf of Miss Eula Guinne for the Dungotty party to dine at Blackthorn Hall, Thursday next.

of Kitross. The day after that, he set off for
Dungotty to issue an invitation on behalf of
Miss Eula Guinne for the Dungotty party
to dine at Blackthorn Hall Thursday next.

CHAPTER TWELVE

Catriona remembered nothing of her ride
back to Dungotty, as she was utterly lost in
her thoughts. What had begun as a lark for
her was turning into something much more.
In the beginning, Montrose had been a
challenge, a mystery to be solved. But now
she was seeing a fully formed man, and not
just a mystery. A dangerously dark, alluring
man.

Emotions and desires were stirring in her,
filling her up and sinking into her imagina-
tion. She could feel his lips on hers even
though they had long since parted. She
could still taste him, even though she was
far from Blackthorn Hall. She couldn't
seem to control her thoughts about the dark
Duke of Montrose and imagining all the
things she ought not to imagine. His naked
body. Those dark eyes staring down at her
as he pierced her with his cock.

Those images took Catriona's breath away.

None of these thoughts were rational, and certainly none of them particularly smart. Moreover, they left her feeling ravenous and helpless and perhaps even a bit hopeless. It wasn't fair that he should kiss her like that when nothing could come of it. Why *had* he kissed her, anyway?

She arrived at Dungotty just before dusk and swept into the entrance hall, shrugging out of her riding coat, her hat and her gloves, and piling them up in Rumpel's waiting arms.

"If I may, madam, I couldn't help but notice your bandage," he said. "Shall I summon a physician?"

"What?" She glanced down — she'd forgotten the cut on her arm. "No, thank you. If I can survive nearly being shot through with an arrow, I can survive a wee wound, aye? Will you serve supper in my rooms, then, Rumpel? It's been a long day, it has."

He bowed in acknowledgment, and Catriona hurried up the stairs. Once inside her room, she threw open the curtains and cranked open the windows. She closed her eyes and leaned across the sill to feel the cool dusk air on her skin. Her face and chest felt as if they were flaming, had felt that way since Montrose had bandaged her arm. All she could see was him kneeling beside her, taking care with the cut on her arm, his hands wide and warm, his touch unnervingly gentle.

She turned from the window and went to her wardrobe to find something less confining than the gown she was wearing — she felt constricted, as if she couldn't properly breathe. As she was rummaging through her things, there was a knock at her door, followed by it opening. "Catriona?"

Catriona leaned back so that she could see Chasity around the open door of her wardrobe. "Aye?"

Chasity swirled inside, carefully shut the door behind her, then flung herself down onto her side on Catriona's bed. "Tell me *everything.*"

Catriona did not want to talk about what she'd experienced at Blackthorn Hall. She wanted to hold it close to her heart, let it knit into her bones. She held out a green silk gown beside a plain brown muslin, examining them. "I was very nearly shot."

"I beg your pardon?"

"I was very nearly struck with an arrow. Miss Guinne's aim accidentally strayed, and she came verra close to piercing me clean through."

Chasity gasped and pushed herself up. *"No,"* she said gravely. "How did it miss you?"

"Aye, that's the interesting part of this tale. Montrose appeared from nowhere and brought me to the ground so quickly that I canna even say how close the arrow came to actually hitting me." She held up her bandaged arm to show Chasity the evidence of her near miss. "But I heard it go over my head."

Chasity gaped at her. "He *threw* you to the ground?"

"He didna *throw* me. He brought me down with him."

"I am all *astonishment,"* Chasity gushed, and fell onto her back. "I would have more readily believed that *he* was the one who tried to shoot you. My mother said you are naïve if you think you might escape the same fate as his wife."

Catriona returned the green silk into the wardrobe, then stepped behind the painted screen to change into the brown muslin. She wriggled out of her trews. "He's been nothing but a gentleman in my presence. And besides, I donna believe it of him — I donna believe he could harm as much as a bunny."

209

Chasity snorted. "What of his wife? Some harm has come to *her,* surely you don't disagree."

It was a fair question, and truthfully, Catriona didn't know what to think of the wife now. "The lass mentioned her in passing," she said as she undressed.

"She *did?* What did she say?"

"She said Lady Montrose was her cousin, but had gone from Blackthorn Hall, and that she missed her. And yet, she didna show the slightest sign of anguish, aye?" Still, the exchange had raised more questions in Catriona's mind. Why had Eula's cousin felt that days passed like weeks at Blackthorn Hall? What did *gone* really mean? If the woman was not dead, where was she? Why had she left her young cousin behind? Did Eula know what had become of her?

She had undressed down to her chemise when she heard another knock on her door. "There's Rumpel come round with my supper. Will you let him in, Chasity?" she asked, and dressed.

"Chasity, darling! I had expected my niece." Uncle Knox's voice filled Catriona's room.

Chasity must have pointed, because a moment later Uncle Knox startled Catriona

210

when he spoke just on the other side of her screen. "Rumpel says you've been seriously injured, darling! I must know what has happened!"

"I've no' been seriously injured," Catriona said with a laugh.

"But she was very nearly *killed* with an arrow!" Chasity exclaimed.

"What? It's true that the duke tried to *shoot* you? Rumpel has told me all! By God, that man will rue the day —"

"No!" Catriona cried, and laughed at the absurdity of this conversation. " 'Twas no' the duke, uncle," she said, and stepped from around the screen and presented her back to him for lacing. " 'Twas the wee lass, that's who. Her arrow went astray, and the duke saved my life by bringing me to the ground. In the fall, I —"

"What's this?" the countess cried, sweeping into Catriona's room through the door her uncle had left standing wide-open. "An injury at the hands of the Duke of Montrose? How *dare* he sup at our table, then lay a hand on you!"

"I will call him out to defend you, madam," Vasily announced just behind her, and bowed low, as if he were accepting her charge to defend her honor.

"By the saints!" Uncle Knox said loudly.

"I shall have you all know that it is not *our* table, it is *my* table, and if there is any calling out to do, *I* will be the one to do it, but that furthermore, apparently there has been a misunderstanding!"

"What misunderstanding?"

Now had arrived Mrs. Templeton.

"The duke tried to kill her!" Vasily announced.

"No!" Catriona shouted, gaining everyone's attention. "The duke has caused me no harm whatsoever! If a crime has been committed, it's been committed by our verra own Rumpel, on my word! If you must know, the duke *saved* me from an arrow's point, and I have a small cut to my arm from the fall." She held her bandaged arm aloft once more. "That's all that has happened this day."

"Your supper, madam."

Her room was so crowded that the poor footman could not enter.

"Let him through!" Uncle Knox commanded, and as best they could, the crowd squeezed to one side so that the young man could place her tray on her table. When he'd left, the rest of them remained standing in her room, their gazes fixed on Catriona. She slowly realized they would not leave until they'd heard everything.

"All right," she said with a sigh. "Here it is, then." She told them about the misguided arrow and her fall to the ground. She explained they had returned to Blackthorn Hall so that they might bandage her arm, and while there, she noticed again the portrait of Lady Montrose. She repeated Eula's comment and then said, "That's all of it."

"And what was the duke's response?" the countess asked. "Did he deny that his wife was no longer at Blackthorn Hall?"

"He said no' a word."

"He did not deny that she'd gone?" Mrs. Templeton asked, her gaze narrowing on Catriona as if she suspected her of colluding with the duke in the disappearance of his wife.

"Madam, as sure as I stand before you, he said no' a word."

"I don't know what to make of it," the countess said. "I have known many strange men, have I not, Vasily?"

"Indeed."

"But I've never heard of one as impossible to understand as this duke. If he didn't murder his wife, why does he not simply say so? How is it possible that she's disappeared and no one can say what has become of her? He is hiding something,

213

quite obviously."

"I think he is easier to understand at every meeting," Catriona said, perhaps a bit more defensively than she had intended. She did not miss the look that the countess and her cousin exchanged.

"Perhaps these *meetings* are clouding your judgment," Mrs. Templeton said with a sniff. "Why do you go to Blackthorn Hall alone? Why not call when in the company of your uncle?"

" 'Tis no' always convenient," Catriona said pertly. She was better acquainted with the duke than any of these people, and she would not abide their derision. She picked up her brush and began to run it through her hair.

"*You* may be very certain he is not an evil man, Miss Mackenzie, but Vasily and I've heard talk of him in Crieff," the countess said. "The last time anyone saw his wife alive was the night of a heated argument between husband and wife. No one has seen her since."

"Who said so?" Catriona asked curiously.

"The innkeeper, Mr. Brimble. He told me, and I daresay he is in a position to know."

"They say the duke is a heavy gambler," offered Vasily. "Perhaps he *sold* his wife."

All eyes, filled with incredulity, turned

214

toward the Russian. "What?" he asked, casting his arms wide. "It's possible."

Catriona sighed. "If you donna mind, all of you, I'm rather tired, aye?" she said, determined not to listen to another word of this preposterous conversation.

"Of course you are," said Uncle Knox. "To think you were so close to being dead!"

"I wasna so close," Catriona tried, but no one was listening to her.

"The duke should take heed," Mrs. Templeton said sternly. "He ought to be made to pay for his indiscretions."

"For the last time, it wasna him who shot the arrow. It was the *lass*," Catriona said.

"Perhaps he told her to do it," Chasity said in a low, menacing voice.

For the love of God, if they didn't leave her room now, Catriona might very well say some things she would much regret on the morrow. She gave her uncle a beseeching look.

"All right, then," he said. "My niece would have her peace now. Come on, all of you, out you go." He ushered them out like so many geese, arguing among themselves about the duke's guilt in any number of things.

When they had all quit the room, Uncle Knox turned back to Catriona. "Are you all right?" he asked. "My sister would never forgive me if something were to befall her spirited daughter."

Catriona smiled. "I'm quite all right, Uncle Knox. Only weary."

"Is there anything I can do for you?" he asked.

"No. *Yes.* Yes, please, uncle. Can you find a copy of the book *The Governess*?"

He blinked. "By Sarah Fielding, isn't it? A children's book."

"Aye, the verra one."

"An interesting choice for reading, my love, but of course. Whatever you need. Get some rest now." He went out.

Uncle Knox thought the book was for her, and Catriona had let him think it — she suspected he'd not like helping her devise another reason to return to Blackthorn Hall. But she had to return. Not to discover what happened to Lady Montrose, but because she had a dangerously overwhelming desire to feel the duke's touch against her skin again.

Two days later, everyone had gathered in the Dungotty drawing room late in the afternoon for tea when Rumpel raced into the room in the manner someone might approach a commander to report that he was surrounded on all sides and his surrender was demanded.

"Good God, what is it, Rumpel? You look like you've been chased by the devil himself!" Uncle Knox said.

"The Duke of Montrose, milord. He's at the door."

Catriona's heart seized. Uncle Knox brought his feet down from the ottoman so hard that his teacup rattled. "At the door!" he exclaimed, and hastily stood.

"Here! Without invitation?" Mrs. Templeton cried.

"Bring him in, bring him in," Uncle Knox said, gesturing grandly.

Catriona didn't know what to do with her teacup. She set it aside and stood, and ran her suddenly damp palms down her skirt.

"*Sit,* Miss Mackenzie," the countess whispered.

Catriona sat.

A moment later, the sure footfall of the duke sounded in the corridor. He entered behind Rumpel, who announced, "The Duke of Mon—"

"Yes, yes, we all know who he is," Uncle Knox said. "Your grace! How good of you to come!" He reached for the duke's hand and shook it heartily. "Shall we pour you tea?"

"No, thank you," he said. He clasped his hands at his back, and his dark eyes made a swift tour of the room, landing on Catriona for a brief moment. "I have come on behalf of Miss Eula Guinne, my ward. I should like to extend an invitation for you and your party to dine at Blackthorn Hall Thursday next at seven."

Catriona's heart skipped. She looked around the room, at the varying expressions of surprise and confusion.

"*All* of us?" Uncle Knox asked.

"Not me," said Lord Furness, who had not bothered to rise from his prime seat at the window. "I mean to return to England as soon as Wednesday."

Good riddance, Catriona thought.

Montrose ignored Furness. His gaze flicked over her, and he said, "All of you, aye, if you are so inclined."

No one spoke. Uncle Knox looked around expectantly at his guests.

Montrose glanced down. "Perhaps you need time to consider your plans," he said, and looked up. "If you will deliver your reply by way of messenger . . . ?"

"Yes, by all means," Uncle Knox said. "Thank you very much, your grace."

"We are honored," Lady Orlov said.

He nodded. He glanced at Catriona once

more. She looked helplessly to her uncle, silently willing him to say something a wee bit more encouraging to the duke.

He must have read her thoughts, because he said quickly, "You may expect our reply within the day, your grace. We're a bit at sixes and sevens, what with travel plans and so forth."

"Of course."

"You're certain you'll not take tea?"

"No, thank you. I must take my leave." He gave Catriona one last look, one she was certain everyone noticed, one that slipped into her body and spread like melting honey. "Good day," he said, and turned on his heel and strode from the door.

No one spoke until they heard the front door open and his footfall fade away. Only then did Catriona leap from her seat and run to the window in time to see him ride away, his horse thundering up the drive.

"Well, *that* was unexpected," Mrs. Templeton said. "I thank you, Norwood, for not accepting for us all. I should not like to dine at his house."

"Why not?" Lady Orlov asked.

"His reputation, obviously," Mrs. Templeton said.

"The invitation has come from Miss Eula Guinne," Uncle Knox pointed out. "I would suspect as Chasity and Catriona are the youngest of us, he should like their company for his young ward. But he could scarcely extend the invitation to the two of them without extending it to us all."

"We will not attend," Chasity's father said firmly.

Chasity gasped. "*What?* But I *want* to go, Pappa! Catriona will attend, won't you, Catriona?"

"I, uh . . . aye, I will attend," she said, and felt her cheeks reddening, as if she'd just admitted to them all that he'd kissed her.

"Haven't you spent enough time at Blackthorn Hall?" Mrs. Templeton asked snidely.

"Thank you, Mrs. Templeton, for your thoughtful attention to my niece's whereabouts, but she is a woman grown, and if she cares to dine at Blackthorn Hall, then by all means, she should dine there."

Mrs. Templeton reddened.

"Will you attend, Uncle Knox?" Catriona asked.

"Alas, I have made prior plans," Uncle Knox said.

"Please, *Pappa,*" Chasity begged. "It's not the duke who invites us, but Miss Guinne. He'll not even be present, I am sure of it." She looked to Catriona for confirmation. Catriona winced.

220

"I think it abominable that he would invite anyone to dine, given his history," her father retorted, and he looked to his wife for confirmation. She winced, too. "What?" he demanded. "What would you say, madam?"

"I would say that I see no harm in it," Mrs. Wilke-Smythe said.

"No harm! You think the man is a murderer, or have you forgotten? And you would send our only daughter into his den?"

"But we'll be with her, as will Miss Mackenzie. And you mustn't forget that he is a duke."

Lord Furness gasped. "Madam! Do you intend to seek a match between your daughter and *that* foul man all for the sake of his title?"

"Miss Mackenzie thinks him innocent, and perhaps I do, too. And we've no other prospects for her at present."

"Mamma!" Chasity exclaimed with a look of horrified embarrassment.

Her husband searched for support of his position in those around him. Finding none, he sighed. "I'll think on it."

"Pappa —"

"I have said I will think on it, Chasity, and that is the best I can do for you now. I had loftier goals for you other than a murderous Scotch duke."

Catriona swallowed down a retort.

"Well, no one has asked *me,* and I should like to attend, too," the countess said. "Vasily?"

"The earl and I have a prior commitment with a gaming hell, which is infinitely more pleasing than the prospect of sitting about all evening while ladies natter on."

"It is decided, then," said Uncle Knox. "The Wilke-Smythes, Countess Orlov and Miss Mackenzie will be delighted to dine with Miss Eula Guinne. Shall I pen the reply?"

Mr. Wilke-Smythe sighed with defeat.

"I will send it, Uncle," Catriona said, as she needed an expedient excuse to leave this room so that she might think about Montrose. How he'd looked at her. How he'd come all this way to extend the invitation himself instead of sending a messenger. And she would like to do her thinking in peace.

As it turned out, she thought about it all afternoon, long after the reply had been sent. But when she slipped underneath the coverlet of her bed that evening, she felt a wee bit sour in the belly. She was thinking about something else. Something that made her feel a bit queasy: the notion that Miss Chasity Wilke-Smythe could be offered up to Montrose as a suitable bride. She didn't like that. She didn't like it at all. No, it was worse than that, wasn't it? That was how much her feelings about the dark duke had changed — the thought was not to be borne at all.

CHAPTER THIRTEEN

Thursday dawned dark and gray, the air heavy. Hamlin had walked down to his latest hammering project — the gardening shed — and didn't like the way the air felt so thick and wet. That generally signaled quite a lot of rain was to fall. It had rained all week, and his lake was swollen, his fountain overflowing.

Just like the lake in him was swollen and overflowing and in desperate need of release.

He had read the letter that had come from Dungotty more than once. It was written in Miss Mackenzie's flourishing script, complete with the same sort of blots and smudges as he'd seen in the last note he'd received from her. It made him smile to know that the one thing the woman was incapable of doing was writing neatly.

To His Grace, the Honorable Duke of Montrose, Thank you for the invitation to

224

dine with Miss Eula Guinne on Thursday evening. Unfortunately, Lord Norwood and Mr. Orlov must honor a prior commitment to a gaming hell, as holding to one's commitment is the true measure of character. If the Lord shines his countenance upon us, Lord Furness will have returned to England, and Lady Templeton will be assailed with a dreadful headache just as we are to leave.

Hamlin had chuckled.

The Wilke-Smythes, Countess Orlov and myself would be delighted to dine with Miss Eula and are quite looking forward to it. Sincerely yours, CM

So was he quite looking forward to it. Hamlin had seen to all the details of tonight's supper — a roasted goose, asparagus grown in his own hothouse, rice from India. He tried to imagine the events of the evening — a lot of chatter, a lot of wine. He did not relish the idea of small talk with the English couple. He did not want the eager attention of their earnest daughter, or that of the countess. What he wished for was a moment alone with Miss Mackenzie. He told himself he intended to apologize for his boorish behavior.

But the devil in him knew that he hoped for another kiss.

Light rain began to fall in the afternoon. Hamlin did some work in his study, then realized he'd not seen Eula all day, which was unusual — she was underfoot more often than not. Then again, she had a pair of new kittens to occupy her, and he assumed that was what had kept her out of his study.

He went to see about her and found her seated on a bench at her vanity while Miss Burns curled her hair for the evening. He had to admit that in spite of the woman's thick accent — there had been moments where she'd sounded to be speaking gibberish — she had proved herself a capable lady's maid. Eula's appearance had vastly improved as a result of Miss Burns's attention to her clothing and hair.

Eula had her head down and was playing with one of the two kittens on her lap. The other would undoubtedly present itself when Hamlin least expected it, darting across his path to attack his shoe like the shadow of the devil.

"I shall have you in the red drawing room at seven, lass," he said.

She glanced up at him and startled Hamlin by her appearance. Her cheeks were red, her eyes shining with fever. "Can you guess which one this is?" she asked, holding up the kitten.

"No," he said, and walked to her bench, squatted down beside her and put the back of his hand against her forehead. She was burning.

"This one is Perry. Walter has gone to hunt mice."

"Walter is scarcely bigger than a mouse himself," he muttered, and glanced at Miss Burns. "She is feverish."

"Aye, your grace. She'll noo' abide her beid."

"She'll abide it now. Ready her for bed." He stood up and walked to the bell pull and yanked on it.

"I donna want to go to bed!" Eula cried out. "We're to have a party!"

"No' you, lass. You're burning with fever."

"No!" she cried, and shot up from the bench, running out of reach of Miss Burns. But she was no match for Hamlin, who caught her easily. "Heed me now, love. Do you feel well enough to listen to adults talk?"

"Aye," she said weakly, but sniffed with despair.

"And do you want to infect our guests with your fever? Would you have all of Dungotty come down with an ague?"

227

She groaned and shook her head.

He bent down before her, pushed her hair from her eyes. "I'll bring Miss Mackenzie up to see you, aye? You may show her your kittens. But you're too ill for company and need to be abed."

In the truest sign that she was ill, Eula dropped her head and nodded. She didn't have the strength to put up an argument. "I wanted to have a supper party," she said, and tears began to leak from her eyes.

"I know," he said, and kissed her burning forehead, then picked her up and carried her to her bed.

Eula had been a different lass since Bain had appeared with the kittens he'd collected from a barn cat at one of the tenants' crofts. He wished he'd acted sooner in getting the kittens. He wished he'd put aside his notions about what should or should not reside in a house, for it was really a trifling thing, and he'd had no idea a pair of kittens would make Eula so deliriously happy. He had Miss Mackenzie to thank for that, he supposed, as she had helped Eula make her case.

Eula was just as happy that they were to receive guests. Of course, Hamlin knew she was lonely and lacked diversion, but he'd not expected her to be so jubilant over the prospect of supper guests. But from the moment they'd received the affirmative reply from Dungotty, she'd been breathless.

"We've no' had guests in *forever*," she'd said as she'd twirled around on one foot, watching the skirt of her gown flare out in the middle of his study. "We'll use the best porcelain, aye? Cousin Glenna used the best porcelain."

"Aye," he said.

"And the crystal, Montrose."

"Your grace. And the crystal."

Later, she'd asked him about the silver, and if the dishes would be served by Stuart and a footman, or put on the table in the manner they often dined, which apparently she found wanting in the performance of a supper party. Hamlin encouraged her to discuss her concerns with Stuart directly, but she seemed to prefer to discuss them with him.

When this event was over and done, his relief from the sheer volume of questions presented to him each day would be great.

He rounded up the kittens, and while Miss Burns helped to undress Eula, he put the kittens in a wooden box at the foot of her bed. When he went out of her room, Eula was lying on her side, forlornly stroking their fur.

He dressed for the evening, his mood soured now that Eula had fallen ill. This evening had been for Eula. Well, for him, too, but for her, as well. He worried about the lass, wondered if he ought to send for a doctor.

He toyed with the idea of sending a message that the supper was canceled. But his desire nudged in hard against his concern for Eula. The only thing he knew with certainty was that he wanted to be in Miss Mackenzie's presence. He wanted to assure himself that the heat he'd felt in his chest had been real, that she was as comely as she was in his mind's eye, that the stars shining in her eyes had not been imagined.

He sent a footman for Bain. His secretary had a keen eye for clothing, and given a different set of circumstances, he would have made an excellent valet.

Mr. Bain had been away all day and still bore a bit of the windswept look as he chose a gold waistcoat and white neckcloth for Hamlin. Hamlin's formal tails were still on the valet stand, and Bain began to brush the garment down. "By the bye, your grace, I have heard that MacLaren remains uncertain about his recommendation to Caithness," he said as he worked on the coat.

"Why?"

230

"He believes your marital history might be an impediment, aye?"

Hamlin slipped a signet ring onto his finger, mulling over what Bain had just said.

"Argyll, however, has defended you," Bain added casually.

Hamlin glanced at the younger man.

"He believes that women must be treated with a firm hand, for if they are allowed to follow their inferior instincts, they will inevitably require correction. He advocates that a firmer hand is better than a softer one and will lead to less confusion."

The end of Hamlin's marriage had nothing to do with how firm or soft his hand was — he'd never raised it, would never consider raising it.

Bain held out the coat for him to slip on.

"Thank you," Hamlin said. He stared at himself in the mirror. "Who is with Argyll and who is with MacLaren?"

Bain swept an invisible speck of lint off Hamlin's shoulder. "Most are with Argyll. One or two are with MacLaren yet." He stood back to eye Hamlin's appearance. "There is still time," he added as he straightened Hamlin's cuff.

There was still time to gather the votes, Bain meant, but in actuality, there wasn't much of it. The vote was a month away.

Before Hamlin went downstairs, he looked in on Eula. She had refused to eat, Miss Burns said, but she was sleeping, the two black kittens curled against her back.

Rain was falling harder now, pelting the enormous windows that framed the staircase. Hamlin walked through the dining room to have a look at the table settings, although he needn't have bothered, as Stuart was impeccable in the service of guests. Hamlin had the distinct impression that Stuart was looking forward to the supper as much as Eula.

He carried on to the drawing room and helped himself to a brandy.

Stuart stepped in to stoke the fire at the hearth. "The weather has turned foul, your grace," he announced.

Hamlin wondered if anyone would come. He supposed a messenger would have been sent by now if the weather would prevent them from coming.

It was an interminable wait. Hamlin drank his brandy, tried to read. Seven o'clock came and went quickly. He believed he would spend another evening playing chess alone, but he heard a commotion near the front of the house and made his way to the foyer.

As Hamlin walked down the carpeted hall,

he heard the sounds of the torrential rain and wind through the opened front doors, Stuart's voice, followed by the rise of a feminine voice. When he entered the foyer, he saw only Miss Mackenzie, and behind her, a carriage pulling away from the portico.

"*Feasgar math,*" she said, curtsying. Her eyes, as always, were shining with happiness. Or did he read too much into it? "I beg your pardon for my tardiness, aye? The horses were a wee bit reluctant to step out."

"Think nothing of it."

"I must look a fright, aye?" she said cheerfully as she removed her cloak.

"No' at all," Hamlin said. In fact, she looked so bonny that he had to remind himself to ask about the others. "I beg your pardon, but have you come alone?"

"I have," she said, and handed her cloak to Stuart, then tried to smooth her petticoat. "Have the others no' come, then? I was to Crieff today and arranged to meet them here. Beg your pardon, sir," she said to Stuart, "may I take something from the pocket of my cloak?" She reached into the pocket and removed a small book, tied with ribbon. "As it happens, the bookshop in Crieff had precisely what I was looking for. I've a gift for Miss Guinne."

Her smile was sinking into Hamlin and taking root. She was dressed in a gown of pink-and-green silk with tiny white roses embroidered throughout and across the stomacher. The sleeves ended with fine white lace that matched the color of the tiny roses. Her hair was artfully arranged, a cascade of slender curls down her back and around her face, the rest of it piled atop her head and woven through with pearls. She was so bloody bonny to him that he was left momentarily speechless. His head was filling with images of that very lovely gown peeling off her body, one piece at a time.

"It's a book," she said. She leaned to one side to see around him. "Has she come down?"

"No," he said, finding himself once more. "She, uh . . . she has taken ill."

"Ill! *Mi Diah,* nothing serious, I hope."

"I donna know," he said, frowning. "She's fevered."

"May I see her? Please," she said earnestly. "I've brought her a gift, I have, and I should like to look in on her."

He nodded. "It would cheer her."

He escorted Miss Mackenzie to Eula's rooms, knocked softly on the door and opened it. Miss Burns was seated in a chair with the light of a single candle to illuminate her sewing. She stood up, curtsied.

"Good evening, Miss Burns," Miss Mackenzie whispered. "How is our lass, then?"

"She's got a bit of a sneefle," Miss Burns said.

Miss Mackenzie went to Eula's bedside.

"Keep your distance, Miss Mackenzie," Hamlin warned her, and came behind her, leaning over her to touch Eula's forehead.

Miss Mackenzie went down on her knees beside Eula's bed and stroked her cheek.

"Miss Mackenzie," Eula said sleepily.

Miss Mackenzie gasped softly and picked up one of the kittens. "What's this, then?" she asked. "You've a kitten!"

"I've *two*," Eula said. "But Walter doesna like to show himself. This one is Perry."

"Walter is here," Miss Mackenzie said, and reached over Eula to pick up the second black kitten. Both of them began to mewl. "Aye, what bonny kittens. They'll make you fine companions."

Eula nodded. She pushed herself up on her elbow. "Is that for me?" she asked, having spotted the ribbon-bound book.

"Aye," Miss Mackenzie said as Hamlin collected the kittens from her arms. She held out the book to Eula. "I went all the way to Crieff to fetch it, I did, because I know you'll be verra well diverted by it. It's

235

called *The Governess; or, The Little Female Academy,* by Miss Sarah Fielding. It's about a boarding school for lassies just like you." Miss Mackenzie handed her the package, and without a moment's hesitation, Eula yanked on the ribbon, let it flutter to her bed and opened it.

"Thank you!" she said.

"Perhaps we might save the book till the morrow, Eula," Hamlin said, and stroked her head. It pained him to see her ill, to see the light from her eyes replaced with fever. "You need to rest."

"Aye, that you do, Miss Guinne," Miss Mackenzie said. "Promise me you'll wait until the morrow to read it."

"Mmm," Eula listlessly agreed, but she held the book to her chest as she sank back into her pillows and closed her eyes. Miss Mackenzie touched her hand, then pushed herself to standing.

"Should I summon a doctor?" Hamlin whispered.

Miss Mackenzie shook her head. "She's come down with a cold, that's all." She turned to Miss Burns. "Chamomile tea if she wakes, to settle her belly. If she's hungry, send for a broth made from chicken, roses and grain meal, aye?"

Miss Burns nodded.

236

Hamlin opened the door to the hall, and Miss Mackenzie slipped out before him. He turned back to Miss Burns. "Send for me if she worsens."

He escorted Miss Mackenzie down to the drawing room. "You have some knowledge of healing, do you?" he asked as they descended the stairs.

"Only what I've learned at the abbey. There is always a sick child among them, but the women, they've learned the remedies, they have." She looked up at him. "You worry for her, aye? I think there is naught to fear. The bairns, they fall hard and rise quickly. She'll be chasing kittens down the halls in a day or two."

Hamlin prayed she was right.

They reached the drawing room, where Hamlin noted it was almost eight o'clock now, and still no sign of the others. He nodded at a waiting footman to serve wine. He needed something to help dull his awareness of this woman and her slender neck. He moved away as the footman served her wine, and looked at the rain coming down in sheets.

"It's dreadful weather," Miss Mackenzie said from somewhere behind him. "I hope the driver hasna met with trouble. I was longer in Crieff than I meant to be."

"It's no' far to Dungotty," he assured her. Although it had felt like an ocean existed between Blackthorn Hall and Dungotty these last few days, a wasteland between him and his desire.

Miss Mackenzie joined him at the window. She leaned across the sill, craning her neck in the direction of the road. Hamlin's gaze was on her figure, plump in all the right places, one delicious curve after the other. He so longed to touch her skin that his hand itched with it.

"They ought to have arrived by now," she said.

Personally, Hamlin hoped they'd be delayed a week.

A loud crack of thunder sounded, followed by a release of more torrential rain. With a start, Miss Mackenzie drew back from the window and turned a wide-eyed look to Hamlin. "I've no' seen a storm as bad as this."

"Blackthorn Hall has stood for more than one hundred years, aye?" he said soothingly. "We'll no' float away."

She smiled self-consciously.

He put his hand on her arm. "Donna be uneasy."

She looked into his eyes. "I donna think," she said, her gaze falling to his lips, "that I could be more at ease."

He meant to speak. To tell her he was at ease, too, that she put him at ease in spite of his initial instincts about her, in spite of his fears about her and her intentions. But he was startled by a loud banging on the front door, someone pounding with determination.

Miss Mackenzie started. "Oh!" she said, and laughed with relief, her hand over her heart. "At last, they've come, determined to make a grand entrance, aye?"

Hamlin didn't think that sort of pounding was the way the Wilke-Smythes would enter Blackthorn Hall. "If you'll excuse me," he said, and went to investigate.

His suspicion proved true — it was not the Wilke-Smythes dripping on his floor, but a diminutive man in a mud-spattered coat. "Beg your pardon, your grace. An urgent message from milord Norwood." He reached inside his cloak pocket to withdraw a soggy folded letter.

Hamlin took the letter and read it. When he'd finished, he carefully folded it again. "Thank you," he said to the man, and to Stuart, "Give him supper and a place to sleep, aye? He'll be our guest tonight."

The man glanced around him, his gaze wandering to the massive crystal chandelier.

"Thank you, your grace," he said, his voice full of awe and, Hamlin guessed, relief that he would not be forced back into the storm.

But it was he who ought to be thanking him, Hamlin thought as he returned to the drawing room. He was grateful that he would not have to suffer the English family or the Russian countess. The perfect evening, his private dream of an evening, had just opened up to him.

Miss Mackenzie turned expectantly when he entered the room. "Have they come, then?"

"No." He handed her the note. " 'Tis from your uncle."

Miss Mackenzie read the letter from Norwood, in which he'd written that the river was rising and there was water standing on the roads, making it impassable in places. None of them could possibly venture out and sent their deepest regrets. Norwood also asked if Hamlin would be so kind as to shelter his most favored niece for the night at Blackthorn Hall. He very much regretted the imposition, but it was not safe for her to travel home.

"Oh, dear," Miss Mackenzie said when she'd read it, and looked up at Hamlin. "What am I to do?"

"As your uncle asks, aye? It's no' safe for

240

you to go out. You are verra welcome here, of course."

She looked around the drawing room. "But . . . is there no one else here, then?"

Had he misread the kiss between them completely? He had thought she might be as desirous of time alone as he was. "Are you frightened of me?" he asked, prepared to explain to her that she had nothing to fear from him, that the rumors were not even remotely true.

But Miss Mackenzie surprised him with a burst of laughter. "Of *you*? No, your grace, I'm no' afraid of you. I merely wondered if perhaps we might have that game of chess after all." She smiled devilishly.

Something unmoored in Hamlin and set sail into uncharted waters. He smiled, too, could feel that smile shining in him. "Indeed, madam, we will have that match. Shall we dine? Aubin has gone to a great deal of effort, and I'd no' harm his feelings. He'll be offended well enough that the party has been reduced to only two."

She laughed. "Aye. I'm ravenous."

He offered his arm to her. Miss Mackenzie laid her hand lightly on it, the weight of it no more than a feather, and Hamlin imagined escorting her to the supper table every evening. His mind was racing, turning over on itself, redesigning the evening he'd planned. He had precisely what he wanted; he had this woman to himself. A little more than a week ago, he'd thought her too bold for her own good. Tonight, he thought her the best company he could possibly ask for, and felt almost desperate that she feel the same way.

It was not until they turned the corner that he realized the black shadows he saw from the corner of his eye were the two kittens, racing after the train of Catriona's gown, trying to catch it.

He was like those tiny kittens, trying to catch her spirit and hold on to it. He hoped he was at least as successful as the tiny felines, but he privately feared the secrets that weighed him down would cause him to stumble and watch her slip away.

CHAPTER FOURTEEN

The meal was superb. Catriona was certain she'd never tasted food so well prepared, and she was not shy about eating what was served. The goose was succulent, the asparagus a pleasant surprise. And there was a wonderful cake to finish the meal.

The Blackthorn Hall dining room was not as large as the one at Norwood Park — that one would seat three dozen — but she preferred this one. It was intimate and warm, and the fire in the hearth thankfully drowned out the sound of rain lashing at the windows.

The extra place settings had been cleared away, and the two of them sat at one end of the table. Stuart and a footman served them in perfect unison. They spoke of Miss Guinne's illness while they dined, of childhood illnesses they had endured. Montrose claimed he had never had an ague.

"Impossible!" she cried.

"Entirely possible," he countered.

"Perhaps if you were an only child. Were you an only child, then?"

"I've a younger brother, the Viscount Brownglen. But as the heir, I was separated from him if he fell ill."

"Ah. I've three brothers and one sister, and if one of us was struck down, all of us were," she said. She told him about a room at the top of Balhaire, long and narrow, where the five of them would lie in their sickbeds to keep from infecting the rest of the castle. "We use it still," she said with a laugh. "I've many nieces and nephews."

"Your childhood sounds as if it was idyllic," he remarked.

"It was," she agreed. "It was before the rebellion, of course." She shrugged, thinking back to the time of greater fortune than what her family enjoyed now. "We've always been together. And what of your childhood, your grace? Was it idyllic?"

He glanced thoughtfully at his plate and shook his head. "My mother died when Charles and I were verra young. My father was stern and scarcely around that I recall. We were left to the care of governesses and tutors."

"Oh." She felt a swell of sorrow for him. Her family was tight-knit, particularly during the dark days following the failed Jacobite rebellion of 1745. "I'm sorry for you."

He smiled sheepishly. "Thank you, but that's the way of a duke's family, as I know it. The duke produces the obligatory heir and the spare, and leaves them to the seat to be reared properly."

She knew enough from her mother's upbringing to know that was true. "Has your father been dead long, then?"

"Thirteen years."

He didn't say more, and she didn't press him. She had the sense it was not a pleasant memory for him and turned the conversation to horses.

When they finished the cake, Catriona leaned back in her chair and put her hand over her belly. "That was delicious, your grace. I must compliment Aubin the next opportunity I have. I'd no' have thought him the sort to turn out a meal such as this, aye?"

Montrose chuckled. "He came to Blackthorn Hall claiming to have great culinary skill. I said he must prove it was so. I made him prove it for a full week before he demanded an answer from me."

Catriona laughed roundly, then smiled at him with genuine, earned affection. How could anyone suspect this man of anything untoward? "What shall we do now, your grace?" she asked him. "Shall we prove our skill at chess?"

He looked up from his brandy, and in the light of the fire, his eyes were as black as the deep of the night. Those dark eyes moved over her, lingering here and there. "Nothing would delight me more," he said quietly.

Catriona's pulse quickened — she was enthralled. She couldn't think of anything that would delight her more, either.

They strolled to the salon, wandering along through the wide hall, Catriona pausing to examine paintings and vases on display on consoles beneath the sconces, Montrose happy to tell her a brief history of the pieces.

A footman had gone before them to the salon, and the gaming table had been placed directly before the hearth. The fire provided a warm glow, and a candelabrum with a trio of beeswax candles provided the light for the match.

Montrose pulled out a chair for Catriona, and as she was taking her seat, he casually ran his hand down her arm. He might as well have touched fire to her skin — it could not have felt any less a flare.

He sat across from her and moved the

chess pieces to their beginning places. The footman stood across the room, his back to the wall, his gaze set on a spot well above their heads. And yet, when Montrose raised his index finger, the footman instantly moved to pour wine for them.

"Thank you, Adam, that will be all for now," the duke said, his voice sultry and low. "Tell Stuart that I should like the blue guest room readied for Miss Mackenzie."

"Aye, your grace," the footman said, and went out.

They were alone. Blessedly alone.

A clap of thunder rattled the windowpanes and her bones, startling her. She looked to the windows. "I hope all is well at Dungotty," she muttered, rubbing her arms.

"You were determined to leave Dungotty after a fortnight rather than face a summer filled with the possibility of balls, as I recall." He glanced up, his eyes shining with amusement.

"What a fine memory you have, your grace," she said laughingly. "My uncle was determined to have me for a time. He needs me to assist him if he is to stop the forfeiture of the abbey."

"What a curious abbey it is," he mused as he finished setting the pieces.

Yes, the abbey. Catriona was suddenly

struck — she'd not thought of the abbey in two days. "You donna approve, is that it? I'm no' surprised — gentlemen of your standing rarely do."

He paused and looked at her again. "Gentlemen of my standing? Do you mean dukes, then? You do me a disservice, Miss Mackenzie. I happen to believe your devotion to your abbey is an extraordinary feat of courage and compassion."

She stared at him with surprise. Was he teasing her? Making light of what she'd done? But he steadily held her gaze, his expression not one of disdain, but interest. "Do you, really?" she asked, incredulous.

"I'd no' say so if I didna mean it."

Desire for this man began to sizzle in her. For so long she'd heard nothing but despair or condemnation for the abbey. But this dark, dangerous duke had just called it an extraordinary feat. She gazed at him unabashedly. The air seemed to crackle around her. She was fascinated with the way the light shone on his face, how in this light, his eyes didn't look so forebodingly black, but fathomless. As if there was a vast landscape beneath them, with peaks and valleys and rivers and dark corners and sunny meadows, all places no one had ever seen.

"Thank you," she said when she remembered herself. "I would that your good opinion was shared by others."

"I recognize there are those who donna wish to see the sort of people you house at your abbey, Miss Mackenzie. But you must believe there are more men, good men, who'd no' care to see the less fortunate wandering the earth in search of shelter. Particularly the weaker sex and their fatherless children, aye?"

"That's exactly the issue," Catriona said, sitting up, her devotion to Kishorn Abbey stirring in her. "Where would they be, then, were it no' for the abbey? They'd be selling their flesh, or dying in the streets, their children turned out to pickpocket."

"Aye, I understand. You are passionate about your cause."

Yes, she was passionate about the abbey and the people who had sought shelter and warmth there. "I *am* passionate," she said. "I am passionate about everything for which I take interest." Unthinkingly, her gaze slipped to his lips.

A silence followed her remark. The room felt charged, as if a bolt of lightning had struck inside. Montrose held her gaze, his fathomless eyes probing hers. He slowly released a soft breath and leaned back. Something was thrumming between them

249

— a fire. A raging storm. *Something.* Catriona could not recall a single time in her life she had felt such stark, unbridled energy between herself and another person.

"I am likewise passionate about many things," he said at last. "That's why I seek a seat in the House of Lords, aye."

"To help women and children?"

"To help all of Scotland. There are many in need. But it goes beyond that, aye? If we donna mind ourselves, if we donna look to the future, we will always be subservient to the English and treated like litter runts."

"Aye," she agreed, her voice full of wonder. Her beliefs rarely aligned with anyone else. Everyone said she was too bold, wanted too much.

His gaze darkened and moved down her body. "And like you, I am passionate about many things," he said low.

The sizzle in her was growing, spreading through her belly and into her chest. His gaze was so potent and full of heat. Her pulse was quickening, and she glanced at the board, hiding her fluster, because there was a great passion gripping her right now. One that was so big and deep that she feared she would not be able to escape it this time. "Is it your move?"

"The move has been yours all along."

The heat between them had leapt across the table and landed squarely in her groin. She swallowed down the thrill his words gave her. She was aware of how closely he studied her, how his eyes were peeling away her skin and muscle and bone and seeing right into her. She was too keenly aware of the duke's presence, massive and dense, filling every bit of this room. She reached for her wine to steady her sudden case of nerves, but the glass was nearly empty. Had she drunk it already?

She finally decided her move and made it.

He smiled lopsidedly. "A queen's gambit. That was a dangerous move, lass."

"Aye." She picked up her wineglass and drained the last of it.

He chuckled. He moved a knight and removed her pawn from the board. "Do you know what I find curious?"

That she was shimmering in her seat? That she could scarcely see the chessboard because she was so aware of him? She shook her head.

He smiled at her. Perhaps she'd had too much wine this evening, but she suddenly thought him the most handsome gentleman she'd ever seen. He was transformed when he smiled, a different man altogether. The dark duke became the bonny duke. "I find it curious that you are allowed to follow your ideals. Most women in your position would have been long married by now. But you, the daughter of a powerful Highland laird, are no' married. No' raising your brood."

The sizzle suddenly left her. *Et tu, Brute?* She sighed with weary disappointment. "This again, is it?" she muttered.

"Pardon?"

"You and all of Scotland find it curious I've no' married, aye? Poor Catriona Mackenzie, they say, quite on the shelf she is."

"I never said such a thing."

"But you are thinking it, are you no'?"

"I am —"

"Well, I *tried,*" she blurted before he could explain himself and humiliate her further. She was light-headed now. "God knows I've tried."

"I see. I —"

"No, you donna see at all, your grace, if you will pardon me for saying so. *You've* lived a life of privilege, have you no'? You undoubtedly had any number of debutantes desperate to meet you with the hope of gaining an offer. You canna possibly know what it was like when *I* reached a marrying age. Everyone said, oh, but she's so like Griselda, she'll listen to no man, no' that

252

lass. Aye, it's true, I was quite independent, that I was, but I was no' like Auntie Zelda at all. *She* never wanted to marry, but *I* did. I wanted it verra much, to have what my brothers and sister had, to have a brood as you call it, to bring them to my father's house and share in the moments that matter in a family. But there was a bloody rebellion brewing when I came of age, and half the men went off to fight the king, and the others fled, and those who remained, they were . . . they were . . ."

She didn't know what they were, other than not suitable for her.

"I tried," she said again. "But as the years have gone by, I'm now too old."

"Too old!" He laughed. "You're verra young yet."

"But I'm no'," she said. She suddenly sat up and said in a low voice, "Two years ago, when I was one and thirty, my mother attempted to arrange a match for me with an Englishman, a baron. But when his family discovered my age, they were uneasy. What if I was too old to bear children or to carry them to term? What if I failed to deliver them an heir? That's all I mattered to them — I was naught more than a womb, and everyone knows a woman is most fertile a decade younger than me."

The duke suddenly reached across the table for her hand and wrapped his fingers around hers. "I'm sorry. I didna mean to cause you distress. I'm verra sorry you've been hurt in this way."

She shook her head.

Montrose brought her hand to his mouth and kissed the back of it. Her rant was forgotten, the burn for him remembered. What did it all matter now? She was not married, she'd never be married and she was here now, with this man, with voracious desire swirling through her.

"I beg your pardon, if you thought I was complaining," she said. "I meant only to say that I tried to be married, but it eluded me. But I am a lucky one, I am — I live life as I please. My aunt taught me that is entirely possible, even for the daughter of a powerful laird. It is my great fortune that my family sustains me."

He stroked her hand with his thumb. Such a small gesture, and yet it felt almost erotic. She swallowed and said, "It's only fair that I, as you've inquired after mine, might inquire after your life, aye?"

He stroked her hand again. "All right, then. What would you know?"

Here it was, her moment of truth, her chance to inquire about the thing that had been on her mind since she'd first laid eyes on him. A shiver of anticipation raced down her spine. She sat up, gripped his hand, looked him directly in the eye and asked, "What happened to your wife, your grace?"

Montrose did not flinch. He didn't seem angered by the question, but he looked as if he were debating what to say. "Quite a lot is said by people who know nothing of my affairs, aye? I warned you no' to listen to gossip," he said.

She said nothing but waited for him to say more.

"Do you believe I've done something to her?" he asked.

"No," she said, and clutched his hand tighter. "No, I *donna* believe it. I've no' ever believed it."

He studied her a moment. "No harm has come to her," he said at last. "But she is gone."

Catriona's mind leapt to all the things that might mean. Where had she gone? Was she dead? Had she taken her own life? Could *that* be the reason for all the secrecy?

"For what it's worth, I tried, too," he said, and laced his fingers with hers.

"Pardon?"

"I tried to make her happy, but it proved impossible."

The air was buzzing around Catriona. The sensation of his touch was spreading up her arm while she tried to imagine what had made the duchess unhappy.

"The truth is that I want, and have long wanted, the same as you. I wanted what I had been led to expect I'd have — a family, a happy life, aye? But I was no' enough for her." He swallowed, as if he couldn't stomach the truth.

Catriona was stunned. Was that what had happened? She didn't want him? Catriona knew his marriage was likely arranged, but it still seemed impossible — he was handsome, he was kind — well, at least he had been to her — and while he could be aloof, he was a duke for heaven's sake. What woman didn't want the affection of a duke?

"And like you, I've long accepted it, aye? Perhaps I could have done more. Perhaps I did too much. I donna know why things happened as it did, but I've accepted it."

She didn't know why things had happened as they had, either, but she had accepted it, like him. Catriona suddenly surged forward, leaning across the gaming table, knocking chess pieces off their squares so that her face was inches from his. "I donna know her, quite obviously, but I think the fault was no' yours, your grace."

He smiled sadly and cupped her face with his hand. "I'm afraid it was."

Catriona could feel his sadness. She could feel it because she knew it — that dull ache that dwelt in her always.

"But I thank you, Miss Mackenzie, for believing me. You are quite alone in that."

"Catriona," she said, and surged closer, bracing herself on the table to kiss him. She boldly, without a second thought, kissed the dark duke.

He caught her by the shoulders and stood, pulling her to her feet with him and then into his arms. He held her face, his eyes tender and soft and shining with undeserved reverence. He stroked her cheek, her temple, her brow. "You've made me mad with longing, do you know that?" he asked roughly. "I've thought of nothing but you these last days."

"Me, too," she said breathlessly.

He bent his head and kissed her. "But I'll no' dishonor you, Catriona. Never."

Her name sounded like a heavenly whisper when he said it, and Catriona closed her eyes and breathed the moment in, certain she'd never desired a man quite so thoroughly. She'd confessed all to him, and he had not shunned her. He *wanted* her. She longed for things she had no right to know

— the weight of his body on hers, the feel of him moving inside her, the warmth of his breath and his lips on her breasts.

His hand went round her waist, holding her tighter, and she realized her desire for the dark duke had made her damnably weak. Who *was* she at this moment? She'd held herself above her most prurient desires for thirty-three years, but she was standing on a precipice. She would abandon her chastity for this man — that was the measure of how much she desired him. There was nothing left of her but a burning craving for his touch.

Hamlin stroked her cheek, her hair. "What am I to do with you, then?" he muttered.

"Do with me what you like," she answered honestly, and cupped his face in her hands. "Do with me what *I* want. You said the move had always been mine."

He shook his head. " 'Tis no' right —"

"There *is* no right for me," she said, and slipped her arms around his neck. "Did you no' hear me, then? I spoke true, Montrose — I've tried. But I am three and thirty and I'll no' have this opportunity again."

He groaned, grabbed her face in between his hands, kissed her hard. Then he grabbed her hand. "Come," he said, and began to walk from the room, tugging her behind him. At the door, he held up his hand to her. "Wait." He opened the door and looked out in the corridor. Then he pulled her along with him, striding from the room, turning right instead of left, up a flight of stairs she had not seen before this evening. They jogged up another set of steps and emerged in a wide hall where candles blazed in sconces. He quickened his step to the point she had to hurry along to keep up with him. She felt fifteen years old again, sneaking out of Balhaire and around to the stables for a kiss with Egan MacDonald. Part of her wanted to laugh like a naughty child. Part of her wanted to cry out with alarm.

All of her wanted whatever came next.

At the end of the hall, he opened a door and pushed her into a room ahead of him. An enormous bed was at the center of the room, its brocade canopy matching the drapes. A table with upholstered chairs was situated near the windows, and a settee before the hearth. The walls were bare, save a few smaller portraits of what looked like people from another time and one very large, very lovely painting of a man, his horse and a dog in a deep glen.

This was *his* room. The master suite. It was masculine, the colors dark and rich.

Before her surroundings could sink into her, the duke put his finger to his lips, then left her, disappearing into an adjoining room. She looked down at the thick burgundy carpet at her feet. Her heart was beating wildly, her breaths coming in tiny pants. She heard a door open somewhere, the duke's low voice, and then, before she could draw another breath, he returned.

He shut the door between his bedroom and the adjoining room and then stood there a moment, gazing at her in disbelief, as if he couldn't believe she was here, either. His arms were at his sides, and he kept stretching the fingers of one hand, then gripping them, then stretching them again.

Catriona didn't know what to do with herself. She held her hands at her waist, waiting. "Your grace, I —"

"Hamlin," he said, and reached for her, drawing her close to him. He kissed the corner of her mouth. "Call me Hamlin," he murmured, and kissed her cheek.

So many emotions began to roil in her, setting her adrift. *Hamlin,* she whispered, and let his name sink with her into a lake of warm desire. "Hamlin."

He began to kiss her, gently at first, feathering her eyes and cheeks with kisses, moving then to her ear, nibbling at her lobe.

But his tongue quickly became a flame, licking and tantalizing her beyond her ability to endure, leaving a trail of fire down her neck that burned in her groin.

He lifted his head, and with his eyes locked on hers, he began to untie the ribbons that laced her gown across her stomacher. She stood mutely, watching the pleasure he took in this single act. He pushed the gown from her shoulders, and it slid down her body, landing in a pool at her feet. She tossed her stomacher aside as he reached for the ties of her petticoat.

Catriona began to unbutton his waistcoat. His eyes were two obsidian pools, devouring her as he removed her petticoat, and the under-petticoat, until she wore nothing but her chemise.

He paused then, as if he were afraid to go any further. He yanked impatiently at his neckcloth, discarding it as quickly as he'd discarded his coat and waistcoat, all the while taking her in, his eyes lingering on every part of her body through the thin chemise.

Catriona was anxious but filled with yearning, too. She wanted to feel his hands on her. Her thoughts were wildly, uncontrollably lustful, but she couldn't seem to stop them. She'd dived into this well and was sinking deeper and deeper into longing.

She grabbed the fabric of her chemise and pulled it over her head and tossed it aside. Hamlin drew a sharp intake of breath. His gaze raked over her body, now completely bare but her stockings, held up by two ribbon garters above her knees.

He very deliberately put his arm around her waist and cupped her bare breast. He kissed her again, but far more urgently than before, plumbing deeper into her. Catriona was instantly swept along with his ardor, her body divorcing her mind and riding along a sensuous path of pleasure.

They were moving. Or rather, with his arm around her waist, he had lifted her from her feet and was carrying her. The next thing she knew she was on the bed, and his hands were exploring her body, sliding down her breasts, between her legs, around her hips. She was kissing him, too, her fingers fluttering over the hard planes and curves of his body, memorizing the beauty of the male physique.

He lifted his head, his gaze brimming with desire. "Do you know how perfect you are, Catriona? How in every way you are the truest of desire?"

She sighed dreamily, pushed his hair from his face, long since come undone from its bob. With his hand on her breast and the thirst for her so clear in his eyes, Catriona felt herself slipping away from reason. She lifted a knee, stroked his face and tenderly kissed his lips.

Hamlin's breathing turned ragged as he moved down her body. With his teeth he untied one stocking garter, and then the other, then kissed the inside of her thigh before moving in between her legs.

Catriona gasped at the explosive sensation of his tongue and grasped his shoulders, clinging desperately to him as he pleasured her with his mouth and tongue. She was crumbling, piece by piece, and then he rose up, drew her nipple into his mouth and put himself firmly between her legs. She could feel his cock hard against her leg, then pressing into her. He slowly guided himself inside her, pushing gingerly. Catriona was floating again, adrift in erotic sensations, in the sights and sounds and smells of it. She couldn't seem to catch her breath, and when he pushed all the way into her, she scarcely noticed the moment of pain, for he had slipped his hand in between them and was stroking her as he moved inside her.

She pressed against him as he moved, her mouth on his shoulder, his throat, his chest, swimming against the current of her release.

This was too surreal, too pleasurable to let go of it so soon, but in the end, she couldn't keep her hunger from exploding in a rain of radiant light.

He was moving faster, pinning her to the bed now, his mouth on hers, then in her hair. With a groan of ecstasy, he pulled out of her just as he erupted and spilled over her bare stomach.

The sensations, the regard she had for him that felt not of this earth, left her reeling. A lush cloud surrounded them, and as she sought her breath, she wondered how could something so wildly carnal feel so right? How could every fiber in her shimmer with exquisite fever?

When his breathing had returned to normal, he rolled onto his side and picked up her hand, holding it tightly. He was stretched out, his body long and lean, the muscles in him curving into soft spaces at his knees and just below his belly.

"Ah, *Catriona*," he muttered raggedly.

Hamlin.

She rolled into his side, rested her head on his shoulder. Her hair seemed to swirl around them. One of her stockings had been pushed down to her ankle. His breeches were still draped around one leg, and his stockings as mismatched as hers. Catriona giggled.

He stroked her hair. "What do you find amusing, then?"

She lifted her head and kissed his bare chest. "All of it." She sat up and pulled the rest of the pins from her hair, letting the tresses fall down her back. Hamlin grabbed a fistful of hair and pulled her back down to him, and wrapped his arms around her as he kissed her. "Where have you been?" he whispered into her ear.

She'd been waiting.

She'd been waiting for exactly this.

CHAPTER FIFTEEN

They played a silly game as they lay deep under the covers of Hamlin's bed, one that Catriona had devised. One of them would name a subject, the other would respond, then name the next subject. Favorite pastime. Favorite dessert. Favorite book. Favorite place. Favorite dog.

Hamlin had never been as content as this. Certainly not in the eight years he'd been married to Glenna, to whom his marriage had been arranged. Even though he'd shared her bed, they had slept apart from the beginning, at her insistence.

He had never known the esteem between two people could be as romantic as this. He had never expected to be so besotted. And now that it had happened to him, there was a niggling in the back of his mind that he didn't know what to do with it. All he knew was that he never wanted to leave this bed. He wanted to remain here with Catriona,

266

giggling like children and exploring one another, for the rest of his days.

But as the night wore on, he became increasingly aware of the morning approaching. Of the reality of his life dawning with the sun. First, it was imperative that he move her to the guest room before anyone saw them or suspected what had happened with her. In the last year he'd lost many of his staff. He had retained the most loyal to him, but there were new members, and he didn't trust them as yet. He didn't trust more rumors to circulate, more untoward things to be said about him.

The second candle had burned down to a nub when he put his arm around Catriona's middle and pulled her back to his chest, his hand sliding down between her legs. He kissed the back of her neck. "I must escort you to our guest quarters now, aye?"

"I donna want to go," she said, and rolled over so that she was facing him.

"I donna want you to go. But I'll no' give any fodder to gossip. It could be disastrous for us both were we discovered."

She smiled, touched her finger to his lips. "You're *protecting* me," she said, sounding delighted.

"Aye." Of course he was. But it was hard — he couldn't look at her beautiful face, or feel her golden hair brush against his skin and not want to touch her, to make love to her. He moaned with the agony of having to leave her and rolled her onto her back, moving on top of her. He was impossibly aroused again. He was a beast let out of its cage, his appetite ferocious, and he began to kiss a trail down her body. When he at last entered her, he took his time with long, patient strokes, prolonging the experience for as long as they could bear it. But the power of their desire quickly consumed them. Catriona clawed at his sheets; riding along with him in the current they had created. Desire and longing spiraled tighter and tighter to a mind-numbing release that crashed over them in one tremendously violent wave.

Hamlin was spent. Utterly spent. He cupped her face, kissed her tenderly. "You have my heart, Catriona," he murmured. "But now you must go, aye?"

He threw back the sheets and climbed out of bed. He went to his wardrobe, pulled a sleep shirt over his head and handed her her chemise. He picked up her clothing, wrapped her in a blanket and kissed her forehead. "I'll send Miss Burns to your room later to help you dress."

With her clothes in one arm, the other

around her shoulders, he snuck her down the hallway to the guest room — one he'd chosen specifically because it was closest to the master suite. He showered her with kisses, then opened the door. Catriona slipped inside.

"Comb your hair," he teased her, raking his fingers through her tresses.

With a giggle, she kissed the tip of his nose and closed the door.

Hamlin returned to his room and fell, exhausted, onto the bed.

It seemed he'd only just closed his eyes when a footman appeared to wake him. It was Old Gregory, an elderly gentleman who had been in Hamlin's employ for years. He walked with a distinct shuffle now but was as loyal as any servant Hamlin had ever employed.

Hamlin dressed. As he went out, he paused and said, "The linens are to be washed, Gregory. I must have nicked myself with the barber's knife and spilled a bit of blood."

"Aye, your grace," Gregory said, and shuffled toward the bed.

From his room, Hamlin went to Eula's. Miss Burns had been replaced by Mrs. Weaver. Eula was sleeping, the sound of her breath rattled and stuffy. "How is she?" he asked, pressing a palm against her cheek.

"Better, I think. She took a bit of broth earlier."

The kittens were wandering around her bed, mewling for milk. He sighed and said, "Mind the kittens as well, Mrs. Weaver. Eula will have both our heads if you donna."

"Aye, your grace."

Hamlin carried on, down the stairs and into the breakfast room. It had stopped raining, thank the saints, but the day was wet and cold, and the drive muddy.

He was joined after a quarter of an hour by Catriona. She was beaming when she walked into the dining room. She had brushed her hair and had tied it loosely at her nape. *"Mdainn mhath!"* she said gaily. "I hope you'll no' mind, your grace, but I looked in on Miss Guinne. I think her fever is down."

"Aye, I think it is. Please, sit," he said, gesturing to the table.

She sat down and helped herself to some bread. "You must forgive me, for I'm utterly ravenous this bonny morning." She paused, glanced slyly at Stuart and added, "I'm so happy the rain has come to an end."

"Pardon, your grace."

Hamlin had not seen Old Gregory enter the breakfast room, as his gaze was quite firmly attached to Catriona. Old Gregory was holding a silver tray, and on it, one of Catriona's shoes, covered in gold silk to match her gown.

"I've discovered a single shoe belonging to a lady."

Hamlin froze. He dared not look at Stuart or the footman.

"Oh, aye, 'tis mine," Catriona said with airy carelessness. "I've a terrible habit of removing my shoes and I did so last night, at the gaming table. I thought I'd picked both of them up."

"But the shoe —"

"Thank you, Gregory. You may leave it there," Hamlin said, gesturing vaguely near the door. "Miss Mackenzie will retrieve it after breakfast."

Catriona glanced around the room at a confused Old Gregory, an unsmiling Stuart and another footman who dared not look at any of them. "You will all forgive my Highland manners, will you no'? I've come to breakfast quite barefoot."

"Think nothing of it," Hamlin said quickly. "Stuart, eggs and ham for our guest, then."

Stuart nodded and returned to the sideboard. Hamlin exchanged a look with Catriona — like him, she was near to bursting out with laughter.

They managed to maintain an air of casual discourse as they breakfasted until Bain arrived. That sobered them both. Hamlin introduced his secretary to Catriona, and Bain took his seat cautiously, as if he was aware he was interrupting something private. He had business to discuss, he said. Letters that had come. And even though Hamlin managed to keep the conversation to general topics, he felt conspicuous. He thought it fairly obvious he did not wish for Bain's presence. He thought it fairly obvious he wanted Catriona and Blackthorn Hall to himself. But alas, the people paid to ensure the dukedom of Montrose performed as it ought would not shirk their duties.

They were finishing breakfast when they heard the unmistakable sound of a team approaching on the drive. Bain stood and went to the window. "It looks to be a Dungotty carriage," he said.

He sounded, Hamlin thought, relieved by it. Hamlin was panicked by it. He was not ready for these few hours of true happiness to end. How would he return to the solitary life he led, hammering away his days?

"Dungotty!" Catriona repeated, surprised and, Hamlin thought, disappointed.

"I'll see to it," Bain said, and cast a look

at Hamlin as he went out.

Stuart picked up the used dishes on the table, and when he turned his back to the table, Hamlin grasped Catriona's hand and leaned toward her. "There is a ruin at the bend in the river," he whispered. "It's accessible only by foot or horse, four miles into the forest, aye? Meet me there tomorrow at half past two."

He let go of her hand just as Stuart turned back to the table with a plate for Catriona.

Voices could be heard from the foyer, and with a tight smile for Catriona, Hamlin said, "I best see who has come." He stood from his seat and went round to help her out of hers, but at that moment, the dining room door burst open, and in sailed the Earl of Norwood followed by Mr. Bain.

"Good morning, good morning!" the earl called loudly, as if he expected dozens instead of the four people in the room.

"Uncle Knox!" Catriona exclaimed.

"I beg your pardon, your grace, for coming to fetch my niece so late in the morning," he said graciously, even though it was only half past nine. "You'd not believe what poor condition I found the roads."

"You should no' have risked it," Hamlin said coolly. "I would have seen her safely home, aye?"

"Of course, but I could not in good conscience have left that duty to you, sir. You've been too hospitable as it is. How have you fared, darling?" he asked, turning to Catriona.

"Quite well," she said. "The duke has been the perfect host. We played a wee bit of chess to pass the time."

"You didn't beat him too soundly, I should hope. The duke always wins, is that not so, your grace? And the lass?" he asked, glancing around. "How did she enjoy the evening?"

"Unfortunately, she has taken ill," Catriona said.

"Oh, dear," Norwood said, and turned to Hamlin. "Nothing too serious, I hope."

"I think no'."

"Well, then, Catriona, darling, we best go on and leave these fine people to their day and to tend the child, yes? Have you everything?"

"I, uh . . . ." She laughed, a little self-consciously. "I donna have my shoe. *Shoes.*"

"Pardon?"

"I've come barefoot to breakfast. I'll just fetch them, shall I?" she added quickly before her uncle questioned her further. She stood abruptly, dipped a quick curtsy and fled the room, grabbing up the shoe they had managed to miss in the middle of the night.

Norwood stared at the door where she'd gone out for a moment, then turned to Hamlin. "That was quite a storm we experienced last night, was it not? Hail and thunder, enough to make one believe the roof would fly off."

"Aye," Hamlin said.

"You had a fine evening in spite of it, if I understand things, is that not so?" Norwood asked coolly.

Hamlin blinked. Norwood clearly suspected something, and he didn't quite know what to say.

"Miss Mackenzie has a particular gift of making every evening pass quickly, my lord," Bain said. Hamlin had almost forgotten he was here. "I hope I donna speak out of turn when I say the duke and I enjoyed her company immensely."

Hamlin looked at Bain, but his secretary had his gaze fixed on the window.

"Yes, well, she's a special young woman, indeed she is," Norwood said, and cast a quick, appraising look at Hamlin. "I'll no' take another moment of your time, your grace. Again, my sincere apologies for last evening, your grace."

Hamlin could feel the heat of discovery climbing up the back of his neck. "None are necessary."

Norwood nodded curtly and looked toward the door, clearly wanting to take his leave.

They stood in awkward silence until Catriona appeared again, breathless in her haste, both shoes firmly on her feet.

"Thank you, your grace, for a lovely evening," she said. "You were so verra kind to entertain me."

"The pleasure was mine," he said, and bowed.

Norwood held out his arm to her. "Shall we? It might take us a bit to reach Dungotty, what with the roads."

She slipped her hand into the crook of her uncle's elbow and smiled again at Hamlin and said goodbye to Bain.

Hamlin followed them out, of course, quite like a puppy, uncertain what to say, how to convey to her without words how very sorry he was to see her go.

In the foyer, Stuart held out her cloak. As she slipped into the cloak, Hamlin noticed that her petticoat was on backward. But she buttoned the cloak at her throat, covering her gown. "I do hope Miss Guinne makes a full recovery," she said to Hamlin.

"Aye, she will, thanks to your suggestions. You must call on her to see for yourself that she is recovered."

"Yes, we'll certainly call on Miss Guinne," Norwood said. His hand was on the small of Catriona's back, and he was hustling her out the door. They'd made it halfway down the steps when Hamlin saw her hat and called after her. "Miss Mackenzie, you've forgotten your hat."

"Oh!" she said, putting her hand on the top of her head. "That I have." She jogged up the steps to fetch it.

"Tomorrow," he reminded her.

"Aye," she whispered, and with a gleam in her eye, she winked at him, then, with her hat in hand, hurried down to her uncle, who promptly put her in the coach and, without so much as a look backward, sent his driver on.

As the carriage pulled away from Blackthorn Hall, Hamlin could swear he felt something pull away from him. He turned around, saw Stuart and Bain in the foyer, both of them eyeing him shrewdly. But if nothing else, Hamlin knew very well how to hide his true feelings. One did not live with Glenna as long as he had without learning to tamp them down. "What business have we?" he asked Bain.

"Correspondence, your grace."

"Verra well. My study, then."

He walked briskly alongside his secretary, his thoughts as far from Blackthorn Hall as they could possibly be. He felt strangely bereft. Not only because Catriona had gone, but in the cold wake of her absence, he had no idea what he was to do with her. Take her as a mistress? No — his feelings ran too deep for that. As a wife? That would cause trouble for his bid for the House of Lords, if for no other reason than her abbey, and God knew the fact that she was a Highlander would not be viewed with pleasure among most of the Scottish peers. Giant wheels had been slowly turning toward gaining that seat, and Hamlin didn't know how to stop them or even if he should.

What he did know deeply in his shuttered heart was that he'd not felt this way about a woman in all his life.

He was not willing to lose the feeling. Not for Parliament, not for anything else.

CHAPTER SIXTEEN

Uncle Knox kept looking at Catriona as they drove back to Dungotty. She wisely — at least she thought it was wise — nattered away about her evening at Blackthorn, and thus did not allow him to speak. It was a tactic she'd learned long ago — if one kept talking, and didn't allow for questions, the listening party would soon fade into a whirl of details. She spoke about Eula, and her fever, what she'd advised them to do. She chatted about the kittens, relived the meal in excruciating detail, dish by dish, then reviewed what little chess they'd played by expounding on her theory of how to win at chess. They had all but reached Dungotty by the time she took a breath.

"Where did you sleep?" her uncle asked her, managing to get his question in after all.

If he thought she would confess that she'd slept in the duke's bed, he was mad. "In a guest room. It was done in blue and white silk, verra pretty, it was, and were I to be at Dungotty much longer, I'd ask my dearest uncle if he might entertain the idea of making my room over with blue and white silk."

"I am your only uncle," he pointed out.

"I'd ask kindly all the same," she said, and poked his arm. "Aye, and how did you pass the time at Dungotty? The storm was frightful, was it no'? You must have been on tenterhooks."

"We were fine. We fretted terribly about you, though, darling."

"Me! The duke himself said that Blackthorn Hall had no' floated away in more than a hundred years and would no' in that storm."

"Mmm," her uncle drawled. He turned his gaze to the window, uncharacteristically subdued.

As they pulled into the drive at Dungotty, the front door was flung open, and half the inhabitants spilled out onto the bricked entrance. "Catriona! You're well!" Chasity cried. "What happened? Were you frightened?"

"Frightened?! No," she said, pushing past them and into the entry. "I'm glad I was there, in truth, for Miss Guinne has taken ill, and I spent most of the evening with her." She realized instantly that this was quite different than what she'd told her uncle and winced inwardly. She was a horrible liar.

"What? The young girl is ill?" Chasity exclaimed.

"Aye, she's come down with fever. I think it a cold, for she was better this morning, that she was, but it gave me a bit of a fright when I saw her yesterday evening."

Chasity's eyes had gone wide with alarm, but the countess, in stark contrast, narrowed a discerning gaze on Catriona. "So it was only you and that murderous duke and a feverish girl in that very large house?" she asked as she followed Catriona into the salon.

"*No,*" Catriona scoffed. "There were scads of servants, aye? And his secretary. And the man from Dungotty."

"I told the earl he ought to have insisted that his man bring you home, and straightaway," Mrs. Templeton said. "Those servants will talk, you may mark my words, and they will not speak kindly of you, Miss Mackenzie. Many assumptions will be made."

This irked Catriona, but she made herself laugh all the same. "I'll no' care if they are," she said gaily, then pinned bloody Mrs.

Templeton with a dark look. "You seem surprised, madam. Do you think no one speaks unkindly of me now? Or that no one has made untoward speculation as to why I've never received an offer of marriage?" She shrugged. "What is one more tale?"

Mrs. Templeton was clearly aghast. She gaped at Uncle Knox, then at Catriona. "You are a *Philistine,* Miss Mackenzie!" she exclaimed.

"Mrs. Templeton!" her uncle said sternly. "How dare you speak to my niece so harshly!"

The woman looked about her with wild disbelief, then turned and flounced from the room.

Lady Orlov chuckled with amusement. "She ought to have returned to her blessed England with Lord Furness."

"She ought never to have come," said Vasily. He was dressed to go out, his boots highly polished and his coat freshly pressed. "I am happy to see you safely returned to us, Miss Mackenzie, but if you will excuse me, I still have an appointment at the gaming hell." With a click of his heels, he bowed, then strode out the door.

Mr. and Mrs. Wilke-Smythe, having seen for themselves that Catriona was alive and well, likewise wandered out of the salon.

"I have business to attend," her uncle said, and leaned over to kiss the top of her head. But he lingered a moment. "I am very glad you are safe at home, where you belong, darling," he said, and then followed the others out.

When everyone was gone but Chasity and Lady Orlov, Chasity pounced on Catriona. "I must know *everything* that happened," she said. "Did you learn anything about his wife?"

"No," Catriona said. "But he offered that she was gone."

"Gone?"

"Quite gone, from the look of things."

"He said that? He said *gone*?" Chasity pressed. "Did you ask him what he meant?"

Catriona collapsed onto the settee and shook her head. She longed for a hot bath, and a change of clothes, and to sleep, ah, yes, to sleep and dream of what had happened to her in the last twenty-four hours. She was in the midst of a grand adventure and these women were interfering with it.

"But what does that *mean*?" Chasity asked of both of them.

"I should think it means *gone*," Lady Orlov said. "Why must we persist in this charade? If we were in Russia, and the man was accused of killing his wife, he'd have hanged by now."

"What! You think he should *hang*?" Chasity cried. "But he's a duke!"

"My *point,* dear girl, is that he has obviously *not* killed his wife, because he is walking among us, and I see no point in belaboring it, time and again."

"I agree," Catriona said.

"But he's a *duke,*" Chasity said again. "My father says that dukes may behave as they please with no consequence."

Lady Orlov muttered something in Russian.

"I think I will rest now, aye?" Catriona said, and stood. She smiled at them in what she fervently hoped they would understand was her way of asking them to leave her be, but, unfortunately, both women rose and followed along behind her, arguing about what sort of privilege a duke in Scotland might truly possess.

Catriona didn't listen to them. She was preoccupied in admiring the vision of Hamlin she carried in her mind's eye. That was all she wanted, to think of Hamlin.

The next day was sunny and warm, and the only sign of the heavy rains was the rushing river. Catriona quietly bid her time, lingering over breakfast with Vasily, playing Whist with the Wilke-Smythes. But shortly after luncheon, she dressed for riding. Her boots clomped along the floor as she made her way to the front of the house — loud enough, apparently, to alert her uncle that she was leaving. He stepped out of his study before she could pass it. "Riding, are you?"

"Aye," she said. "I've been cooped inside for too long, I have. I mean to take some air."

"I see. And where, exactly, do you mean to ride?"

What had come over him? He had never cared a whit about where she went or what she did.

"Ah . . ." She glanced at the door. "No particular place."

His gaze flicked over her, and she wondered if he noticed she was wearing a new riding habit. "A letter has come to you from your sister, Vivienne," he said.

"Vivienne?" A letter from her sister filled her with joy.

Her uncle gestured for her to come into his study and handed her the missive.

Catriona eagerly broke the seal and read her sister's familiar scrawl. She reported on the activity at Balhaire. Her oldest children, Maira and Bruce, were to France, to visit an old friend of Vivienne's husband, Monsieur Leclair. Catriona's father had suffered a bout of croup but was recovered. One of the dogs had died quite suddenly, and it looked as if he'd gone in his sleep near the hearth.

Vivienne also wrote that Mr. Stephen Whitson had come round again, and had delivered the royal decree that Kishorn was forfeited, signed by the Lord Advocate, and must be vacated by the end of the year. *Father believes we should waste no time in finding them suitable situations,* Vivienne wrote.

"Oh, no," Catriona whispered, and glanced up at Uncle Knox. "Pappa wants to find the women places to go. He means to let Kishorn be seized. Uncle Knox, what will we do?"

"Are the terms the same?" her uncle asked.

"Aye. We must vacate before the end of the year."

He nodded and looked thoughtfully toward the window for a long moment. "I inquired as to the Lord Advocate's plans after you arrived. What did he say? That he would be in Edinburgh and should like to see Dungotty, was that it?" He sifted through some papers on his desk. "Ah, here it is," he said, and held up a letter.

286

Catriona smiled. "Is there anyone you donna know, uncle?"

"Oh, I'm sure there is, tucked away here and there," he said matter-of-factly. "But I've made it my life's work to know. You didn't know my father, but had you known him, you'd understand why. Now, I propose we call on Mr. Dundas as soon as possible. We may ask him what can be done and arrange a visit to Dungotty at the same time. Two birds, one stone, as they say."

"Thank you, Uncle Knox," she said, and stood from her seat. She walked to him and kissed his cheek.

"Perhaps you ought to ride with someone," her uncle suggested. "Isn't Chasity a passable rider?"

"Chasity has informed me that she doesna care for horses and will only ride if a handsome caller comes round with a saddle for her. And anyway, I prefer to ride alone. No one to tell me to have a care." She smiled.

Her uncle sighed wearily, as if they'd had this conversation before. "I can't persuade you?"

What an odd thing to say. Uncle Knox had always encouraged her independence. "Why would you want to persuade me, then?"

"Catriona." He took her hand in both of

287

his. "May I speak frankly?"

No. She didn't want him to speak frankly, for whatever it was would not be good. "Uh . . ."

He gestured for her to resume her seat. He smiled sadly at her and leaned forward and touched her knee. "My darling, I've always held a special place in my heart for you. You know that, do you not?"

"Of course."

"I have loved your spirit since you were a child. Admired it. Protected it where I could."

She laughed anxiously. "A dearer uncle I could no' have had," she agreed.

"I suspect that you have developed . . . feelings for Montrose —"

"What?" she sputtered, and could feel the heat flooding her face. "No, uncle —"

"And if you have, I'll not condemn you. Esteem comes upon a person when he least expects it and at times when it is not convenient. I know this to be true, for it happened to me, many years ago, before you were born. Your aunt Zelda and I —"

Catriona shot to her feet. *What?*

"It was a brief affair, but a passionate one," he said, and for a moment, he looked a wee bit misty-eyed. "Unfortunately, for many reasons, it was not meant to be."

Catriona was shocked. She knew something had happened between them, but she'd assumed it was a bit of bad business. A deal gone wrong, perhaps. But *lovers*? "Does my mother know?"

"I can't say for certain, but I would imagine that at the very least, she suspects it. Your father knows," he said with a snort. "It was he who put an end to it." He gazed thoughtfully at the window.

"Mi Diah," Catriona whispered, and put her hands to her face.

"Arran understood it would not end well, and that his cousin would be the injured party. I didn't agree with him at the time, but in hindsight, I know that he was quite right. Zelda would never have been happy in England, and I never in Scotland, and the longer we dabbled at our affair, the harder it would've become to disentangle without harm."

"Did you *love* her?" Catriona asked in a near whisper, as this revelation had opened up a door through which she was almost afraid to walk.

"Oh, I loved her, but not in the way you mean. I think we both agreed it was enchantment. Which brings me to you, darling."

"Me?" Catriona cried. Then gasped. "Am

I your *love* child?"

"For heaven's sake, of course not!" he thundered. He caught her hand and squeezed it. "Heed me now, Cat. I fear you are heading down a similar path. The duke . . . he may say things that sound lovely to you, that might even sound like promises."

Her face was all at once on fire, and she tried to take her hand back, but Uncle Knox held tight. How could he know? How could he *possibly* know?

"There are two things I beg you to keep in mind. One, we don't know what happened to the man's wife. No matter what he says, no one knows, and it's not difficult at all for the diabolical to lie."

"Uncle Knox!"

"Two, and I say this with great love, my darling, but even if he loved you beyond compare, he would never be at liberty to make an offer to you."

Catriona's heart seized and lodged in her throat. She was dumbfounded. She'd not even thought of it, but now that her uncle had said it, she felt a swell of indignation. If only she could summon the words she needed to tell him so, but her shock was so great she was speechless.

"It's not to do with you, do you understand? Montrose needs a different sort of woman on his arm in London. There would be too many questions about a Highland lass, and the abbey, well ... it hardly recommends you. Not to mention the rumors of smuggling with your brothers, and my own father's treason. Well, I'll say the list is quite long and leave it at that."

She gaped at him, her mind rushing almost as hard as the blood in her veins.

"Oh, dear, I've hurt you," he said, and stroked her cheek, but Catriona jerked away from him.

"I don't say these things to distress you, love. I say them so that you might put your expectations in line with cold, hard truth. I mean to be as honest with you as your father was me. Painful though it was to hear, it was for the best. Your aunt would have agreed."

She shook her head. She stood up.

"Catriona!"

"Aye, I understand, uncle." She started for the door, walking almost blindly, her mind anywhere but in her head.

With a weary sigh, her uncle rubbed his forehead. "Please, darling, have a care. For your heart and your virtue."

Oh, aye, her bloody virtue. She wanted to scream at him and ask him what use her

291

bloody virtue was to her? What use was her heart, for that matter, if she would keep it all to herself? She walked out the door and carried on, marching, really, toward the stable.

She wasn't angry with her uncle — she actually appreciated his honesty. But she was livid with her fate in this life. It stung her to know that, because of where she was from, and the actions of her family before her, and the help she had tried to give women less fortunate than her, she would be considered unacceptable for a duke. Aye, and what had she expected?

Nothing.

Nothing at all.

Her expectations had been so degraded over the years that she rarely expected anything. And she certainly hadn't been thinking of what she expected when Hamlin had kissed her. She certainly hadn't been concerned with her expectations when she'd made love to him.

Her thoughts were spinning as she waited for a horse to be saddled, and then hurting her head as she set out across the meadow.

She ought to ask herself what she expected now. Did she really have no expectations? She ought to think about what would happen now that she had given herself to him

— and he to her. Had she maybe thought of a future with him, if only for a fleeting moment? Or was she being purposely dull-witted, pretending to want only the experience?

Catriona didn't want to ask herself those questions. She didn't want to think about anything other than how happy she had felt these last two days. She didn't want to notice anything other than the feel of the wind in her hair, and the sun on her skin.

Hamlin had made no promises to her, and she'd asked him for nothing. She'd been swept up in the sensations and the thrill of his adoration, in her own deep feelings for him. She understood Uncle Knox's warning to her, but at this moment in her life, she chose to ignore it.

She would rather have the experience of Hamlin than not.

Her horse was laboring when she finally spotted the ruin at the curve of the river. A remnant of a wall circled around what looked like an old, crumbling keep, and in the middle of what she assumed was a bailey was an enormous yew tree, grown so tall that it covered half the keep. She could see a black horse tethered beneath a copse of trees outside the wall, and sent her horse to a walk up the hill. When she reached what was left of the wall, she slid off her horse, picked her way through the rubble and stepped through what had once been a door or window.

Hamlin was here. He stood with his back to her, at another opening that had surely been a window to the glen below, the hem of his coat flapping in the breeze.

"Hamlin."

He jerked around. Myriad emotions skated over his handsome face — relief, she thought. Happiness. And esteem, true esteem. *For her.* Her heart swung off its mooring and sailed, and Catriona ran, leaping into his arms, her lips landing on his. He kissed her hungrily, as if he'd not seen her in days, then set her down and ran his hand over her head. "Catriona, thank God." He swept his hands down her arms, his gaze following the path. "*Thank God.* You came."

She laughed, threw her arms around his neck and kissed him again.

Of course she'd come. Nothing would have kept her away.

CHAPTER SEVENTEEN

Aubin had looked at Hamlin with wild disbelief when he'd asked him to prepare some food that he might take with him on horseback.

"*Oui,*" he'd said slowly, as if he suspected Hamlin had lost his mind. "For *le petit porcelet* and yourself, then?"

Hamlin had never heard Aubin refer to Eula as the little piglet before — perhaps he'd left the lass too long in the man's company, even if he had spoken the words with affection. "No," he'd said. "For me."

"Ah," Aubin had said, and shifted his gaze to the wooden table where he was chopping carrots, as if to avoid Hamlin's direct stare. "*Oui,* your grace. At once."

Was it so hard to believe that a man might want to stop along a riverbank and have a bite to eat? Apparently it was, because Bain had been waiting for Hamlin in the foyer, his arms folded across his chest, his weight on one hip, looking quite impatient. Hamlin had wondered idly what thing he'd left undone that would have put his secretary in high dudgeon, but he chose to ignore him rather than ask. He'd accepted his hat from Stuart and fit it on his head.

"Might I inquire as to when you'll return, your grace?" Bain had asked, clearly unwilling to be ignored.

"I donna know."

"There is a matter of the meeting with the Duke of Argyll," he'd said snippily.

"What meeting?"

"The one I mentioned to you yesterday after your guest had left, aye? He would like to speak with you about the upcoming vote."

Hamlin had not recalled, but then again, he'd been staring at the window, his mind on Catriona and the extraordinary night they'd shared. He'd been thinking about how deep his attachment to her went, or reliving those moments with her, or summoning up the sound of her laughter from somewhere deep in his heart.

Perhaps his isolation for more than a year had somehow led to an addling of his brain.

"When is the meeting?" he'd asked, refusing to acknowledge whether he recalled or not.

"Friday morning, in Crieff, your grace.

We should discuss our objectives, aye?" he'd said as Hamlin put out his hand for his riding gloves.

Just at that moment, Aubin had appeared, carrying a bundle wrapped in a cheesecloth. "Your food, your grace."

Hamlin had snatched the bundle from him. "Aye, thank you." He was not blind — he'd seen the look that Bain and Aubin had exchanged, and he'd suddenly wanted away from Blackthorn Hall, from all the people who thought he ought to act a certain way because of who he was and the things that had happened to him. Well, Hamlin was weary of putting up a façade around his life. He had fit his hands into his gloves, then turned to face the men gathered behind him. "Inform Miss Guinne I shall join her for supper," he'd said to Stuart. "We'll have something light, Aubin. Her stomach is tender yet."

Aubin had bowed his head in acknowledgment.

He'd made himself look at the young buck that was Bain. "We'll discuss Argyll when I return," he'd said, and swept past the lot of them, out onto the portico, then jogging down the steps to the drive, where one of the grooms had his mount waiting for him.

He'd reached the ruins in no time at all,

riding as if he were being chased by English soldiers, and once there, he'd begun to fret. What if she didn't come? What if her regard for him had changed with the light of the sun and the influence of her uncle, who had clearly suspected what had happened between them? What if she was sent home to the Highlands? Was he to resume his singular life? Pretend nothing had happened? Forget that he'd had the most astounding escapade of his life? Ignore the tumult of his thoughts, the near desperation to experience the intimacy again?

But then he'd heard the scrape of a boot and his name, softly said, and he'd turned, and there she was, her smile as luminous as ever, her eyes full of affection, and he'd sailed away with the fantasy of her. He'd caught her up, kissed her until she laughingly begged him for mercy.

He'd taken a blanket from a saddlebag, had laid it in the middle of the ruin beneath the yew tree and had brought out the food.

Catriona exclaimed with delight. "You've made a picnic!"

"I have tried," he sheepishly admitted. "There's no wine, unfortunately — I was afraid to ask Aubin for it."

She laughed. They sat side by side, munching on cheese, nuts and figs. "How are you?" he asked. "Are you well?"

"I am verra well. And you?"

"As well as I've ever been," he said. He touched her hand. "Have you had any second thoughts, Catriona?"

She looked at him with surprise. "No! Why, have you?"

"None, never," he said quickly, grabbing up her hand. "I've had only inappropriate thoughts," he said, and kissed her temple.

She laughed. "How is Eula?"

"Much improved," he said. "The lass wants out of her bed, she does, but the doctor has cautioned against it. She's read the book you brought her and complains there is nothing to occupy her and wishes very much to talk to you."

"May I call, then?" Catriona asked. "Perhaps with Miss Wilke-Smythe?"

Hamlin thought of the young Englishwoman, and the close attention she paid to him.

"You donna care for Chasity?"

"I would rather you come alone, aye? I want to be with *you,* Catriona."

She smiled ruefully. "We both know that's impossible. If I call on Miss Guinne alone, it will only spark more speculation than there has already been given that I was stranded in your house overnight."

"Aye, of course, you are right." He squeezed her hand affectionately. He would well imagine Nichol Bain's apoplexy if she were to come alone.

"But how will I see you, then?" she asked. "Am I wrong to want it? Do I ask too much?"

"No, no," he said, and with a sigh, he cupped her face. "I'll think of something, I will. Be patient with me, lass. It's no' particularly easy for a man in my position to . . ." He hesitated. What did he intend to say? That it wasn't easy for him to take a lover? Was that what she was to him — a lover? It felt more than that. It felt large and unformed, but important, and he didn't really want to know the truth at present. He wanted only to experience it. He wanted only to be with her, delight in her presence. Make her smile, or laugh. Kiss her. Touch her . . .

"To be seen with a woman like me?" she asked, finishing his thought.

"I didna mean that," he said, shaking his head, but that wasn't entirely true. He could hear Bain's warnings if he was to suddenly and openly keep company with Miss Mackenzie of Balhaire. "I meant that it's no' easy for me to be away from you," he amended, and kissed her.

But Catriona pushed him backward and stared at him seriously. And then she came to her feet and took a few steps away from him.

Hamlin leapt to his feet and followed her. "What have I said?"

"Nothing. You've said *nothing.* But there is no need for you to, is there? I know the truth, Hamlin. I am no' naïve."

"What truth?"

"I do no' regret a moment with you, aye? No' one. But I know I am a disadvantage to your cause, and you are a disadvantage to my reputation. We are . . . We are the *worst* possible people for one another. We are."

What she said so bluntly was unfortunately true. She turned toward him, waiting for his response. Perhaps waiting for him to deny it. Or to offer her more than he could.

"Will you say nothing now?" she demanded.

"What would you have me say?" he asked her plaintively. "Would you have me deny it? Pretend that all is well?"

Her shoulders slumped. "No. But I hoped —"

"Catriona, heed me." He took a step toward her. "This," he said, gesturing between them, "is precarious at the moment. My chance for the seat in the House of Lords is precarious. I must be above reproach, do you see?"

"What of the rumors of your wife?" she challenged him.

"*Especially* given the rumors," he said evenly. His conscience was shouting at him from the bottom of a deep well that he had to end this with Catriona, for all the reasons he just said, but the warning was drowned in his selfishness. He wanted her to remain in this affair they'd started for his own gratification. It was a deplorable reason.

"What is it?" she asked, peering at him closely.

Hamlin glanced up. "This is detrimental to you," he said, biting out the words. "I know it is, and yet I canna bring myself to say the words that, by *any* measure of moral decency, I ought to say."

"What words?"

"That we should end this here and now," he said. "That I have brought you low and that you deserve far better, Catriona. And yet, I canna say those words to you, no' earnestly, for my esteem for you runs wide and deep and appears to be much stronger than my conscience, aye?"

She stared at him as if trying to understand him. She kept him in agony as she silently studied him, and he assumed that she would take his warning, would put an end to their short affair. He would have the memory of the best night of his life, and he would have to console himself with that.

But Catriona didn't say that. She sighed with exasperation, put her hands to her hips. "I'm well acquainted with the necessity of appearances, that I am," she said, and sounded as if she were a returning soldier from the front of the war on appearances. "But have you no' guessed that I donna care what is said of me, Hamlin?"

His heart gave a tiny little leap of joy that quickly disappeared into a swell of guilt. "But you *must* care —"

"Why? I donna care. I told you, I'm three and thirty. There is verra little anyone can say of me now, is there? My family will no' turn me out. Highland society will no' turn their backs. My prospects for marriage were dashed long ago and buried when I took up Zelda's cause. What more can be said of me? *You* are the one who must be concerned."

He tried to make sense of what she said, to find his moral footing in it.

"What are we to do now?" she whispered. "I want to see you, Hamlin, I do. I want to be with you. Is there no way for us, then? I donna care if we must hide."

In that moment, Hamlin didn't care about his seat in the House of Lords, or his isolation from society, or anything but her. He took her face in his hands. "We'll find a way, aye? We'll meet here for a time. The weather is good, the ruins remote — I rarely see anyone ride so far into the hills as this."

"Here?" she said, looking around her.

Hamlin put his arms around her shoulders and pulled her into his embrace. He kissed her neck and her ear as he moved his hand up over her ribs, to her breast. *"Here,"* he said.

"Aye, I am beginning to see the appeal of here," she murmured beneath his lips.

Their concerns about what was happening between them, and where, and how it might continue, was forgotten for the remainder of the afternoon.

They met at the ruins four times that week alone — enough that the residents of Dungotty were beginning to question Catriona's riding, she told him one afternoon. They were lying on a blanket under the boughs of the yew tree that had grown in the middle of the ruins. He had his back propped against the tree and was stroking her hair, which he'd freed to hang loose over her shoulders.

Clouds were sliding in from the west, turning the light around them to gray. Rain was coming, which meant the ruins would be unavailable to them.

"Chasity is quite cross with me," Catriona said as she idly played with the hem of his shirt. "She's no' a thing to occupy her but the countess, and they've quarreled about the silliest things. Vasily is *wild* with curiosity about where I ride, and threatens to follow me."

Hamlin looked at her with alarm.

"Donna worry," she said airily. "The poor man canna catch me on horseback. He is adept at preening on the back of a horse as he saunters along. But no' riding." She laughed at her own jest.

"I donna like that they question you," he said with all seriousness. He didn't like any suspicion swirling around her.

"They're bored. They've nothing to occupy them most days. In fact, Mrs. Templeton is returning to England on the morrow."

"Oh?" Hamlin asked idly, and caressed her bare shoulder.

"She said her daughter had sent word she was needed. But in truth, I think her hope of snaring my uncle as her next husband has been unsuccessful. She is admitting defeat. Nevertheless, we're to all dine

305

together this evening to wish her well."

Hamlin smiled and kissed the top of her head.

"What of you?" she asked, and twisted about in his arms to see his face. "What has Stuart to say of your many absences?"

"Stuart is a consummate professional," he said. "It is my secretary that is displeased. He has all but accused me of ignoring my duties."

Catriona gasped. "He didna!"

Hamlin laughed. "Aye, he's right, Catriona," he said, and brushed away a strand of hair that draped over her eye. "But I'll no' give these afternoons away, no' for him or anyone else. Next to Eula, they are the one bright spot of my existence."

She laughed. "Next to Eula, mine, too."

They spent their hours in the summer sun learning each other, physically, emotionally, spiritually. Hamlin so enjoyed Catriona — she challenged him, she made him laugh. She was truly a bright light, a woman with the gift of lively conversation and ideas. Of course, he loved kissing her, making love to her, even in the crude circumstances of the ruins. But it wasn't the physical aspect that drew him to her. It was simply her.

She was, he believed, the companion of his heart.

She asked about his plans for the House of Lords and listened raptly. She engaged him in discourse about government and theology, music and art, travel and solitude. They played silly little games that made them both laugh like children.

Who would have thought that a man of his stature, with the privileges he'd experienced in his life, with his title and wealth and holdings, would spend the most glorious week of his nearly forty years with a Highland woman in the middle of old ruins?

And yet, he wouldn't have changed a moment of it. Not a single moment.

Hamlin didn't know it, but he would come to understand far too late that he'd allowed himself to exist in the realm of fantasy up on that hill in the middle of that ruin.

CHAPTER EIGHTEEN

A message came from Blackthorn on Saturday that Miss Eula Guinne was much improved and desired to thank Miss Mackenzie for her book in person. If Miss Mackenzie were so inclined, it would be Miss Guinne's pleasure to receive her and her friends Monday afternoon for tea.

"What friends?" Chasity asked eagerly. "Does the letter name them?"

"No," Catriona said. "I suppose you, aye?"

"Yes!" Chasity said with glee.

"And what of me?" Countess Orlov asked. "Am I not also your friend?"

"Aye, you are," Catriona said, although she did not sense any genuine affection from the countess as she did from Chasity.

"Mamma, you must be included, as well," Chasity suggested.

Diah, Catriona did not want the entire Dungotty household to attend. She glanced at Chasity's mother, who was busy at her needlework. "Mrs. Wilke-Smythe, would you care to join us?"

"Well," she said, and put down her sewing, "I suppose I ought to if Chasity desires to go. Her father would not care for her to go alone."

"She'd no' be alone," Catriona pointed out.

"I mean, in the company of a proper chaperone," Mrs. Wilke-Smythe clarified with an air of condescension Catriona did not care for.

"I am a countess!" Lady Orlov said haughtily. "I am a perfectly suitable chaperone! Do you think that only your countrymen are capable of guarding your precious virtues?"

"I hardly think she meant offense, madam," said Uncle Knox from the corner of the room, where he was reading.

"I most certainly did not," Mrs. Wilke-Smythe sniffed.

"And yet, you sound as if you do mean to give offense," Uncle Knox added, and smiled at her over the top of his spectacles.

"Ha!" cried the countess triumphantly.

"If I may, I suggest that as Chasity and Catriona are the youngest, and the most suitable for Miss Guinne's company, that they, and they alone, accept the invitation,"

Uncle Knox said. He threw up his hand before Chasity's mother could object. "I will send one of my men along to ensure that your daughter is properly protected and is not compromised so that you might have to seek satisfaction from the duke by way of marriage." He raised his book again. "I happen to quite like the man, if you must know. I saw him in Crieff two days past, and he inquired after us all and said he should like to have us all to dine."

Catriona bit back a smile. Hamlin had told her about encountering Uncle Knox in the village and their conversation. What Uncle Knox hadn't said was that he was the one to have suggested the supper. "I scarcely knew what to say," Hamlin had said laughingly. "He extended an invitation to dine at Dungotty, but before I could utter a word, he'd gone completely round the bend and said that while it would be his great honor to have me in his home once more, there were so many restless guests at Dungotty that perhaps they might all be more comfortable at Blackthorn Hall's superior accommodations, and he'd wait to hear from me as to a suitable date."

Catriona had laughed with delight. "I think my uncle has grown weary of his houseguests," she'd said.

"Shall I pen the response?" she asked her uncle now.

"Thank you, darling, but I will respond for us all," he said, and pinned her with a look.

Uncle Knox had not said more to her about Hamlin since that afternoon in his study. But he watched her like a hawk, always knew when she rode out. She was also aware that another letter had come from her mother, and had seen one addressed to her in the tray that held the mail for Rumpel to take to the post. She could well imagine the content of those letters and cringed at the thought of returning to Balhaire.

Funny, since she'd begun her illicit affair, she didn't like to think of Balhaire. She'd scarcely thought of the abbey at all, as her thoughts were taken up with more tenderhearted matters. But that didn't mean she harbored any illusions. Catriona would return home, probably sooner rather than later. She worried about the abbey, worried that her charges had all they needed. Vivienne had written her again, telling her that Rhona MacFarlane had reported a trio of men had come to the abbey to have a look around. Catriona didn't know who they were or why they'd come, but it pointed up to her that she was needed at home. She was needed to carry on Zelda's work.

When she thought of Balhaire, and the abbey, and all that she must, tentacles of guilt caught hold. Her heart was rent in two — half of it lodged here, with a man who made her burst with happiness, who had given her the splendorous gift of intimacy. She felt things for him that she had never experienced. Was it enchantment, the sort Uncle Knox had described to her? Or was it love?

What if it *was* love? Was it the same love she had for Balhaire, for the work she and Zelda had done? If this was love, a new sort of love, did it outweigh everything else she loved?

And what about the other half of her heart, the half that was presently neglected but still very much part of her? The half that was rooted in the Highlands and with the people she loved best? Sometimes, at night, Catriona lay sleepless in her bed, her mind creeping into her restlessness and telling her it was time to go home, her heart refusing to listen. But when the sun came up, all she could think of was seeing Hamlin again, of feeling his arms around her, his lips against her skin. He was the pull of the moon on the sea of her longing, and it was impossible to resist.

She was torn between the woman she'd been until now, and the woman she was suddenly becoming. She couldn't say which was truer to her heart.

She couldn't say. For the first time in years, she could not, with confidence, say who she was.

On Monday afternoon, Chasity and Catriona arrived at Blackthorn Hall for tea and were greeted at the door by Stuart. He showed them to a sunlit room just off the gardens. The French doors had been opened to the spectacular greenery and roses blooming there, the fountain a soothing noise. Eula, with a bit of pink in her cheeks, looked the picture of health. She had a wee cough now and again but seemed returned to near perfect physical constitution. She curtsied. "Thank you for coming," she said, as if she'd rehearsed it.

"Aye, but thank *you* for the invitation," Catriona said. "May I introduce my friend Miss Chasity Wilke-Smythe."

Eula was already looking at Chasity with awe, and little wonder — Chasity was quite fair, which made her look a wee bit like an angel. "Good afternoon, Miss Guinne."

"Will you no' come in?" Eula asked, and

swept her arm wide, to indicate the small room. Oh, aye, she'd been rehearsing her debut as hostess.

She was also eager to demonstrate her tea-serving skills and was just about to begin the business of pouring when Hamlin entered the room. Catriona and Chasity stood at once and curtsied. "Your grace," Chasity said solemnly.

Catriona smiled. "Your grace," she said, a bit impishly.

"Good afternoon, ladies. How pleased we are to have you for tea."

"I'm to pour now," Eula said, her voice full of warning, as if the duke should stand back.

"By all means," he said, gesturing for her to continue.

She carefully filled four cups of tea, then picked up a china plate where squares of cake had been laid out. "May I offer you cake? Aubin has made it. He's our cook, and my riding instructor, and he's from France."

"Oh," Chasity said, and winked at Catriona. "He's *French*." She helped herself to a piece of the cake, as did Catriona. Hamlin waved it off.

"I like your hair," Eula said to Chasity before picking up her own teacup.

Chasity touched her hair. "Thank you. I like yours, too. What a lovely color."

"Aye, it's very pretty," Eula agreed. "Miss Burns arranged it. She's my *lady's* maid. Miss Mackenzie found her for me."

"Yes, I heard of it," Chasity said, and gave Catriona another look.

"We canna thank you enough for bringing Miss Burns to our attention," Hamlin said. "She has been helpful to us both, has she no', Eula?"

"Oh, she has. She knows all about hair, and what gowns to wear, and she knows how to sew. She's from Glasgow," Eula said.

"Is she?" Chasity responded.

A kitten suddenly shot out from beneath the settee, attacked Chasity's shoe and then darted out of the room, just narrowly missing Stuart as he entered.

"That was my kitten Perry," Eula explained. "I have another one, and his name is Walter. But he doesna like to come out."

Stuart bent over Hamlin's shoulder and whispered in his ear. An expression of confusion moved across Hamlin's face but quickly turned inscrutable. He leaned forward to put his teacup aside. "I beg your pardon, Eula. Ladies, if you will excuse me." He quit the room, Stuart on his heels.

Catriona watched him go, curious as to

what was happening.

"Where is Walter?" Chasity asked Eula.

"Maybe he's in the garden. He likes the sun." She looked toward the open doors.

"I had a cat," Chasity offered, and began to relate to Eula a tale of Mr. Whiskers. Catriona could not have been less interested in the trials and tribulations of a long-dead cat, and stood up, wandering to the open doors to look out.

Chasity eventually ended her rambling about the cat, and Eula said, "Aubin said the tea has come all the way from India. He showed me where India is on a map, and it's *verra* far from Scotland."

"It's quite good," Chasity said.

"Would you like to see my painting?" Eula asked. "It's in the garden."

"Yes, please."

Eula appeared at the open door where Catriona was standing and slipped her hand into Catriona's to pull her along.

The courtyard was a small square in the midst of the many mazes of corridors of Blackthorn Hall, surrounded by four walls rising three stories high. Most of the windows had been opened to a very fine summer day. In the middle of the garden was an easel, a stool and a canvas.

"I painted it," Eula said, pointing to the

rose. "Mr. Kenworth taught me. He said it's verra good."

Mr. Kenworth was right — it was actually quite good. It was clearly the work of a child, but Eula's talent for art was apparent.

"All you have to do is look at the lines," Eula was saying, but in the course of her lengthy explanation of how great art was made, a raised voice floated out one of the open windows and seemed to hang over them. A man was talking very loudly, and while it was impossible to know what he was saying, the tone was clearly angry.

Catriona and Chasity looked at each other. Catriona wondered if Chasity had recognized that the voice belonged to Hamlin.

"Mr. Kenworth says that one day, my painting will hang in the salon, and I know where, too, for Montrose took my cousin's portrait down and now there's an empty spot."

"Whose portrait?" Chasity asked.

"My cousin, Glenna. She was his wife," Eula explained.

The voice rose again. It sounded like a curse word.

"Perhaps we ought to go inside, aye?" Catriona asked.

"Who is that?" Chasity asked. "Who is shouting?"

"Montrose," Eula said. "Sometimes he is cross."

Cross? Catriona had never seen any hint of it.

Chasity put her hand on Catriona's arm and squeezed, then asked, "Does he shout a lot, Miss Guinne?"

Eula frowned, as if she were thinking about it, then shook her head. "He *never* shouts, no' really. He's verra quiet."

Chasity's hand dropped. "Oh."

"But he shouted at my cousin once," Eula continued as they stepped into the garden room.

Catriona's pulse began to pound. She didn't want to hear this. She didn't want to hear a single untoward word said of him. She *especially* didn't want Chasity to hear it. "Shall we pour more tea?" she asked. "I should like more of that *delicious* cake —"

"I beg your pardon, Miss Guinne, but did you say the duke shouted at your cousin, Lady Montrose?"

"Aye," Eula said, as if there were nothing unusual about it.

"What on earth did he shout about?"

"I donna know," the lass said with a shrug. "She was shouting, too. I heard them all the way down the hall, I did."

"How about that cake?" Catriona tried, but Chasity shot her a look.

"I donna think there is more cake," Eula said, looking around for the plate. "Miss Wilke-Smythe ate it all."

"I didna eat it *all*," Chasity said. "Miss Guinne, did you ever ask your cousin about the shouting?" Chasity asked.

"Chasity," Catriona said low. At what point had she become an inquisitor?

"No," Eula said, and sat in a chair. "She was gone the next day. She's never come back."

"She's never come back!" Chasity said. "Why do you —"

"Chasity!" Catriona said loudly. "How do you find the tea?"

"The what?" Chasity asked, startled out of her line of inquiry.

Eula suddenly gasped. "Look! There's Walter!" She leapt from her seat and rushed after the elusive kitten.

Chasity took the opportunity to grab Catriona's arm again. "Did you hear what the girl said?"

"Aye, I heard it," Catriona said, yanking her arm free. "Leave her be, Chasity. She's a lass."

"But has anyone thought to question her

as to the whereabouts of her cousin?"

Catriona didn't answer, as Eula was suddenly before them again, holding an identical black kitten to the one that had attacked Chasity's shoe earlier. "This is Walter. He comes out at night, but hardly at all during the day."

"Why, he's beautiful!" Chasity said, and took the cat from Eula's arms and placed him in her lap. She began to stroke its fur. "Miss Guinne, forgive me, but I have forgotten — where did your cousin go?"

"Hmm?" Eula asked, and looked up from her fascination with the purring kitten. "I donna know. Montrose says she's gone, and she'll no' come back again."

Chasity gasped and turned a wide-eyed look to Catriona. Fortunately, Eula didn't seem to notice — she leaned over Chasity to pick up the kitten. But Walter was of a different mind and scratched the lass, and she dropped Walter in turn. The kitten darted into the hall and disappeared.

"Have you any other paintings you'd like to show us?" Catriona asked brightly before Chasity could begin her line of questioning again.

"Aye. I finished a painting, and Montrose allowed me to hang it in the dining room. Do you want to see it?"

"Aye, of course we do," Catriona said, and stood, took Eula by the hand and started for the door, ending any chance Chasity had of probing deeper.

They were moving down the hallway when a bell was rung in some distant room. A moment later, Stuart hurried past them.

"The dining room is here," Eula said. She went in first. "I'll find a candle!" she called to them.

As they stood waiting, they had clear sight of the foyer. A man appeared in the foyer; his coat was rumpled and his hat looking as if he'd dropped it in the road at some point. He carried a satchel that he slung over his shoulder. As Stuart handed him his gloves, Hamlin strode into view. He stood with his legs braced apart, his arms folded, and watched the man depart.

"Here it is!" Eula said, and light suddenly flared from the dining room.

"Oh, dear," Chasity murmured, and slipped into the dining room. But Catriona hesitated. Only for a moment, but long enough for Hamlin to turn his head and see her there. His jaw was clenched, his brows knitted in a thunderous frown. *The dark duke.* He gave her no acknowledgment but turned on his heel and disappeared to wherever he'd come from.

Catriona stepped into the dining room and pasted a smile on her face as Eula showed them her best work of art to date — a painting of a teacup and saucer.

"I like the colors," Chasity said.

"Would you like to watch me dance?" Eula asked, and held her arms aloft, as if she meant to dance around the dining table. "I've a new dance instructor. He's danced before the *king,*" she said, and began to move to music only she could hear.

Catriona and Chasity watched her twirl around the dining table, but Catriona scarcely saw a thing, as her mind's eye was filled with Hamlin. Why had he looked so dark?

When at last Stuart came and informed Eula it was time to dress for supper, Catriona and Chasity said their goodbyes and departed in the Dungotty coach. There was no sign of Hamlin.

"Well?" Chasity asked once they were alone. "What do you make of it?"

"Of what?"

"For heaven's sake, Catriona, you know very well what," Chasity said. "I think he did it. I think that girl holds the key to the mystery."

Chasity firmly believed it, for she announced it the moment they arrived at

Dungotty. They'd arrived just in time for supper, over which she eagerly relayed the entire visit, complete with the shouting, and Eula's admission that the duke and duchess had quarreled the night before she disappeared.

"What do you think?" she asked them all when she'd finished her tale.

"I think he's done something to her," Lady Orlov said flatly. "The innkeeper said they'd argued there, too, if you recall."

"Why must we always accuse the gentleman?" Vasily said. "Perhaps *she* has done something to *him*."

"What could she have possibly done to him?" Mr. Wilke-Smythe said with a snort. "He's still living in a house as big as a castle. He's still a duke. Women have no power or authority in this world, sir. Had she done something to him, she would be hanging from a tree in the village square."

No one disagreed. Catriona wanted to disagree, but to defend him now would only draw speculation about her.

"I know the girl is speaking the truth," Lady Orlov said ominously. "As it happens, I have exchanged a few words with a woman who once served the duke."

"I should like to know how you would have occasion to speak to a servant of

323

Blackthorn Hall," Mrs. Wilke-Smythe said accusingly.

"In Crieff, if you must know," she said. "Vasily and I met a serving wench who had served the duke's chambers." She looked to Vasily to vouch that this was true, and he nodded.

"She said the fighting could be heard in every hall that night, and afterward, they never saw the lady again. He simply called them together and said Lady Montrose had departed Blackthorn Hall, had her things gathered and sent to Lord knows where. No one knows why she disappeared. Or *how*." She gave Catriona a catlike smile and asked, "Do you *still* believe him innocent, Miss Mackenzie?"

Catriona bristled. "Aye, I do. He's been verra kind to me."

"Well, well," Vasily said, leaning back in his chair, his whisky at his fingertips. "Will you all look at Miss Mackenzie! I think she is smitten with the duke."

"I'm no'!" Catriona protested, and knew the moment she protested, that she had given herself away. She was always the one to laugh off the largest of insults or innuendo, and when she didn't, everyone noticed. "I simply find it verra hard to believe that he caused his wife even a wee

324

bit of harm."

"There, you see?" Vasily said to the rest of them. "She defends him."

"I donna defend him. I offer my opinion," she tried, but it was too late.

"You do!" Chasity said, her eyes wide. "You *esteem* him!"

Catriona panicked. She looked to Uncle Knox, but he was staring into his cup. "I donna esteem him," she said, as if that was ridiculous. "How could I? I scarcely know him at all, do I?"

No one looked convinced.

Catriona felt a tic of panic in her breast. "Verra well, you've guessed my secret. I'm *enchanted.*"

Everyone gasped. Even Uncle Knox glanced up.

Catriona forced a laugh but found her footing. "Do you find fault in it, then?" she asked gaily. "He's a handsome man, is he no'? I am enchanted by the mere idea of him. But I do *no'* esteem him. I scarcely know him at all."

"I am very happy you don't esteem him, my darling, and it's only a case of enchantment, for I have received word that the Lord Advocate will see us. We are to Edinburgh next week."

Catriona's supper suddenly turned sour

in her belly. "We will? That's wonderful, Uncle Knox!" she said, feigning excitement. But all she could think was that the news signaled the end of her time at Dungotty.

"Yes, I think it will do you good to see something other than Dungotty and the woods for a change. Perhaps it will rid your mind of this enchantment."

"Ah, that," Catriona said, and picked up a glass of wine. "Consider it rid. I've no' been to Edinburgh in a verra long time, and I can think of nothing more diverting."

As talk fell to Edinburgh, Catriona pretended to be held riveted by the conversation, speaking often, asking her uncle so many questions that even her head spun with them.

But all she could really think was that she needed to see Hamlin again. She wanted to know what had happened, but no matter what else, she needed to see him, to touch him, to see his black eyes shining at her. The thought of not having her wish made the sourness in her belly even worse.

It was true, then — her enchantment had turned to lovesickness.

CHAPTER NINETEEN

Hamlin was on the roof of the gardener's shed hammering shingles. "There is no need," his carpenter said nervously. "We've repaired it, your grace."

"I'll have a look all the same, Mr. Watson, aye?" Hamlin drove another nail into a shingle that was already secure. If he wasn't careful, he'd drive so many nails that he'd split the shingle in two. When it became apparent to him, even in his disquieted state of mind, that he was doing more harm than good, Hamlin surrendered. He climbed down the ladder, looked around at his men and said, "What else needs repair, then?"

After some frantic discussion, Mr. Watson mentioned that a window frame in the orangery needed replacing.

"Aye, let's replace it, then."

Hamlin's restlessness had to do with an unfortunate turn of events, culminating with the humiliating need to ask Bain to see that a message was delivered to Catriona.

Bain had looked at him as if he had never seen him before that moment, had no idea who he was.

"What is it, then?" Hamlin had snapped. "Is there some reason you are no' able to do as I ask?"

"No, your grace," he'd said, and had taken the hastily penned, carefully folded note. But his gaze had flicked over Hamlin when he did.

"What?" Hamlin had coldly demanded.

"We've a meeting concerning the banking issue with Lords Perth, Caithness and Mr. MacLaren, aye?"

"What of it?" Hamlin had asked, although he knew the answer. Bain was concerned about appearances.

"Given the recent events, I would suggest we prepare for any topic that might arise, aye?"

"Do we no' always discuss any topic that might arise?" Hamlin had shot back.

Bain had looked as if he wanted to say more, and Hamlin could guess that the man wanted to beg him to cease this dangerous affair. But this time, his secretary wisely kept his opinion to himself. "I will see that the message is delivered, your grace," he'd said curtly, and had gone out.

Hamlin knew he was being unreasonable, but he didn't care. It had been two days since his solicitor had come, two days since he'd been forcibly dragged back in his mind to think of Glenna, to recall the worst time of his life at the best time of his life.

Of course Glenna was not dead, as everyone surmised — she was very much alive and living not so far from him at all, a fact he was rudely forced to recall with the visit from Mr. Dundy. It was humiliating enough that she'd left Blackthorn Hall with her lover. It was mortifying enough that he'd dissolved his so-called marital union at her behest. And now she had risen like a ghost to mortify him again.

Their marriage had been doomed from the start, although he'd been too blind to see it. His marriage had been arranged, as he knew it would be from the time he was old enough to understand such things. A ducal empire was improved through advantageous marriages. After a handful of suppers and walkabouts with Glenna, who seemed perfectly content in his company, the marriage deal had been struck. His father, God rest him, had been fond of her. "Aye, she's a jewel, that one, a grand addition to the Graham name, aye?"

Hamlin had liked Glenna well enough,

and he'd supposed he would like her more once they were married, just as his father had suggested. But Glenna had begun to complain the moment their vows were said.

He was thankful his father did not live long enough to see his son cuckolded. Certainly there was no heir, and he had added a lump of coal to the Graham name, not a jewel. For eight years, he'd endured his marriage in name only. He'd tried his best to appease his wife, but she would not be appeased. He'd tried to ignore her, and she would not be ignored. On the outside, she presented a happy home. She was vibrant and lively, an excellent hostess, quick to laugh, and performed the sort of charitable works in the shire that were expected of a duchess. But behind closed doors, she was desperately unhappy with what she viewed as their many incompatibilities. Hamlin, she said, did not understand her. He did not see her spirit. He was a person who inhabited her bed from time to time, but for whom she could not muster any true affection.

Hamlin had never known what was at the root of their incompatibility — it was his opinion she never knew him well enough to have come to the conclusion. But in spite of her feelings for him, he had cared about her in some respects. And he'd trusted her to a certain extent.

He never suspected infidelity.

He supposed that was the thing that angered him most — he'd gone about his business like a fool, trying to pretend all was well, alternately appeasing her or removing himself from her presence, but all the while believing she would honor her vows. He'd even been foolish enough to believe that she would eventually come to accept it and they would have a happy marital life. That was his desire. Maybe when they had a child she would warm to him. Maybe she'd been so young when they'd married that she only needed time to mature. And he'd trusted her.

And now, because of her, he found it difficult to trust anyone else.

Her perfidy had gone on for some time, by her own admission. The man who had captured her heart was not someone known to Hamlin. He was a tradesman, perhaps a merchant — a nebulous figure in Hamlin's mind — but he was apparently a man who, Glenna had asserted, would one day be as wealthy as Hamlin. He was a man for whom she'd declared she felt "such intense emotions that she could *never* in *all her life* feel for Hamlin."

He could not stop her from leaving in the manner she had. No threats, no recriminations could dissuade her from the love story she was convinced she was living. Oh, aye, it was an all-consuming love, she'd shouted at him. She and this faceless man were very much in love and were not forced into a union as she'd been previously. They would be *happy,* which she had *never been* with Hamlin.

"I never wanted to marry you," she'd shrieked at him.

"Then by God, why did you agree to it?" he'd bellowed at her.

"What choice did I have?" she'd screamed.

A million choices it had seemed to him. Any choice other than to marry him if she'd found him so utterly irreconcilable to her soul.

"What of Eula?" he'd asked her. "You are all the lass has in the world."

"I canna take the child," Glenna had said immediately and without the slightest compunction. That had prompted another round of loud argument, but the end was inevitable — Glenna had left him, running into the arms of her lover, and at her behest, her plea, he had ended the marriage as she desired.

The Duke of Perth, his late father's closest friend, had been the one to help Hamlin obtain a divorce. It was quick and relatively painless, on the grounds of marital desertion. Glenna and the faceless lover had taken a small house in Edinburgh, where, presumably, he employed his trade.

It was likewise Lord Perth who'd recommended Hamlin keep the unpleasant matter to himself. At the time, there'd been quite a lot of talk already circulating about where on earth the bonny Lady Montrose had gone. But Perth reminded Hamlin that if he desired a position in the House of Lords, it was best that the men voting him into that seat did not know he'd been cuckolded and had then granted a divorce to the woman who had humiliated him. "Naturally, you had to do it," he'd said kindly. "But a titled man will sooner understand sending a bothersome wife away before he will understand how a powerful man such as yourself might have been hoodwinked by a woman. It weakens your position."

Hamlin had been taken aback by Perth's assessment that, essentially, to dispose of one's wife was acceptable, but if the wife was the one to do the disposing, a man was considered weak.

The idea had suited him, because Hamlin

had not been eager to announce his divorce. He was mortified by it, utterly abashed that he'd failed so miserably at the business of matrimony, and, in all honesty, he didn't fully understand why. He still did not understand what reprehensible thing he'd done to deserve Glenna's scorn, other than breathing. So he'd taken Perth's advice, and when someone inquired after Lady Montrose, he answered vaguely. He said she'd gone, and left it at that. His position as duke afforded him the ability to handle things this way. No one but Eula dared to question him.

So Hamlin had said nothing. Nothing at all.

He should have known the rumors would take on a life of their own. He could not have predicted they would turn so dark, but in retrospect, he blamed himself. He'd been dejected, distrustful of all and brooding, which had fed the rumors. But he'd not been able to help himself.

And into that gray world had charged Catriona Mackenzie, nearly running him over in what one might have assumed was a runaway carriage, given the recklessness with which she drove. That cabriolet had delivered to him the happiness that had long eluded him and had transported him to a higher plane. Catriona was a joy to him, and his feelings for her were growing by leaps and bounds. He'd not thought where those feelings might take him, not yet — he simply wanted to enjoy the sunshine for a time, to feel the swell of true affection and esteem.

But then his solicitor had come. *Curse Dundy.* He was one of the few who knew the truth about his wife.

"Lady Montrose has been to see me," he'd said casually in Hamlin's study on the day he'd shown up unexpectedly at Blackthorn Hall.

"There is no Lady Montrose," Hamlin had curtly reminded him.

"I beg your pardon, your grace, of course no'," he'd said with an apologetic nod of his head.

"Why?" Hamlin had asked. "What did she want, then?"

"Money. I explained to her that naturally I couldna honor her request without your express permission. She was verra tearful, she was. It seems her benefactor has left her."

"Her benefactor," Hamlin had said with a chuckle of derision.

"She was no' the grand lady anymore, your grace. She had a rather weary look about her."

What did Dundy think, that he would care how she appeared now? "You should have refused her. Why come all this way to ask when you know I will refuse her, then?"

Dundy had cleared his throat. "I didna refuse her, your grace."

Hamlin had suddenly went cold.

Dundy had sat up a little straighter. "She is aware that there has been no public mention of the dissolution of your marriage, aye?"

"I donna care," Hamlin had said.

"She is also aware that you seek a seat in the House of Lords."

Hamlin had suddenly realized what the man was implying, and he'd felt a sick twist in his belly.

"I suggested she seek help from family."

Hamlin had looked away from Dundy. "The only family she has is a lass of ten years," he'd muttered.

"Aye, so she said," Dundy had agreed. "I thought it prudent to give her a wee bit of coin money until she is able to determine what she is to do."

Hamlin had jerked his gaze to the solicitor. "I beg your pardon?"

"A small amount, your grace. Fifty pounds."

Hamlin had come out of his chair. "What right have you to give away my money?" he'd seethed.

"None," Dundy had said calmly. "But I thought to err on the side of protecting your privacy until I had opportunity to speak with you, aye? If I'd no' taken action, I believe she meant to take the whole affair public and sully your good name."

Hamlin had stared at him, trying to make sense of it. He'd given Glenna what she'd wanted, and she would seek to harm him still?

"I think the matter is done," Dundy had said. "She seemed pleased with the amount and, furthermore, seemed to think her differences with the gentleman might be resolved."

"He's no gentleman," Hamlin had snapped, and stalked to the window. He had drawn a deep breath. And then another. She was a snake. She might have slithered away for now, but she would always slither back. His heart was pounding, his rage mounting. Why must she come back now? Why now, when he'd found happiness?

"Did she ask after Eula?" he had asked stiffly.

Dundy had cleared his throat. "No."

Hamlin had closed his eyes and uttered a

curse. Glenna Guinne Graham was the most reprehensible person he'd ever known.

It had been two days since Hamlin had chased Dundy and his rain cloud out of Blackthorn Hall, and since then, Hamlin had calmed himself somewhat. What he needed, he'd realized, was Catriona's touch. What would ground him, would make him feel himself again, was her smile. He needed her to remember what he had *now,* and not a painful past.

He told himself all he had to do was survive the vote that would occur in a fortnight. Then he didn't care what Glenna did. She could announce to all the world that he'd divorced her if she liked. He would denounce her if it came to it, and suffer the repercussions, but by God, he would not be held hostage by her.

So he'd asked Bain to deliver a message to Catriona, and Bain had looked at him in the way that he had, and Hamlin had wanted to demand what it was Bain expected of him. He was a healthy man, for God's sake, and he couldn't deny his desires any better than Bain could, and God knew Bain did not deny his desires.

On Wednesday, Catriona arrived at Blackthorn Hall in the company of the people

Hamlin had requested of her in his note. Catriona was driving the cabriolet, which came as no surprise to him. But the modiste and her assistant looked a wee bit dazed as they stepped carefully out of the carriage.

Hamlin hardly noticed them at all. He could not take his gaze from Catriona. It felt an age instead of days since he'd last seen her, and she looked bonnier than ever. He wanted to grab her up and bury his face in her neck, but instead, he clasped his hands at his back and bowed his head.

"Madainn mhath!" she called brightly. "My Lord Montrose, may I introduce Mrs. Fraser and her assistant, Mr. Carver. She has brought some fabric samples I'm certain Miss Guinne will like."

"For *me*?" Eula asked with delight.

"Aye, for you," Hamlin said, and ran his palm over her head. "You've grown a foot, I think."

"Have I?" Eula asked, and unthinkingly put a hand to the top of her head, as if she might be able to feel how much she'd grown.

"I asked Miss Mackenzie if she would be so kind as to help us find someone to outfit you properly."

"I should be delighted and honored, your grace," Mrs. Fraser said, sinking into a curtsy. "How many gowns would you like to commission?"

Hamlin glanced at Catriona, who pressed four fingers next to her temple, as if she were contemplating something quite important.

"Four. One evening, three day," he said quickly.

"Verra well. If it suits your grace, we'll start with a few measurements and then look at some fabrics?"

"Aye, by all means. You'll no' need me for that." He gestured toward the front door, where a footman was waiting. "Adam will show you to a room to begin your work, aye?"

"Thank you," Mrs. Fraser said, and she and Mr. Carver gathered their things and walked up the steps to the footman. Eula grabbed Catriona's hand and skipped up the steps behind them. But in the foyer, before Catriona and Eula could disappear into a room, Hamlin said, "Pardon, Miss Mackenzie. Your uncle left his walking stick when last he came to call. I believe Stuart has it. You might fetch it before you go, aye?"

"His walking stick!" Catriona laughed with great amusement, her eyes twinkling at him. "Aye, he's looked high and low for it and will be rightly pleased to have it returned to him. Thank you, your grace."

He nodded, resisting the urge to smile at her theatrics, and moved as if he intended to walk on, but paused again. "Ah. I recall that Stuart will be leaving Blackthorn Hall in the next half hour or so for the village."

"Oh! I'll fetch it from him just as soon as we are all settled here. *Thank* you."

He bit his tongue to keep from smiling and turned in the opposite direction. He walked to the other side of the stairwell, free from prying eyes, as Bain was out and Stuart had indeed been sent on a fool's errand — delivering ham and bread to poor Mr. Bartles, who would not remember that anyone had called by the morrow.

After an interminable wait of a quarter of an hour, Catriona stepped out of the salon. She saw Hamlin lurking in the shadows of the staircase, glanced all around, then flew on tiptoes toward him. As soon as she reached him, he pulled her around the stairs, then, with his hand on the small of her back, ushered her quickly down a narrow hallway and up an even narrower passage.

"Where are we going?" she asked, giggling.

"*Shh,*" he cautioned her. They went up two flights on the servants' stairs, emerging into a darkened corridor. He led her down to the end and opened the door to the last room on the right. It was cold and dark and musty inside. There were no candles, no fire in the hearth, the blinds shut, the drapes drawn, the furniture covered in dust cloths. He let go of Catriona's hand so that he could open one window to have enough light to see.

"What is this room?" she asked, looking around her.

" 'Twas my grandmother's salon. It's sat unused all these years."

"Oh," she said, and looked at him curiously.

He chuckled. "I've no sentimental attachment to the room, if that's what you think. It's only that Blackthorn Hall is so large that there's no' a use for every room."

"What a wretched problem for a duke to have," Catriona said.

He laughed, grabbed her up and spun her around, putting her back against the wall, suddenly out of his mind with want.

"A *walking* stick?" she said, and laughed.

Hamlin kissed her, moving down her body, his lips trailing a path across her warm, scented skin. He gathered her skirt in his hand and lifted it so that he could touch her leg above her stocking. With a

342

sultry gasp, Catriona pressed against him, slipped her arms around his neck and kissed him.

Hamlin was instantly hard and moved between her legs as he fumbled to free himself. They were frantic, wild for each other, their hands and mouths everywhere. She wrapped one leg around his waist and cried out with pleasure when he drove into her.

Their coupling was mad, purely hedonistic pleasure, as if the fury of their lovemaking wasn't furious enough. When they were sated, they collapsed onto the rug beside each other. Catriona giggled infectiously, and in the next moment, Hamlin was laughing, too.

She rolled onto her side and propped her head on her hand so she could look down at him. She traced her finger across his chin. "What happened to you, then?" she asked, and began to pull his neckcloth free. "I feared I'd no' hear from you."

"Aye, I've been occupied," he said. He stroked her neck.

"You seemed distressed when I saw you last," she said, and kissed his chin.

" 'Twas nothing," he said vaguely. He did not want that day to enter this room. Not in this moment.

"Are you certain?" she asked.

"Catriona," Hamlin said, and suddenly sat up, rolling her onto her back. He kissed her tenderly, his lips lingering on hers, feeling the softness in her. "Donna pry, aye?" he murmured.

She pushed him back a bit and stared into his eyes, as if seeking some explanation. But she suddenly smiled and said, "Then next time, donna make me wait so long." She grinned.

So did Hamlin. He rolled onto his back with her, bringing her on top of him. "My sincerest apologies, madam," he growled, and kissed her, but this time with a little less urgency and a little more meaning.

CHAPTER TWENTY

In the days that followed their tryst at Blackthorn Hall, Catriona and Hamlin were blessed with weather that was unfailingly warm and sunny and found time to meet at the ruins. The colorful bog myrtle scented the air, and crossbills chattered over their heads. As fanciful as it seemed, it was their private slice of heaven.

They lived each moment for each other. They didn't speak of the past or the future — that all seemed inconsequential at the ruins. What mattered to Catriona was the here and now, the moments of passion, the glorious feeling of being in love.

Aye, she was in love — she recognized all the signs from other moments in her life when she'd come so very close to it. She'd been young when her sister, Vivienne, had fallen very much in love with and married their distant cousin, Marcas Mackenzie. Catriona could remember how she'd envied her sister's dreamy state, the way she'd smile at everyone around her as if she were the Madonna, bestowing her light and goodness on the less fortunate. Vivienne was serene in her happiness.

Even at that young age, Catriona had understood what Vivienne was feeling. But she'd learned in the years that followed that Viv's happiness wasn't as easy to find as she had thought. Every year that passed, Catriona longed for it, dreamed of it. Here, at last, at long last, it was hers.

She thought of Hamlin constantly, waited impatiently for the next moment she could be with him and was never happier than when she was in his presence.

She hoped and believed that Hamlin felt the same about her.

Uncle Knox extended an invitation to Hamlin to dine at Dungotty on the occasion of the announced departure of the countess and her cousin. Vasily was finding the bucolic countryside a wee bit tedious for his tastes. He was a gambler, and he'd convinced his cousin the time had come to move to greener fields. They were to London, where the countess had a "dear friend" in whose house they might reside for a time.

"Haven't they a house of their own?" Chasity had whispered to Catriona.

Catriona had wondered the same.

Shortly after Lady Orlov announced that she and Vasily would depart, Mr. Wilke-Smythe informed Uncle Knox that he and his family would return to England at the same time Uncle Knox and Catriona made the trip to Edinburgh. "My wife desires to bring in a dressmaker to outfit my daughter for the Season at what I assume will be a dear cost," he'd said, clearly unhappy with the prospect.

Hamlin had accepted Uncle Knox's invitation, and when he arrived, he had the same demeanor he'd carried the first time he'd dined at Dungotty. He greeted Catriona cordially, declined an offer of whisky. He was reserved during the course of the meal, quietly listening to the chatter, answering the questions put to him without expounding. Catriona stole a glimpse of him at every opportunity, but Hamlin was a master at keeping his thoughts and his attentions to himself. No one gathered around that dining table could possibly suspect what had been happening between Catriona and Hamlin.

It wasn't until later, when they'd retired to the salon to hear another musicale performed by the Wilke-Smythes, that Hamlin surreptitiously touched her hand with his little finger to let her know he was there. It was a touch so small that she should not have noticed it at all, and yet it sent a shock of sparks sizzling and sputtering through her veins.

It was excruciating to be so constrained, to be prohibited by societal expectations and morals. Catriona would have liked nothing better than for everyone to know her true feelings for Hamlin, but she couldn't possibly, not without damaging his reputation and hers.

On the other hand, having this secret was delicious and tantalizing. She thought about how Hamlin touched her, how reverent and ardent he was in his desire for her. She imagined how the people in this room would collapse with shock if they knew, and had to work to suppress her smile.

When the Wilke-Smythes had at last finished their warbling, Mr. Wilke-Smythe offered Hamlin a brandy and asked, "What do you think of the vote, your grace? Will you earn your seat in the House of Lords?"

Catriona was shocked by Mr. Wilke-Smythe's interest. She'd had the feeling all evening that he was at last warming to Hamlin. She had the unsettling thought that perhaps he'd decided the cost of dressing Chasity for another Season in the hopes of landing her an offer of marriage was too great. Perhaps he thought she would be the perfect Scottish duchess, and would ignore the rumor that the duke had murdered his wife.

"It looks promising, aye," Hamlin said.

That was precisely what was happening, Catriona realized — she'd been so desperate for a glance from Hamlin that she hadn't been fully cognizant of how attentive Chasity had been of him, too. She'd tried to engage him in conversation more than once, but for heaven's sake, Chasity was naïve if she thought that she might capture the attention of a man like Hamlin with talk of the gloves she found in Crieff that she simply must have. Hamlin preferred to speak of things that mattered, such as the banking regulations, which he'd explained to Catriona as having the potential to be unfair to Scotland. Or the freedom of Scottish merchants to trade with whom they pleased, which she also understood, as her family had been forced to smuggle in goods before the rebellion. Or how important it was to the economy to expand the markets for Scottish wool and beef.

Hamlin did not care about a pair of gloves.

Poor Chasity didn't know about these things, but Catriona did. Her family had openly discussed national issues for years. When one's father was responsible for a clan, one took note of the obstacles facing the clan, and those issues were always economic. Moreover, her father had always treated his daughters equal to his sons, bringing them in to discuss matters near and dear to his heart. Catriona understood Hamlin completely. She understood how a cause could root itself into one's being. *She* was the one who could be a helpmate for Hamlin. Not Chasity.

A tiny voice in her thoughts reminded her that a cause firmly rooted in *her* being demanded her help. She was already a helpmate — to more than a dozen women at Kishorn Abbey. Was it possible to be both? It didn't feel like it, and she pushed the tiny voice down, burying it for the evening.

When Hamlin took his leave, Catriona walked with her uncle to the door to see him off. Hamlin smiled at Catriona, took her hand in his and bent over it. His lips lingered warm and soft on her skin, and when he lifted his head, she could feel the regard flowing between them.

"Thank you so for coming, your grace," she said, smiling at him.

"The pleasure has been all mine. I should

like to return your hospitality, if I may," he said, and let Catriona's hand slip from his palm, his fingers tangling with hers for a brief second. "I should like to invite all of your party to dine at Blackthorn on Friday."

"Weather permitting," Uncle Knox said with a chuckle. "Thank you, your grace. We'd be delighted."

"Good evening, Miss Mackenzie. Lord Norwood."

"Good evening," Uncle Knox said, and slipped his arm around Catriona's waist and pulled her into his side. They watched Hamlin jog down the steps and move fluidly into his coach. The driver tapped the lead horse with his crop, and they were off.

Catriona turned to her uncle. He sighed, cupped her chin. "Compose yourself before we return to our guests, darling. Your smile is so bright they'll think a comet has slid across our night sky."

Good Lord, was it so obvious? She hastily ran her fingers over her cheeks, as if she could erase the heat in them. Uncle Knox was right — she was too giddy, too happy. She was giving away their secret. So what if she did? She was convinced there was nothing in this world that could wreck her happiness.

■ ■ ■ ■

Two days before they were to Edinburgh, Catriona and Chasity took the cabriolet into Crieff. Chasity was determined to have the kid leather gloves and had convinced Catrionia she should, too. "You've worn through your gloves what with all the riding. And you're getting freckles, Catriona," she'd scolded her.

"Aye," Catriona had said, and was unable to suppress a giggle about it.

As they moved down the road from Dungotty, Catriona driving, a lone rider approached them traveling in the opposite direction.

"Who is that?" Chasity asked, squinting at him.

The rider took his hat off his head and waved at them, as if he desired them to stop.

Catriona reined the team to a halt.

"Aye, g'day, g'day," he said, and bowed as low as he could over his saddle without toppling off his horse, and revealing his balding crown in the process. He straightened up, returned the hat to his head and beamed at Catriona and Chasity. His coat was covered in the grime of the road, and his boots looked as worn and muddied as if he'd walked here through the moors.

"Would you be so kind as to point me toward Blackthorn Hall? I'm a wee bit turned about, that I am."

"This is the road to Dungotty," Catriona informed him. "The road to Blackthorn Hall is just there, a mile or so in the direction you came, aye?" She pointed down the road.

The man twisted about in his saddle and peered behind him. "A mile, you say?" he asked, sounding confused.

"Aye, a mile. Look for a row of yew trees."

"Well, then, old Charles, we've come too far, we have," he said to his horse, and proceeded to turn the horse about. But he was a poor rider, and it took several attempts before the old horse consented to retracing its steps. "Thank you!" he said, and spurred the horse onward, lurching and waving at once.

"How could he have missed a road so wide across?" Catriona wondered aloud.

"What business has a man like him at Blackthorn Hall, do you suppose?" Chasity asked as Catriona set the team to a trot once more.

"I couldna guess," Catriona said. She was afraid to guess.

The man apparently found the road, for

he'd disappeared by the time they passed the entrance to Blackthorn Hall. He was entirely forgotten once they reached Crieff.

He was forgotten until the next morning, when Hamlin's secretary arrived at Dungotty. Catriona suspected Mr. Bain was the sort of man who knew he was unreadable and liked it that way. Whatever he thought of her, or anyone for that matter, he kept competently to himself. But then again, he had a way of looking at her that made her feel as though he saw right through her, knew all of her darkest secrets.

He bowed low to Uncle Knox, then with his hands clasped at his back, he said, "I beg your pardon, milord, but his grace the Duke of Montrose regrets that he must rescind his offer to dine at Blackthorn Hall this evening, as he has been unexpectedly called away."

"Called away?" Catriona said before she could think.

"How unfortunate," Uncle Knox said. "We were very much looking forward to the evening. All is well, I hope?"

"Aye, as far as I am aware, milord."

"Our regards to the duke. Thank you for coming all this way to inform us," Uncle Knox said, and nodded at Rumpel to see him out.

Mr. Bain turned to go, but Catriona blurted, "There's no note?"

He slowly turned back, his pale green eyes piercing hers. "None, madam. He asked that I deliver the message in person."

"Of course," she said contritely. She was thinking too much — of course he would not send a note with his secretary, not to her directly. He would send one discreetly, with a messenger. Or a groom. A note would come, today or tomorrow, she was certain of it. He knew she would depart for Edinburgh soon and he'd not allow her to go without a word from him.

"Frankly, I am grateful" Uncle Knox said after Mr. Bain had taken his leave. "We're at sixes and sevens as it is, what with everyone departing at once."

What had happened to Hamlin? What could have occurred that would necessitate sending his secretary and not informing her himself?

No note arrived that afternoon. Or that evening.

Tomorrow, then. Still, that did not keep Catriona from becoming consumed with his sudden disappearance. She conjured up any number of reasons for it — it had to do with the upcoming vote. Or nothing to do with it. Or perhaps the authorities had come and

355

taken him away for murdering his wife after all, and she'd been blind to the truth. Or perhaps he'd simply grown tired of her.

Her need to see him, to know what happened, was increasingly urgent.

It was a gift from the heavens, then, when the modiste Mrs. Fraser and her assistant, Mr. Carver, arrived unexpectedly at Dungotty the following afternoon. Mrs. Fraser had a gown for Eula. "I do beg your pardon, Miss Mackenzie," she said apologetically as Mr. Carver positioned the gown on the settee.

"No' at all," Catriona said.

"I'm to fit the lass today, and I thought . . . that is, if you donna mind, then, would you have a look? I've no' made a dress for a duke before."

The gown was bonny, the color of it cream, adorned with pink ribbons that Eula would adore.

"Is it appropriate for Miss Guinne?" the modiste asked anxiously. "Will it suit?"

" 'Tis *bòidheach*, Mrs. Fraser. A bonnier gown I've no' seen," Catriona said with all sincerity.

The woman blushed self-consciously and gestured for Mr. Carver to wrap it up again. "Aye, thank you kindly, Miss Mackenzie. I'm a wee bit flustered at the idea of present-

356

ing it, that I am."

Catriona seized her opportunity. "Would you like me to come along?" she asked casually. "I'd no' mind, if it will put you at ease."

"Oh," Mrs. Fraser said uncertainly.

"In the event there is any trouble," Catriona added as she pretended to examine the hem of the garment as Mr. Carver prepared the box.

"Trouble," Mrs. Fraser repeated.

"I donna expect there will be, mind you, but if the lass should happen to find fault — after all, she's only ten years, aye? But if she did, I should be able to speak to her and persuade her."

Mrs. Fraser and her assistant exchanged a look. "Would you mind terribly?" she asked.

Catriona smiled. "I'll fetch my coat, aye?"

At Blackthorn Hall, they were greeted at the door by Stuart, who immediately showed them into the garden room, where Eula was busy at her art lessons with Mr. Kenworth. She dropped her brush when she saw who had come, and skipped across the room, excited to see her new gown.

After a suitable bit of exclamation at the gown, Mr. Kenworth saw that his lesson was done for, and excused himself. Mrs. Fraser took Eula into another room to put the garment on. She appeared a moment later, her arms spread wide, twisting and turning one way and then the other, admiring the flare of the petticoat. "It's bonny, is it no', Miss Mackenzie?"

"Aye, the bonniest," Catriona agreed. "Stand still for Mr. Carver, lass," she said as Mr. Carver went down on his knees to mark the hem and seam adjustments.

Eula stood perfectly still as Mrs. Fraser and Mr. Carver reviewed the gown, tucking it in here and straightening there.

"Perhaps you'd like the duke to see it, aye?" Catriona suggested.

"Aye, but he's no' here," Eula said. "He's gone."

"Oh," Catriona said. *Gone?* Where was he? She wandered to Eula's canvas and tried to look at the teapot Eula had been painting. "Where's he gone off to, then?" she asked casually, as if she didn't really care for the answer but was making polite conversation.

"I donna know," Eula said. "I'm to stay with Aubin and Miss Burns until he returns."

"Aye, and when will that be?"

For some reason, Mrs. Fraser looked up at Catriona from her work on the sleeve of the gown.

Heat crept up Catriona's cheeks. She

358

leaned closer to the canvas as if she was studying Eula's technique. "I only ask as he will want to approve the gowns, will he no'?"

"He said if Miss Burns likes them, so shall he."

If *Miss Burns* liked them? How long did he intend to be gone, then? How could he have left without uttering a single word? What in God's name had the strange man on the road said to him to make him leave so unexpectedly? Catriona burned with curiosity and creeping humiliation. How dare he leave her like this, as if she weren't worthy of the slightest consideration?

When she returned to Dungotty, her head was filled with doubts. She discovered that Uncle Knox was uncharacteristically cross with her for leaving without a word. He'd planned a farewell supper for the Wilke-Smythes, and Catriona was late for it and had to rush to change into evening clothes and join them.

She scarcely slept that night, imagining the worst of everything, then abruptly chastising herself for being foolish. Did she think dukes were not called away from time to time? He was an important, powerful man, a political figure, and it was certainly possible a matter of great urgency did not leave him time to pen a note to his illicit lover.

Lover.

It was the first time Catriona had thought of herself in that way. Until this moment, they had belonged to each other. But just because she'd not named herself in this didn't mean it wasn't true. She was an illicit lover.

The Wilke-Smythes departed first the following morning. Tearful goodbyes from Chasity were followed by her father's gruff promises that he'd invite Catriona to England. Uncle Knox and Catriona departed soon thereafter. Catriona was too despondent to natter away and feigned a headache, which her uncle believed to be the result of so much bouncing about on the pitted roads to Edinburgh.

Once they arrived, they were received at the home of the Marquis of Tweeddale on Canongate, whose father had been a close friend to Uncle Knox. The marquis, a man significantly younger than Uncle Knox, kept eyeing Catriona as if he would very much like to lick her from head to toe. The marchioness greeted Catriona with cool indifference and looked at her as if she would like to put her on a spit and roast her.

"I beg your pardon," Catriona said. "I've an awful headache from the drive."

"It's all that bumping about, I tell you," Uncle Knox said.

"By all means, you ought to retire," Lady Tweeddale said, and gestured grandly for her butler. "Show Miss Mackenzie to her room and have a broth sent up to her, as well as some compresses." To Catriona she said, "Perhaps you will have recovered by morning, Miss Mackenzie."

"Thank you." Catriona should have been insulted to be sent away like that, but she was relieved to be away from the Tweeddales. Unfortunately, her early retirement led to another sleepless night, through which she tossed and turned on a lumpy mattress. She rose at dawn, dressed her body and her hair, and when she could stand it not another moment, she descended the stairs and prepared to go out and have a walk about to ease the tension in her.

Mr. Hume, the butler, met her in the foyer. "If I may, Miss Mackenzie," he said as he reached to open the door for her. "Donna go so far to the north, aye? There's been a bit of tomfoolery near the poorhouse and the kirk. Best to stay on the Canongate."

Catriona nodded, but her thoughts were

muddled, and she paid no heed to the direction she walked. At one end of the Canongate was Edinburgh Castle. At the other, Holyrood Palace. She walked, lost in thought. So lost in thought, apparently, that she found herself in a section of the town where the homes were plain and small, and crowded in beside one another. Laundry hung in the mews, and children ran with chickens, loose dogs and the occasional pig in the street. She turned a circle, trying to find the castle so to get her bearings. When she spotted the towers of the castle, she let out a breath of relief and started back the way she'd apparently come. But as she was walking down the street, retracing her steps, a man emerged from one of the houses. He was tall and well dressed, and when he turned back to the open door of the house, she saw the black bob of his hair beneath his hat.

Catriona stopped mid-stride, her breath in her throat. She was staring at Hamlin on the stoop of that house. Her mind couldn't make sense of it. She couldn't imagine what he was doing there, of all places. If he was in Edinburgh, why had he not told her? Why was he at this house, and not a grander one on the Canongate? Why was he in Edinburgh at all, particularly knowing she was coming here? She took a step forward, intending to call out, to wave, but before she could, a woman stepped out onto the stoop, too, and this time Catriona's heart stopped.

She knew that woman. Her portrait had hung in the salon at Blackthorn Hall until recently. Her ginger hair looked almost faded in the morning light, and even her gown seemed to wilt around her. But there was no mistaking Lady Montrose.

Catriona's heart sank to her toes. Her gut began to churn, turning over on itself to the point she feared she might be ill. Her face burned with shame and humiliation and fury. She wanted to crawl into a corner and hide, but she was standing on the street. She didn't know what to do, which way to go. She couldn't head toward Edinburgh Castle without passing him and his wife, who was *not* gone, thank you, but very here, in the flesh. So she whirled around and began racing blindly down the street, nearly colliding with a woman carrying a basket, who shouted at her.

It didn't make sense. Nothing made sense. He'd said she was gone. *Gone.* What had she thought gone meant? Dead? Out of his reach? *Diah,* was she his wife *yet*? Had Catriona's unpardonable sin been made unpardonably worse with adultery? What had he done, cast his wife out? Had he put a *duchess* in that small, mean house? And if she was as alive as this, why hadn't he denied the rumors about her death?

Everything was spinning in her head and gut, but the worst of it was the wrenching pain in her heart.

CHAPTER TWENTY-ONE

Hamlin returned to Blackthorn Hall in a mood that was not as black as when he'd left, but one that would brook no questions. That turned out to be impossible, however, as Nichol Bain was waiting for him. Hamlin could see him pacing in the foyer as he came off his horse and removed his bag from the back of the saddle. He came to attention when Hamlin entered the foyer and handed his things to Stuart. "Welcome back, your grace," he said evenly.

"Bain." He looked at Stuart. "Bring a bucket of ale to my study, aye? As big a bucket as you might find, then. Fill it to the bloody top."

"Aye, your grace," the unflappable Stuart responded.

Hamlin turned toward his study. Bain followed behind him without invitation. That was the sort of man Bain was — he came whether he was wanted or not. That was the

sort of man Hamlin had knowingly employed, and he'd had no regrets until this
moment.

In the study, he collapsed into his chair
behind his desk with a weary sigh. Bain
stood, anxiously waiting. When Hamlin
didn't offer him anything, he sighed. "Will
you make me beg for your news, then?"

"I find it remarkable how freely you speak
with a duke," Hamlin snapped irritably.

Bain didn't blink as much as an eyelash.
He steadily returned Hamlin's gaze, waiting.

"Verra well. I found her, I did."

"And?"

"And . . . her lover has left her, and she is
desperate. She means to hold me hostage
with her threats, but I have turned the tables
on her, that I have, sir. I invited her to say
what she likes — I donna care."

Bain seemed frozen for several moments.
Then he looked wildly about the room, as if
searching for his response. Or perhaps
something with which to club Hamlin. "We
must contain this," he blurted. "The seat
—"

"Mr. Bain, if you've no' yet understood
me, let me speak plainly — I donna give a
bloody damn about the seat if it means being held hostage by that woman."

366

A knock at the door ended the conversation as far as Hamlin was concerned — Stuart entered with a pitcher of ale and two mugs. He poured Hamlin a mug, then glanced at Bain, who shook his head.

When Stuart had gone out, Bain planted his hands on the desk and leaned across it. "I understand your ire, your grace, God knows that I do. But we've worked so hard for this."

"It was no' meant to be, apparently," Hamlin said, and lifted the tankard, drinking deeply.

"Do I have your leave to . . . to repair this situation?"

Hamlin scoffed. "What can you possibly do about it, lad?" He drained the tankard, and when he had finished, he drew his sleeve across his mouth. He slid the empty tankard across his desk and nodded at Bain to refill it. "You're fortunate, that you are, Mr. Bain, do you know it? You're no' bound to marry and produce an heir in the name of a dukedom. Your freedom is quite real and quite your own. You may seek your happiness wherever you find it and rejoice in it. I must wear this bloody mantle."

"It may appear so, your grace, but we all have our crosses to bear, aye? Have I your leave?" he stubbornly insisted.

Hamlin waved a hand at him. "Do what you like, then. But on my honor, I will no' *pay* her to leave me be."

"You will lose the seat," Bain said flatly. "After the work you've done, you will lose it."

Hamlin shrugged. "As I said, so be it."

"This can be remedied," Bain said.

"If it amuses you to *remedy* it, then by all means, remedy it," Hamlin said curtly.

"Montrose!"

Eula raced through the door and to his desk.

Hamlin grinned. He stood up and caught her before she crashed into him, holding her tightly to him.

"You're *hugging* me," she said, laughing. "You never hug me!"

"That's because you're rarely far from my side, are you? I've missed you, Eula."

"Guess what? My gowns are almost finished. Do you want to see my painting of a teapot? Mr. Kenworth says I am *verra* talented."

He smiled and kissed her cheek before putting her on her feet. "Perhaps after supper, aye? Go now, finish your lessons, and you may tell me all about your painting then."

"All right," she said. She kissed his cheek

in return. It surprised Hamlin, for he was not the only one who suffered from an inability to show affection. She skipped out, pausing to poke Bain in the belly. Generally, Bain smiled at her or rolled his eyes. But today, he hardly seemed to notice her. His gaze was fixed on Hamlin.

It was for Eula's sake that Hamlin had felt such a surge of red fury when the bumbling messenger had arrived at Blackthorn Hall with Glenna's message of extortion. What had Glenna paid that fool to deliver her threat? Hamlin had demanded to know where Glenna was, but the man claimed not to recall. Hamlin had left for Edinburgh that very afternoon, seething with indignation.

Neither did his solicitor know precisely where Glenna lived. But Hamlin had his own ways, his own men, and he'd found the lying wench. She was living in a house much smaller than any house she'd ever lived in, but Glenna was haughty. She liked it there, she'd said.

He had asked Glenna, in the midst of their heated argument, how she could be so callous when it came to the lass. "She is your cousin's daughter, your only living relative," he'd said. "How can you turn your back on her?"

"I hardly knew my cousin, much less her

369

bairn," Glenna had said haughtily. "And besides, the lass is well cared for at Blackthorn Hall, better than I could care for her. It's hardly fair, really — *I'm* the one with no one to look after me."

He'd found the sheer depth of her selfishness breathtaking. Glenna was not a well woman — she was lacking any sort of compassion for anyone but herself.

"What do you want?" he'd asked her, curious as to how far she would go to torment him.

"Five thousand pounds," she'd said without a moment's hesitation.

Her audacity was staggering. "No," he'd said flatly.

"Five thousand pounds and I'll leave you be, Hamlin. Is that no' what you want?"

"Aye, it is what I want," he'd agreed. "God save me, I want it more than I could possibly convey to you. But I know you'll no' end it there, Glenna. You'll come round again, just like a rat. But know this — you'll no' intimidate me with your demands." He'd quit the room, disgusted, uncertain of why he'd come at all, of what he thought he might have possibly accomplished in appealing to the worst sort of person.

But Glenna was a desperate woman and had rushed after him, onto the stoop. "You will regret this, Hamlin. Everyone will know you're a cuckold, they will! You'll lose your precious seat in the House of Lords and no one will care! No one!"

"Do what you please, madam," he'd said coolly. "I donna give a damn."

"I'll come to the vote," she'd threatened him. "I'll make sure that everyone knows the sort of man you really are!"

He'd tipped his hat to her. "Farewell, Glenna." He'd started down the steps, away from her.

"I hate you," she'd said to his back.

Hamlin had actually laughed at that remark. There was one thing, and one thing only, that he understood about Glenna, and it was that she hated him.

He'd returned to his townhouse in Edinburgh and had stormed around his study with great agitation. That agitation had given way to drink, and he'd gotten pissed that night, allowing himself to wallow in pity. But the next morning, he'd risen as himself once more. He was resigned to the fact that he would not have his seat in the House of Lords. It was a blow to his heart — there were many things he'd hoped to accomplish, that would have given his life true purpose.

Once he realized there was no way to

salvage his reputation if she were to come forward, he didn't bloody well care what Glenna did.

But Bain cared. He rode out that evening with some vague vow to return with a solution at hand.

That evening, Hamlin was pleased to dine with Eula and realized how her girlish chatter was a salve to the old wound Glenna had opened again. He watched the lass as she told him her news with great animation and wondered how he'd ever thought her a burden. He was glad he'd never located a distant relative to take her. He was thankful that he'd had her to share the last awful year of his life.

"Mr. Kenworth says I'm verra talented," she said, as if it were fact and not the least bit boastful.

"I donna doubt it."

"Do you like my gown, then?" she said, and held her arms out on either side of her, as if he could appreciate her gown in spite of her being seated behind a table.

"Aye, it is beautiful, Eula. *You* are beautiful."

She nodded, apparently pleased with that, and picked up her fork again. "I think I shall be an artist and no' an archer."

"The world will rejoice."

She smiled at his quip. "Aubin says if I want to shoot arrows, he'll take me far from man or beast."

"A wise man."

"Do you think Miss Mackenzie will mind, then, if I donna take up the archer's bow?"

"I think she'll be pleased with your decision to be an artist, that's what," he said. "You must ask her next time she comes round, aye?"

"Aye. But she'll no' come for a time. She's gone to Edinburra."

Bloody hell, he'd forgotten it — he was struck with a pang of conscience that he'd not sent word to her about his absence. She was surely wondering what had become of him these last four days. But the attempt at blackmail had filled him with such blind rage he'd not thought everything through.

"Where did you go, your grace?" Eula asked.

Hamlin shifted his gaze to her. "It doesna matter," he said simply.

She looked at her plate. "I should like to see Edinburra one day. My cousin promised to take me there."

"Did she?" Hamlin asked curiously. "When did she promise it?"

Eula looked at her plate. "She promised before she left. She said she would have a new house there, and when she was settled, I should come and live with her and her friend."

This news astounded Hamlin, and he stared at Eula in disbelief. "Why have you no' said this to me before?"

Eula shrugged and pushed her potatoes around her plate. "I didna remember it."

Didn't remember it, indeed. He watched her moving her potatoes around her plate, rolling them from one side to the other.

"Eula? Why did you no' tell me that she'd made you this important promise?"

Eula glanced at him from the corner of her eye. "I was afraid."

"Of your cousin?" he asked, not understanding her.

"No' of her. Of you."

He blanched. He reached for her chin, forcing her to look at him. She had never shown him the slightest hesitation, or the slightest fear of him. "You were afraid of *me*?"

"I was afraid you'd make me go to her and her friend," she said softly.

Something warm sluiced through his veins. "Eula, lass." He took her hand in his, squeezing it. "You're here at Blackthorn Hall, with me, aye? And here you shall remain."

She gave him a look of unusual cynicism. "Always?"

"*Always.* Do you understand, then? No one can take you from me."

She slowly smiled. She sat up straighter. "May we invite Miss Mackenzie to tea when she returns from Edinburra?"

He let go her hand. "We may. I'll ask Stuart to discover when she will return and send an invitation round."

Eula picked up her fork and speared a potato, her appetite suddenly returned.

Everyone had secrets, it seemed. He wondered what all the lass had seen, what had made her fear being sent to Glenna. He resented Glenna all the more for it. Eula was her blood. How could she be so callous in her affection for a child?

Two days later, Stuart informed the duke that Norwood and his niece had indeed returned to Dungotty the previous day. An invitation to tea was dispatched, inviting Miss Mackenzie to join Miss Guinne for tea at Blackthorn Hall the following afternoon. The reply was swiftly relayed back to him in the flowing, blotted script he'd come to recognize as Catriona's. *Please thank Miss Guinne for her kind offer, but alas, I am far too occupied with the preparation for my*

*return to Balhaire and cannot possibly attend.
CM*

Not only was the note quite distant and cold, the words *return to Balhaire* startled him.

Hamlin rode out that very afternoon for Dungotty. When he arrived, the butler informed him, "His Lordship has ventured into Crieff on this fine afternoon, your grace. He is not expected to return before the supper hour."

"Then I'll have a word with Miss Mackenzie, aye?" he'd said.

The butler had seemed a bit uncertain about that but had taken his hat and gloves, had shown him to a small salon and had gone to fetch the mistress all the same.

Hamlin heard her coming down the hall. She was not walking daintily, but in great strides, and at a wee bit of a clip, as if on a march. She shoved the door open and fairly burst into the room. He expected her incandescent smile, a cry of delight. That was not at all how she greeted him.

Hamlin smiled.

Her brows dipped into a dark frown.

"You're cross," he said, confused. "I beg your pardon, I should have sent word I'd be away, but a matter had arisen verra quickly —"

"You think I'm cross that you dis-appeared?" She laughed coldly.

What in blazes was wrong with her? She confounded him. "Aye," he said. What else could have created such a pique in her as this? And why did she laugh at him with such derision?

"I will grant you it was badly done to go off without so much as a word, aye," she agreed as her hands found her hips in a manner he did not care for at all. "But I would have forgiven you that."

"Then . . . what?" he asked, helplessly casting his arms wide. "Do you really mean to return to Balhaire?"

"What if I am? What do you care?"

"I care!" he said, surprised by that. "Catriona, I —"

She suddenly launched across the room and hit him squarely in the chest with the flats of both palms with such force that he took a step backward. He saw it then, the sheen of furious tears in her eyes. He caught her by the arms before she could strike him again. "My God, Catriona, what has made you so cross?"

"I saw you," she whispered, and squirmed out of his hold.

"Saw me? Saw me where?"

Her eyes were glistening with the sort of

fury that he'd only ever known a woman to bear. "She's no' *gone,* Hamlin. She is verra much alive! I saw her, as pretty as a portrait in Edinburra, and I saw *you* with her!"

It felt like his insides were tumbling down into rubble. How was it possible that Catriona had seen him? "Did you *follow* me?" he asked incredulously.

"What? How could I have followed you? I didna know you had left!" she said, her voice raised with frustration.

Hamlin glanced at the open door. He moved swiftly to close it, then turned around to face her. " 'Tis no' what you think, Catriona."

"Ha!" she said. "Is it no', Hamlin?" she challenged him. "You've turned her out! Admit it! You've cast her aside as if she were so much rubbish! Why did you no' tell me? Why have you allowed everyone to believe you *murdered* her? Why did you allow me to *believe* —"

She choked on a sob.

Hamlin reached for her, but she slapped him away and put her back to him.

"I didna turn her out," he said as evenly as he could, but his heart was pounding so hard as to make him breathless. "I tried all that I knew to keep her at Blackthorn Hall, on my word I did. But the truth, Catriona, is that she left me. She and her lover —"

Catriona whirled about, wide-eyed. Her chest was rising with each tortured breath, her eyes wide and searching. *"What?"*

He shrugged. "I told you the truth, aye? The Lady Montrose was never happy in her marriage. She sought happiness elsewhere."

She could only stare at him, clearly dumbstruck.

"At her request, I divorced her," he said, his voice going lower, filling with shame.

"Divorce," she whispered, her eyes going wide. "You divorced her?"

"Aye. She begged me to, she did. She'd no' have a prayer of gaining one on her own."

"Does Eula know?"

He sighed. That was more complicated. "No' everything. No one knows, save three people."

"But why? Why pretend, why no' be truthful?"

"The seat," he said morosely. "The bloody seat."

"I donna understand."

He thought how to explain it. "The Duke of Perth was my father's closest friend and ally, and he has long since been the one I turn to for advice, aye? It was his advice . . ." He paused to drag his fingers through his hair. "He advised me that men would understand if I'd sent away an unruly wife. But that those same men would think less of me had I'd been cuckolded. Which I had. And I know it to be true."

Catriona looked at the floor, then at the ceiling. Her hands found her hips again, and she chewed on her bottom lip. And then, without a word, she turned away, went to the sideboard and poured two whiskies. She handed him one. "You best tell me all, then."

So he did. They sat together on the settee, and he told her about Glenna's unhappiness, which she'd expressed to him only after the vows had been said.

"Aye, of course," Catriona said darkly. "Better to wed a duke than to love him."

"I suppose," he said, without emotion. He'd long come to grips with the idea that he'd been duped. He explained that he could never find the path that would make her happy. How Eula had come, and the responsibility to see after her cousin's only surviving child was an annoyance to her. How she'd finally left and had begged him to set her free. That, he'd done without regard for the seat in the House of Lords — he'd wanted nothing to do with Glenna, either.

"How wretched that must have been for you," Catriona said softly.

It was wretched, all right. He told Catriona how he'd sought the advice of the elderly duke, and how he'd taken his advice. "It was easy to do," he said. "I wanted the seat. And no one questioned me. I was no' forced to explain what had happened, which, I will admit, was to my liking. But I never assumed the rumors would grow into such monstrous accusations against me."

"Why did you no' tell me?" she asked. "I would no' have judged you."

He looked at her solemn face and wished he could go back in time and tell her everything. "Aye, you would no' have judged me, I know." He pressed his palm to her cheek. "I was selfish. When I was with you, Catriona, I didna think of her. I didna want to think of her, and it never seemed imperative."

She turned her face and kissed his palm, then moved slightly. "When would it have seemed imperative?"

It was a fair question. "I canna rightly say. The only thing that matters to me is how happy you've made me these last few weeks, *leannan*. It has been a joy, a pleasure beyond my wildest imagining, aye? It never occurred to me that she'd come back into my life and try to extort money from me or threaten to expose the truth."

"What will you do?"

He shrugged and leaned forward to kiss her forehead. "No' a thing, aye? She can say of me what she likes. None of it is as damning as what's been rumored."

"But what of the seat? The vote is within the fortnight."

"It's a seat," he said. "The only thing that matters to me is you."

Catriona studied him a moment. She turned and pushed him backward, kept pushing until he was lying on his back on the settee. "I donna care about her," she whispered, and lifted her skirts to straddle his lap. She took his head in her hands and kissed him.

Hamlin groaned. He caught her shoulders and pushed her away. "Donna do this, no' here. Someone will come."

"They'll no' come." She kissed his eyes, his cheeks, his mouth.

He groaned again, full of longing and raw need. " 'Tis no' wise," he muttered.

"It was never wise, *mo chridhe,*" she murmured.

She'd never called him a term of endearment. He didn't know Gaelic save a few phrases, but he thought she'd called him

her heart. *Her heart.* His heart fluttered —
he had believed he'd never know this depth
of emotion, and as she began to move
against him, tantalizing him, making him
hard, he could feel something in him pro-
testing. She'd called him her heart and
he . . . he was weak, that was what. Bloody
well weak. "Donna go home to Balhaire,"
he said. "No' yet."

"Donna speak of it, no' now," she whispered, and bit his lip, then lifted her hips
and, with a bit of help from him, slid down
onto his shaft.

Hamlin didn't speak of it. He didn't think
of it. He was lost.

CHAPTER TWENTY-TWO

Over the course of the next two days, Catriona spent as much time as she could in Hamlin's company. She met him at the ruins, where he'd been followed by his hunting dogs. They laughed at the antics of the two when they tussled over a stick. They made love under the yew, and Catriona was happy and sated and in love. She had learned every inch of Hamlin, from the stubborn curl of hair that escaped his bob, to the curious tattoo on one shoulder, which he laughingly told her had been acquired one drunken night during his Grand Tour of the continent as a young man. She knew the soft patch of skin in the crease of his elbow, the small scar above his knee. She knew that a flick of tongue behind his earlobe drove him mad and that he rarely hunted because his vision blurred the farther away his prey was.

She didn't think about anything but being

with him when she was with him, but at night . . . well, at night, alone in her bed, the veil on her fantasy was lifted, and she lay restlessly, watching her life float by in a series of images.

She wondered when it would have become imperative for him to tell her about his divorce? He had never really answered her about that. Catriona was also at turns angry and maudlin about his secret. She'd known from the beginning that their affair was temporary, a summer she'd never forget, and that he owed her no explanation. And yet, there was much more to her feelings. Perhaps she ought to have pressed him, to demand to know when, if ever, he would have told her about his former marriage. But to what end? Had she not been warned that nothing could come of this? Did she think Hamlin would jeopardize his reputation or his potential seat in the House of Lords for her? And would she not return to Balhaire as she'd planned all along, and really, sooner rather than later? Did she not have her promise to Zelda to see after the abbey? Had that not become more imperative after her trip to Edinburgh?

Her audience with the Lord Advocate had not been terribly encouraging. Having heard the reason for their call, he'd shaken his head before Uncle Knox could even make his plea on her behalf. As she'd explained it to Hamlin that afternoon in the ruins, "He said there was no goodwill for Scotland in London. That the land where the abbey sits would be better used for sheep, and there were enough English lords who desired a foothold for that verra purpose."

"Is there nothing that can be done?" Hamlin had asked.

"He promised to bring up our case with the king, but that he believed it would come to naught. But he granted another six months to vacate the abbey. He said I would be wise to prepare myself for the worst."

Hamlin hadn't said much, and Catriona assumed that he thought much like Uncle Knox had thought about it — when Catriona had asked her uncle his opinion on the return to Dungotty, he'd thought a long time and then had said, "I think that Zelda's heart was bigger than practical. It was always a costly proposition, was it not?"

"You think I ought to let it go, then," she'd said dejectedly.

Her uncle had patted her knee. "I think it not sustainable."

Catriona had been perturbed that her uncle didn't share her view of the necessity to fight for Kishorn. But even still, she had known in some part of her soul that he was right. The abbey was in disrepair, they were entirely dependent on the charity of others and the abbey was so remote that the women and their children were removed from society and gainful employment. It was not a true solution for the plight of those women and children.

"What do you mean to do, then?" Hamlin asked her that afternoon when she explained the Lord Advocate's answer to him.

How refreshing that Hamlin didn't tell her what she ought to do or think, as her brothers or father would have done, as the men who wanted her land would have done. "Uncle Knox thinks it will become an unwelcome complication for my family if I push the Lord Advocate. But what of the women and their children? Where are they to go? What are they to do?"

Hamlin had no answer for her. He stared into the distance, as if contemplating her question.

"I've been gone too long," she said quietly.

Hamlin said nothing.

She'd been gone two months now, and if they would be forced to give it over to the Crown, there was much work to be done. She had to find places for them all. She couldn't stay at Dungotty forever — even

Uncle Knox had announced he planned to return to England before autumn. Catriona had been putting off the inevitable, but time was running out for her and Hamlin.

She wanted to be in every moment of this extraordinary experience, absorbing it, imprinting it into her heart. She didn't want to think too closely about the secrets they'd kept from each other, or anything that didn't really matter when one lived in the moment. Those things only mattered when there was more to come of a love affair. Not when time was running out and they were grasping at the last rays of their sunlight.

It hurt her heart to think of leaving him. Aye, her uncle had warned her in the beginning, but Catriona had allowed her heart to swell with love for the duke anyway. She couldn't help it.

But she wouldn't think of that now. Not today. Not tomorrow, or the day after that. She had every moment of the rest of her life to nurse her regrets.

Hamlin had invited Catriona and her uncle once again to dine at Blackthorn Hall. "If we canna dine at Blackthorn on the third attempt, I will believe it is cursed," he'd said with a smile.

On the night they were expected, Catriona

dressed in her best gown, a blue silk with embroidered green vines and leaves, a pearly white petticoat with the same vines. They arrived at Blackthorn in the cabriolet and were met by two liveried footmen. Eula, wearing her new evening gown, stood framed in the open door, too excited to receive her guests in the salon as a grand lady might.

Miss Burns had turned the lass out very prettily. Her gown had been fitted, and her hair a wee tower on her head, threaded with pink ribbons that matched those on her gown. She curtsied deeply, her arms spread wide. "You are most welcome," she said solemnly.

"It is our great honor," Catriona said, just as solemnly.

Eula giggled. "I've learned a new dance," she said as they followed Stuart to the salon. "Aubin will play the pianoforte so that I may perform. Montrose said I might."

"Aubin has musical talents in addition to everything else?" Catriona asked with surprise.

"Aubin can do anything, he can," Eula said. "I mean to marry him when I'm of age."

"We'll have no talk of matrimony just yet." It was Hamlin who spoke as they entered

389

the salon. He was standing at the hearth and was wearing, much to Catriona's surprise, a tartan plaid and a formal coat. She paused to take him in — of all the men she'd seen in plaids in her life, she had never seen one wear it so well, and it caused her heart to skip a beat or two.

"Your grace, you are a Scotsman indeed," her uncle said.

"Aye," he said with a smile. "In honor of our Highland guest," he said, looking at Catriona.

She could not possibly have loved him more.

" 'Twas my idea," Eula said as she walked a slow circle around the duke. "Aubin said everyone knows the Highland regiments wear them, and Montrose —"

"His grace," Hamlin murmured.

"His grace had one in his wardrobe."

"One might inquire what a lass was doing in a gentleman's wardrobe," Hamlin said, but he smiled so fondly at Eula that Catriona realized something all at once. He loved Eula. She could see it in the way he looked at her, smiled at her. It was the same way he looked at Catriona and smiled at her.

Hamlin loved her.

They dined on lamb and parsnips cooked

to such perfection that Uncle Knox asked for more. The wine flowed freely, thanks to Stuart's attention, and the four of them laughed as if they were old friends. They toasted Hamlin, who would face the vote for the House of Lords next week. Uncle Knox regaled them all with a story about running from the king's soldiers as a young man, and sliding into a shed to hide, only to discover the shed housed the family pigs.

They laughed until their bellies ached, and Catriona could look around that table, with the flickering light of the candles, the smell of roasted lamb in the air, a warm fire in the hearth at her back, and imagine what might have been. She could imagine Hamlin on the dais with her family at Balhaire. Or here, with more children around them. A family had always been her greatest desire, and that want had not ebbed with time. If anything, it had only grown. She wanted to matter to someone in a way that transcended sister and daughter.

There was so much laughter that evening, so much warmth. Catriona had never seen Hamlin so relaxed, or Eula so animated with delight. She was feeling soft, thinking how perfect the dinner was to mark the end of the summer, when the sounds of commotion reached them.

"Is it the shutters, then?" Eula asked Montrose.

"I donna know, lass," he said, and poured more wine.

A moment later, a footman appeared. When he opened the dining room door, they could hear voices, male and female alike, one of them exclaiming over the other.

"Your grace, you are needed," the footman said.

Hamlin looked at the footman with an expression of sheer apprehension. "If you will excuse me, aye?" he said to his guests, and followed the footman out.

Catriona looked at Eula. The lass, who was so eager for visitors, was staring at her plate. She shifted her gaze to Uncle Knox. He understood her better than anyone at times — and he knew what she was thinking. "Stay," he said sternly. " 'Tis no' your affair."

Catriona didn't stay. She stood up.

"No!" Eula suddenly cried, and tried to lunge for Catriona's hand. "Stay here, Miss Mackenzie. *Please.*"

Now Catriona was alarmed. "Donna fear, Miss Guinne. I'll return straightaway." She ran her hand over Eula's shoulder, but Eula grabbed her hand and held tightly.

So Catriona took the lass with her. She

stepped into the hall and saw at once that her worst fear had come true. Catriona was stunned — the commotion was the return of the former Lady Montrose. Catriona could feel Uncle Knox at her back, and Eula leaning against her side. Together, the three of them stared at the people down the hall — Hamlin, standing separately from the others. Mr. Bain. An elderly gentleman in a coat of superfine and a felt hat Catriona had never seen before. And a woman with ginger hair.

Lady Montrose's cheeks were flushed and her smile sparkling. The servants of Blackthorn Hall were appearing from everywhere, hastening into the foyer, hugging their former mistress at her invitation. She was speaking to each and every one of them as if they were long-lost friends, reunited at long last.

"It is so good to be returned to Blackthorn Hall!" she said gaily. "I should no' have left. You must forgive me, all of you."

Uncle Knox put his hand on Catriona's shoulder.

Lady Montrose turned and saw them standing in the hall. Her gaze went to Eula, and with a cry of delight, she bent down, her arms wide. "Eula, darling!"

Eula shrank deeper into Catriona's side.

Lady Montrose laughed. "Donna be shy, lass. Come kiss your cousin, aye?"

"Leave her be," Hamlin said quietly.

Lady Montrose slashed a look across Hamlin that made Catriona shiver. She looked at Hamlin; his gaze met hers. His eyes had gone cold, and his face was devoid of color. Catriona did not understand what was happening, and she was desperate to understand, but Uncle Knox took her firmly in hand. "Your grace, we will take our leave. You have unexpected guests, and we'll not be a bother."

"You are no bother, my lord," he said gruffly.

"Nevertheless," he said, and with his hand now gripping Catriona's elbow, forcing her to let go of Eula's hand as he propelled her forward.

Catriona looked at Mr. Bain. Had he done this? He steadily returned Catriona's gaze, but whatever he thought of it, she couldn't determine. He was expressionless. Utterly expressionless.

"Please, you mustna interrupt your supper for *me,*" Lady Montrose said. "I've come quite unannounced, I have."

"*Why* have you come?" Hamlin demanded.

"Perhaps we ought to retire to your study,

your grace," said the elderly man. "There is much to discuss."

Hamlin gave the man a dark glance. He seemed to remember himself and said, "If I may, my Lord Perth, I should like to introduce Lord Norwood and his niece Miss Mackenzie."

Catriona was in such a state of shock at what was happening before her eyes that she couldn't think to even curtsy. Uncle Knox moved forward with her, exchanged the pleasantries for her. The woman, who was currently hugging Mrs. Weaver to her, was not introduced.

Why was she here? It made no sense — she had returned to Blackthorn Hall like a long-lost, prodigal daughter.

"Stuart, have you anything I might eat?" she asked as she unfastened her cloak. "I've traveled all day and I'm famished. And some wine, Stuart. Eula, darling, will you not join me?"

Hamlin gave Mr. Bain a blistering look. Mr. Bain instantly took Lady Montrose by the arm and led her in the opposite direction of the dining room. Lord Perth glanced at Hamlin as he followed, his gaze questioning.

"I'll be along," Hamlin said quietly, and watched the older man follow after Lady

Montrose and Mr. Bain. Then he turned toward Eula and motioned her forward. Eula ran to him, throwing her arms around his waist and burying her face in his belly. Hamlin squatted down beside her, put his arms around her and whispered in her ear. When he stood again, he handed her over to a startled Miss Burns, who had only just arrived into the excitement.

Then he turned to Catriona. "I beg your pardon, Catriona," he said. "I was no' expecting —"

"No, of course you were not," Uncle Knox said. "We understand, do we not, Cat, darling?"

No, she didn't understand. She was swimming in a sea of confusion and hurt and didn't understand anything other than the woman he'd divorced had returned to Blackthorn Hall as if she were queen here.

Hamlin suddenly took her hand and bent over it, his lips lingering on her knuckles, heedless of Uncle Knox, who abruptly walked away and pretended to examine a painting. "I'll send word to you as soon as I am able, aye?" He leaned in and kissed her cheek. And then he stepped back, his face shuttering, the aloof, distant duke returning. "Thank you, my lord," he said to her uncle.

Uncle Knox turned about and moved instantly, catching Catriona's wrist, pulling her close to him so that he could put his arm around her and keep her close. "Thank you, your grace, for a lovely evening."

Hamlin nodded, and with his hands clasped behind his back, he watched them walk out the door, and kept watching until a footman had closed the door behind them.

In the cabriolet, Uncle Knox pulled the curtain between them and the groom, and sank against the squabs. "What in God's name has happened this evening?"

"It was his wife," Catriona said.

"She's alive, then, is she?"

Catriona smiled bitterly. "Aye, she is. She . . . she took a lover and left him, and he divorced her."

"Well, then," Uncle Knox said. "I suppose that's a bit more palatable than murder, but he can't be happy to see her returned. One wonders why she has. Why now? It has to do with the vote, I should think."

Catriona didn't know, and at that moment, she didn't care. She felt an unbearable weight in her chest, squeezing the breath from her. She hadn't imagined how her love would end, but she would never have guessed it would be like this. She could not keep the tears from sliding down her cheeks. She bent over her lap trying desperately not to cry. She had no right to cry; she'd known from the beginning what this was. But that didn't make it hurt any less.

"Oh, my love," Uncle Knox cooed, and put his arm around her shoulders and pulled her into his side. "My poor dear girl," he said, and Catriona turned her face into his coat and sobbed.

CHAPTER TWENTY-THREE

Hamlin was livid. How dare Bain seek
Glenna out and bring her here? How dare
Perth abet him in that? He strode down the
hallway to his study and slammed the door
behind with fury once he entered. Glenna
jumped and looked nervously to Perth and
Bain. But the two men returned Hamlin's
heated gaze with stoic determination.

"Is this your doing, then?" Hamlin accused Bain as he gestured to Glenna.

"You gave me leave to put the situation to
rights, your grace," he said with his bloody
untroubled demeanor.

"This is no' to *rights,* sir. This is blackmail!"

"I donna care for it any more than you,"
Glenna said haughtily, as if, by some incom-
prehensible measure, she was the injured
party. "Do you think I wanted to come back
to this mausoleum? And why are you

dressed like that, as if you live in a Highland cave?"

"If I may," Lord Perth said.

No, you may not. But Hamlin owed the man his respect and debt of gratitude for having advised him so unselfishly after his father died. He clenched his jaw, gave him a curt nod.

"If I may have your leave, your grace, I'll sit," Perth said, and gingerly lowered himself onto a leather armchair. "I'm no' a young man who might stand for hours." He settled into his seat, crossed his hand over his belly and said, "Now, then. Lady Montrose —"

"She is *no'* Lady Montrose," Hamlin said acidly.

Glenna rolled her eyes.

"Quite right," Perth conceded. "The former Mrs. Graham is in dire straits, your grace. She hasn't a farthing to her name, aye?"

"That is no' true," Hamlin said. "She managed to extort fifty pounds from my solicitor."

"I gave it to Charlie," she said.

The blood in Hamlin's veins roiled at the mention of her lover.

"But it wasna enough. I told you it wasna enough. Now he's had to go to Glasgow to find work, he has, and I —"

400

"Mrs. Graham," Lord Perth said curtly.

She pressed her lips together and sat on the edge of a chair beside Perth, her head down, like a disobedient child.

Lord Perth shifted his gaze to Hamlin. He looked rather sad, really. "Your former wife and I have come to an agreement. In exchange for her cooperation, I shall grant her a handsome sum to take herself and —" he paused to look at Glenna "— and *Charlie* away, aye?"

Hamlin gaped at him. "You've *what*? No, your grace, there is no need for you to do so."

"There is every need, Montrose. It is my desire to see you in the House of Lords. The reappearance of your wife will put to bed the rumors about you. Naturally, people will assume you had a lover's tiff and are reconciled. Once the vote is taken, you may trundle off to London, and she will trundle off to God knows wherever a thousand pounds will take her. You may say whatever you like about the dissolution of your marriage then, aye? Whatever you say will no' be contradicted by the former Mrs. Graham, lest she'd like to see her lover accused of infidelity and kidnapping and live without a farthing."

Hamlin couldn't believe what he was hearing. He looked at the three of them, staring up at him as if this were a perfectly reasonable thing to do. *"No,"* he said with great indignation.

"For God's sake, Hamlin," Glenna complained. "I've said I'll do what I must. What more do you want?"

"What do I *want*? I want to go back to the day I met you, madam, and start all again. I'll no' pretend," he said flatly. "I'll no' lay claim to a version of events that is no' true. I'll no' *pretend* to have reconciled!"

"Your grace," Bain interjected, "might I have a word?"

Hamlin swung a dark gaze to his secretary. Or rather, his former secretary as of this moment. *"What?"*

"Privately, if you please, aye?" He gestured to the other end of the room.

"What is it?" Glenna said, looking at Bain, then at Hamlin. "What secrets are you sharing?"

"Mrs. Graham, you will fare far better if you keep your mouth shut," Perth advised.

Hamlin stalked to the other end of the room. Bain followed along as if they were out for a stroll. When they were out of earshot, Hamlin said, "You've disappointed me, Nichol. I trusted you, and you have bloody well betrayed me."

402

"I understand," he said simply.

Hamlin's rage flared. "Do you, indeed? Then understand this, lad — I've no bloody use for you now."

"I would have been surprised at any other outcome, your grace. However, we have an agreement I will see you through the vote. If I may speak to that?"

The man had so much gall it was a wonder no one had shot him before now. Hamlin gestured impatiently for him to speak.

"You bear a great deal of affection for Miss Mackenzie," he said.

Hamlin's heart lurched in his chest. "Mind yourself," he said low, seething. " 'Tis none of your affair."

"Indeed it is no'," he agreed so bloody calmly. "But it has no' gone unnoticed by others. Will you no' be of better service to her from a position in the Lords?"

Hamlin glared at him. Catriona had nothing to do with the House of Lords, and he didn't care if others had noticed.

As if reading his mind, Bain said, "I am thinking specifically of the abbey at Kishorn."

Hamlin arched a brow above the other. "How in God's name do you know of that?"

"There is talk around Crieff, aye? None of the English or Russians could be trusted

403

to keep the slightest secret. I am given to understand that she is quite passionate about the wards there and I should think, for the span of a few days, you might bear your former wife's presence if only with the eye toward helping Miss Mackenzie in her cause in the future."

Hamlin pointed a finger into Bain's face. "Stay out of it," he said sharply. "And stay away from Miss Mackenzie."

"I've no intention of approaching her, your grace. But I will submit that I think you can be of better use to the abbey and its friends if you are in the House of Lords. You can be of no use to her at all if you are disgraced."

"Disgraced?" He was once again appalled by Bain's audacity.

Bain shrugged. "It does no' give me pleasure to say it, but if you allow the former Mrs. Graham to say what she pleases, you will be disgraced and live on in solitude. Further . . ." He paused, glanced down for a moment. "Further, it is entirely possible that if you fail to follow Lord Perth's advice in this, your affair with Miss Mackenzie could be exposed, aye?"

Hamlin found it outrageous that this man, in such bald-faced manner, would say such a thing. "Do you *threaten* me, Bain?" he

404

asked incredulously.

"No' for a moment. But you must keep in mind that Mrs. Graham has seen her. Eula has seen her many times at Blackthorn Hall. So have others. It would no' take more than a wee bit of gossip and bit of brain to put the pieces together, aye?"

Hamlin was stunned. He seethed with rage and betrayal and worse, the knowledge that what Bain said was entirely possible. But to pretend? "Have you no' gathered by now that I am an honest man, Mr. Bain?" he asked, his rage barely contained.

"Aye, that you are, your grace, beyond compare. No one will fault you for this extraordinary turn of events, as Mrs. Graham is prepared to assign all blame to herself. The men who cast their votes will think you noble, aye? A man who has no' uttered a single ill word about his wife when he had every reason to do so. MacLaren, in particular, will be moved by it. Moreover, no' a word of what I've just said is untrue. You've no' said a public word against her. She is to blame for the failure of your marriage."

"Get out of my sight," Hamlin bit out. "Before I wrap my hands around your bloody throat, aye?"

Bain nodded as if he'd just been wished a

good day, and returned to the others.

Hamlin clenched his fists, took several breaths. This was beyond comprehension — he had to find his bearings, he had to think rationally. But something Bain said kept ringing in his ears. *Live on in solitude.* He'd found happiness. After so many years of longing for it, he had it in his hand, and he was desperately loath to lose it.

He was just as desperate not to expose Catriona to disgrace.

After several moments, he turned and looked at the others.

Perth watched him closely, his eyes narrowed. Glenna was staring at the floor, looking as unmoored as Hamlin felt. And Bain, naturally, stood behind them, his hands clasped at his back, his expression serene. Hamlin could tell them all to go to hell, but Bain was right — if he did that, the world would turn against him. Glenna would make certain of it. And Eula? What of the lass? Anything he did would affect her, as well. He saw no good options for Eula, either, except for the path that Bain had laid out. Pretend to be reconciled until the vote, for the sake of appearances. For the sake of keeping the roof on the house he'd built with Eula and Catriona.

Catriona. What in God's name would he

tell her? Bain was right that he could help her save the abbey if he was in the House of Lords, or at least find some options that would accommodate her wards. It was the most he could do, and yet Hamlin would rather tell her anything but what had happened here tonight. Because he loved Catriona, and he would walk on fire-red coals rather than hurt her. He wanted to be with her, but Glenna had made that impossible.

The servants loved Glenna. Bain was right there, too — Hamlin was a fool if he believed only Bain suspected. Someone would say just enough to expose his affair with Catriona, and Glenna would not hesitate to use that knowledge to extort something from him.

With his fists clenched, Hamlin approached the other end of the room. "I've two demands," he said flatly.

"Aye?" Perth asked.

"Eula Guinne remains with me." He looked at Glenna.

Glenna snorted. "Is *that* all? Aye, of course. I've no place for her."

"The other demand?" Perth asked.

"As soon as I depart for Edinburgh for the vote, she must leave," he said, nodding at Glenna.

"With pleasure," Glenna said. She stood up. "Is there anything to eat, then? I've a wretched headache." She walked out of the library as if she still lived here, as if she were still duchess.

Hamlin's stomach turned. He thought of Eula, of how the lass would take the news. He thought of Catriona. *Catriona, Catriona* . . .

He'd known from the beginning that theirs was a love story that was not meant to be. But he hadn't imagined it to be so bloody painful in the end.

CHAPTER TWENTY-FOUR

Word traveled quickly — Lady Montrose had returned, and everyone, down to the lad who fed the pigs, was jubilant. "She's a true lady, that she is," the lad said to Catriona when she walked down to the stables the following afternoon for a mount. She happened to overhear a groom and the lad speaking about it. The groom had been the one to drive the coach she and Uncle Knox had left Blackthorn Hall in that night, and, naturally, had seen the commotion of the returning duchess.

"Have I interrupted?" she asked curtly when neither young man noticed her.

"No' at all, madam," the lad said. "Have you heard, then, that the Lady Montrose has returned?"

Oh, aye. She'd heard.

In the days that followed, it didn't seem to matter that Hamlin's former wife confessed, to anyone who would listen, that she

409

had left of her own accord, that she'd needed time to think and that her husband, her dear husband, the duke, had been gracious during that uncomfortable time. Catriona heard nothing but happy curiosity that she'd returned, unharmed.

Mrs. MacLaren told Catriona the entire tale through breathless gulps of tea one afternoon. She and her husband had called with the news, unaware that Catriona and her uncle already knew that the world had collapsed. "You were right all along, Miss Mackenzie — the duke would no' have harmed a single hair on his bonny wife's head. How *dreadful* that anyone believed it of him!"

Funny she was so quick to say so now.

"It's most extraordinary, really. You canna imagine my great surprise when the duchess walked into the public room at the inn. She was in the company of my dearest friend, Mrs. MacGill, she was, and the two of them talking as if she'd no' been gone this long year! The duchess greeted me warmly and asked after my husband, and my sister, who passed months ago, and said she was so verra sorry she'd no' been at Blackthorn Hall to offer proper condolences. She seemed to want to say more, did she no', darling?" she said, directing this question to her husband. "Naturally, we invited her to join us."

"Naturally, she was delighted to do so, aye?" Catriona drawled.

"Indeed she was! Now, then, you are no' acquainted with Mrs. MacGill, but she is no' the sort of woman to let questions go unasked —"

"She's a busybody, she is," Mr. MacLaren interjected. "Sticks her nose in all the places it doesna belong."

"Mrs. MacGill inquired, without the slightest hesitation, where the duchess had *been* all this time, and, Miss Mackenzie, you'd no' believe the tale."

"She might," Uncle Knox said, although the MacLarens didn't seem to hear him.

"She was verra frank, really, and said that it was all her doing. She accepted the duke's offer of marriage when she was so verra young, as we *all* do." She paused there, realizing what she said, blinking like a lamb. "I didna mean —"

"I didna take offense," Catriona said, perhaps a wee bit curtly.

"She was young, and she didna think of it *properly*. She didna consider all that marriage was, really, and —"

"And Mrs. MacGill interjected, quite rudely, if you ask me, 'What was there to

411

think about then? You were a duchess,' "
Mr. MacLaren said, mimicking a woman's
voice.

"Aye, she did," Mrs. MacLaren said,
shooting a look at her husband. " 'Twas a
fair question, was it no'? No matter, the
duchess said — and this I understand quite
utterly — that she couldna help wonder if
perhaps she'd missed something in agreeing
to marriage at such a young age."

"What do you mean, you utterly understand it?" Mr. MacLaren blustered.

Mrs. MacLaren waved an impatient hand
at him. "She said that while she and the
duke were perfectly compatible, theirs was
no' a love match, and she wondered if she'd
no' missed her opportunity for love, do you
see?"

"I donna see at all," Mr. MacLaren said,
clearly annoyed with the reasoning.

"It's evident, is it no'? The dukes and
whatno', they rarely marry for *love*. They
marry for connections, they do. And a
dukedom is so important for future heirs.
He couldna marry just anyone, could he?
He had to marry a woman with important
social connections, which, of course, the
Guinnes had until their unfortunate death
in the fire."

Catriona blanched. She set aside her tea,

feeling queasy.

"That was her reasoning?" Uncle Knox asked, clearly perturbed. "She determined she'd not married for love, and that she must try again?"

"She expressed her misgivings to her husband, and though he didna care for her decision to separate and live freely, he nevertheless honored his vows to her. Naturally, she soon realized what she'd left behind and, in her own words, came crawling back to Blackthorn Hall to beg for his forgiveness."

Bloody snake came slinking back, that's what.

"This is the point, then," Mr. MacLaren said. "MacGill, that old harridan, bluntly inquired what the lady supposed her husband would do, now that she'd come crawling back."

"Mrs. MacGill didna inquire so bluntly," his wife chastised him. "But the duchess was contrite in her response, the poor dear."

The poor dear! Catriona bit down on her tongue to keep from saying her thoughts aloud.

"She said she didna know what would happen, if he'd even allow her to stay or turn her out after what she'd done, but that she would strive each and every day to earn

413

his forgiveness. If you ask me, the duchess is to be commended for taking responsibility for her bad behavior, is she no'? We all make mistakes, aye? Marriage can be verra hard."

"What? It's no' been the least bit hard for me," MacLaren said, to which his wife rolled her eyes at Catriona.

"If you ask *me,* the one to be commended here is no' Lady Montrose, but the duke," Mr. MacLaren continued. "I've new respect for him, I do. He's weathered the terrible things said about him with his head held high, that he has. A finer man you'd no' meet."

"You believed he had something to do with her disappearance, or have you forgotten?" Uncle Knox challenged his friend.

"Pardon?" MacLaren said, startled. "Did I? Well, he's proven me quite wrong, has he no'? I told Caithness just yesterday that a finer man he'd no' find for the seat in the Lords and to cast his vote in favor. No' a moment's hesitation did I give it."

"This has all the markings of a grand love story," Mrs. MacLaren said. "But I rather think you suspected it all along, did you no', Miss Mackenzie?"

"Me?"

"You never believed him capable of mur-

414

der," Mrs. MacLaren reminded her.

"No, but I . . . I didna think this," she said with a flick of her wrist. How she wished the MacLarens would take their leave. How she wished they would disappear with all their glowing praise of the Duke and Duchess of Montrose. She wasn't a duchess any longer! How was it that a woman could leave her husband for another man, demand a divorce, extort money and still be treated like a triumphant warrior returning home? It was too much to be borne.

"*No* one could imagine that, I daresay," Mrs. MacLaren agreed. "But here they are, properly reunited, and I am confident they will find their way to one another! Would it no' be the most blessed event if an heir was to arrive as a result of their reunion?" This, Mrs. MacLaren asked, with the excitement of a child at Christmas.

"I do agree London will be beneficial for them both," her husband said. "A bonny place to patch up their differences, aye?"

"Well, surely everyone hopes it will be so. You'd no' believe how many are calling at Blackthorn Hall. Why, we passed two carriages turning onto the drive, did we no', darling?"

"We did indeed."

Catriona's face felt hot. *She* felt hot. She resisted the urge to tug at her bodice. She hadn't spoken to Hamlin, not since that awful night. At least she understood why, thanks to the MacLarens — he could not extract himself from the debacle. She understood what he was up against, how important appearances were to him right now.

"I suppose we ought to call, Cat, would you agree?" Uncle Knox asked.

The question startled her.

"To wish the couple well before we take our leave of Dungotty," he added.

"Take your leave!" Mrs. MacLaren cried. "But you canna go!"

"Aye, we must," Uncle Knox said, and rose from his chair, putting an end to this interminable tea. "Cat desires to return to Balhaire, and I to England before the autumn sets in." He held out his hand to Mrs. MacLaren, which forced her to put down her teacup and rise. "You'd not imagine what all must be done to prepare for our departure, but thank you, both of you, for bringing us the extraordinary news. We will pay our call to Blackthorn Hall."

"But . . . we'll see you 'ere you leave, will we no'?" Mr. MacLaren asked as Uncle Knox ushered them to the door, which Rumpel had conveniently opened.

416

"Of course," Uncle Knox said, and stepped out into the hall with them.

When they had gone, Uncle Knox returned to the salon and walked to Catriona, his arms open, and took her into his embrace. "Don't despair, darling."

"No," she said simply. She had gone well past the point of despair into complete numbness. She asked to be excused from supper and went to bed with a cloth on her head. But there was no remedy for her. What hurt in her was incurable.

The next morning, Uncle Knox took the carriage to Stirling for some business. "Come with me," he urged her.

Catriona shook her head. She hadn't even dressed her hair, finding the task of it too much to contemplate. "You were quite right, uncle — there is too much to be done here."

He sighed with resignation and kissed her forehead. "I'll be gone all day."

"I'll be all right," she said again, and pointed to the bolts of cloth she and Uncle Knox had bought in Crieff. The cloth was for the ladies at Kishorn Abbey. Catriona also had a few patterns she'd bargained from Mrs. Fraser. "I've so much to pack."

There was indeed more than enough work

to keep her occupied, but when Uncle Knox departed, Catriona left the packing to Rumpel. She was restless and felt incapable of the slightest productive thought — every bit of her head and heart had been taken up by Hamlin.

When she couldn't bear all the aimless wandering around Dungotty, she called for a horse to be saddled. Riding was what cleared her head and helped her think. She wanted to go to the ruins one last time. She guessed seeing it would make the weight on her chest feel that much heavier, make her breath feel that much shorter, but Catriona needed to pour the salt on her wound. She needed to feel the sharp, bitter edges of it.

It took nearly an hour to reach the ruins. She tethered her horse and walked in through one of the archways in the wall and into the center and gazed up at the yew tree. How odd that the summer should begin in a ruin and end in one. It seemed terribly prophetic that all she held dear — Kishorn, her aunt's memory, Hamlin — should end in *ruins*.

She shook her head, folded her arms over her middle and squatted down, staving off a swell of nausea. Her despair was so deep she felt as if she might faint.

"Catriona."

Her first thought was that she was hearing things. But then she heard the footfall, and when she glanced up, Hamlin was leaning over her, helping her up.

His expression was thunderous, but not with anger — with desire. They reached for each other at the same moment, and then she was in his arms, and he had lifted her off her feet and was kissing her.

"Are you here alone? How did you know?" she demanded breathlessly.

"Aye, of course I'm alone. I didna know. But I've come every afternoon, hoping."

Catriona caressed his cheek, his hair. "But I thought . . . I assumed —"

"My God, how I've missed you," he said, and kissed her hard, with what felt like passion and remorse all balled into one. He kissed her in a way he'd never really kissed her before, as if he thought he'd never see her again.

Catriona pushed hard against his chest. "You shouldna be here. If you are discovered —"

"What if I am?" he said curtly. "I donna care, Catriona. Let the whole world know what I feel for you."

Her heart leapt painfully. "Donna say that!" she pleaded with him, but he'd moved her so that her back was against the trunk

419

of the yew tree. He pinned her there, his gaze greedily feasting on her body and arousing her with the fiery, lustful look in his eye.

"It's over, Hamlin," she said. She could scarcely breathe, she was so ignited. "We must face the truth —"

"Donna tell me what I must face," he said, and dipped his head to kiss her bosom, biting the swell of her breast. His breath was hot on her skin, and an inferno flared in her veins. "Nothing is over, Catriona. *Nothing.*"

He grabbed her wrists in one hand and pinned her arms overhead against the tree. He was pressed against her, and Catriona could feel all of him, every hard plane, every muscle, his rock-hard erection. His hand and his mouth were everywhere on her, making her heart race, her blood leap, her groin somersault. She closed her eyes and tried to drag air into her lungs again.

He pressed his erection against her as he nibbled her ear, then began to fumble for his trousers. She gathered her petticoat and yanked it up, then undid the trews she wore to ride and felt them slide down her legs to her ankles.

The mad rush to be with each other was intoxicating, an explosion of color in her thoughts, of fire in her body. Hamlin slipped his hand between her legs, slid his fingers inside her, and she gasped loudly with pleasure. She closed her eyes, leaned her head against the tree as he moved his fingers inside her. "I am lost," she said. "I donna want to prolong the agony of you, but I canna stop."

He pressed against her and cupped her chin to kiss her again. But his kiss was abruptly tender and sweet, and the inferno of desire in her disintegrated into primal thirst.

Everything in her surrendered to him. Her blood stirred violently as he pulled her hair free of its pins, then claimed a breast with his hand and mouth. She gave in completely to the stroke of his fingers, and then his body, moving fluidly, rocking her toward the moment of oblivion.

She'd abandoned every rational thought to wild passion, allowed herself to be swept away beneath the boughs of that yew tree until the need for release was clawing at her throat and her chest.

The conflagration was so intense that she cried out and choked at once, her voice garbled. Her body was shimmering as she tangled her fingers in his hair and burned with pleasure everywhere he touched her until he'd found his own release.

They collapsed onto the ground, exhausted, Catriona on top of Hamlin.

Hamlin's hair had come undone from its queue. He leaned against the trunk of the yew, his eyes closed, his arms tightly around her. Catriona pressed her cheek against his chest. "I'll no' keep her," he said, his voice rumbling deep in his chest. "You know that, do you no'?"

Catriona swallowed. "Aye, but you must for now."

Hamlin sat up, took her by the shoulders. "I love you, Catriona. Do you know that I do? Can you feel it? I *love* you."

His declaration, so desired by her, sounded almost desperate. "And I love you, Hamlin." Tears were beginning to cloud her vision. "I canna convey how much I do." She stroked his hair back from his face. "But this was never going to be, was it? Did we no' know it all along? Is that no' why we never spoke of it?"

"I knew no such thing," he tried.

"Aye, you did," she said. "You were always bound for London. And I was always to return to Balhaire and Kishorn Abbey. We lived each day as if it were our last because we both knew an end would come —"

"For God's sake, I am a bloody duke, I can do as I please."

She touched her fingers to his lips, then kissed the corner of his mouth. "None of us can do as we please, Hamlin."

He abruptly let her go and scrambled to his feet. He walked to one of the holes in the crumbling wall. He stood there, one arm braced against what was left of the wall, and stared out at the lush, green valley below. Catriona followed him. She put her arms around his waist and pressed her cheek to his back. "Promise me one thing — promise me you'll no' forget me."

"For the love of God, Catriona, I could never forget you. I could never forget you, for if I did, you might verra well forget me." He twisted around and wrapped her in his arms, holding her tightly against him. "I've never loved anyone as I have loved you. I've never known such happiness in my life, aye?"

She closed her eyes, squeezing back the tears. "Neither have I," she whispered. "With all my heart."

He slipped his fingers under her face and made her look up at him. "When do you leave?"

"In two days."

"The day before I leave for Edinburra and the vote, then. Will you come and see Eula before you go?"

Catriona didn't know if she could bear the thought of stepping into Blackthorn Hall again, but she had only to think of that lass. She nodded. "What will you do once the vote is taken?" she asked quietly.

He shook his head as his gaze moved over her face. "She is no' my wife. She will no' live as my wife."

That should have soothed Catriona, but it didn't. It made her sadder. "I do love you," she said, her voice shaking. "You've shown me the best days of my life."

"And you leave me bewitched," he said hoarsely. "My love for you will never end, Catriona. Never."

She thought that would be the hardest thing of all — it would be agony knowing there was a man in the world who loved her, the one man she could not have.

CHAPTER TWENTY-FIVE

For Hamlin, the next day was filled with the sheer agony of a broken heart and the necessity of having to receive callers as the vote for the House of Lords neared. It was torture to stand in a room while Glenna pretended to be contrite and so very sorry for her bad behavior, when all he could think of was Catriona, and those moments under the yew tree. She'd been so beautiful, with her hair wild about her, her eyes shining with such pleasure.

He had to appear as if he was a measured man, which, weeks ago, he might have been. But he was so filled with resentment it was hard for him to be anything other than distant. He despised Glenna with all of his being and couldn't wait for the moment he could remove her from his sight permanently.

Glenna, however, was bold, and without any apparent remorse. She'd brazenly commissioned three new gowns, knowing Hamlin would not utter a word before the vote was taken. She cared nothing for Eula, and while she tolerated the child's presence, she otherwise hardly seemed to notice her at all. Eula, Hamlin noted, had not touched her painting in a week. She kept to her rooms and her kittens and Miss Burns. Hamlin didn't pretend to fathom how deeply this strange turn of events might have influenced the lass, but the blame for her melancholy belonged to Glenna. That, he was certain.

Two days before Hamlin was to leave for the vote in Edinburgh, Glenna sought him out in his study and announced very matter-of-factly that she would accompany him to London after the vote.

Hamlin lifted his head from his correspondence. "I beg your pardon?"

Before she could answer, Stuart appeared. "Your grace, His Lordship the Earl of Norwood and his niece calling."

Thank God. Hamlin rose from his seat. "Show them into the salon, aye?" He walked around his desk. "You'll no' accompany me to London, Glenna. You will be long gone from Blackthorn Hall by then."

"But I've no' been to London."

Was she mad? He couldn't possibly care

426

where she'd been or hadn't been. "I donna care."

"Why are you rushing off? Who is this Norwood?"

He ignored her as he strode across the room.

"Is it the woman you were dining with when I returned?" she demanded. "Is that what makes you run like a wee lad?"

He paused. He glanced back at her. "I would advise you to send for tea and calm yourself, madam."

"But I'm talking to you!" she said angrily. "Whoever it is may wait."

"We've nothing to talk about," Hamlin reminded her. He resumed his walk to the door.

"You're a fool, Hamlin. I'm with child!"

Those words halted him mid-stride. He whipped around and glared at her. Who *was* this woman? She was not the woman he'd married — surely he would have noticed her utter lack of compassion or character.

Glenna was suddenly tearful. "I didna want to tell you this way, but you left me no choice. You'd no' *listen*."

"It would seem that you should hasten back to *Charlie* posthaste, aye? How fortunate that your carriage will carry you to wherever you will go in two days' time."

"But that's just it, Hamlin. Charlie is gone," she said, her bottom lip trembling.

Hamlin couldn't believe what he was hearing. She thought she would find sympathy in *him*? He shook his head incredulously. "That is your trouble, Glenna. No' mine." He turned and walked out of the study, striding down the hallway to Catriona.

"It's *your* trouble, too, Hamlin!" Glenna shrieked from somewhere behind him.

He paid her no heed. He walked on, turning into the salon, and feeling the smile on his face at once when he saw Catriona squatting beside Eula, Norwood standing near the window. "Good afternoon," he said.

"Your grace." Norwood bowed.

Catriona rose to her feet and curtsied. "How do you do, your grace?" she said, and her smile, that bloody bonny smile, illuminated the room.

"You'll no' ignore me!"

Hamlin whipped around, startled by Glenna's sudden appearance. Tears were streaming down her face. "Madam, go to your rooms," he said sternly.

"I'll no' go! I'll no' allow you to treat me so ill, Hamlin! What am I to do? Are you truly so heartless as to toss me aside when I carry a bairn?"

Catriona gasped at the same moment Eula

cried out, *"No!"*

"Good Lord," Norwood muttered.

"For all that is holy, go," Hamlin said again.

But Glenna was a stubborn wench, and she didn't move as much as a muscle. "I'll no' allow you to treat me ill."

"I beg your pardon, your grace," Catriona said. He glanced at her over his shoulder. "May I take Miss Guinne from the room?" She was holding Eula's hand, and Eula, the poor lass, was staring with horror at Glenna, her eyes full of unshed tears.

"Please," he said.

She put her arm around Eula and walked calmly to the door. She stepped out into the hall with the lass, bent down and whispered something to her, gave her a hug and then sent her on.

"We'll call again," Norwood said. He was almost to the door.

"Please, my lord," Hamlin said, holding up a hand. "Please stay."

"I don't think —"

"Aye, stay," Glenna said angrily. "I should have witness to his cruelty! I've nowhere to go, and he knows it. No one will take me, no' with a child in my belly! No one will let me a room, and everyone will whisper! But if I stay with *you,* they will think it is *your* child. I've no family but *you,* Hamlin."

"I am no' your family!" he roared at her. "You made certain of it!"

"If I may?" Catriona asked, her voice high. She was nervous, Hamlin realized. Little wonder — Glenna looked like a madwoman.

"Catriona, donna trouble yourself," Hamlin said.

"Catriona!" Glenna said. "Are you so familiar as to call this woman by her given name?"

"I beg your pardon, Mrs. Graham," Norwood said. "But that does not seem the most prudent battle you ought to engage in at present."

"I know a place for her," Catriona blurted. "I know where she might go."

Hamlin stared at her. What was she talking about? "No," he said. "This is a private matter, and you'll no' concern yourself —"

"Kishorn Abbey," she interrupted him.

"Ha! A nunnery," Glenna said petulantly.

" 'Tis no' a nunnery," Catriona said. Her voice was shaking, as if she found it difficult to speak. "It's a place where women such as yourself are welcomed and cared for. A place you might seek comfort, aye?"

"I donna need your comfort. I've never heard of this abbey and I'll no' go."

"And what, precisely, is your alternative?"

Uncle Knox asked.

Glenna opened her mouth as if she had an answer, but Glenna had no answers. She looked at Hamlin, as if she expected him to save her.

Hamlin would not save her. He walked to where she was standing. He took her hand and held it in both of his. "Make no mistake, Glenna — I will forego a seat in the Lords without a bloody thought, aye? I will give up all of Blackthorn Hall if it comes to that. You canna threaten me and I will no' take responsibility for your love child. You've been offered a place to go where you will be cared for. You can accept the kindness offered to you, or you can make your threats and suffer the consequences. You will leave Blackthorn Hall one way or another, but how you go is your choice." He let go of her hand.

Glenna's bottom lip began to tremble. She suddenly buried her face in her hands and sobbed.

Hamlin sighed and helped her to a settee. He turned to Catriona. "Thank you. You donna have to do this."

"All right, I'll go," Glenna said tearfully. "I'd walk to the ends of the earth to be away from here. And *you,*" she said, glaring at Hamlin. "How do I arrive at this . . . abbey?"

431

Catriona's face was pale. "I leave on the morrow. You may accompany me if you like."

"*You?*" Glenna began to sob again, bending over her lap. "I've been abandoned, and now I will be cast out for the sin of following my heart!"

Catriona turned away from Glenna, to her uncle. "Shall we go, then?" she asked softly.

Norwood nodded. Hamlin moved to escort them out, but Glenna said, "Hamlin? Are you truly so uncaring?"

Glenna's capacity for self-pity was astounding. "I cared for far too long, Glenna. You should thank the Lord I've no' delivered you to the streets of Edinburra with your love child as your lover has done, aye?" He turned his back to her and walked Catriona and Norwood out.

In the foyer, Norwood was collecting his hat and gloves while Catriona stood quietly by. She looked shocked. There was no hint of her effervescent smile, but instead, an expression of great sorrow.

Hamlin hated that look. He hated more that he was responsible for her sorrow. "Catriona," he said softly. "You need no' do this, no' for me."

"It is done," she said wearily.

"It is done," Norwood agreed. "And

432

really, what choice do you or your former wife have in the matter? Be grateful to my niece for her incomparable generosity and know that you will never know a better person." Norwood didn't wait for a reply but stalked out the front door.

"I know," Hamlin said. "God pity me, how I know." His throat burned, his eyes burned. "You've done this for me, Catriona, but you've done too much."

She shook her head. A tear slid from the corner of her eye, and she swiped at it. "I've only done what Zelda did for many other women. Your . . . Mrs. Graham has no place to go." She shifted her gaze to the open door, to the figure of her uncle on the drive, waiting for her.

"I will spend my life making it up to you in earnest, aye?"

"I donna ask you for anything, Hamlin."

"My God, Catriona . . ." He took her hand. "Look at me. Please. What will I do when you are far away from me?"

Her eyes filled with tears. "What will *I* do? I should go. My uncle is waiting."

He couldn't let her go like this. He pulled her into his body and kissed her. She sagged against him for a moment, as if the weight of her disappointment was too much to bear. But in the next moment, she was gone.

Disappeared. A morning vapor lifting with the sun and vanishing from his sight.

He would never forget what she'd just done for him. She'd shown him the happiness he'd craved, and now she'd just saved him from a brewing scandal. And for that, he was handing her his former wife with a bastard child growing in her belly.

He would never forgive himself for having done this to her.

He would forever be in her debt.

But he would not accept her help blindly and without consequence. She deserved better. She deserved everything. Hamlin didn't know how in that moment, but he was determined that she would not regret him.

He was determined that she would not forget him.

CHAPTER TWENTY-SIX

On the long trip to Balhaire, Catriona found herself wondering more than once what possibly had kept Hamlin from killing his former wife. Personally, she imagined it every day in a variety of ways and had settled on a push off the cliff over the cove at Balhaire as her favorite fantasy, only because she could imagine Glenna's fine silk gown billowing out around her like wings that would not save her.

It was easier to think about that than her broken heart, and fortunately for her, Glenna Guinne Graham was quite possibly the most miserable person Catriona had ever met in her life.

It was easy to despise Glenna for what she'd done to ruin the last few days with Hamlin. It was even easier when Glenna complained about every single thing. The carriage was not to her liking. The inns where they stayed were not suitable. The food was despicable. She couldn't understand how anyone could travel without a maid. She refused to help with the slightest task and could not be counted on to carry even her portmanteau. When Catriona informed her that she'd have to share in the work at the abbey, Glenna had laughed gaily and said, "That's absurd."

Moreover, the long hours spent in the coach together led to a lot of questions. Glenna was curious about the abbey, and after coaxing Catriona to tell her the story of how it came to be, and the women who lived there now, she scoffed at it, declared it untoward and passed judgment on the women who, like her, had found themselves in a predicament.

"They are no' unlike you," Catriona pointed out, her rage scarcely contained.

"Like me!" Glenna had said, alarmed. "I am a *duchess,*" she said, as if that somehow gave her license to infidelity and bastard children. "*I've* been cast out."

Catriona debated whether she ought to point out that she was no' a duchess any longer and instead opted to ask a question that was burning in her. "Were you cast out, then?" she asked skeptically.

Glenna shot her a look. "I donna know what you call it in the Highlands, but, aye,

I've been cast out."

"Did you no' cast yourself out?" Catriona pressed.

"You donna know what I endured!" Glenna cried, and launched into a tirade of how she and Hamlin lacked compatibility, which, when she had exhausted herself and her reasoning, boiled down to the fact that Hamlin was too quiet and too fond of books or some such nonsense.

But Charlie, well, there was a man for the ages. He was a fine physical specimen, Glenna noted with a wink for Catriona and a secret little smile that, if nothing else, kept her silent for several minutes as she looked out the window. "We were *quite* compatible," she said, and her cheeks colored.

Diah, it was enough to make a woman ill.

Catriona never said much as Glenna ranted and spoke at length about her lover, her life and her many expectations. But on the last day of their journey, Glenna woke up in an irritable mood, and instead of talking as she did most days, she spent a good amount of time glaring at Catriona.

At last, Catriona could bear it no more. "What?" she demanded. "Why do you stare at me in that way, then?"

"You love him."

"Pardon?"

437

"You love my husband," Glenna said.

Catriona sighed. She folded her arms across her middle. "I canna love your husband, madam, because you donna *have* a husband."

"Aye, all right, he's no longer my husband, but I was married to him for eight interminable years, and you *love* him."

Catriona said nothing.

Glenna suddenly smiled. "He'll no' marry you, if that's what you think. You'll no' be a duchess."

Catriona laughed. "I never thought I would."

"Did you no', perhaps just a wee bit, then? Well, he could never marry you, no' with this abbey business, and him in the House of Lords. It would ruin him in Parliament, aye? Peers are no' to associate with the wrong sorts of persons, are they."

"I'm the wrong sort of person, am I?" Catriona scoffed.

"You're a Highlander!" Glenna said, as if that was akin to a leper. "The English believe Highlanders to be wild animals." She shrugged.

Catriona smiled sardonically. "If you think to upset me, you'll be sorely disappointed. There is naught you can say to me that's no' been said, or whispered, or implied."

Glenna looked surprised. "I didna mean to offend, Catriona, but to warn you."

Her words of "warning" were quite offensive.

One late afternoon, they could finally see the tops of the towers at Balhaire rising up above the tree line. Catriona's heart swelled with affection — she was happy to be home. She couldn't wait to be in the great hall with her family and their dogs. Her heart had been wrenched in half, but if there was one place on this earth that could repair it, it was Balhaire. As they turned onto the road that would take them up the hill, Glenna wrinkled her nose. "It's ghastly! It's positively medieval. Are there knights inside? Will they pour burning oil on us from the battlements as we cross the bridge?" She shuddered. "I donna know how people live in such heaps of stone."

Catriona turned her attention from her home to Glenna. "*Mi Diah,* why are you so bloody horrid?"

"Horrid!" Glenna exclaimed. "I donna think I'm horrid. I'm *honest.* Frankly, I wish there were more like me."

"Well, I am verra thankful there are no' more like you," Catriona said.

As soon as the carriage rolled to a halt, she flung open the door and leapt out before any groom could arrive, and began striding for the entrance to the main keep.

Frang, their longtime butler, was at the door and greeted her, "*Fàilte,* Miss Catriona!"

"Thank you, Frang," she said impatiently, and slipped past him with a squeeze to his arm, then ran to the great hall.

It was empty, the hearth cold. She whirled about, almost colliding with Frang. "Where are they, then? Where is my family?"

"In your father's study."

She ran down the narrow corridor, spilling into her father's study so suddenly that her mother cried out in alarm. "Cat, darling!" She threw her arms around her daughter.

Catriona buried her face in her mother's shoulder. She heard the clump of her father's cane, and the heavy drag of his bad leg. A moment later, she felt his arms around her, too. "We are so grateful to have you home, lass," he said.

"I'm so grateful to be home," she said, her voice shaking with emotion. "I've never been so happy to be at Balhaire."

"Darling," her mother said, and cupped Catriona's face, forcing her to look at her. "What's wrong?"

Catriona shook her head. *Everything.*

440

Everything about my life is wrong. "It's been a hard journey, aye?"

"I beg your pardon, is there no one to greet me?"

Catriona closed her eyes with a groan. Glenna had followed her to the study and walked inside, looking around her. "No' a servant or anyone to see after me?" she said accusingly.

Catriona's parents gaped at Glenna.

Glenna didn't seem to notice. She clucked her tongue at Catriona. "How rude of you no' to make a proper introduction, Catriona. I'm Lady Montrose."

"You are the former Lady Montrose," Catriona said wearily.

"Why do *you* look so bereaved?" Glenna asked. "I'm the one who's suffered. Will no one offer me a glass of water? Or to sit? My back is aching after that wretched ride."

Catriona's parents turned their confused gazes to her.

Catriona wanted to explain. But as Glenna made her way to the settee and sat, Catriona found herself incapable of speech. Tears welled in her eyes, and she swallowed hard, trying to keep them at bay. She said, "It's been a *verra* long journey."

Catriona's mother was a masterful hostess.

She saw immediately that Catriona was distressed and took matters into her hands. She escorted Glenna to a guest room and sent a meal up to her. She was also provided a companion with whom she could speak freely and for as long as she liked — the maid Fiona Garrison, a lass who was near to deaf and was content to work on her embroidery as Glenna nattered on with her complaints.

For Catriona, her mother had a bath drawn. When Catriona had bathed, and her hair had been put up, and she'd dressed in a clean gown, she came down to the great hall, where her family was waiting for her, all of them eager to greet her and hear her news. It was the salve she needed — she felt loved.

Her brother Cailean and his wife, Daisy, were at Balhaire, and Cailean hugged her tightly to him. "I'm glad to see you home, where you belong, aye?" he said.

Catriona didn't know if she belonged here or not. She didn't know where she belonged.

Her brothers Aulay and Rabbie teased her about the amount of sun she'd had this summer, theorizing she'd spent more time racing about on horseback than anything else. Her nieces and nephews were there, too, all eager to know if Uncle Knox had

sent them anything. Of course he had —
they all received a crown.

Vivienne was very relieved to see her.
"You'd no' believe all that you've missed,"
her sister confided as some of the clan
members began to filter into the great hall.
"There has been quite the scandal in my
husband's family —"

Catriona didn't hear what the scandal
might have been because one of the clans-
men grabbed her up and whirled her around
in a big bear hug. "Aye, we've missed you,
lass, that we have," he said, grinning from
ear to ear.

More people came to greet her, and soon
the ale was flowing freely, and the smell of
roast pork made her stomach growl.

Over supper, Catriona filled her family in
as best she could about what had happened
with the Lord Advocate, which, she quickly
learned, they already knew, as Uncle Knox
had sent a letter ahead of her to her father.

Catriona couldn't help but wonder what
else Uncle Knox had told them. But if they
knew about Hamlin, none of them said a
word, and for that, Catriona was very thankful. She wasn't ready to speak about him.
She *couldn't* speak about him, not without
the risk of falling to pieces. Eventually, when
the time was right, she would tell her

mother and sister. But tonight, the only thing that mattered was being with her family again, feeling safe and loved and cherished.

Even Glenna couldn't ruin Catriona's homecoming. She appeared in the great hall before the meal was served, complaining that no one had told her to come down. She was miffed that she was not invited to dine on the dais with the family, and instead was made to sit with her deaf companion. Lottie, Aulay's wife, took pity on her and sat with her for a time. But even Lottie, who had the tolerance of Job, returned to the dais, her eyes wide. "She's *wretched*," she said, her voice full of wonder.

"Donna fear," Catriona said. "She's to the abbey at morning's first light."

Lottie lifted her tankard and tapped Catriona's. "Thank the saints for that."

With a good night's sleep in her own bed, Catriona's mood was improved the next morning. Particularly when she walked into Glenna's room at first light and threw the drapes open on her window.

Glenna howled at the intrusion.

"Come on, then," Catriona said. "We're a boat ride away from your final resting place."

"My *what*?" Glenna exclaimed.

Catriona smiled sweetly. "I mean, Kishorn Abbey."

"Good," Glenna said petulantly. "I donna like it here in this drafty castle with its musty smells and strange sounds at night." She stretched her arms high overhead. "Will someone bring breakfast, then?"

Catriona rolled her eyes and walked out to prepare for the boat trip to Kishorn Abbey.

When Glenna first laid eyes on the abbey, she looked distraught. She stared, slack-jawed, at the decrepit buildings, as if she couldn't comprehend it.

Catriona gleefully ran up the ancient steps to the abbey. Rhona MacFarlane was the first to reach her and greeted her with a hug. "How happy we are you've come home!" she exclaimed. "Come, see the others."

"Aye, I will," Catriona said. "But, first, may I introduce Glenna Guinne Graham," she said, and gestured for Glenna to join them, which she did, complaining about the danger of falling as she picked her way up the steps. "Glenna has come to the abbey to stay," Catriona said.

"*Fàilte!*" Rhona said, and opened her arms to Glenna.

Glenna stared at her as if she were covered with muck.

Rhona lowered her arms.

"Glenna is with child," Catriona said.

"I beg your pardon!" Glenna protested.

"And she's no place to go. So she has come here, seeking a roof over her head. Is that no' right, Glenna?" she asked, and looked pointedly at her charge.

Glenna sighed. "Aye, it is."

"You are most welcome here, aye?" Rhona said, and put her arm around Glenna, ignoring how Glenna tried to pull free. "I've a perfect room for you, with a view of the loch."

They walked through the ruins, through a flock of chickens running about, past the milk cows meandering into the old narthex, and past women and their children at work. One by one the women stopped what they were doing and nodded at Glenna, called out a greeting to Catriona.

Glenna kept her gaze on the path before her, looking, oddly, a wee bit frightened.

The room Rhona showed them to was plain, but had a small bed, a bureau with a basin and a window that overlooked the loch.

"This is to be my room?" Glenna asked,

looking around. "It's small. Is there nothing larger?"

"Nothing larger. It's a safe place for you, Glenna," Catriona reminded her.

Glenna walked to the bed and sat. And then she lay down, rolled onto her side and put her back to Catriona and Rhona. Catriona almost chastised Glenna for being so rude, but Rhona shook her head and drew her out of the room.

"I beg your pardon, Rhona," Catriona said. "She's a wee brat."

"Donna fret, Miss Catriona. She's no' the first of us to be unhappy with the place her life has led her. Come now, we'll have some tea. I have news!"

"Aye," Catriona said. "So do I."

They went to the common room, where several women joined them, one of them brewing tea, another cutting cake. They took seats around a rough-hewn table that Rabbie had made for them.

"I'm afraid I've bad news," Catriona said, wincing as she looked around at their hopeful faces. "My uncle Knox, the Earl of Norwood, gained us an audience with the Lord Advocate."

"Oh, aye," Rhona said with a wave of her hand. "That, we know."

"You know? How?"

447

"Lady Mackenzie came to Kishorn to tell us, she did."

Catriona looked around at their faces. They did not seem to be bothered by her news, not one of them. "So you know that we might have a wee bit of time, but likely will no' be able to keep the abbey, then?" she asked, to make sure they understood.

The women nodded.

"But . . . but do you understand what it means?" she pressed.

"Aye," Rhona said cheerfully. At Catriona's disconcerted look, Rhona reached across the table and squeezed her hand. "We've a plan, Miss Mackenzie, a fine one, aye?"

"A plan? What plan?"

"We're to be weavers!" blurted one of the women who was heavy with child.

Catriona was confused. *Weavers?*

"It's true!" Rhona said gleefully. "Did no one tell you, then? It was Mrs. Aulay's idea, it was. She told us that her father once determined their clan would produce flax linen, but though he purchased the looms, he had no flax. It didna go as planned, the poor lad."

Catriona had heard quite a lot about Lottie's late father and was not surprised that he had struck out to make flax linen

448

without flax. "I don't understand."

"That tale gave her the idea, and when she considered how many sheep were wandering about, and how much wool was being shorn at Balhaire, she wondered, why no' spin it and weave it, then? Why no' make the woolen cloth instead of sending it off? Lottie Mackenzie is a clever lass, she is."

Catriona shook her head. "But how? We know nothing of weaving."

"We donna know it, no. But it happens that the MacGregors do a wee bit of weaving, they do, and Captain Mackenzie, well, he had a chat with them, and it seems as it's no' so difficult, no' when one has the wheels and looms, and Mr. Rabbie Mackenzie, he said he could verra well make the wheels and looms if he had a pattern, and naturally, the MacGregors did. So . . . we're to be weavers!"

The women looked at her with eager faces. They were pleased with the plan, and Catriona had to admit, it was as good as any. Gainful employment. A product they could sell. Catriona wanted to be thrilled for them, but something was niggling at her — they hadn't needed her to determine what to do. Together with her family, all of whom had promised to look after the abbey while she was away, they'd devised their future without her.

"But . . . but where will you live?"

"Auchenard," said one. "Until we've another place, that is. Lord Chatwick has said he'd be pleased for us to reside there, as he rarely comes to Auchenard."

Auchenard was an old hunting lodge the family owned and where Daisy and Cailean had forged their love for each other. The lodge belonged to Daisy's son by her first marriage, to Ellis, Lord Chatwick. It was true that Auchenard, just down the loch from Rabbie and Bernadette, sat empty most of the time, and Catriona wondered why she and Zelda hadn't thought of it.

Rhona and the others laid out the details of their plan to Catriona that afternoon. It appeared they'd thought everything through, and with Catriona's family to fill in the gaps, it was readily apparent that . . . well, they didn't need her.

Kishorn Abbey didn't need her anymore.

When it came time to return to Balhaire, Catriona walked slowly through the ruins. She paused in the middle, looking around her. For more than a year, she'd devoted all her time to the abbey and the residents here. It was hard to believe that it would disappear, and these women, who had given her such purpose in her own life, had found their voice and their path. That's what Catriona had wanted for them, wasn't it? Aye, it was . . . but she couldn't help but feel sad and a wee bit dejected that it had happened without her.

Rhona strolled beside her, talking about looms and wool cloth, oblivious to Catriona's grief. They reached the entrance and Rhona said, "Ah, there's the lad who will row you, then. Time to go, aye?"

She meant, of course, that it was time for Catriona to return to Balhaire. But the question echoed in Catriona's head. *Time to go. Time to leave this part of your life behind.*

"Oh, dear, I almost forgot!" Rhona said. "One moment, Miss Catriona." She hurried into the habitable side of the abbey and, in a few moments, appeared again, waving a folded paper at her. "I near forgot! This is for you! I promised I'd no' give it to you until the future of the abbey was decided, aye?"

Catriona looked at the letter and recognized Zelda's flowing hand. She gasped — Zelda had left her a letter after all, and she took it with a fresh surge of grief. She smiled gratefully at Rhona. "*Thank* you. I thought . . ." Her words trailed off.

Rhona smiled with great empathy. If anyone understood what Zelda had meant

451

to Catriona, it was Rhona. Zelda had meant the same to her in some ways. "You'll come again to see after Mrs. Graham, aye?"

Catriona looked at the abbey. What was there for her now? "I'll be here until the end, that I will, Rhona."

Rhona gave her a tight hug, then waved as Catriona walked down the steps to the water's edge.

On the return to Balhaire, Catriona read the letter Zelda had left her:

My dearest Catriona, the apple of my eye, as near to my own child as if I had birthed you. My greatest desire was to give you everything I know, but as I lie here on my deathbed and think of my own life, I know there is one last thing I must impart — you must live with no regrets, leannan. You've been given the gift of a privileged life, and you must live it and love it. No looking to the past. No mourning what might have been, for whatever has been was meant to be. No worrying for the future, for whatever will be is meant to be. No fretting over wagging tongues. I'd not have lived my life as I did, with many loves, and many disappointments, and many joys, had I looked back or fretted over talk or worried what was ahead.

My days are growing shorter, and soon there will be none left, and I have no regrets for a life well lived. Now I move to the next astounding thing. You will be sad when the abbey comes to its end, and I suspect you will fight against it. I hope you will live with no regrets, and that you'll not look back, but only forward to the next astounding thing. Above all, do not listen to what others say of you — that is the truest freedom of spirit you can know. Mo chridhe, how much joy you have given me.

Your loving Zelda

Catriona read the letter twice more before she folded it and put it in her pocket. She loved Zelda so very much . . . but she was not Zelda.

She couldn't help but look back at the summer of Hamlin and not regret it. It was incredibly painful to have loved so hard only to have lost that love. She wished for one more day with Zelda, one chance to ask her how she'd endured the loss of Uncle Knox. She wished she could ask how Zelda had possibly believed there were more astounding things to happen for her after that loss.

To Catriona, it seemed that the best of

her life had come and gone under a yew tree.

And now that the abbey would be no more, there was nothing for her. Nothing to look forward to, nothing to give her joy, nothing at all ahead of her.

CHAPTER TWENTY-SEVEN

A fortnight had passed since Catriona's return to Balhaire. Three and a half weeks since she'd left Dungotty. Twenty-two days since she'd last laid eyes on Hamlin, and every day that passed she felt more breathless than the last. As if she could not breathe properly. As if her lungs had all but collapsed on her.

Catriona managed to keep her wits about her by throwing herself into the task of learning about the business of making wool cloth. In fact, she'd just come from the Isle of Skye, where she and her sister-in-law Bernadette had paid a call to Catriona's dear friend Lizzie MacDonald and Lizzie's brother, Ivor MacDonald. Ivor had, at varying points of Catriona's life, tried to court her. He was in the business of exporting cloth now, and when he wasn't blushing at her over a bolt of it, he was explaining to her the market for it.

Ivor MacDonald was a good man. But he was not the duke.

Catriona and Bernie were returned to the shore on the mainland and were picking up their things when Bernie noticed a ship in the cove. "Who has come?" she asked curiously.

Catriona turned to look at the ship. It was unfamiliar, flying a British flag. "I donna know. Shall we have a look, then?"

"Not me," Bernie said. "I'm famished! I could scarcely stomach Lizzie's tea cakes. Did she make them with mud, do you suppose?"

Catriona laughed. "The tragedy is that she fancies herself a good cook."

Bernie shuddered, then laughed. "I'll see you in the hall, shall I?"

Catriona waved her on and started in the direction of the cove, but when she reached the top of the path, she noticed a man walking up. He was at the bottom of the path, but Catriona would recognize that auburn hair anywhere. *That* was Mr. Bain. She blamed him for the appearance of Glenna Graham in her life.

She stood with her arms akimbo as he made his way up the path. "What are you doing here, then?"

"Aye, *feasgar math,* Miss Mackenzie."

She stared at him with shock. "You speak Gaelic?"

He smiled in a manner that suggested he had a secret. "I've come in the company of your uncle, Lord Norwood."

"*What?* My uncle! He's no' expected! But why have *you* come with him?"

"I've taken a position in his household, madam."

"*An diabhal toirt leis thu!*" she exclaimed without thinking.

"The devil will no' take me today," he said with a cheeky half smile.

Catriona was shocked that he was in her uncle's employ and spoke Gaelic. What else was the man hiding? "Where is my uncle?" she demanded.

Mr. Bain turned, and there behind him, she saw her uncle laboring up the hill and cursing every step.

"Uncle!" she cried with delight, and brushed past Mr. Bain. "We were no' expecting you!"

"Yes, darling, I know, you were not. For the love of God, is there no one who can help an old man up this bloody hill?"

"If it please, my lord, I'll have a litter sent down," Mr. Bain said.

"You'll do no such thing," Catriona scoffed. "I will help him." She put Uncle

Knox's arm around her shoulders and began to walk with him. "What a delightful surprise, Uncle Knox. Did Mamma send for you?"

"She did not. I have come because I have important news and thought it best to deliver it myself. And to see my sister before I am too old to make this wretched journey."

"What news?"

He paused halfway up the path to catch his breath. "All right," he conceded. "I'll tell you, as you ought to hear it before anyone else, darling. First, you should know that the vote was taken, and your Montrose is now a sworn member of the House of Lords."

She blinked. Of course she'd wondered. She'd tried to picture it, but other than seeing Hamlin's face, she'd been unsuccessful. She had no understanding of how those things went, of how votes like that were taken.

"Have you nothing to say?" Uncle Knox asked.

"No, I . . . I am no' surprised, aye? But you could have sent a letter, uncle. You didna come all this way to tell me that."

"No, indeed." He sucked in several more breaths, his gaze fixed on her face. A smile slowly appeared, crinkling in the corners of his eyes. "I didna come to tell you that — I came to tell you *how* he became a member of Parliament."

"The vote," she said.

"Aye, the vote, but there was a bit of mayhem before the vote was taken, as Montrose refused to accept the vote without first clarifying a few things for the gentlemen who would cast their votes."

She couldn't guess what her uncle was talking about. "What things?" she asked, her brows sinking into a frown.

"First, he insisted on telling the truth about his former wife. He told them quite plainly that he'd been cuckolded and left high and dry, so to speak, with the care of her ward. And then he explained that she had come back to him with another man's child in her belly."

Catriona gasped. She gaped at Uncle Knox. "He *didna*! I donna believe you!"

"Believe me, for it is true. I witnessed it with my very own eyes, I did."

"You? Why were you at the vote?"

"Well," he said with a bit of a shrug, "I had some business with Mr. Bain. But never mind that — Montrose certainly did say that," he said, his grin growing wider. "He went on to say that had it not been for Kishorn Abbey, he would have been forced to take the adultress and her bastard child in, as it was the only decent thing to do, and that with their vote, he intended to fight for all of Scotland, for the meek and the poor as well as the privileged among us, and if any of them took issue with his cause, they ought not to vote for him."

Catriona covered her gaping mouth in disbelief.

Uncle Knox put his hand on her arm. "But they *did*, Cat. They voted for him. All but Caithness, that is, who, I have heard, felt a bit duped by MacLaren. Nevertheless, Montrose was voted in with the slimmest of margins, and he is to London now."

Catriona laughed with delight. Pride and love surged through her, and she wished she could tell Hamlin how proud she was. "Thank you, Uncle Knox. Thank you for coming all this way to tell me. You've made me verra happy with this news." She hugged her uncle.

"You think I came all this way to tell you that?" he asked, and laughed. "No, darling. I have come on an errand for the Duke of Montrose himself."

"What errand?" she asked. She couldn't imagine what errand might lead her uncle here.

"Well, God save us all, lass, no man could

find Balhaire without a guide, could he? You're bloody well far into the Highlands, aren't you?"

It took a moment for his meaning to register with Catriona. Her stomach dropped. She was suddenly shaking, her thoughts raging about her head like a summer storm. She gripped Uncle Knox's arms. "What do you mean, uncle? Speak plain — is he here?" she asked, her voice quaking with hope.

Uncle Knox pointed to the cove.

Catriona gasped. She lifted her skirts and began running down the path. "Mind you donna break an ankle, darling!" Uncle Knox shouted after her.

Catriona paid him no need. She flew down to the sandy beach at the cove, running as fast as her legs would carry her, fast enough that her hair was falling from its coif. She ran until her chest was burning and she couldn't drag air into her lungs.

There was no one on the beach, but a small boat was rowing in from the ship.

A figure on the boat suddenly rose to his feet. Catriona couldn't believe her eyes, but that figure was Hamlin. He had come to Balhaire.

He had come to Balhaire.

Emotion overwhelmed her. She sank to

her knees in the sand and tried to make herself breathe through her disbelief, her absolute astonishment. She had thought she'd never see him again. She had thought she'd never lay eyes on the love of her life again.

As the boat neared the shore, Hamlin leapt over the side and into thigh-high water, splashing his way to her.

Catriona gained her feet and ran into the surf to greet him.

"My God, Catriona," he said, grabbing her up, holding her to him, his face buried in her hair. "*My God,* I feared I'd never hold you again."

Catriona couldn't catch her breath. "You came for me," she choked out.

"Of course I did, my darling. After what you did for me, how could I leave you? How could I live another moment without you?" He suddenly picked her up, walked to shore with her and put her on her feet. And then he kissed her. Openly. Fully. He didn't care that tongues would wag. He didn't look back. He was looking to the next astonishing thing.

Catriona kissed him, too. She dug her fingers into his arms, afraid to let go of him.

Hamlin at last broke the kiss. He caressed her cheek and then sank down onto a knee before her.

"What are you doing, then?"

"Is it no' obvious? I am asking you — no, *begging* you — to be my wife, Catriona Mackenzie. Come to London, work with me, alongside me. Be my love, my mistress and the mother of my children, aye?"

She felt as if she were in the midst of a dream. How could one go from such despair to dizzying heights of happiness?

Hamlin took her silence as hesitation. He took her hand. "You were right, lass — we never spoke of it. There was too much to say, and we never spoke because there was too much to live in each moment, aye?"

Overwhelmed, and her heart filled to bursting, Catriona sank onto her knees before him.

"Will you no' speak?" he asked, his palm on her cheek.

"I canna breathe," she said. "I've no' taken a proper breath since I last saw you."

"*Breathe,* then. I'm here, aye? I've come for you, and I'll no' leave without you. Say *yes,* Catriona."

"Yes," she whispered, and gulped for air again. "A thousand times, aye."

He laughed. He drew her into his embrace, and the two of them tumbled into the sand. And for the first time in weeks, Catriona felt as if she could at last breathe.

EPILOGUE

There was, as one might expect, quite an uproar at Balhaire when Catriona appeared with a strange man who she gleefully introduced as her fiancé. Uncle Knox stepped in to right the ship. He'd kept Catriona's secret, had not written her mother about her daughter's enviable summer, but was more than happy to relate the tale now, complete with embellishments and a few events Catriona was certain didn't happen.

Hamlin finished the story by asking Catriona's father for her hand.

Her family was in awe. They kept looking at Hamlin as if he were an apparition. Why wouldn't they? Their daughter, their sister, their niece, whom they'd long since put on the shelf, had caught a duke. And not just any duke, mind, but one who sat in the House of Lords and shared her sensibilities about justice.

"It's as if you're marrying Zelda!" Rabbie

exclaimed in awe.

Catriona was going to marry the best man she'd ever known in her life, which was saying quite a lot, as the best men she knew were gathered in the great hall, celebrating her joy. The only people missing were Eula and Miss Burns, whom Hamlin reported were waiting impatiently for word at Blackthorn Hall, and would meet them in London.

"London?" Vivienne exclaimed. "But I canna do without you here, Catriona!"

"Aye, you can," Marcas said, and kissed her cheek. "Allow Catriona to know the happiness we've known, aye?"

There was no posting of the banns for the happy couple, as Hamlin was due to be in London in a month's time for the start of the Little Season, and Uncle Knox wanted to return to England. They were allowed, under Scottish law, an "irregular" marriage, which occurred at Balhaire at the end of the week. A week after that, Catriona set sail with her husband, bound for London.

It had all happened so fast and in such a flurry that she was still in a state of breathless astonishment. They were housed in Uncle Knox's London townhome until Hamlin found a suitable home of their own. As he undertook his new duties, Catriona undertook hers — she was an unlikely duchess, mistress of a grand household, all responsibilities she took quite seriously.

There were more surprises — after a month, Catriona discovered to her great delight that she was carrying Hamlin's child. She wasn't too old after all, apparently, and they were both delirious with joy.

But not everything was golden. The truth about Hamlin's first marriage began to circulate around London's Mayfair district, and people whispered about the new duke, a divorced man, married to a Highlander. "Donna listen to the talk," Catriona soothed Hamlin one night, when the weight of the gossip seemed to eat at him. "That is the greatest freedom there is, to no' care what is said of you, aye?"

He'd chuckled and pulled her into his embrace. "How are you so wise? The only opinion I care for is yours, *leannan*."

What the gossips and scandalmongers didn't know was that Hamlin had returned Glenna's family home and dowry to her. He was not heartless, and he understood that Glenna would have a bairn to look after. It had been Bain's suggestion, the last one he made to Hamlin before he was summarily let go from his post. But curiously, Catriona and Hamlin received word from her mother that Glenna desired not to leave Auchenard quite yet. She wanted to help the women establish their weaving. It seemed that against all odds, she'd found friends at Kishorn Abbey.

"How is it *possible*?" Catriona asked Hamlin, fully shocked by that turn of events. "She's the most unpleasant woman I've ever known."

They were lying in bed, his hand on her belly. "Maybe the child has softened her, aye? I donna know. But I hope to heaven it is a true calling, for her sake and the sake of her bairn."

Eula flourished in London. She had friends now, lassies who invited her to tea and strolled with her in the park at Grosvenor Square, and whispered with her about the lads who followed them around on their long, gangly legs.

Hamlin became quite involved in his work and took a particular interest in the reformation of the Poor Laws. He met long hours seeking reform with lords and ministers on the lack of uniformity across parishes in laws designed to help the destitute.

But no matter how hard Hamlin worked toward a cause, he never lost sight of his wife. He was an attentive, loving husband, and Catriona often marveled that he was her husband. All those years spent mourning a marriage, when in truth, she'd only had to wait a little longer for the perfect man.

Catriona settled into life in London in fits and starts. London society was much different than life in the Highlands, and London ladies at first viewed her with equal parts fascination and disdain. But as she grew rounder and worked harder to gain entry, social acquaintances began to warm to her. She was not without friends, although none as close to her as a sister or cousin. And they were English — for a woman taught on her father's knee to never trust an Englishman, she was slow to find her place in London society.

Just before Catriona was due to begin her confinement, Uncle Knox came to visit without his new agent, Mr. Bain.

"Why must you keep him?" Catriona demanded. "Surely there are other agents."

Uncle Knox laughed. "Will you never forgive him? If you ask me, if he hadn't brought Mrs. Graham around, there is a high likelihood you'd not be living in this fine house with a child in you."

Catriona sniffed. She supposed he was right. "Well, then? Where is he?"

"I have dispatched him to Balhaire,"

Uncle Knox said. "It seems that Marcas Mackenzie's niece is in a wee bit of trouble that needs sorting out."

Catriona had received many letters from home, and Vivienne had loudly complained about Marcas's niece. Catriona was in the dark as to what the scandal was all about, but she knew it was causing strife.

Her mother wrote often, too, with news of Kishorn Abbey and the budding weaving business at Auchenard. The women who had remained were quite happy with their craft. But some had left, looking for more society and a better wage.

The talk of Hamlin and his previous marriage began to fade into the background as Catriona's due date neared. It was summer again, and she could scarcely stand, she was so large. She was miserable — no bed or chair was comfortable, and even Hamlin's massaging of her feet couldn't soothe her. They said she was unusually large, and it felt as if her bairn kicked her on one end and punched her on the other all day long. "I'll bear a horse," she said.

A terrible storm passed over London the night Catriona's water broke. She was thankful that Hamlin was home at the time, meeting with his advisers about the Poor Laws. A midwife was summoned, and so began the excruciating, tedious night. Catriona was certain she'd not survive it, that her body would be rent in two. But just as the sun was coming up over the rooftops and the water from the night's rain glistened in the trees and in the square, the mystery of the pummeling Catriona had endured was revealed to them all. She was astonished to deliver not one, but *two* healthy boys, identical to one another, with hair and eyes as black as their father's.

She could not have been happier. And as she watched Hamlin holding his newborn sons, the tears of joy shining in his eyes, she thought of Zelda's words. *Do not look back, but ahead, to the next astounding thing.*

At the time, she'd believed the astounding thing was behind her. But looking at her family now, and feeling the swell of love so intense that it made her weep, she couldn't wait for the next astounding thing.

underage or in a hurry.

Hamlin and Osmond were in a hurry.

AUTHOR'S NOTE

Marriage and divorce laws differed between England and Scotland in the 18th century. In England, divorce generally needed some sort of Parliamentary dispensation. In Scotland, either man or woman could divorce on the grounds of desertion, which is what my Duke of Montrose sought in seeking his divorce.

In England, marriage was supposed to be done in a church, with banns posted so that anyone with grounds might object, and was not accepted as a true marriage if not performed by clergy. In Scotland, however, there were both civil and church weddings, and "irregular" marriages that were based purely on consent. In other words, a man and woman had to consent to be married to each other in the presence of a witness. This is why eloping to Gretna Green, just over the border from England, became popular if an English or Welsh couple was underage or in a hurry.

Hamlin and Catriona were in a hurry.

GLOSSARY

Twenty years ago, on one of my first trips to Scotland, I picked up *Everyday Gaelic* by Morag MacNeill, in addition to some linguistic texts and a Gaelic-English dictionary. What I learned from those purchases is that Scottish Gaelic is not for everyday use. I don't know how anyone but a native speaker could ever become proficient — it's a tough language. But that hasn't stopped me from sprinkling Scottish Gaelic terms and phrases throughout my manuscripts like a boss. While I've tried to be accurate with gender and grammar, I'm no expert. So please take the instances where I use Scottish Gaelic with the grain of rock salt it deserves. Pronounce the words as you see fit because I don't know how to say them, either. My apologies to Scottish Gaelic speakers everywhere.

French:

Le petite porcelet: akin to saying piglet, a term of endearment for a child

Scottish Gaelic:

Airson gràdh Dhè: for the love of God

An diabhal toirt leis thu: the devil take you

Bòidheach: beautiful

Criosd: Christ

Diah/Mi Diah: God/my God

Fàilte/Fàilte dhachlaigh: welcome/welcome home

Fèille: feast, festival

Feasgar math: good afternoon

Leannan: sweetheart

Madainn mhath: good morning

M'eudail: my darling, my dear

Mo chridhe: my heart

Nighean: daughter

Sassenach: foreigner, most commonly used to indicate English

ABOUT THE AUTHOR

Julia London is a NYT, USA Today and Publisher's Weekly bestselling author of historical and contemporary romance. She is a six-time finalist for the RITA Award of excellence in romantic fiction, and the recipient of RT Bookclub's Best Historical Novel. Visit Julia online:

www.julialondon.com/newsletter
www.facebook.com/julialondon
www.twitter.com/julialondon
www.instagram.com/julia_f_london